ALSO BY PETER LEFCOURT

The

MANHATTAN BEACH

PROJECT

A Novel

PETER LEFCOURT

Simon & Schuster

New York   London   Toronto   Sydney

SIMON & SCHUSTER
Rockefeller Center
1230 Avenue of the Americas
New York, NY 10020

SIMON & SCHUSTER and colophon are registered trademarks
of Simon & Schuster, Inc.

For information regarding special discounts for bulk purchases,
please contact Simon & Schuster Special Sales at
1-800-456-6798 or business@simonandschuster.com

Designed by Jeanette Olender

Manufactured in the United States of America

10 9 8 7 6 5 4 3 2

Library of Congress Cataloging-in-Publication Data
Lefcourt, Peter.
    The Manhattan Beach project : a novel / Peter Lefcourt.
        p.   cm.
     I. Title.
    PS3562.E3737M36 2005
    813'.54—dc22   2004058311

ISBN 0-7432-4920-8

For Terri

As always, forever . . .

Acknowledgments

I'd like to thank the following people, for the following reasons: my publisher, David Rosenthal, for refusing to be a bean counter; my editor, Geoffrey Kloske, for his wit and his not being afraid to put his blue pencil where his mouth is; my hero, Charlie Berns, for refusing to die in a timely manner; my friend Dan Preniszni, one book too late; and Michael Eisner, for going down with the ship.

In Hollywood you're never quite as dead as people give you credit for . . .

Charlie Berns

Great boldness is never without some absurdity.

Francis Bacon

ONE

Sharing

Three years, nine months and twenty-four days after winning an Academy Award for producing the best picture of the year, Charlie Berns was sitting on a folding chair in a second-floor room at the Brentwood Unitarian Church Annex listening to a woman with smeared lipstick and a bad postnasal drip tell him, and the other thirteen people in the room, that she had just charged $1,496 worth of cashmere sweaters on a VISA card she had received in the mail and failed to destroy.

"I was just a week short of eighteen months debt-free . . ."

The woman, who looked as if she had slept in her car with the heater on, collapsed back into a heap and began to pull compulsively on her hair.

"Thank you for sharing, Sheila," the group leader Phyllis said. "Anyone else want to share?"

She looked straight at Charlie as she said this. Charlie looked right back at her. There was no way he was going to get up there and tell this group of deadbeats that after making $2.65 million in back-end profits for producing the picture, he had let it all ride on the NAS-DAQ in February of 2000. That his broker at the time, Teddy Herbentin, kept calling it a market correction until the 2.65 mil dissolved into low five figures and Charlie had cashed out to pay his back property taxes. That the next picture he developed collapsed under the collective weight of four different writers, a million-plus in before the studio pulled the plug. That the book he optioned with what remained of the back-end money, an exposé on sweatshops in Honduras, turned out to be a complete fabrication by the author, who had gotten all his information off some unreliable Web sites and was being sued by the Hondurans, as well as by the publisher. That the woman he had been living with, Deidre Hearn—a thirty-eight-year-old development executive who had been sent to shut down his Oscar-winning picture and instead wound up working on it with him—had been killed by a faulty electric transformer on his automatic sprinkler system, electrocuted on the Fourth of July last year when she had tried to repair a broken sprinkler head and her wet hand had made contact with the exposed terminal of the transformer that his gardener had been promising to fix for months.

Nor was he going to share the fact that he was living in his nephew Lionel's pool house, driving Lionel's personal assistant's sister's car while she was recovering from periodontal surgery—a 1989 Honda Civic with one functioning headlight—communicating on a cell phone that he had gotten on promotion with a kited credit card and was there in this Debtors Anonymous meeting only because his debt consolidator had insisted he attend as a condition of his protecting Charlie from the dogpack of creditors that descended on his mailbox daily.

This was the third meeting he had been to, and he had yet to open his mouth, except to wolf down bagels during the after-meeting social period. He hadn't gotten past the first of the twelve steps: *We admitted that we were powerless over debt—that our lives had become unmanageable.*

As far as Charlie was concerned, his problems had nothing to do with being powerless over debt: it was the debt that was making him powerless, a semantic distinction that did not seem to fall under any of the twelve steps displayed prominently on the church annex room wall. If it hadn't been for that three-year-and-counting market correction; if he had gotten a decent script of two to produce; if he hadn't become severely depressed after Deidre died trying to save his lawn; plus a few dozen other ifs, he would still be living in his 4,900 square feet in the Beverly Hills flats, driving the SEL560 and employing a small army of people to deal with his life for him.

He had gone to his debt consolidator, Xuang Duc, a Vietnamese with a green card and no-frills English, only because his creditors had started to call him at all hours at Lionel's, his last known phone number, and Lionel told him to please do something about it asap because he, Lionel, did not want to have to change his phone number.

And it was Xuang Duc who had suggested that he see a mental health professional and had furnished him with a list of people who would treat people temporarily unable to pay. When he started having suicidal thoughts, Charlie took out the list and scanned it, looking for someone convenient to Brentwood. He avoided driving to places in more remote areas of the city because he was using an expired Union 76 gas card, whose existence he had not disclosed to Xuang Duc, as he was supposed to, and which would certainly be shut down soon.

This was not the first time that Charlie Berns had considered pulling the plug. A year and a half before winning the Best Picture Oscar, he had actually hooked up a hose to the exhaust pipe of his about-to-be-repossessed Mercedes and fed it through the doggie door of his Beverly Hills house, after having taped up all the windows meticulously with gaffer's tape. It was only the fortuitous arrival of his nephew Lionel, just off the Greyhound from New Jersey, that had kept Charlie from drifting into oblivion on the fumes of his fuel-injected engine.

And it was Lionel's script based on the life of the nineteenth-century British prime minister Benjamin Disraeli that Charlie had optioned, had a drunken hack named Madison Kearney rewrite into a Middle Eastern action movie called *Lev Disraeli: Freedom Fighter*, got the studio to invest fifty million dollars in against domestic box office after he managed to get a black action star with a fleeting interest in Zionism to commit to the picture, which started shooting in Belgrade, cheating Tel Aviv, until the action star got kidnapped by Macedonian separatists and Charlie had to shoot the original Disraeli script on a hidden location in Yugoslavia, cheating 1870s London, without the studio's knowing where they were until it was too late and they realized they had a best-picture candidate in the beautifully produced, talky melodrama that eventually won the big one while Charlie sat in the Shrine Auditorium catatonic in his rented

3

tuxedo barely able to make it to the stage to accept his award in front of a planetwide TV audience.

All that was water under the bridge. Though you would have thought, as Charlie often did, that the Oscar would have at least allowed him to skate for a couple of years, enjoying fat studio housekeeping deals while developing his next picture. But he hadn't counted on the new lean and mean bottom-line studio management philosophy brought on by vertical integration and balance sheet accountability, his girlfriend getting shocked to death on his front lawn, the NASDAQ's going south, or the general law of diminishing returns as he passed birthdays that progressively defined him as an endangered species in the youth-sucking ecology of the film business.

So there he was, on the second floor of the Brentwood Unitarian Church Annex, staring down the group leader, a reedy women named Phyllis who was five years into recovery after having maxed out every charge card she could get her hands on. There were only twenty minutes left before coffee and bagels, and he wasn't going to crack now.

A woman wearing aviator glasses with a Band-Aid holding them together, a Milwaukee Brewers windbreaker and sweatpants, raised her hand.

"Thank you, Wilma," Phyllis said, all the time keeping her eyes on Charlie.

"Well," said Wilma, "I finally told Carl to move out. I had six years invested in that relationship and like I said last meeting it was suffocating me I could barely breathe you have no idea . . ."

When the collection basket came around, Charlie contributed two dollars—a dollar less than Phyllis suggested but, given the fact that he had seven dollars in his pocket, a generous contribution nonetheless in that it amounted to a significant percentage of his net worth—and then stiffed it when they sent the basket back around a second time to make up what they claimed they needed to cover the coffee and the bagels.

When sharing was over, Phyllis asked people to raise their hands if they were willing to be called before the next meeting, and everyone but Charlie and a guy sitting across the room from him dutifully raised their hands. He was a short, wiry guy, maybe late forties, with bleached teeth, wearing a nicely cut sport jacket, pressed slacks, Italian shoes and tinted glasses.

During coffee and bagel time this man approached Charlie and introduced himself. "Kermit Fenster," he said, violating the rule about using last names.

"How're you doing," Charlie responded.

"You're in the entertainment business, aren't you?"

Charlie flinched.

"How do I know that? I know that because I am blessed with a photographic memory for faces. I can remember someone I met at a cocktail party sixteen years ago."

"Have we met?"

"I saw you on TV. At the Academy Awards, I'm saying three, maybe four years ago. Course, you were wearing a tux at the time and had a couple of less miles on the odometer."

He took out a tin of Altoids, offered Charlie one.

"No thanks."

"I could use a twelve-step to get off *this* shit. Listen, I'd like to talk to you about something."

"I'm really not in the business anymore."

"Just want to pick your brain."

"Maybe next time. I've got to take off now," Charlie said, looking pointedly at the door.

Kermit Fenster took out a thick wallet and handed him a business card.

"Give me a ring when you got a moment. We'll grab a cup of coffee."

"Sure thing," said Charlie, heading for the door.

As he walked down the hall, he passed the AA meeting room next door. Through the glass he could see someone sharing. From the man's expression of excruciatingly contrite sincerity, Charlie put him between Step Four (*We made a searching and fearless moral investigation of ourselves*) and Step Five (*We admitted to God, as we understand Him, to ourselves, and to another human being the exact nature of our wrongs*).

* * *

For ten minutes Charlie sat in the Honda at an expired parking meter, keeping an eye in the rearview for the traffic gestapo vehicle while he tried to remember which ATM he could hit. The complex kiting system he had devised for his remaining credit cards involved intricate timing. One false move and it could all come tumbling down on him. He could drive back to Lionel's and review the monthly statements, but Lionel lived way up in Mandeville Canyon, ten miles up and back, and the gas gauge was to the left of E.

He riffled through his small stack of charge cards, trying to intuit which one had a little breathing room on it. Closing his eyes, he strained to visualize the name of the company to whom he wrote the check on the overdrawn City National checking account which he mailed off at the beginning of the month, the third, maybe, which would mean they got the check for the minimum amount due on the fourth or the fifth, which would mean that he was good to the end of the billing cycle, which was the seventeenth, which was two weeks ago, nine days before the due date which would be yesterday, which. . . . His mind skidded off the rails. These computations were getting more and more complex, especially when you had four different cards working and three bank accounts.

Not only was this system perilous, it was, as Xuang Duc had pointed out, ultimately self-defeating. Kiting credit cards was like walking from one melting ice floe to another. He was paying 19.90 percent interest on the ATM advances and merely sinking deeper and deeper into the abyss. "You making banks very rich," Xuang Duc had explained. "Where else they going to get 20 percent on their money?"

Charlie tried the MasterCard in an ATM on San Vicente, inserting it like he was putting a dollar in a slot machine, and when that didn't pay off, he tried the VISA and hit it for $80. As it turned out, he needed the eighty because the Union 76 pump spit out his gas card, and he had to give them cash in advance before they turned the spigot back on. He filled the tank only one quarter full. It was indicative of his frame of mind these days that he thought a full tank of gas was an improvident investment in his future.

Charlie did a Taco Bell drive-through for their 99-cent special. As he sat eating his lunch, he considered whether he should blow off Judith, his pro bono therapist, with whom he had a three o'clock appointment. But if he did, he would have to account to Xuang Duc, to whom Judith would report his absence. If he blew off both Judith *and* Xuang Duc, then he'd have to account only to VISA and Master-Card.

Judith Dinkman lived in a $1.4 million bungalow south of Olympic in Baja Beverly Hills. Her office was a converted garage apartment, furnished in brightly painted IKEA colors with travel posters on the walls. His therapist greeted him at the door with her usual motherly look, her tortoiseshell glasses hanging over her ample bosom on a gold chain. They sat opposite each other, on matching director's chairs.

"So," she said, "what's happening?"

"Not a whole lot."

"Why is that?"

"There's not much going on in my life. I go to DA meetings, then I meet with my debt consolidator, then I meet with you. What kind of life is that?"

"Isn't that the question?"

"If I had a life, I could talk about it. But I don't have a life."

"That's what we need to talk about. Why *don't* you have a life?"

"I can't get a job."

"And why can't you get a job?"

"I can't get a job because I spend all my time going to meetings to discuss why I can't get a job."

They went around in circles like this all the time. The same questions, the same answers. He might as well phone it in.

"All right," she said, "don't come back. I mean, there's no point in doing this unless you're willing to work at it, is there?"

"Okay, you win."

"I don't win anything. This isn't about me."

"You're right. I'm sorry. It's just that I don't like doing this."

"You're not supposed to like it. If you like it, you're not doing it right."

He nodded, took a deep breath. It was time to share.

"So, I went to another meeting this morning. I listened to a lot of fucked-up people talking about themselves. It made me feel pretty together actually. And then afterwards this guy came up to me, said he recognized me from seeing me get the Oscar on TV. Which was very strange because that was almost four years ago and no one else in this town seems to remember it."

"What did he say?"

"He said he wanted to talk to me about something."

"What did you do?"

"Took his card."

"Are you going to talk to him?"

"I don't know. I mean, he doesn't look like Michael J. Anthony."

"Who?"

"Michael J. Anthony. He was the guy who gave away the money on *The Millionaire*. He worked for John Beresford Tipton, and he would go up to this stranger that they had preselected and tell that person that his name was Michael J. Anthony and that he was going to give him a million dollars—was this before your time?"

"Yes."

"Because if I had a million dollars I wouldn't be having this problem."

"Charlie, it's not about the money. We're past that."

Every week in DA they said it was not about the money. Xuang Duc had said that to him, as well, at their first meeting in the debt consolidator's small office in Glendale. Charlie had sat across the desk as the Vietnamese with the pocket protector and the wrinkle-free slacks explained to him, in his erratic, machine-gun English, that debt was only conquerable by behavior modification.

He had asked Charlie to bring all his bills, credit cards and bank statements to their first meeting. Charlie had held four of his sixteen cards out, plus three of his seven bank accounts. Xuang Duc played the calculator like a concert pianist, totaling up Charlie's outstanding debts, calculating the interest, then entering it all into a program on his computer that calculated the one monthly charge he would have to pay the company that Xuang Duc worked for in lieu of all the other debts. He printed it out and handed it to Charlie. It was an unsettling number.

"It look big only because it's total of all your obligations. But you add them up, you paying a lot more. Look at *that* number. Column six."

Charlie looked at that number.

"You saving 16.8 percent on the face, 9.3 percent after you pay us. Plus you don't have people calling you all hours, and you get credit rating clean."

Charlie wrote a check for the initial consultation and signed a number of forms he didn't bother reading, which enabled Xuang Duc's company to make monthly automatic withdrawals from Charlie's bank account.

The withdrawals came on the tenth of the month, another variable he would have to keep in consideration for his complex juggling of funds. He'd ATM on the ninth and make a cash deposit at the bank to cover the automatic withdrawal—

"Charlie, did you hear me?"

Judith's voice pulled his attention back to Baja Beverly Hills.

"What was that?"

"I said that we both know that this is not just about money. So are we going to talk about what it's about, or just keep going around in circles?"

"How come you're doing this for nothing?"

"We're not here to talk about me."

"Well, yeah, but I think it's strange that you're not getting paid."

"All right. That's it. We're finished."

She rose from her seat like a large wave, filling the space with her shapeless navy blue dress. "Get out."

"You're throwing me out?'

"You bet."

Charlie looked up at her hovering over him, her eyes moist with anger.

"You don't want me to come on Thursday?"

"Nope."

"Next Tuesday?"

"No."

"So this is what—tough love?"

"There's no love at all in this. Adios, Charlie."

* * *

Charlie drove west on Sunset, through the Beverly Hills flats, feeling a little shaky. He had just been fired by his therapist. Frankly, he didn't blame her. He was a pain in the ass, a charity-case pain in the ass, no less.

Well, there went Tuesday and Thursday afternoons. He'd think of something else to do with the time. He could always join another twelve-step. There were meetings every day of the week. There was a Gamblers Anonymous that met Tuesdays and Thursdays in Santa Monica. He'd been in the movie business. He could relate to that.

On a whim, he turned right onto Alpine and pulled up in front of his old house. The bank had foreclosed for a song. Since Charlie had about a dollar fifty worth of equity left in the house, having refied it till it bled, he let it go without a struggle.

The house had been remodeled by the new owner. What had once been a nominally Mediterranean house, stucco and Spanish tile roof, had been transformed into a dark blue French chateau, with faux Norman shutters, crenellated roof and a marble statue of a Charles de Gaulle in full dress uniform with a képi on his head on the front lawn.

Charlie's throat caught as he looked at the front lawn, planted with some sort of completely un-Normanlike succulents. They had ripped up his lawn—the lawn that Deidre had given her life to try to save.

Deidre. He could have talked about *her* with Judith. Deidre would never have let things come to this. She had no patience for his self-pity. "Charlie, you're full of shit," she would tell him. Lovingly. Gently. With that little cracked smile of hers, that smile that he had loved more than anything he could remember. As he sat there in the Honda and stared at the lawn, the very lawn that she had been trying to revive when she stuck her wet hands into the exposed circuitry of the broken transformer, small warm tears clouded over his vision.

The small warm tears became warmer and less small. It wasn't long before he was bawling loudly in the front seat of the car, undoubtedly a strange sight to anyone who may have been looking out the window of the navy blue chateau because somebody inside the house had, in fact, been looking out the stained-glass front window and, seeing a strange man crying loudly in a beat-up Honda in front of their house, called the Beverly Hills police.

Minutes later a tall blond motorcycle cop was shining a flashlight in his eyes.

"You want to step outside the vehicle, sir."

When Charlie did not react immediately, the storm trooper moved closer, his hand on his weapon, and repeated the command.

Charlie stepped out of the vehicle. The cop, whose name, appropriately, was Heimler, asked him for identification.

Charlie produced his driver's license, which still had the Alpine Drive address. Heimler examined it, looked at Charlie, looked at the house and the house number, and said, "Do you live here?"

"No."

"How come your driver's license has this address?"

"I used to live here."

"What are you doing here now?"

"Reminiscing."

Heimler curled his lip, unhappy with this answer.

"I lost the house to the bank," Charlie explained. "I didn't have enough in to refie again so I just let them take it. Anyway, I'm in Debtors Anonymous, so I'm working on the problem. I was on my way home from my therapist when I passed the street and thought I'd have a look at the house. It used to be Mediterranean, believe it or not."

"Where do you live now?'

"Top of Mandeville Canyon. With my nephew Lionel. Actually, in his pool house. You see, I gave him his first job, four years ago. He wrote the script for *Dizzy and Will*. Won Best Picture. You happen to see it?"

The cop shook his head, handed Charlie back his driver's license and said, "You need to get your address changed on your driver's license."

"Sure," said Charlie. "I've got a lot of time on my hands."

Sergeant Heimler stood in front of the house, arms folded, and watched as Charlie got in his car, did a U-turn, and headed back to Sunset. He waited five more minutes to make sure he didn't return.

* * *

Later that night, as Charlie sat watching *CSI: El Paso* in the pool house beside the Olympic-length lap pool behind Lionel's sprawling Greek Revival home on the top of Mandeville Canyon, his nephew slid the glass door open and walked in. Charlie looked up and saw his sister Bea's son wearing a cashmere sweater, designer jeans and socks. Lionel had a personal shopper, as well as a personal assistant, a workout coach, manager, agent, lawyer, accountant, stockbroker, decorator, pool man, gardener, housekeeper, dog walker and closet organizer. Charlie eyeballed his nephew's above-the-line expenses for this platoon of people at a couple of hundred thou a year easy.

Lionel Traven, né Travitz, was pushing twenty-five and, in a large part due to his having written Charlie's Oscar-winning movie four years ago, was an A-Plus List screenwriter. He was so hot that he had five different scripts stockpiled at the moment—all of them high-profile projects with major talent attached. The amount of money potentially represented by these jobs was enough to present challenging tax problems, causing him to purchase a share of a negative cash-flow medical building in Costa Mesa and a sizable position in some very volatile Indonesian rubber stock futures.

"Hey, Uncle Charlie. How're you doing?"

"All right, Lionel."

"Got a moment?"

Charlie hit the "mute" button on the TV just as Jason Priestley stuck the coyote excrement under the electron microscope. Lionel put his hands in his pockets, flexed his jaws uncomfortably, which signaled to Charlie that he was about to hear bad news.

"Uh . . . here's the thing. Shari?"

Charlie nodded. This was the way that you had a conversation with Lionel. He would utter a series or short interrogative phrases, and you would nod until he continued.

"She's been living with me?"

Shari had been hired to organize Lionel's closets and had managed to parlay this into a live-in position. Lionel's closets all looked like file cabinets. After alphabetizing his spice rack, she had color-coordinated his sweater drawer.

12

"Well, she's thinking of branching out into general organization?"

Nod.

"You know, help people get organized? Arrange their offices? Their schedules? Their priorities?"

Nod.

"So she kind of would like to have an office to work out of? You know what I mean?"

Nod.

"And she thought that the pool house would be perfect?"

Nod.

"So . . . you know, we were kind of thinking what your plans were?"

"Plans?" he uttered, batting the ball back to Lionel's side of the court.

"Uh-huh. Like . . . are you going to be like moving out soon?"

"Moving out?"

"Uh-huh . . ."

"Where?"

"Like to an apartment somewhere or a house?"

"Oh."

A protracted moment of strained silence passed. Charlie considered pointing out to his nephew that, unlike Shari, he, Charlie, was family, that it was in a large part thanks to him, Charlie, that Lionel now owned part of a negative cash-flow medical building in Costa Mesa.

"Maybe you could like find a place in the Oakwood Apartments? They're, like, convenient to the studios? For your meetings?"

Charlie hadn't had a meeting at a studio in months. The only meetings he went to now were meetings at which people got up and spilled their guts. The Oakwood Apartments were furnished lodgings, basically Embassy Suites with Internet access and optional maid service. They were expensive, depressing, full of people getting divorced or out from the East Coast for a month or two. Charlie couldn't make a week's rent, let alone a month's.

"When does Shari need the space by?"

"Like asap?"

"All right. I'll look for a place."

"Great? Oh yeah, and Rita's off the painkiller for her gum surgery?"

"Good."

"So she's going to need her car back?"

"Right."

"See you later?"

And his nephew gave him a cheerful wave and retreated to the
main house. Charlie kept the "mute" button on and stared blankly
at the screen. Dana Delany was taking off her lab coat, looking a little chunky in a pair of baggy woolen slacks. Charlie would have
fired the wardrobe mistress for letting Dana Delany wear those
slacks.

He leaned back on the couch and closed his eyes. Very slowly he
exhaled, as if he were trying to conserve his breath. He hadn't
thought that things could get any worse. But they just had.

He was now not only broke and carless. He was homeless.

Two

Starbucks

Charlie's first-month-free-1,000-anytime-minutes cell phone went off before nine o'clock the following morning. It was not his best hour, even before he was broke and homeless, and as he rolled over on the lumpy pullout couch, he wondered who could possibly be calling him on this phone. But Charlie was at the point in his life where he couldn't afford *not* answering a phone. You never knew. It could be Michael J. Anthony.

The phone was on its ninth ring—a computer-generated rendition of "Für Elise"—before he tracked it down buried in the pocket of yesterday's trousers.

"Hello."

"Charlie?"

"Who's this?"

"Kermit Fenster."

"Who?"

"We're in the same DA meeting. We spoke yesterday, remember?"

The wiry guy with the tinted glasses who had approached him during coffee and bagel time.

"How'd you get this number?"

"You got a free hour today?" Fenster asked, ignoring the question.

Then Charlie remembered that he put the number down on the sign-up sheet for the DA meeting. It was indicative of his desperation at the moment that Charlie had given the number in the event that some deadbeat studio executive needing a producer for a go movie would show up at DA for some sharing.

"I don't know."

"There's a Starbucks on San Vicente and Barrington. How about noon?"

"I've got some things I need to do—"

"See you then."

And Fenster hung up, having, Charlie realized, completely ignored everything he had said. Charlie looked at his watch, a non-pawnable digital Timex. 9:14 a.m. Generally, he didn't get out of bed till after ten, which made the day shorter and therefore more manageable. Things were looking a little gray at 9:14 a.m. The sun hadn't burned off the cloud cover yet.

Putting on a pair of jogging pants and a UCLA sweatshirt, he slid open the door and circumnavigated the pool, which was being acid washed by Mr. Kim, Lionel's anal-compulsive Korean pool man. The pool was so clean it looked like undulating aqua Jell-O. Charlie waved nonchalantly at Mr. Kim, who did not return his salutation.

He entered the kitchen by the back door. At the sink washing up the breakfast dishes was Glinka, Lionel's depressed Estonian cleaning lady. She did not return Charlie's salutation either. He went to the cupboard and confronted the breathtaking order that Shari had imposed. Canned goods were organized alphabetically, with type of food being a category, and brand name and flavor being subcategories. So that to find Campbell's celery soup, for example, you located the soup section first, then the Campbell's and then found celery between beef barley and consommé. The Cheerios were located in the dry cereal section, between All-Bran and Frosted Flakes.

The refrigerator was organized by basic food groups. The proteins were on the first shelf, then the carbohydrates, the leafy vegetables, fruits (citrus and non-citrus), and so forth on the shelves in descending order. Charlie found the milk, displayed according to fat content, starting with regular, then going to 2 percent fat, 1 percent fat and fat-free.

As he sat under the sullen glare of Glinka, eating his cereal, he considered whether he should bother meeting Kermit Fenster at Starbucks. The guy probably wanted to pitch him some script his wife had written. There was, moreover, the practical problem of getting there. Shari's sister wanted her Honda back. It was close to five miles just to get to Sunset and another two to Brentwood.

Charlie went to the cupboard, where he found jars of instant coffee, organized into two categories: caffeinated and noncaffeinated. Within the caffeinated subgroup there was American, Colombian, East Indian and French, in that order. He chose Colombian, spooned a healthy amount into a Miramax For Your Consideration mug and added water from the instant hot water tap.

Coffee cup in hand, he headed to the bathroom off the kitchen, also known as the yellow bathroom. Each of the six bathrooms in the house had a unique color scheme with the towels matching the exquisite tile work done by five Armenian brothers and their father and written off by Lionel's accountant as a research expense on one of his scripts that featured an Armenian hitman.

Charlie was about to enter the yellow bathroom when Shari came down the hallway, carrying a stack of yellow towels and several rolls of yellow toilet paper.

"Would you mind using the rose bathroom? I'm restocking the yellow bathroom's towels."

She continued, in the way of explanation, "There are a couple of rose towels that need to be washed, and tomorrow is the day that the rose bathroom towels get washed, so this way we can start the yellow bathroom's cycle off with a full set of towels, you see?"

He was about to suggest that he could use the rose towels in the yellow bathroom without disturbing the towel washing cycle, but he knew that she would knot her eyebrows in displeasure as she always did whenever he said anything the least bit contrary to her. She already didn't like him. There was no point in antagonizing her further while he still had her sister's car keys.

Charlie nodded and continued down the hall, past the small den to the larger den, off which was located the rose bathroom, thankful that she hadn't said anything about her sister's car. Maybe he could get another day or two out of it.

In the end, it was the availability of the Honda with its eighth of a tank of gas that made Charlie decide to meet Kermit Fenster at Starbucks. After his shower in the rose bathroom, Charlie hurriedly dried off with a rose towel, then hurried back to the pool house, threw on some clothes, and pulled the Honda out of the drive and down Mandeville. A hundred yards past the house, he put it into neutral, shut off the motor, and coasted the rest of the way to Sunset.

* * *

Kermit Fenster was not at Starbucks at noon. Nor at 12:15. Charlie had invested $1.75 of his shrinking liquid capital in a tall latte grande. Around him people sat alone at the molded plastic tables, reading newspapers, cell phoning, Palm Piloting, staring blankly off into the neutral climate-controlled ether.

Los Angeles café society. In spite of the caffeine, the average pulse rate in the place was below 50. Besides the staccato desultory cell phone conversations, the only other sounds were the occasional *whosh* of the espresso machine and the white noise of the ventilation.

"Für Elise" gurgled from his pocket. He fished the phone out and heard Kermit Fenster's voice on the other end.

"Charlie, it's Kermit Fenster. I'm running a little late."

"How late?"

"Don't go away."

And he disconnected. Charlie left the phone on the table and drained the latte grande. He ought to leave. Not that his time was at all that valuable. But he didn't like being jerked around. And this guy who didn't answer questions seemed by all appearances to be a major jerk-off artist.

He could still make a one-o'clock matinee of a movie. The tickets were only $7.50 for the first show. But was there anything he really wanted to see?

Since Charlie had drifted to the outer precincts of the movie business, he spent less and less time actually seeing movies. He found that he couldn't sit through the vapid tent poles that Hollywood was producing these days. The industry had become an assembly line for sequential software, manufacturing roman-numeral movies or pretentious wetdreams from hot auteur directors that nobody actually went to see but which kept the talent happy so that they would do more tent poles.

Not that the films that Charlie Berns had produced were great works of art. With the exception of his Oscar-winning picture, a complete fluke that he had backed into thanks to a sequence of highly improbable circumstances, most of his movies were trash. But they were honest trash. You got what you paid for. You got action, blood and gore, tits and ass, whatever was advertised.

In the few interviews he had done following the Oscar, during that fleeting moment when he had some clout and recognition before the window of opportunity was nailed shut, Charlie was always honest to a fault. He said that he believed that movies were entertainment, not art, that success was largely an accident of time and place, and that all he wanted to do was to make a living. This matter-of-factness was one of the reasons that his agent at the time—an insect with a bad sinus infection named Brad Emprin—told him that his career was slowly but ineluctably heading south, from where, he implied, it had come from.

The last call that Brad Emprin returned, three days after Charlie had left word, was from his cell phone on his way home at 7:45 p.m. in the Sepulveda Pass, and consisted of a short homily, interrupted by cell phone static from the Santa Monica Mountains, about the law of diminishing returns with respect to heat. Heat, Brad Emprin had said, was the most ephemeral of qualities in the movie business. Here today, gone this afternoon. Strike while the iron is hot. Don't rest on your laurels. Reinvent yourself every day anew . . .

At 12:50, Kermit Fenster walked in the door. He spotted Charlie in the corner, came over and sat down.

"What're you having?" he asked, without a word of apology or explanation for the fact that he was nearly an hour late.

"Nothing. I already had a couple of latte grandes."

"Two latte grandes," Fenster called to the Aztec behind the counter, took off an expensive suede jacket and draped it over the back of his chair and smiled. His bleached teeth were so white that Charlie felt like he was looking right into a pair of high-beam headlights.

"*Willy and Ben,* that was the name of the picture, wasn't it?"

"Actually, it was *Dizzy and Will.*"

"Hell of a picture. What did it do?"

"About two and a quarter worldwide."

"No shit. I'd a thought it was over three."

Fenster went to collect the coffees. Charlie watched him take a thick roll of bills out of his pocket to pay for the lattes. He sat back down, handed Charlie his latte, and put a bunch of sugar packets and napkins on the table. As Fenster stirred two sugars into his coffee, Charlie took a closer look at him. Under the aqueous neon lighting, the man looked older than Charlie had originally thought when he had met him at DA, over fifty at least, maybe even sixty. His face was tanned, the skin stretched by a recent face-lift, but you could see some age in the spiderwebs at the corners of his eyes and a couple of incipient liver spots on his forehead. He was thin, compactly built, with small nervous hands and a good head of lightly dyed hair. His clothes were expensive, more eastern than California, and he was sporting a large emerald ring on his right hand.

"So, tell me something, Charlie, you watch TV?"

"Not a whole lot," Charlie lied. Given his disposable income, he logged a lot of hours in the pool house in front of Lionel's twenty-seven-inch Sony.

"What do you watch?"

"I kind of surf around a lot."

"You watch that reality stuff?"

"Like *American Idol*?"

"Uh-huh. Hottest thing on TV. People can't get enough of that shit. And from what I hear, you can make it for next to nothing."

"Apparently."

"So, how would you like to get into the reality TV business?"

"Me?"

"Who am I having a coffee with?"

"Look, it's very nice of you to think of me, but I don't know the first thing about producing television."

"What's to know? You produced an Academy Award–winning movie, didn't you? This ought to be a whole lot easier."

Charlie eyed the exit. He could say that he had to put more money in the meter and make a run for it. But what else did he have to do at the moment? As the DA people liked to say, if you don't change your direction, you'll wind up where you're going, which, according to his ex-therapist Judith Dinkman, was not a good place.

"You have to open doors, Charlie, even if you don't know what's behind them, or else you'll spend your whole life in the hallway."

So Charlie asked, "What did you have in mind?"

Fenster looked around him, as if he were about to divulge a state secret.

"Uzbekistan," he said, in a low, almost whispered voice.

"What?"

"Uzbekistan," Fenster repeated. "Central Asia. Former Soviet Socialist Republic, population 24 million, area 447,400 square kilometers, GNP $23,490,000,000, or about $1,010 per capita. One of only two doubly landlocked countries in the world. The other one is Liechtenstein."

"Didn't know that."

"You want another coffee?"

"No thanks."

Fenster signaled for two more latte grandes, then leaned in toward Charlie and looked directly into his bloodshot eyes. "This is strictly need to know, what I'm going to tell you. It goes no further than this table. There could be some serious collateral damage if certain people and situations are compromised, you understand what I'm saying?"

Charlie nodded self-protectively. The guy was obviously off his rocker, and Charlie didn't want to agitate him unnecessarily.

"I'm a CIA operative. Central Asian desk. Seventeen months in Tashkent. I've been all over the area—Tajikistan, Turkmenistan, Kazakhstan, Kyrgyzstan—all the Stans, including Afghanistan. I helped kick the Taliban the fuck out of there."

"Uh-huh."

"Lots of interesting things going on over there these days. You got your shaky governments, you got your rebels, you got your Russian mafia, you got your Islamic fundamentalists, you got your drug cartels, you got your warlords. We got interests there because of the oil. The Russians think they still own it. Besides the oil, there're gold reserves, there's opium being transshipped from China. There are ecological disasters about to happen—the Aral Sea is drying up, losing 7.5 square kilometers a year from too much irrigation. So what do you think?"

"About what?"

"Central Asia, Uzbekistan in particular."

"As a TV reality show?"

"Isn't that what we're talking about?"

"Well, I don't know—"

"You don't know? The place is perfect. It's exotic, it's dangerous, you take your life in your hands just drinking the water . . ."

"Do you have a concept?"

"What I was thinking was one of these reality programs about the day-to-day life of a warlord—you know, follow him around, film him with his family, getting tributes from neighboring villages, running guns, taking a cut out of the dope trade, consolidating his power. You call it *Warlord*. How can you not watch that?"

"Well, it's certainly . . . intriguing . . ."

"Charlie, do me a favor. Don't tell me something I already know."

"Do you think an American audience would relate to this?"

"You kidding? It's a fucking Western. It's Dodge City. Everyone carries a gun. The sheriff's scared shit to enforce the law. It's completely unpredictable. Think of Genghis Khan, think of Attila the Hun . . . I have all the contacts. You want anything in the entire region, I know how to get it."

"What about your job?"

"My job?"

"With the CIA."

"I'm not at liberty to discuss that."

Fenster went and got two more latte grandes and placed one in front of Charlie even though he hadn't touched the first one. He took a big sip, wiped his mouth with a napkin and looked around him again.

"So you want in?"

"Look, I don't know what I bring to the table."

"You're going to sell this."

"I told you, I don't know anything about television."

"Come on. You've worked in this town for a long time. You know people who, if *they* can't do it, know people who *can*. All you have to do is get us in the door at a network and sell it. I'll do the rest. I'll get us a warlord, local facilities, the muscle. Whatever you want. If you can buy or steal it in Uzbekistan, Kazakhstan, Turkmenistan, I can get it."

"I think it could be a hard sell."

"Charlie, what step are you on?"

"Step?"

"The twelve steps. Which one are you on?"

"I'm not really sure."

"Take a look at number thirteen."

"What's that?"

"When somebody throws you the ball, run with it."

He held Charlie's look for a long moment.

"Let me think about it," Charlie said finally, if only to break the spell.

"Don't think about it too long, because this is a ground-floor opportunity. You're not interested, I'll get someone else. In this town you can throw a stone and hit a producer."

Charlie looked at his watch pointedly and said, "Thanks very much, Kermit, but I really do have to go."

"I'm giving you a seventy-two-hour window. I want to hear from you by this time Monday or else I'm going to Jerry Bruckheimer."

Fenster reached into his wallet, removed a card and handed it to Charlie. It had CENTRAL INTELLIGENCE AGENCY written on it, CENTRAL ASIAN DESK, Fenster's name and a phone number with a 703 area code.

"Thanks," Charlie said, "I'll be in touch."

"Step thirteen, Charlie. Don't drop the ball."

* * *

Though Charlie had nothing to do in town, he did not want to drive back up Mandeville for fear of having the Honda confiscated. Being carless was worse than being homeless in Los Angeles. You could always sleep in your car.

He mapped out a game plan for the remainder of the day before he could slink back to Lionel's under the cover of night: Taco Bell for the 99-cent lunch, then the Brentwood Public Library for the afternoon of random reading, an hour or two in the Westside Pavilion window shopping, then two pizza slices at Piece O' Pizza before going up the hill to the twenty-seven-inch Sony.

He started the Honda up and squinted at the gas gauge. There was a fraction of light before he hit absolute E. Charlie had become an expert on reading gas gauges. He knew from experience that there was Empty and then there was *Empty*. He estimated one and a half more trips up and down, maybe two if he coasted down the hill.

In the Brentwood Library he whiled away the afternoon reading a Harlequin romance novel. At the Westside Pavilion he got his sunglasses adjusted for nothing at Sunglass Hut and checked out the sales on sweat socks. He was sitting over a Diet Coke in the food court, watching the flora and fauna of a mall afternoon through lidded eyes when "Für Elise" sounded.

"Hello?"

"Uncle Charlie?"

"Yeah, Lionel."

"The car?"

"Oh, right, listen, I thought I'd get it washed. You know, as a token of my appreciation to Shari's sister Rita for lending it to me."

"That's nice of you? But she really needs it? She has a follow-up appointment at her periodontist's? Tomorrow morning? In Encino?"

"Okay, I'll bring it back tonight."

"How's the apartment hunting going?"

"I'm looking."

He left the mall and drove off a gallon of gas before heading up Mandeville and retiring to the pool house. It was after ten o'clock when he surfed on to a rerun of *The Sopranos*. Tony was having problems collecting on a skimming racket from the building workers' union, and then he comes home and his kid starts to dump on him and his wife's concerned about their nest egg being buried in plastic bags in the backyard. He was eating a lot of junk food and not looking well and having a recurrence of his anxiety attacks.

It was fascinating to watch a guy with that much power struggling against such everyday problems. Even though this guy routinely chopped people up and buried them in the Jersey salt flats, you found yourself rooting for him.

When it was over Charlie shut the set off and took a guerrilla trip to the yellow bathroom. As he dried his face with one of the clean new yellow towels, prematurely starting the yellow towel cycle, he saw it all laid out in front of him. It was one of those flashes of insight that hit you unexpectedly like a wave of exhilaration. It had been so long since Charlie experienced anything remotely like exhilaration that he felt a little dizzy. He kept the idea wrapped up tight until he had gotten into bed on the lumpy pullout sofa.

And then for at least an hour before he finally drifted off to sleep, he went over and over the idea, expanding on it until he was convinced it was the best idea he had had in at least a year. If not five.

THREE

ABCD

Hidden away in an industrial section of Manhattan Beach, about fifteen miles from the ABC Television Building in Burbank, was a rogue division of the network called, innocuously enough, ABCD—American Broadcasting Company Development. The existence of ABCD was so secret that much of the parent company hierarchy, not to mention the network itself, was unaware of it. Even the CEO had only a vague notion that this skunkworks existed beyond the small line item in the budget that he signed off on quarterly under the column titled "Development Expenses."

In order to create a shield around the CEO and around the other high-level executives at both the network and the parent company, the details of just what was going on in Manhattan Beach were kept from them. It was a strategy that had worked successfully for the Reagan White House, when the president was kept out of the loop about Iran-Contra in order to maintain his deniability.

The creation of ABCD was a response to the network's shrinking audience share and unappetizing demographics, which were exerting relentless downward pressure on the parent company's stock price and increasing its vulnerability to being gobbled up by some cash-rich bottom feeder. The CEO had recently been ignominiously booted from the chairman of the board's job by a group of disgruntled stockholders, and his tenure on the CEO job was thought to be tenuous.

The division was an attempt to stop the bleeding by creating a superweapon to deal with the problems quickly and overwhelmingly —in the way that the atomic bomb stopped the bleeding in 1945. It was essentially a top-secret research and development program. The people who worked there were required to sign agreements not to reveal the nature of the work done in this division. Like the nuclear scientists working on the Manhattan Project in Los Alamos during World War Two, they were engaged in highly sensitive work developing the type of television projects that were so radical that public knowledge of them could lead to embarrassment of the parent company—the very same people who every night, 365 nights out of the year, sponsored a group of actors dressed as friendly animals parading down a plastic Main Street in Anaheim for tourists from the world over.

Along with ABCD, there was the traditional development division at ABC, on Riverside Drive in Burbank, which bought scripts and made pilots for the network—sitcoms and cop shows and, more and more of late, the kind of audience-pleasing reality shows that were popular. This division, headed by a thirty-two-year-old hot shot named Kara Kotch, went about its work unaware that just a few miles south of LAX was a shadow division also developing product for the same network. They were actually a front for ABCD, though a front that had no idea what was going on in back and would have been shocked to know that a nice slice of the network's development resources was being devoted to this rogue operation in Manhattan Beach.

The cover for the division was alternative media. As far as anyone who worked at ABC knew, the people in Manhattan Beach were engaged in some think tank gaming to expand the network's presence into Internet programming, virtual video, satellite transmission—the whole futuristic, quasi-sci-fi part of the business. They had no idea that ABCD was engaged in experimental programming designed to plug the holes in the network's regular lineup and could, conceivably, replace them.

To camouflage its existence further, ABCD did not advertise the fact that it was not actually located in Burbank. The direct-dial phone numbers of all the offices had 818 area codes as well as the 363 prefixes that preceded all of the network numbers. The leading executives had offices in the Burbank headquarters as well as in the Manhattan Beach facility. These superfluous offices on Riverside

Drive were occupied only when a meeting with someone outside the division was unavoidable; they were manned by secure ABCD personnel who were trained to make sure that the executive in question was always away from his desk or at an outside meeting if someone from the network happened to wander up to the fifth floor looking for one of them.

ABCD's specialty was the ERS, or extreme reality show, a prime-time version of extreme sports, in which plausibility and taste were stretched to accommodate the kind of lower-than-lowest-common-denominator television that viewers would be unable to resist. Once these shows were developed and produced, they were to be test-aired on closed-circuit cable channels to see how people reacted to them—the TV version of doing medical experiments on mice to see how they would be tolerated by humans. If in the judgment of the ABCD research people, they were hitting their demographic targets, they would be slipped into the network's prime-time schedule to jump-start the ratings.

The division's work was still largely in the start-up stage. There was only one program that was remotely ready to be produced, let alone be aired. It was a program called *Kidnapped*, in which an unsuspecting person was filmed being abducted and being kept sequestered at a secret location for twenty-four hours, while the victim's family would be contacted for ransom demands. With the audience registering their opinions online about whether or not the person was going to be ransomed, the subject would learn just how his friends and family felt about him before being told it was all in good fun, set free for a tearful reunion with his loved ones and given a series of prizes for his or her sportsmanship.

The problem to be resolved with *Kidnapped* was how to avoid the victim's pressing charges against the producers for abduction. The ABCD lawyers had proposed getting the victim to sign a hold-harmless agreement before getting the prizes, but they were concerned about the *ex post facto* nature of the agreement and the possibility that grand juries would indict in spite of the agreement. So the program lay in limbo while the lawyers went back and forth on it.

The ABCD development exec behind *Kidnapped* was a forty-four-year-old refugee from the movie business named Norman Hudris, who had been, coincidentally, at the studio that had produced Charlie Berns's Academy Award–winning movie, *Dizzy and Will*, and had watched his own career, like Charlie's, slip slowly but steadily south as time passed, drifting downward to a job in Standards and Practices at NBC, the Antarctica of the TV business.

Then Norman Hudris had been approached one day by an old studio colleague of his, Howard Draper. Howard Draper was a man blessed with patrician looks, impeccable taste and little else. He looked good in Brooks Brothers, knew his way around a wine list and didn't double fault at tennis.

Howard Draper's position at ABCD was only slightly less protectively distanced from the action than the CEO's. He took pains to stay, if not completely out of the loop, then at least in the outer quadrant. The treatment for *Kidnapped* never crossed his desk, and the memos from the lawyers were e-mailed to him and then immediately deleted after he read them. One young attorney had to be let go because he had inadvertently put Howard Draper's name on the c.c. list for a memo. They confiscated his nonduplicable key, erased his hard disk and scraped his ABCD parking sticker off the windshield with a solvent that left no traces.

Norman Hudris had regular meetings with Howard Draper in which he had to be careful not to tell his boss anything compromising while, at the same time, telling him enough so that Howard Draper could get through *his* meetings with the money people around the corner. This systematic passing up of selective disinformation benefited everyone involved except the people at the bottom of the pyramid and the company's stockholders, whose stock was so depressed anyway it didn't make a whole lot of difference. And should the division come up with the big hit, everyone would come out smelling sweet.

The network's health plan was one of the principal reasons that Norman Hudris took the job at ABCD. After the studio he worked for had been sold to the Japanese, who immediately belt-tightened and consolidated his job, he had spent nearly eighteen months out of work, protected only by the leaky umbrella of a cut-rate HMO which required him to use Eastern European doctors with questionable medical degrees.

When you had the type of health problems that Norman Hudris had, you needed top-notch treatment. He suffered from a number of chronic conditions—cardiac arrhythmia, prostatitis, thyroid imbalance, pancreatic insufficiency, urticaria, bleeding gums, to name just a few. Sometimes he wished that he had one really serious problem, like cancer, instead of all these nickel-and-dime problems that were collectively debilitating him but not killing him.

Howard Draper, of course, enjoyed glowing health. So that when they had their monthly lunch at, for security reasons, a remote Greek restaurant in Glendale, where nobody from the business ate, Norman Hudris avoided discussing his health problems.

They were always a very delicate proposition, these lunches at the Hercules Taverna on Brand Avenue. The challenge was to fill his boss in on the projects in development in such a general way that Howard Draper would have only a vague idea of what was going on in his own division but not enough detail to compromise him should a firestorm break out. It was a fire-break in the line of command, with each person involved kept only on the perimeter of the loop by the person directly beneath him. At ABCD, the only thing more dangerous than being out of the loop was being *in* the loop.

"We're . . . moving ahead on a number of fronts," Norman Hudris said as he took a small bite of his *htapothi vrasto.*

"Good," responded Howard Draper, chasing his blanched olives with a large sip of acrid Retsina.

"There are some promising projects in the works."

"Glad to hear it. Any time frame?"

"Nothing firm. We wouldn't want to rush any of this too quickly into the pipeline."

"Of course. You think maybe by the end of the second quarter?"

"Third at the latest. There's this one particular pilot that I think could go through the roof . . ." Norman Hudris began.

"Good, good," Howard Draper hurriedly interrupted lest his underling get too specific.

"There are some attendant legal problems. You've read the memos?"

"No," Howard Draper said emphatically. "I haven't read any memos, but I'm sure our lawyers are on top of things."

"It's a little too early to talk about it, though. It's still gestating."

"Good. You can't rush creativity. On the other hand . . . I'm getting a little pressure from the people I report to. The network's first quarter demos are the lowest they've been in fifteen quarters."

"I understand. We'll push things, see if we can get a pilot on film by the end of this quarter."

They ate in silence for a moment, then Howard Draper laid his fork down carefully, neatly on his napkin, and said, "Norman, we need to get something out of the box very soon. Or else . . ." he lowered his voice even though there were only three other people in the restaurant and they were speaking Greek, "there may be no box."

"Is it that bad?"

"We're getting beaten by UPN in Adults 18 to 49."

"Jesus, really? Adults 18 to 49?"

"Uh-huh."

"By UPN?"

"Uh-huh."

"That's a demo you don't want to come in sixth in."

"You certainly don't."

Ten minutes later, having paid the bill in cash, they left in separate cars.

* * *

There were three names on Norman Hudris's call sheet when he returned from his lunch with Howard Draper in Glendale. His colorectal surgeon was returning his call to schedule his semiannual colonoscopy; his dermatologist was returning his call with, he hoped, the results of the biopsy taken on a suspicious-looking mole on his earlobe; and someone named Charlie Berns.

Norman Hudris came up empty on Charlie Berns. He asked his assistant, Tom Soaring Hawk, a Native American hired as a result of the network's recent diversity campaign, if Charlie Berns had mentioned what he was calling about.

"No, he didn't, Norman," Tom Soaring Hawk said in that calm, uninflected voice that Norman was really starting to dislike. Norman was considering having a chat with ABCD's head of Human Resources to see if he could get Tom Soaring Hawk transferred out of the division as a security risk.

"If you don't know who they are, you're supposed to ask what this is regarding."

"I know who he is."

"You *do*?"

"Yes. I Googled him."

"Who is he?"

"He's a producer."

"A producer of what?"

"He won an Academy Award for *Dizzy and Will*."

It all came flooding back to Norman Hudris: the flake who had come to him when he was still in the movie business with a script about Benjamin Disraeli that he somehow had managed to attach Bobby Mason to, that they started off making in Yugoslavia until Bobby Mason got kidnapped by Macedonian separatists and then the guy had gone underground and made the original script with blocked currency and with Jeremy Ikon and Jacqueline Fortier, and actually managed, against all odds, to win the Best Picture Oscar.

After that, Charlie Berns had disappeared off the radar screen. He hadn't made a picture since then. His name was never in the trades. He was not connected with any projects that were being talked about.

Norman Hudris saw no good reason to return Charlie Berns's phone call. He was probably trying to pitch him some TV movie he couldn't sell as a feature. Or hit him up for a job. Or, even worse, suggest lunch so that they could reminisce about the halcyon days when they were both in the picture business.

So Norman Hudris did not return Charlie Berns's phone call. Instead he called his dermatologist and was told that there was no conclusive evidence from the biopsy that the mole on his earlobe was malignant. He was not overly comforted by the language. The word *conclusive* was not reassuring. So he scheduled an appointment to repeat the biopsy. Then he called Dr. Hjort, his colorectal surgeon, and made an appointment for his colonoscopy.

* * *

Charlie Berns had gotten Norman Hudris's phone number by first calling NBC, and then, upon being told that the former Standards and Practices executive no longer worked there, he simply cold-called the other networks and had the ABC switchboard put him through.

Charlie had been in the business long enough to know when he was getting blown off, and when Norman Hudris did not return his phone call by noon the following day, Charlie called the ABC switchboard again.

"Norman Hudris's office," Tom Soaring Hawk announced.

"It's Charlie Berns."

"Mr. Hudris is in meetings all day and—"

"No, he isn't."

"May I ask what this is regarding?"

"Just put him on the phone."

"I'll see if he's available," the assistant said, and he punched the hold button, got up and knocked on his boss's door.

After a moment Norman Hudris called, "What?"

Tom Soaring Hawk opened the door and stood in the doorway. His boss was playing Minesweeper on his computer, staring intently at the screen, no doubt trying to avoid getting blown up by a U-boat.

"Charlie Berns called back."

"Did you tell him I was in a meeting?"

"Yes, but he didn't believe me."

"Oh, for shits sake . . ."

"He's on line three."

Norman knew this because there was only one line blinking. His assistant had the annoying habit of providing superfluous information. "Close the door," he said irritably, then waited fifteen seconds before picking up.

"Hello."

33

"Norman, it's Charlie Berns."

"Hey, how're you doing? It's been a while. What are you up to?"

"I want to come in and pitch you an idea for a series."

"You ought to go see Kara."

"I don't know Kara. I know you."

"Well, Charlie, I'm flattered you would think of me, but I'm sort of in the alternative media division here."

"That's okay with me. This is kind of an alternative idea."

"You want to put something down on paper, e-mail me."

"No. I want to pitch this to you personally. You got any time Monday?"

"We've got staff meetings pretty much all day . . ."

"I'm sure you can slip me in. Late afternoon? About four? Staff meeting should be over by then."

Norman Hudris looked at his calendar. The only thing he had scheduled for the entire day was a morning trip to the dermatologist to take another skin sample from this earlobe.

"Four's okay."

"Leave two passes."

*   *   *

"Division 51," the voice said when Charlie dialed the 703 area code number that Kermit Fenster had given him.

"Fenster?" Charlie spoke softly since he was making the call from Lionel's kitchen, his free 1,000-minute cell phone being limited to local calls.

"Who's this?"

"Charlie Berns."

"Berns. Good to hear from you."

"Where are you?"

"What do you mean *where am I?*"

"The area code of the number you gave me is Virginia."

"That's where the agency is, Berns. Langley, Virginia."

"Oh, I thought you lived *here.*"

"You think over my proposition?"

"As a matter of fact, yes. And I think it may have some virtue."

"Tell me something I don't know."

"Listen, I got in touch with an old friend of mine at ABC and set up a meeting for Monday. Four p.m."

"I'll be there."

"You going to fly in from Virginia?"

"That's why airplanes were invented."

"Here's the idea—"

"I don't need to know the details. That's your department."

"You don't want to know what I'm pitching?"

"Charlie, an efficient machine has no unnecessary parts. If everyone knows only what they're supposed to know, things run a lot more smoothly."

"Okay, but it's all going to depend on finding a warlord."

"You want a warlord in Central Asia? I can get you a dozen. Who's the meeting with?"

"ABC. A guy I used to know, Norman Hudris, is in development there."

"This guy says yes, then what happens?"

"Well, ordinarily, you get development money to bring in a writer to write a pilot script, but this is a reality show, so there is no script. So what we want is money to go over there, scout locations and find our warlord. What do you think it's going to cost to spend a couple of weeks in Uzbekistan?"

"Fifty grand."

"For travel expenses?"

"Fifty thou *plus* travel expenses."

"What's the fifty for?"

"You don't just go into a country in Central Asia and start talking to warlords. There are assets that need funding."

"They're not going to pay fifty thousand dollars plus travel just to find a warlord."

"Charlie, there are two types of people in this world: there are people who get things done, and there are people who tell you why they can't get things done. You're disappointing me."

"Assuming they want to write a check, who do they write it to?"

"Cash."

"ABC is not going to write a check for fifty thousand dollars to cash."

"They like the idea enough they will. Where's the meeting?"

"ABC in Burbank. Norman Hudris's office. I'll have them leave a drive-on pass in your name at Security."

"Have them leave the pass for Dwight Halloran."

"Who's he?'

"You don't need to know."

FOUR

Slouching to Burbank

Charlie Berns awoke the following Monday morning with the problem of finding transportation to Burbank for his meeting with Norman Hudris. Shari's sister Rita, sufficiently recovered from her periodontal surgery to be off Vicodin, had repossessed her car keys, leaving Charlie stranded on top of Mandeville Canyon.

In the kitchen he looked for a phone book in the transportation drawer beneath the kitchen phone. The transportation drawer was directly below the take-out food menu drawer and contained phone books arranged alphabetically by municipalities. Charlie grabbed the phone book for *Santa Monica and Adjacent Neighborhoods Including Brentwood* and retreated into the pool house. Consulting the map, he determined that he would need to take the number 2 bus east along Sunset into Hollywood, get off at Highland and catch the 420 through the Cahuenga Pass, then the 163 north along Barham to Riverside, from where he could take either the 569 east or walk what looked to be about three-quarters of a mile to the studio.

But first he had to get down the hill. The bus map taught Charlie what every poor person in Los Angeles is born knowing: there are no buses that go and up and down the canyons. You had to get to Sunset first before you could get a bus. If Charlie were more observant or got up earlier, he might have noticed the cleaning ladies, or at least those not fortunate enough to own an uninsured pre-1990 Chevy, walking up Mandeville from Sunset every morning with paper bags containing refills of Windex.

He looked out the sliding glass doors to the motor pool at the end of the drive. There was Lionel's jet black Porsche Turbo Carrera GT,

MSRP $181,700, which he wouldn't even let Shari do her makeup in; his off-beige Lexus 430, just detailed; and the cranberry Range Rover, the car he allowed Shari to drive.

Requesting the use of a car, however, would entail disturbing Lionel in his study, where he worked seven days a week on the several scripts he was writing. Charlie knew from experience that Lionel did not like being disturbed while he was working. And since Charlie was supposed to be moving out, it would only remind Lionel that his uncle was still living in the pool house that he was eager to convert to his girlfriend's office.

A solution presented itself in the form of Mr. Kim, who appeared after lunch with his skimmer and kit of chemicals. Charlie prevailed upon the taciturn Korean pool man to give him a lift down the hill as soon as he was finished painstakingly backwashing Lionel's filter and adjusting the acid-pH ratio to some sort of zenlike balance.

Charlie rode shotgun down Mandeville in the pool man's immaculate Toyota Tacoma, got out at Sunset and crossed over to the eastbound bus stop. When a bus came along, it was a number that was not listed on the map in front of the phone book. He got on the bus and took out his wallet.

"How much?"

"A dollar seventy-five," the driver answered, pressing down on the accelerator and nearly knocking him over. Charlie took a ten-dollar bill out of his wallet, tried to give it to the large woman behind the wheel, but she looked at it disdainfully and said, "Exact change only."

"You can't change a ten?"

"What'd I just say?"

"But I don't have exact change."

"Then you're getting off at the next stop."

Charlie turned and faced the dozen or so passengers, sitting there lost in their Spanish-language *Soap Opera Digest*s.

"Anybody got change for a ten?"

No one so much as blinked. The driver was slowing down as she approached the next bus stop. He was about to be left stranded in the grassy, quasi-rural stretch of Sunset that runs through Brentwood, where there was no place to get change for a ten.

"All right," he said, lowering the price like a seller on the floor of the stock exchange with a rapidly sinking security. "How about five dollars in change?"

The bus halted. The driver opened the door at the deserted bus stop. People glared at him with hostility. Because of this deadbeat gringo they were all going to be late.

"Okay. I'll give someone this ten-dollar bill for exact change in quarters." No one budged.

"That's a profit of eight dollars and twenty-five cents!"

A skinny kid in an Oscar de la Hoya tee shirt went into his pocket for a bunch of quarters. Charlie walked down the aisle of the bus to where the kid was sitting and handed him the ten-dollar bill. The kid held it up in the light, like a bank teller checking to see if it was counterfeit, before dumping seven quarters into Charlie's hand.

He trudged back up the aisle under the irritated glare of the other passengers and dropped seven quarters into the fare box. The driver didn't close the door until all seven quarters made the appropriate sound.

"How far is Highland?" he asked.

"This bus don't go there. Transfer to the 302 at Barrington."

* * *

By the time Charlie got off the bus at Riverside Drive in Burbank, he had spent $20 in overpayment for bus fares. For that money he could have called a taxi. It had taken him an hour and forty minutes to get from the foot of Mandeville Canyon to Burbank, a trip he could have done in twenty minutes in a car. He walked the last leg of the journey along Riverside Drive—closer to a mile than three-quarters of a mile, it turned out—and arrived in front of the ABC lot covered with a veneer of perspiration. Though it was January, the temperature in the Valley was up in the seventies, under a sinking grayish sun.

The guards were checking for terrorist bombs by passing mirrors under the car chassis. At least he didn't have to worry about his car chassis. Charlie had his explosives wired to his chest. He started toward the entrance to the building when one of the guards stopped him.

"Help you?"

"I have a four o'clock with Norman Hudris."

"Your name?"

"Charlie Berns."

"Government-issue ID?"

Charlie waded through the kited credit cards till he found his driver's license. The guard compared the photo on the license with the man standing in front of him. The picture was four and a half years old and seemed to be of a man considerably younger.

The fact was that four and a half years ago he *was* considerably younger. These last few years had taken a disproportionate toll on him. Though Charlie Berns was only fifty-seven, he could pass for sixty-five.

"Where did you park your vehicle, Mr. Berns?"

"I don't have a vehicle."

Charlie might as well have said that he didn't have a liver.

"Would you step back outside the gate, sir."

"Check with Norman Hudris's office. They said they would leave a drive-on for me." But as soon as the words were out of his mouth, Charlie realized that at this level of security, things were taken very literally. Apparently, he didn't need a drive-on; he needed a *walk*-on.

Charlie stepped back a few feet until he was, technically at least, off company property and watched the guard discuss the situation with a fellow security guard. Meanwhile, cars started piling up in front of the gate as the two guards tried to decide what to do with this man who wanted to gain access to a studio lot without a vehicle.

Five cars back, at the wheel of a black Hummer H1, Charlie made out the features of Kermit Fenster. Charlie started back toward the guards to retrieve his driver's license, but they stopped him almost immediately.

"Sir, stay behind the gate."

"If you give me back my driver's license, I can get a ride in with a friend. He's the fifth car in line. He's got an appointment too."

The guards looked at each other. It took a moment before the second guard nodded. This seemed to be the solution. Charlie would be entering the lot in a vehicle and therefore no longer in an irregular situation. They could check beneath the vehicle with their mirrors and look in the trunk for bombs.

Charlie walked back past the row of cars till he reached the black Hummer. Fenster pressed a button, the door lock opened and Charlie climbed into the large passenger seat of the ferocious-looking vehicle. They inched forward until they reached the gate. As the second guard passed the mirror underneath the Hummer, the first guard asked Fenster to pop the trunk.

"This car doesn't have a trunk," Fenster said. "It has a cargo bay."

"Would you open the rear of the vehicle?"

Fenster hit a switch under the dashboard to unlock the rear door.

"You know what the payload is on this baby?"

Charlie shook his head.

"Two thousand two hundred pounds. Over a ton. Hundred-ninety-five horsepower engine, four hundred thirty pounds of torque."

They were asked to produce their driver's licenses, and Charlie caught sight of a Florida license. Fenster gave his name to the guard as Dwight Halloran. After they finally got waved through, Fenster-Halloran said, "When you introduce me to the TV guys, use the name Vernon Gough."

"What happened to Dwight Halloran?"

As usual, Fenster did not answer the question. They drove, as directed, to a visitors' parking area, where Fenster parked in a handicapped space. When he got out of the car, Charlie noticed the handicapped plate on the rear of the Hummer.

"There are no airbags in this baby. You know why? Because nothing can stop it. With eighty-five hundred pounds of gross vehicle weight, it's going take out anything in its path."

"That's comforting."

"This is the military version. It's armor-plated. In case some guy on the freeway wants to take a potshot at you."

Inside the building, they went through one more security check, producing their driver's licenses and being given temporary ID badges with their names on them. As they entered the elevator, Fenster took out his wallet and removed a strip of tape, with which he covered the name of Dwight Halloran with another name. His badge now read Vernon Gough.

They rode the elevator to the third floor, got off and proceeded to a reception desk, where a woman wearing a telephone headset and too much makeup was fielding incoming calls. Eventually she came up for air and looked up at them.

"Charlie Berns and Vernon Gough for Norman Hudris," Charlie announced.

"Is your entire meeting here?"

"We *are* the entire meeting."

The woman didn't flinch. She merely hit an extension and said into her headpiece microphone, "I've got a Charlie Berns and a Vernon Gross for Norman."

"Gough," Fenster corrected.

She flicked another button, then said, "Have a seat. They'll come and get you when they're ready."

They sat down on an uncomfortable faux-leather couch in front of a faux-walnut coffee table covered with copies of the trade papers. Fenster picked up a copy of *Variety* with the headline "Majors Maxing Out Minis." He stared at it for a moment, then asked Charlie, "What the hell does that mean? It's fucking Greek."

Charlie tried to compose himself for the pitch. It had been a while since he'd pitched anything. Usually he would be in the meeting with a writer, a book he had optioned, something tangible that he had thought about and discussed at some length. But now he was going in with a half-baked idea and a possible psychopath with three different names and a phony security badge.

Twenty minutes went by. Fenster said, "This SOP, making you wait?"

"Depends on how important you are."

"It's just a power game. I can rise above it. I hung around for two days to see the minister of the interior of Azerbaijan. Waited the fucker out. Power is just a zero-sum game. The more you allow them to have, the less you have."

* * *

It was ten to five when they were finally led back through a long corridor to Norman Hudris's office. A fifty-minute wait was borderline outrageous in this business; it was ten minutes short of a complete blow-off. But Charlie wasn't surprised. It had been clear to him that Norman Hudris did not want to take this meeting in the first place and was doing his best to make that apparent.

But Fenster—a man who had sat outside the minister of the interior of Azerbaijan's office for two days—wasn't going to let it pass without a remark.

"You guys get caught in traffic?" he asked the man he assumed was Norman Hudris as soon as they entered the office. The man turned out to be Geoff Kloske, a junior member of ABCD's development team, invited to the meeting to take notes and help Norman deflect whatever was coming at him.

Geoff Kloske looked a little confused until Norman Hudris emerged from behind his desk and offered his hand. "Hi. Norm Hudris."

Fenster shook it and replied, "Vern Gough, nice to meet you. *Finally.*"

"Sorry about the wait. We had a little fire to put out."

"Must've been a hell of a fire . . ."

Charlie and Norman looked at each other for a moment, each one trying to recall the other's appearance four years ago. They both had forgotten entirely what the other one looked like. In the movie business, the disk drive in the brain responsible for face retention has a very small capacity. The features of the people you work with on one project get overwritten by the features of the people you work with on the next project.

"You're looking good, Charlie," Norman Hudris said.

"So are you, Norman," replied Charlie, wondering how anybody who knew him four years ago could possibly think he was looking good. He wasn't even looking good four years ago.

"This is Geoff Kloske, one of our new directors."

Charlie and Geoff Kloske shook hands.

"I loved *Dizzy and Will*," the young man said, in the type of reverential tone reserved for dinosaurs. The kid looked like he was fifteen. And sounded as if he were talking about *Birth of a Nation*.

"Thank you."

"You making a sequel?"

"Don't think so . . ."

Charlie introduced Fenster as Vernon Gough, his Central Asian consultant.

The four of them took seats at the conversation area in Norman Hudris's office. The office was on the small side and was devoid of any personal touches. It didn't look to Charlie like Norman Hudris had risen very high in the television world, at least not according to the square-footage criterion—a not entirely unreliable measure of clout in Hollywood.

For the next seven minutes they indulged in small talk—gossip, innuendo and anecdotes. This was the customary amount of time for irrelevant conversation at the beginning of all pitch meetings. And it was accepted practice that it was the network executive, the person giving the meeting, who would wrap up this period by saying something on the order of, "So, what have you got for us today?"

But before Norman Hudris could say that, or something like it, Fenster, who had not been participating in the vamping, said, "So, are we here to talk about the Lakers or to sell you a show?"

He said this right in the middle of Norman Hudris's describing being courtside at Staples and watching Jack Nicholson with a babe forty years younger than him. Norman skidded to a halt, flashed an anemic smile, and said, "So, what do you have for us?"

"Charlie's got a fabulous idea," Fenster said, turning to Charlie with an expectant look on his face.

Charlie was on the mound with the ball in his hand. It was time to deliver to the plate. Norman Hudris was standing there, the bat on his shoulder, waiting.

"Okay, so here it is. This is a reality show. I mean, what else is working on television these days, right? Well, it's actually kind of a combination of reality and fiction. It has the best elements of both. But it's non-scripted. Anyway, I met Ker . . . Vern . . . socially . . . and he started talking to me about Central Asia . . ."

Charlie picked up a very subtle, almost imperceptible raising of the eyebrows. Central Asia was not something that whetted their appetites. Ball one.

"It's a really interesting place—kind of anarchic and colorful, not unlike the American West a hundred and fifty years ago. Vern's worked there and he knows everything there is to know about

Uzbekistan, Turkmenistan, Tajikistan and all those places that used to belong to the Soviet Union. They're wild places—run by corrupt governments, Russian mafia, Islamic fundamentalists, warlords with private armies running around collecting tributes and settling scores with rival warlords. It's Dodge City, all these guys with their gangs and guns and the sheriff trying to maintain order . . ."

There were some signs of modest interest. They liked *warlords* and *guns* and *mafia* . . . They were good words.

"So I thought about this idea, you know, how to make this world real and interesting to the television viewer. I mean, does the guy in Dubuque care about what's happening in Central Asia?"

Ball two. Charlie had forgotten one of the primary rules of pitching: never raise negative questions even if they're rhetorical. There's no point in giving executives any more reasons than they already have to say no.

"Of course not. But what he *does* care about is the human struggle to survive in this world. What's it *like* to be a warlord? What kind of problems do you face? How do you consolidate power? How do you *survive* in this world?"

Slowly, he was reeling them back in. They were listening with a certain degree of anticipation.

"So the idea is to do a reality series about the life of a Uzbek warlord—film his daily life, his exacting tribute from the villages he controls, his guerrilla war with the corrupt government forces, his relationships with his lieutenants and his soldiers, and, here's what I think is really interesting: his problems in his everyday life—with his wife, his girlfriend, his children. And the thing is, this will all be real. Real problems, real battles, real bullets . . ."

Even though the executives were leaning in closer, flecks of interest in their eyes, Charlie knew he hadn't quite sold it yet. He was a couple of phrases away from the cigar. He needed to put one more idea into their heads. And he was saving it for last. This was the going to be the clincher. One way or the other.

"Here's the log line," Charlie said, in a quiet voice, letting them amp up their attention a few notches. He waited a few beats for the imaginary drumroll before delivering the hook.

"*The Osbournes* meets *The Sopranos*."

During his salad days, Charlie Berns had played in a weekly poker game. With a fair amount of success. What made Charlie successful was his ability to decipher the body language of other players. These very subtle signs are called tells because they tell you what you need to know about the cards your opponents are holding without their realizing that they're telling you.

In the split second before he could cover it up, Norman Hudris displayed the tell that Charlie Berns had been looking for. Whatever the television executive might say to the contrary, Charlie knew that he had betrayed his interest. He might still turn it down—for any of a dozen pro forma reasons that projects are passed on—but not because he wasn't interested.

Charlie left the log line floating in the room. When it came to pitching, less was definitely more. He sat on the couch and waited for a reaction.

"Uh-huh," Norman Hudris said, after a long moment.

"Uh-huh," Geoff Kloske echoed.

"Beautiful, isn't it?" Kermit Fenster said.

"Well, that's . . . intriguing, I suppose . . ." Norman Hudris said, careful to modulate any enthusiasm with the right tone of caution.

"Interesting," said Geoff Kloske, who looked down at his yellow legal pad on which he had neglected to write anything during the very short pitch.

The two executives looked at each other, trying to discern the other one's level of interest. It was always dangerous, especially for underlings, to express an opinion publicly until they knew how everyone else in the room thought.

Finally, Norman Hudris said, "A couple of questions."

"Sure," said Charlie, who had, he thought, anticipated most of them.

"How do you choose this warlord?"

"No problem," Fenster said before Charlie could open his mouth. "I know warlords all over the area. I could deliver a dozen of them. Two dozen."

"Right," said Charlie, picking up the ball, "We audition them, put the best ones on tape. You choose the guy you like best."

"Sort of like *The Bachelor*, right?" volunteered Geoff Kloske.

"Precisely," said Charlie.

"This warlord," Norman said, "he's not going to speak English, is he?"

"He doesn't even speak Russian, he speaks Uzbek, if we're lucky, maybe a little Arabic," said Fenster.

"We subtitle him," Charlie said quickly. "And anyway, you don't really care what Tony Soprano says, do you? It's always *fucking this* and *fucking that*. It's what he *does*, it's that look in his eyes when he has to deal with a problem, or when he has to off somebody. That's what counts."

"Let me ask you something," said Norman, a little queasily. "Would you actually show real violence?"

"Your call," said Charlie. "I mean, look what they show on *The Sopranos*, not to mention on the eleven o'clock news every night."

"We could edit it . . . tastefully, I suppose . . ."

"Any way you want it. Tasteful or not."

"I mean," said Norman, articulating the unasked question, "there would be limits to what you show. For example, you wouldn't actually show the warlord . . . *killing* someone. Would you?"

"Why not?" said Fenster. "It's reality television, isn't it? So what's wrong with a little reality?"

"Vern's speaking metaphorically, of course. We do have to deal with the FCC."

"Fuck the FCC. A bunch of clowns who sit around Washington selling broadcast licenses to the highest bidder."

"The point is," Charlie said, "we'd have complete control in the editing room. We'd show as much or as little as you want us to."

"Once they get the scent of real blood in their nostrils, they're not going to be happy with ketchup."

"Anyway," said Charlie, eager to get Fenster out of the room, "that's the idea. We'll let you chew on it for a while." And he rose from the couch. The two TV executives rose with him. Fenster stayed seated.

"We need to hear by Wednesday," the Central Asian consultant said, his arms folded in front of him.

"Well . . ." Norman said, "I don't know if we can get back to you that quickly."

"Wednesday we're going to NBC." And Fenster got up, took his parking ticket out of his pocket and offered it to Norman Hudris, "You want to take care of this?"

The TV executive looked at the ticket, then at Fenster and said, "They'll validate it for you at the front desk."

"It's a buck seventy-five every twenty minutes."

"Well, thanks for coming in."

"Thanks for hearing the pitch," said Charlie, edging Fenster toward the door.

"Uh . . . whom do we contact about this?" Geoff Kloske asked.

Charlie tried to remember when the thirty-day free trial for his cell phone was up. But it was the only number he had. He gave it to Geoff Kloske.

"Who's representing you guys?"

"We're actually . . . between agents," Charlie said, now at the door, effectively blocking Fenster from access back into the room.

"We'll be in touch," Norman Hudris said.

"By close of business Wednesday," Fenster fired back and turned and headed for the elevators.

* * *

Plowing through the Cahuenga Pass in the Hummer, Fenster expressed his take on the meeting they had just attended.

"I've heard less bullshit from Bedouins."

"It's just code language," Charlie explained.

"They don't buy it, we go across the street."

"It's a buyer's market. There're a lot of people out there selling shows."

"How many of them can deliver the real thing?"

"We'll need to get a lawyer to draft something, and have him negotiate a deal with the network to protect our own interests."

"You think they're going to fuck with us?"

"They're not going to hand us anything, let alone a sack of cash, without some sort of deal in place. What happens if they develop it further, we go on the air? How much control do they have? Who owns the product?"

"What do you mean—who owns the product? We own the product."

"Not these days. Networks want a piece of the action."

"That's extortion."

"That's the television business."

"They fuck with us, they're in big trouble. I drop a dime, I can have both of them taken care of," Fenster said as he turned the Hummer onto Sunset and headed west into the murky dusk.

FIVE

Souvlaki

In his corner office at DBA, Dynamic Boutique Associates, Brad Emprin was getting a blowjob from a desperate actress named Tamara Berkowitz when the intercom buzzed. He had taken the precaution of locking his office door but had neglected to turn off his intercom, something he didn't know how to do, in any event, even if he'd had the forethought to do it.

It was, frankly, a substandard blowjob, with a little too much hot air for his taste. He'd give it a 4, at best, on the blowjob scale, which was not enough to preclude his responding to the intercom.

"What?"

The Zoloft-enhanced mellowness of his assistant Gina Perfft's voice slithered through the intercom.

"There's a Charlie Berns on two."

"Who?"

"Charlie Berns."

"Take his number."

"He won't leave his number. He said he has a deal at ABC and wants you to negotiate it."

Brad Emprin put his hand on Tamara Berkowitz's head to slow her down, not that she needed a whole lot of slowing down. This blowjob could take two hours the way it was going. She must have thought she was going to get points for artistic merit.

"Who is this guy?"

"Apparently you used to represent him. When you were with Sy Green."

"He has a deal at ABC?"

"That's what he says."

For a moment Brad Emprin considered whether he wanted to blow off the blowjob. It was probably too late. Tamara Berkowitz was already working gamely away, and now he would have to agree to represent her or else risk getting hauled into court on sexual harassment charges even though the blowjob had been totally her idea. She was on her knees before he had said a word.

"Put him through," he said, taking his hand off the pause button. Tamara Berkowitz might as well work through the phone call. It was going to take long enough as it was.

"Charlie, how you doing?" said Brad Emprin, no idea whom he was talking to.

Charlie Berns, who did know whom he was talking to, responded, "I'm okay, Brad."

"What's going on?"

"Yesterday I pitched a series to Norman Hudris at ABC. I need someone to make a deal for my partner and me if he buys it."

"They said yes in the room?"

"Didn't have to. They love it."

"What's the log line?"

"Just call it Charlie Berns Reality Show Project."

"What do you want?"

"At the moment, we want first-class air travel and accommodations, and fifty grand in R&D money. To scout locations and cast it."

"Fifty grand? Where're you going—the south of France?"

"Brad, just call Norman and lay it out for him. It's real simple. That's a five-thousand-dollar phone call for you. That is, if you want to make it."

"Of course I want to make it. I love this project. So . . . you want fifty grand development money and round-trip first-class air and hotel . . . where?"

"Tashkent."

"The Tashkent? Where is that—in Vegas?"

"Uzbekistan."

"*Where?*"

"Central Asia. Two countries north of Afghanistan."

* * *

While Charlie Berns was obtaining representation for Kermit Fenster and him, Norman Hudris was presiding over an ABCD staff meeting in the soundproofed conference room on the third floor of the Manhattan Beach facility. You needed a special key card to gain entrance to this room, where there was an oval table, chairs, a coffee machine and no telephones. The walls were unadorned, the ceiling lit by fluorescent lights.

Norman Hudris hadn't realized just how much he wanted Charlie Berns's project for ABCD until he woke up at 4:00 a.m. in a paroxysm of anxiety about the division's—and, *a fortiori*, his own—prospects for survival. The ice beneath him was getting thinner by the day. Unless the division began to produce results soon, the network would dissolve it, dumping all its personnel on to the retracting marketplace for TV executives.

He did not want to be dumped out on to a shrinking job market at a time like this. His disposable income was rapidly dissolving. The lease on the LS 430 was five months from termination. He had a balloon payment on his house in Coldwater due in the fall.

In attempt to stay afloat, Norman had instituted an austerity program—cutting down on weekend trips to Palm Springs, avoiding pricey Melrose Avenue trattorias, attending every free screening he could. He had dialed down his cable to basic monthly service, using the office TiVo to keep up with HBO programs.

Still, if he wasn't careful, he would wind up in a rented apartment in Van Nuys. That's how thin the margin was. So when he bolted awake at 4:03 a.m. and ran the numbers, as he did every night at this time in the desperate hope that the bottom line would be different, he became more acutely aware of the need to produce a breakthrough show for ABCD.

As soon as Charlie Berns had presented the log line for *Warlord*, Norman Hudris knew that it was a winner. It was the ultimate hybrid, the soap opera violence of *The Sopranos* mixed with the unpredictability of reality television. It covered all the bases: adventure, voyeurism, exotic locales, colorful people.

Though Norman didn't know whether Charlie Berns could actually deliver this show, and he had no reading at all on the loose cannon he had brought in with him as consultant, Norman was persuaded that it was their best shot. And nothing that he was hearing from the development staff this morning was telling him that his assessment was wrong.

Moira Appolny, a reedy, asthmatic woman in her thirties, a refugee from the network's vanishing two-hour movie department, was presenting a concept called *Thirty Days to Live*. The idea was that a doctor told a person during the course of his routine annual physical that he had an incurable illness and only a month to live. You then followed him to see how he dealt with it.

"It has a lot of payoff to it," Moira Appolny was saying, "when you break the news to them that it was all a setup. I mean, you can see the tears already, right?"

"Does the audience know?" Geoff Kloske asked.

"Yes. But the person doesn't. Like *Joe Millionaire*."

"So it's a kamikaze series. You do ten segments and you're finished."

"We could do lawyers, as well. Same idea, the lawyer tells you you're being sued up the wazoo . . . or maybe plumbers—they tell you you're looking at a seventy-five-thousand-dollar job to replace all your pipes . . ."

Norman tuned out. These ideas all had serious legal exposure. His mandate from Howard had been to produce nothing that was actionable. That was the beauty of *Warlord*. Who was going to sue them? The Uzbekistan government? The Russian mafia? The Islamic fundamentalists? The show was litigation-proof. And probably inexpensive. How much money could a warlord want? There were no branch offices of the William Morris Agency in Uzbekistan.

Pleading a conference call he had to take, Norman disbanded the meeting and headed back to his office, where he was handed a list of phone messages by Tom Soaring Hawk.

"Brad Emprin from DBA said that you need to call him before lunch."

"Before lunch?"

"He's representing Charlie Berns."

"Oh fuck. Really?"

"I told him you were in a staff meeting. He said that if he didn't hear from you by noon he was taking the show to NBC."

Norman checked the knockoff Rolex. 11:47. If he tried to get to Howard before talking to Brad Emprin, he would be cutting it close. He'd call the agent first to get the numbers. Then he would do a Greek restaurant lunch with Howard and lay it out.

"All right. Get Brad Emprin for me. On my private line."

"I can't access your private line from my phone," Tom Soaring Hawk reminded him, correctly.

Norman took the phone message into his office, closed the door behind him. He removed his jacket, a silk Armani he had gotten at the Barney's warehouse sale at 60 percent off but still $700 he couldn't afford, sat down and dialed Brad Emprin's phone number.

* * *

The subject of this phone call, meanwhile, was holed up on the top of Mandeville Canyon watching DVDs of *The Sopranos* in his nephew's media room and waiting for his cell phone to ring. He had seventy-two hours before the month's free trial would expire and they would shut him off. After that he would be phoneless as well as homeless and carless.

He watched Tony wander down the driveway in his bathrobe to get his newspaper and wave to the FBI surveillance team in the New Jersey Power and Light truck parked around the corner. Unshaven, the top of his undershirt protruding from the half-open terrycloth robe, the guy had a slovenly sex appeal. They needed to find a warlord with this type of appeal. Some Uzbek version of Gandolfini.

His ruminations were interrupted by "Für Elise." Clicking the DVD player to mute, he picked up the call.

"Hello?"

"Mr. Berns. That you?"

The high-pitched nasal voice of Xuang Duc, his debt consolidator.

"Mr. Berns isn't in at the moment. May I take a message?"

"Mr. Berns. That you. I know."

Charlie put the phone down for ten seconds, then got back on with a different voice. "Hello, Charlie Berns here . . ."

"Mr. Berns. I call you many time, leave message on voice mail. You don't return call."

"Sorry about that. The voice mail on my phone isn't working right. I'll have to take the phone in."

"Mr. Berns, your check bounce."

"No kidding? I'll have my business manager cut a new check right away."

"Mr. Berns, you don't have business manager."

"Look, Xang—"

"It's Xuang."

"Look, *Xuang*, I'm just about to close on a lucrative deal. As soon as I get the check, I'll remit."

"When you get the check?"

"This week sometime."

"What day?"

This guy was relentless. He would hire another debt consolidator to get the Vietnamese off his back. He would kite debt consolidators . . .

"Friday."

"You call me on Friday, Mr. Berns. Otherwise, I institute procedures outlined in your contract."

Charlie hadn't bothered reading the contract and had no idea what these procedures entailed. He pressed a button and cut off Xuang Duc.

What could they do to him? Seize his property? Attach his salary? Take him to Hanoi and work him over? By the time the Vietnamese goons paid him a visit he'd already be out of Dodge. Let them come after him in Uzbekistan. He'd have the warlord take care of them. And film it. Episode 8—the warlord whacks Xuang Duc, tosses the body into the Aral Sea with a cement statue of Ho Chi Minh chained to his ankle.

"Charlie?"

This wasn't the phone. This was Shari. Standing in the doorway.

"Hey, how're you doing?"

"Listen, could you straighten up the pool house a little bit? I want my decorator to have a look, okay? And it would be nice if we could get the hardwood floor guys in there to start stripping the wood next week."

"No problem."

After the warlord did Xuang Duc, Charlie would have him do the closet organizer. Drop pieces of her in the Mojave Desert. Body parts distributed in alphabetical order.

*　*　*

Norman Hudris arrived first at the Hercules Taverna in Glendale and entered through the back door that gave on the parking lot. He took the booth in the rear, next to the kitchen, so that his boss, when he arrived, would have full vision of the front door of the restaurant.

The restaurant, as usual, was nearly deserted. Only two other tables were occupied—both by heavyset men in cheap suits. If there was a Greek mafia, this is where they would hang out.

Norman slid a five-milligram Valium into his mouth and chased it with saliva. He needed to get Howard to approve $50,000 plus travel expenses to Central Asia for the development of *Warlord*. This was a lot of money to be given to two men with no track record and with nothing on paper. And, as usual, he would have to explain the project to Howard without getting too specific.

Howard Draper was twenty minutes late. Sitting down without apology, he said, "Order a bottle of Agiorgitiko. The Retsina always gives me a headache."

They ordered *gharithes vrastes* to start and *stifatho* for a main dish. When the boiled shrimp appetizers arrived, Norman said, "I think I have something hot."

"I hope so."

"How much do you want to know?"

"As little as possible."

"It's a reality program loosely based on *The Sopranos*."

"A mob reality program?"

"Not exactly. It doesn't take place in America."

"Sicily?"

"No. Uzbekistan."

Howard put down his fork and stared across the table. "Are you putting me on?"

"No. The idea, in a nutshell, is—"

"Norman," he nearly shouted, before he could get the rest of the sentence out. "I don't need to know any more. Who brought it in?"

"Charlie Berns."

"Who?"

"Do you remember the producer of *Dizzy and Will*? Won Best Picture four years ago?"

"I thought he was dead."

"Might as well have been. Hasn't done anything since. He came in with this idea and some guy he introduced as a Central Asian consultant who claims he can deliver anything we need in Uzbekistan."

"*The Sopranos* in Uzbekistan? Produced by a man returned from the dead?"

"Howard, this show could break through big time. You follow this warlord around, watch him—"

"How much do they want?"

"Fifty thousand dollars plus first-class air and hotel in Tashkent. You're looking at seventy, seventy-five out the door."

"And we're not even going to get a script for that?"

"It's for expenses. They need to go over there, scout locations, cast the warlord . . ."

Howard Draper took a large pull of Agiorgitiko. "Let me ask you a question. But don't answer it. All right?"

Norman nodded, accustomed to these oblique debriefings.

"Does this warlord actually kill people?"

Norman did as instructed. Howard took another long sip of wine and said, "If he actually kills people, drink some wine."

"What should I do if I'm not sure?"

"Don't buy the show."

Norman took a sip from his wine glass. Howard looked around him cautiously, then, in a lowered tone of voice, "What can we write the money against?"

"Development costs."

"Whom do we write the check to?"

"Cash. We don't want to create a paper trail."

"How do we deal with a fifty-thousand-dollar cash outlay?"

"We write it up on the books as ten separate five-thousand-dollar petty-cash allocations, staggering the dates through the next ten quarters."

"Jesus, Norman, did you ever work at Enron?"

Though it was a rhetorical question, Norman shook his head.

"We need a code name for this project," Howard said.

"What's wrong with *Warlord*?"

"Too specific. How about . . . *Souvlaki*?"

"You want to name a project after a Greek shish kebab?"

"You have a better idea?"

* * *

"Brad Emprin's office."

"Let me speak to him. It's Charlie Berns."

"Will he know what this is regarding?" Tamara Berkowitz asked.

"Yes."

Brad Emprin's new executive assistant—a temporary position until a role worthy of her acting talents became available—buzzed her boss.

"Charlie Berns is on the line. He says you know what this is regarding."

Brad picked up the blinking phone line. "Charlie, I closed twenty minutes ago."

"When will the money become available?"

"On signature of contract."

"That could take weeks. Get me ten grand right away based on a deal memo."

"I'm not sure they're going to agree to that."

"They will."

"How do you know?"

"Because you're going to tell them that if they don't, we're going to NBC."

"Norman's a little nervous about this deal. He's negotiating directly with me instead of turning it over to Business Affairs."

"Have them messenger the front money to your office. In twenty-dollar bills."

"That's a shitload of twenty-dollar bills."

"Five hundred. Help yourself to a grand off the top."

"Jesus, Charlie, can't you write me a check? I mean, the agency doesn't accept cash commissions."

"Don't report it to them."

"What if they find out about this deal?"

"If you don't tell them, why should they?"

"What about . . . the IRS?"

"Your line tapped, Brad?"

"I don't think so."

"Then there's no problem."

* * *

Charlie left messages for Kermit Fenster on both the Virginia and Florida voice mails. Sixteen minutes later Fenster called him back.

"What's going on?"

"They bought it."

"Of course, they bought it. They had hard-ons in the room."

"I'm having an agent draw up a deal memo, preparatory to full contracts. Meanwhile, I'm getting us ten grand up front. In cash. Twenty-dollar bills."

"Get it in euros. Cleaner currency these days. In fact, make the whole deal payable in euros. We'll make another twenty percent on the conversion rate."

"Why do we need euros in Tashkent?"

"We're not going to Tashkent directly. We're going to Bishkek first."

"Where?"

"Bishkek. It's the capital of Kyrgyzstan. We fly in there and take a train to Tashkent."

"Why are we doing that?"

"Charlie, did I tell you how to pitch this show? Did I interfere with your creative integrity in any way? Just leave the logistics to me, all right? Have them book a suite at the Hotel Kontinental. With a *K*. It's on the Erkindik Prospektisi. Telephone is 22 05 98 54. Dial 011 then 00 996 first. Get a room on the fifth floor rear, as far away as possible from the ice machine."

"Hang on a second. Let me write this down."

Fenster repeated the specifics, right down to the telephone number, and Charlie wrote it down.

"What about airlines?"

"British Airways to London. Aeroflot to Moscow. Air Kazakhstan to Bishkek."

"Air Kazakhstan? Aren't we going to *Kyrgyz*stan?"

"Charlie, what'd I just say?"

"Okay. Fine."

"I'm going to need your passport number."

"What for?"

"For your visa, Charlie. Get yourself a diphtheria/tetanus booster, and you might as well get a typhoid and a hepatitis while you're at it."

"Hepatitis?"

"Yeah. A *and* B. And make sure the euros are in used twenty-euro bills with nonconsecutive serial numbers."

After he hung up with Fenster, Charlie called Brad Emprin back and told him about the euros.

"That's going to make it more than fifty grand in dollars," the agent pointed out.

"Cost of doing business."

"Where is Norman Hudris going to get fifty thousand euros?"

"In a bank, Brad. Make sure they're in stacks of twenty-euro bills. Used bills, nonconsecutive serial numbers."

Brad Emprin hung up with Charlie Berns and called Norman Hudris and told him about the euros.

"I thought we were closed."

"This is just boilerplate."

"He wants fucking *euros*?"

"Yeah. In twenty-euro bills. Used bills, nonconsecutive serial numbers."

"Where am I going to get used euros?"

"In a bank, Norman. And while you're there, negotiate a rate. We're going to want the remaining forty grand in euros as well."

*　*　*

Norman Hudris hung up with Brad Emprin and dialed Howard's private number. When his boss picked up he said, "The *Souvlaki* just got more expensive."

"How much more?"

"Check the exchange rate on the euro."

"Huh?"

"They want euros, not dollars. In twenty-euro bills."

"How do we write off fifty thousand euros?"

"The same way we write off the dollars. Petty cash. We're buying our office supplies in Luxembourg. As an economy measure."

It took about five seconds for Howard Draper to do the math. When he did, he said, "I couldn't hear that—the line must be bad," and hung up.

SIX

Tick-Borne Encephalitis

PAYMENT FOR
MEDICAL SERVICES
IS EXPECTED AT
TIME OF
TREATMENT

Charlie Berns sat in the crowded waiting room of West L.A. Medical Services: A Corporation and tried to ignore the plaque prominently displayed on the Plexiglas partition behind which the appointment nurses sat armed with calculators. He had not seen Dr. Vahan Moussekian, a jovial Armenian internist with a liberal prescription pad, for at least a year and a half—ever since his HMO fired him for failure to remit the annual premium.

Dr. Moussekian was one of the few professionals in Los Angeles that Charlie didn't owe money to. His attorney, his accountant, his stockbroker were all suing him for nonremission of fees. Soon his debt consolidator would join the ranks of people pursuing Charlie Berns in one court or another.

The fact that Charlie was clean with the Armenian internist and still on his patients' database enabled him to get in to see the doctor before April 1, the next available appointment. And it was this status that also spared him having to fill out the new patient questionnaire that asked pointed questions about a person's financial references.

"Still on Alpine Drive?" the nurse asked him.

"You bet." Charlie smiled back, already imagining the bill coming back, *addressee unknown* stamped under his name. West L.A. Medical Services: A Corporation could get in line to sue him.

It was forty minutes before he was allowed to penetrate the Plexiglas. He entered the rabbit warren of small consulting rooms and was ushered into one of them, where a nurse took his blood pressure.

"This is really not necessary," Charlie said, but she just continued squeezing the rubber ball and cutting off the circulation to his arm. She wrote the number in his chart, told him to strip down to his shorts and socks, stuck his chart in a box on the door and walked out.

Another forty minutes passed before Dr. Moussekian breezed into the room, his white lab coat over a pair of unpressed gabardine trousers. Charlie's chart in hand, the doctor scanned it quickly, then said with that bland perfunctory doctor's tone of voice, "How're we doing?"

He had taken a bus to get here and borrowed five dollars from his nephew's cleaning lady for carfare. That's how well he was doing.

"I'm not thrilled with your blood pressure," the doctor said, reading the number that the nurse had written down. "You taking any medication?"

"No."

"Diet and exercise?"

"Not terrific . . ."

"I'd like to do an EKG and check your thyroid. I'll have Denise draw some blood. We'll put you on a diuretic and a beta blocker, maybe throw in a ACE inhibitor . . ."

"Doc, I'm just here for some inoculations. I'm going to Central Asia. I was told I need diphtheria and tetanus boosters, typhoid and hepatitis A and B."

The doctor left the office and returned with a reference book.

"Which countries?" he asked.

"Kyrgyzstan and Uzbekistan, for sure."

"How about Tajikistan?"

"Could be."

"Then you'll want to be vaccinated against meningitis. How about Kazakhstan?"

"Don't know."

"We better do yellow fever. When did you get your last polio booster?"

Charlie shrugged.

"Are you going to be doing any trekking?"

"I'm not planning on it."

"Well, just to be on the safe side, we'll throw in tick-borne encephalitis."

* * *

Forty-five minutes later, an exotically punctured Charlie Berns stood at the cash register with a bill for $1,151 worth of consultations, tests and vaccinations. When he told the nurse-accountant that he would not be able to make payment for these medical services at the time they had been rendered, she darkened.

"Who is going to be responsible for today's charges?"

"My business manager. Just send the bill to him. He'll take care of it."

"You should have mentioned something before you saw the doctor."

"Did you ever read the Hippocratic Oath?"

"Excuse me?"

He was way over her head. She shuffled some papers, cleared her throat and said, without looking up at him: "I don't have the name of your business manager in your file."

"Brad Emprin."

"Could you spell that please?"

Charlie spelled his agent's name; then gave the accountant-nurse Brad Emprin's address and phone number at DBA and walked out of the office, another bridge in flames behind him.

* * *

ABCD's head of Business Affairs, Maxine Dyptich, was accustomed to unusual deal memos crossing her desk. But the deal memo for the "Untitled Charlie Berns" project was more bizarre than most. It called for $12,307.07 up front, followed almost immediately by an additional $49,228.28 for "development costs." It also authorized first-class airfare and hotel accommodations to the tune of another $26,120.55.

Besides the fact that these were not round numbers—in her twenty-two years in Business Affairs she had never seen a deal that wasn't rounded off to the nearest hundred dollars, if not the nearest thousand dollars—the money was to be paid out in one check for $12,307.07 and then ten separate checks in the amount of $4,820.05 apiece. All the checks were to be made out to cash.

She called Norman Hudris and asked him how she was to enter the money on the books.

"Petty-cash outlays, one a month for the next ten months."

Maxine Dyptich didn't blink. She had been at the secret division long enough not to question the accounting.

"Just out of curiosity, how come the odd figures?"

"You don't need to know that, Maxine."

"Fine with me. The less you know around here the better."

Maxine Dyptich hung up and proceeded to fill out the vouchers that were required to cut the checks. As usual, she had CNN Financial News on the TV with the sound off. She glanced up absently at the screen to see how the Dow was doing. The morning's prices for the yen and the pound rolled across the bottom of the screen. As the quote for the euro ran by—$1.2307—she turned back to her work. Two seconds later, the lightbulb went off. She grabbed her calculator and entered the number.

Jesus!

Maxine Dyptich thought she had seen it all, but apparently she hadn't. They were writing the goddamn deal in euros. The auditors would be all over it.

She took Norman Hudris's deal memo down the hall and photo-copied it. Then she filed it in a secret folder she kept locked away for the purposes of plea bargaining, if the time came.

* * *

Tamara Berkowitz looked across the desk at the man with the thinning hair and the Adidas gym bag and asked if he had an appointment.

"Just tell him Norman Hudris is here."

"Will he know what this is regarding?"

"Yes." Norman tried not to bark at the woman with the frizzy hair and tit job. She picked up the intercom and buzzed her boss.

Brad Emprin came out of his office to greet him. The agent eyed the Adidas bag nervously and led him quickly inside.

Unlike Norman Hudris's office at ABCD, Brad Emprin's office was big and full of expensively tasteless furniture. It resembled the office of the president of a Persian Gulf bank. The desk alone was nearly the size an small aircraft carrier. The agent was dressed like the 1995 version of Tom Cruise—silk blazer over a black cashmere jersey, jeans and boots that added a few inches to his five-foot, six-inch frame.

"Did you run into anybody in the elevator?"

"Nobody I knew."

"It doesn't look good coming into an agency with a gym bag full of money."

"Look, Brad, can we get through this?"

"Let's do it."

"I'm giving you the up-front money against the deal memo."

"Is it in euros?"

"There's ten thousand euros in there."

Norman opened the Adidas gym bag and removed the 500 twenty-euro notes from underneath his workout clothes. He put the money on Brad Emprin's desk.

"The rest will be forthcoming upon executed contracts."

Brad Emprin looked at the funny-colored used bills stacked up on his desk and shook his head. "That's funny-looking money."

"It was *your* deal point."

"Right. If I didn't know Charlie better, I would think this is some kind of drug deal, huh?" And he laughed his aggressive hyena laugh.

"I'll messenger the contracts to you for signature by the end of the week."

"Cool."

Norman took a last look at the money on Brad Emprin's desk, then turned and headed for the door. Brad hurried to follow him.

"Tamara will validate your parking," he called, but Norman Hudris did not even look back. He'd rather eat the $4.50 for twenty minutes parking than risk further exposure. Brad Emprin watched him head for the elevator before returning to his office, closing and locking the door behind him.

The agent walked over to the stacks of euros on his desk, picked two up, counted out his commission. He put the two stacks of euros into his pocket and the rest in his wall safe, where he kept his vitamin B$_{12}$ ampoules, his Lakers floor seats, his stock options and a pair of fur-lined handcuffs.

*　*　*

As he had done before, Charlie left messages on both of Kermit Fenster's voice mail machines and waited for the call back. This time it took twenty-two minutes before "Für Elise" gurgled in the pool house.

"We closed?" Fenster asked.

"Yes. The front money's with the agent."

"What's the time frame?"

"A week."

"Not sooner?"

"The lawyers need to draft the deal. Besides, I'm supposed to wait ten days to two weeks for my inoculations to take effect."

"You just don't drink the water or get a blood transfusion you'll be fine."

"Kermit, there are a few things we haven't discussed."

"Like what?"

"Like how you and I split up the money."

"What money?"

"The fifty thousand euros, for one thing."

"That money's already spent."

"What are you talking about?"

"How do you think we're going to get a warlord? You think we're going to put an ad in the *Tashkent Times*—Looking for colorful warlord for reality TV program. Good salary and benefits?"

"What about titles?"

"I don't want a title."

"You don't want your name on the screen?"

"What the fuck do I want my name on the screen for?"

"What about the ten grand front money?"

"Hang on to it for the moment."

There was a brief pause, and then Fenster said, "You fuck with me, Charlie, and you'll wind up on the bottom of the Aral Sea."

Fenster laughed. "Don't worry. There's not enough left of the Aral Sea to hide a body in."

* * *

Charlie used what leverage he had—his continued occupation of Lionel's pool house—to borrow a hundred dollars from his nephew, who seemed only too eager to give him the money if it would enable his uncle to get out of the pool house more quickly.

"We on schedule?" Lionel asked him as he counted out five twenties.

"More or less."

"Shari's got the hardwood floor guys coming in on Monday?"

"I'll do my best."

"What's wrong with your arm?"

Charlie was wearing a tee shirt that revealed the swelling in his biceps from all the injections he had gotten.

"I needed some inoculations."

"A little late in the season for a flu shot?"

"Never too late for tick-borne encephalitis."

"What?"

"They were having a special at my doctor's so I got the whole package. Hepatitis A and B, typhoid, meningitis . . ."

"Wow? That's great? You think I should get them?"

"Why not? You never know when you have to make an unscheduled trip to Turkmenistan."

After Lionel was gone, Charlie called his agent and told him to have the money ready for him. Then he indulged in a luxury he hadn't enjoyed for a long time. He picked up the phone and called for a cab.

* * *

Brad Emprin hadn't seen Charlie Berns in nearly four years. Not since the night that Charlie had won the Oscar for *Dizzy and Will,* when he, as a junior agent, was relegated to the next-to-back row at the Shrine Auditorium, the area reserved for accountants and seat warmers. So that when Charlie walked into his office, Brad Emprin barely recognized the upper middle-aged guy wearing a baseball cap and carrying a Saks Fifth Avenue shopping bag.

"Charlie, good to see you. Sit down. Want a drink?"

"No thanks, Brad. I've got a lot of things to do."

"I bet you do. On your way to—where the hell are you going again?"

"Tashkent."

"Terrific place."

"You've been there?"

"No. But I've heard. Listen, if the accommodations aren't first-class, you let me know, all right? I'll cut Norman Hudris a new one."

"I appreciate that. You have the money?"

"You bet. In twenty-euro bills, just like you asked," Brad Emprin said as he went to his wall safe and worked the combination. He extracted the stacks of euros and brought them to his desk, lining them up in a neat row.

"Nine thousand euros, net of commission. Present and accounted for."

Charlie put the stacks into his shopping bag.

"You don't want to count them?"

"That's your job, Brad. How are we doing on the contracts?"

"Working night and day on them. You should have them on Friday. By the way, we need to sign agency papers with you and this guy Gough."

"That's not going to happen."

"Charlie, we're negotiating this deal for you."

"And you're getting a commission, aren't you?"

"Well, yes, but . . . I mean, we'd like to announce the deal, maybe take an ad out in the trades."

"Brad, the less said about this deal the better."

"Uh-huh."

"This is a very unconventional deal."

"Uh-huh. I don't even know what the hell you sold."

"You don't want to know."

"Uh-huh."

"In fact, if I were you I wouldn't tell anybody else at the agency about the deal."

"Uh-huh. What about the commission?"

"Take it to Thomas Cook, change it into dollars and put it in your safe."

"Uh-huh."

"If you keep each transaction under ten thousand dollars, they don't have to report it to the IRS."

"Isn't that—illegal?"

"You bet it is."

* * *

An hour later Charlie walked into Thomas Cook Currency Service, Inc., on Rodeo Drive in Beverly Hills. The place was full of tourists cashing traveler's checks and the odd freelance currency speculator. Charlie took one of the stacks from the paper bag, placed it on the currency exchange counter and asked for U.S. dollars.

The clerk counted out the euros, holding each bill up to a counterfeit detection machine. If the money turned out to be funny, Charlie would be the guy left holding the bag. He'd do eighteen months at a federal minimum-security facility and learn how to do white-collar crime the real way—from the accountants.

Carrying his Saks shopping bag, Charlie walked down Rodeo Drive among the blue-eyed tourists in their bermuda shorts and Universal Studios Tour tee shirts. For the first time in a long while, he had money burning a hole in his pocket. His appetite rose to the occasion.

Ten minutes later he was sitting in an overcrowded pasta place eating undercooked linguini in clam sauce and washing it down with an overpriced merlot. The conversations around him were carried on at breakneck speed, breathy staccato character assassination indulged in over the risotto du jour.

As the wine penetrated his brain, he began to get a feeling he hadn't had in a long time. The feeling of possibility.

He had no idea what he was doing. But in this business did anyone really know what they were doing? You just did it. And with any luck someone saluted it and you went on to the next thing. And you rode that thing as long as you could until they caught on to you.

There was much to do. He would have to discover a warlord whose life was worthy of an hour's worth of attention every week.

He would need to find a director, a crew, editing facilities. He would have to convince ABC to put it on the air. He would have to survive Kermit Fenster and tick-borne encephalitis.

But at that moment, as he sat with his linguini and wine, everything seemed possible. Failure, as Ed Harris said in *Apollo 13*, was not an option.

The rail-thin waitress with the Joan Rivers mouth shouted over the noise. "You want dessert?"

"What do you have?" Charlie shouted back.

"How about the tiramisu?"

"Do it."

"Coffee?"

"A double espresso. And a shot of Amaretto."

Charlie watched her thread her way through the cacophony toward the open kitchen. Then he sat back in the flimsy director's chair and laughed. A year from now he would either be dead or famous. And possibly both.

SEVEN

Air Kazakhstan

At 7:30 p.m. on February 6, Charlie Berns sat in the British Airways first-class lounge at LAX drinking a watery Cosmopolitan and waiting for Kermit Fenster to show up with the remaining forty thousand euros and their visas. Ten days ago they had signed the contracts and taken delivery of the rest of the money, which Fenster said he would take charge of.

"All of it?"

"Let me ask you something, Charlie—you know how to get fifty thousand euros in currency out of the country? In case you haven't noticed, they're a little jumpy at the airports these days. They find it in your baggage, they haul you away for laundering money for Al Qaeda."

Just before he had called the cab for the airport, Charlie went to say good-bye to his nephew. Lionel was sitting in the kitchen drinking a cup of green tea and watching a rerun of *Eight Is Enough* on the small TV on the faux green limestone counter.

"Well, I'm out of your pool house," he announced. "Finally."

"So where're you moving to?" Lionel asked absently, his eyes on Dick Van Patten having a heart-to-heart with one of his daughters over milk and Toll House cookies.

Charlie told him that he was going to Uzbekistan, via Kyrgyzstan."

"I didn't know they made movies in Uzbekistan?"

"They don't."

"So what are you doing there?"

"Casting a TV series."

"No kidding? Who're you looking for?"

"A mixture of James Gandolfini and Yul Brynner."

Lionel searched unsuccessfully for a sliver of irony in Charlie's expression.

"So where should I . . . forward your mail?"

"I don't get any mail."

"So when are you going to be back?"

"I have no idea."

Lionel tore himself away from Dick Van Patten, got up, walked over and gave his uncle an awkward hug.

"Bon voyage?"

* * *

At 8:15, five minutes before they began boarding the 9 p.m. flight to Heathrow, Kermit Fenster walked into the first-class lounge wearing a fleece-collared aviator's jacket, a fisherman's cap and cowboy boots and carrying a Hermès attaché case. Without greeting, he sat down next to Charlie and said, "I hope you didn't check your luggage all the way through to Bishkek, because you'll never see it again."

Charlie's face darkened.

"Don't worry. I'll deal with it."

"What about the money?"

Fenster said in a low but firm voice, "Don't ever ask me that question in public again."

It wasn't until they were thirty-eight thousand feet above the Sierra Nevada that Charlie dared to ask Fenster about his visa.

"You won't need it till we get to Bishkek."

They were sitting in spacious reclining seats in the first-class section of the British Airways 767, drinking single-malt scotch and nibbling on cashews. Around them sat British businessmen in unfashionable suits and movie people in suede and denim. Charlie sat back and let the scotch tickle his brain.

It was going to be a grueling trip. Ten and a half hours to London, a two-hour layover, three hours to Moscow, and then a tight connection for the five-and-a-half-hour Air Kazakhstan flight to Kyrgyzstan. They would be flying through thirteen time zones, over three continents, and arriving a day and a half after they left.

After washing down the roast beef and Yorkshire pudding with a couple of glasses of Chateauneuf du Pape, Charlie dozed off and didn't wake up until their steward Nigel asked him if he would care for a bit of breakfast before landing.

He had slept all the way across the Rockies, Canada, the North Pole and Greenland. Charlie looked at his watch, which was still on L.A. time. It was 6:20, but he couldn't figure for the moment if it was a.m. or p.m. Out the window, the sky was a pale gray and either steadily darkening or steadily lightening.

"What time is it?"

"Greenwich mean minus one," Fenster replied.

Nigel brought them an extravagant breakfast of kippers and eggs. Fenster had only coffee and a croissant. Charlie ate the kippers and immediately regretted it.

Ten minutes later he was in the first-class lavatory recycling the kippers. He emerged white-faced and walked unsteadily back to his seat. Fenster took one look at him and said, "The only place I never eat in this whole fucking world is England. I've had better meals at a kebab stand in Ashgabat."

At Heathrow, they stayed in the transit lounge. Charlie drank a Bass ale to try to steady his stomach, while Fenster read a Robert Ludlum novel. The flight to Moscow was forty minutes late taking off, but the Aeroflot Airbus 300 caught a brisk tailwind, and they got into Moscow, through Russian customs and onto a shabby-looking vintage 737, on time for the final leg of their journey.

The first-class section on Air Kazakhstan was essentially the front two rows of seats. As far as Charlie could tell, everything else was exactly the same. The flight was crowded with dour-looking Russians. The flight attendants were of indeterminate nationality, dark but without pronounced Slavic cheekbones.

It was a bumpy flight, the engines of the old Boeing sounding like a malfunctioning air-conditioning unit. The service, even in first class, was no-frills. The only difference between their meal and the meal in coach was that they took the cellophane off before serving it. Dinner was some sort of lamb stew with yogurt, tepid from the microwave. The vodka, however, was top shelf: 98 proof Stoli and iced to within an inch of its life.

As they were lowering altitude, over the Muyun Kum plateau in southern Kazakhstan, Fenster opened his Hermès attaché case and retrieved a colorfully stamped document and a tube of what looked to Charlie like super glue.

"Give me your passport."

Charlie handed it to Fenster and watched him lower his tray table and carefully glue the document into Charlie's passport.

"This is your visa for Kyrgyzstan. You don't want to show a Kyrgyzstan visa in Moscow. Unless you want to spend two hours at the airport in Moscow being interviewed by Russian police."

The sun was beginning to dissolve behind the clouds over Lake Issyk-Kul when the wheels of the 737 flopped sloppily onto the runway at Manas International Airport in Bishkek. As they taxied toward the gate, Charlie looked out the dirty window. There were patches of snow on the ground and a few odd-looking planes of airlines he had never heard of before.

A mixed quiver of anticipation and anxiety went through him, along with the last flutters of gas from the kippers he had left somewhere over Scotland.

Charlie followed Fenster through Kyrgyz passport control. The guard didn't even blink at his pasted-in visa. They claimed their baggage, which, miraculously, was waiting for them in a pile of luggage lying unceremoniously beside a nonfunctioning conveyor belt.

The airport was drab and drafty, with maudlin Central Asian Muzak playing loud enough to be distracting. At a money-changing kiosk, Fenster changed some euros into Kyrgyz som, the local currency, whose posted exchange rate was 49 to the euro.

The taxi ride into town—in a Soviet-era Škoda, with no functioning springs or rear window—was perilous enough to distract Charlie from the cold wind blowing on his neck. Jet-lagged to the teeth, he watched the sun set from between the gray featureless apartment buildings to the west of the city, as the driver plowed through the mostly empty streets at hair-raising speeds.

They drove up the Erkindik Prospektisi and came to a screeching halt in front of the unimposing façade of the Hotel Kontinental, where the driver and Fenster launched into a loud argument in a mixture of languages. Though Fenster had prenegotiated the fare, the driver apparently now wanted to renegotiate before he would open the trunk and release their baggage.

Without taking his eyes off the driver, Fenster said, "Go into the hotel and tell them I'm getting ripped off by the cab driver."

Charlie got out of the cab and entered the hotel. The lobby was large and dingy. There was some overstuffed furniture and a polished desk behind which stood a man in a very bad suit, flanked by a bellhop dressed like a down-at-the-heels nineteenth-century diplomat.

The man behind the desk made a small bow of his head and revealed a set of yellow teeth. Charlie explained the situation to him. The man nodded, as if this was to be expected, reached down behind the desk, came up with a crowbar and handed it to the bellhop.

Charlie followed the bellhop out to the taxi. Without saying a word to the driver, the bellhop took the crowbar and jimmied open the trunk. The driver got out of the cab and started screaming at the bellhop, who ignored him, loaded their luggage under his arms and walked into the hotel.

"*Dasvidanya*, fuckhead," Fenster told the driver, as they followed the bellhop inside. The desk clerk greeted Fenster familiarly.

"Mr. Halloran, welcome to Bishkek."

"Nice to see you again, Akmatov. How're they hanging?"

"They are hanging good."

"Got HBO in the room?"

"You bet we got, sir. And . . . porno channel from Copenhagen."

"Excellent."

They signed in, Charlie using his real name and Fenster signing in as Keith Keller, of Marblehead, Massachusetts. They followed the bellhop into a small, rickety elevator and went up to the fifth floor. On their way down the hallway they passed the ice machine, a large, loud contraption that wheezed asthmatically.

Their rooms were as far away as possible from the infernal machine. The bellhop unlocked the first one, and Fenster said to Charlie, "I'll meet you downstairs in the bar in an hour. Don't bother to unpack."

He handed the bellhop some money, took his suitcase and disappeared into the room. Charlie's room was large and over-furnished, with a four-poster bed, a chipped desk, an armoire with peeling finish and, the center of attraction, a large-screen TV with various cables coming out of it.

The bellhop put Charlie's valise down on the bed, grunted something at him and exited. Charlie went over to the window and looked down onto the street below. The Erkindik Prospektisi was a wide avenue lined with old sickly oak trees and large unfriendly-looking buildings. At one end of the street was a park; the other end disappeared into the grid of boulevards. The city's architecture was a hybrid of Moslem onion-shaped domes and featureless Soviet utilitarian, an indigestible mélange that gave it the feeling of a poorly conceived stage set.

Charlie was afraid that if he lay down on the bed he wouldn't get up for hours so he turned on the TV. It was tuned to the Danish porno channel. The screen was immediately filled with an extreme close-up of a vagina being penetrated by a dildo. The scene was terribly overlit. And the boom shadow was so pronounced that Charlie wondered if the woman with the strap-on was doing her own sound recording.

* * *

Fenster was not in the bar an hour later when Charlie descended. A man wearing a turban was reading a newspaper in Cyrillic script. Charlie sat down at a table and asked for a beer. The alleged bartender put down his paper, padded over to a refrigerator, took out a bottle presumably of beer and brought it to Charlie.

"Could you open the bottle, please?"

The man shrugged and returned to the bar and to his newspaper. Charlie sat at the table with the unopened bottle of beer with a colorful label that said *Bielovodskoye*. He tried to twist the cap off without success.

"Bottle opener?" He called across the bar, miming the opening of the bottle with an imaginary bottle opener. At this point Fenster showed up. He sat down at the table, took a look at the beer label and said, "You don't want to drink that shit. They cut it with vodka. One glass and you'll be on your ass."

He called to the bartender, "Oblomov. *Dva*."

The guy shuffled back to the refrigerator and brought two bottles of another colorfully labeled beer but still no bottle opener. Fenster took out his Swiss army knife and opened the two bottles of Oblomov.

"Okay, here's what's happening. Tomorrow morning we go to the DHL office and hope that a package containing forty thousand euros is there. If so, we're out of here."

"So that's why we flew to Bishkek first."

"Why else would we be in this hellhole? We avoid customs at Tashkent Airport. Cost us an arm and a leg to bribe our way out of there. We take the train to Tashkent. Eight hours. If we're lucky. We'll go soft class, skip the chickens and the drunk soldiers."

"What do we do tonight?"

"There's a bar with some Latvian pussy."

"I think I'll stay in the hotel."

"You rather yank your chain to the porno channel, suit yourself."

* * *

Charlie spent the night in his room eating potato chips and peanuts, eschewing the porno channel in favor of a Mexican soap opera dubbed in Russian. He fell into a fitful sleep somewhere toward dawn and was awoken by the telephone an hour later.

"We're checking out in fifteen minutes."

A dull headache throbbing in his head, his stomach still tossing and turning, Charlie rode with Fenster through the cold gray Bishkek morning, past Ala-Too Square and Panfilov Park to the DHL office on the Chuy Prospektisi.

Fenster told him to stay in the cab as he went inside what looked like a car rental office with a DHL logo on it. The driver lit a cigarette, then reached into the glove compartment, removed a pint of vodka and took a swig.

Five minutes later Fenster emerged with a DHL package under his arm, got back in the cab and told the driver to take them to the train station. They rattled through the streets, with a DHL package presumably containing forty thousand euros in Fenster's lap, caught the train with two minutes to spare and settled down in a compartment with brocade curtains and soft plush velvet seats that resembled the opera box of a down-at-the-heels czarist Russian civil servant.

The train ride from Bishkek to Tashkent was two and half

hours longer than it should have been because of a delay at the Kyrgyzstan-Uzbekistan border, where drunk Uzbek customs officers with Kalashnikovs went through the cars trying to extort bribes from the passengers for supposed visa infractions.

Fenster was able to buy off the customs officers with a hundred euros. He used the DHL package as a tray to eat his *shashlyk* and noodles. As the train chugged along at fifty miles an hour, Charlie nibbled on onion bread, drank tea and looked out the window at the uninspiring countryside barely visible through the dirty window, protected by wire mesh from rock throwers.

"They hate anything Russian in this country, except vodka," Fenster explained. "They see a Russian train, they throw rocks at it."

In Tashkent they were staying at the Intercontinental. It was on the network's nickel, and Fenster had them book a two-room suite that went for $750 a night.

"It's a five-star hotel. There's a gym and an indoor swimming pool. You can order anything from room service. But you want to stay away from the bouillabaisse. The fish come from the Chirchik River, which is so polluted you can walk across it."

In the taxi from the train station, they passed blocks of Soviet concrete apartment buildings with Uzbek slogans written on them, large parks, parade grounds, and grandiose public monuments. There were pictures everywhere of a darkly complected man with a Stalin moustache, wearing a Moslem skullcap, whom Fenster identified as the president of Uzbekistan.

"His name is Islam Karimov. He was a communist apparatchik who rode the dissolution of the Soviet Union into power. He pretends to be a Moslem—had himself sworn in with his right hand on the Koran, which he's probably never read. He runs a very tight ship. But only in Tashkent, Samarkand and Bukhara. The rest of the country is run by the warlords, the drug dealers and the mafia."

Their suite at the Intercontinental resembled a Vegas high-rollers' suite relocated to Riyadh. The bathrooms were marble tiled with gold gilt faucets. There was a sunken tub, a dozen large white fluffy towels, and inlaid mosaics featuring djinns floating over mosques. On the faux Directoire writing desk was a fax machine. Beside it was a copy of the Koran.

Fenster signed the register as Howard Nevsky of Carson City, Nevada, and asked to have *USA Today* sent up to the room in the morning.

Charlie opened the room service menu as Fenster made several phone calls and grunted monosyllabic replies to whomever he was talking. He hung up and went over to the minibar, took out Chivas and mineral water, poured himself a drink, sat down on the bed and laid things out for Charlie.

"We're flying to Nukus tomorrow afternoon. We've got a meeting with Izbul Kharkov at eight that night, which he won't show up at. Friday morning we'll tell the hotel manager in Nukus that we're leaving, call a taxi, and instead of a taxi, one of Izbul's men will show up and take us out to see his boss."

"Where is Nukus?"

"About a thousand kilometers from here, on the western edge of the Kyzyl Kum desert, on the way to the Aral Sea. It's located in Karakalpakstan, which is supposed to be an autonomous republic within Uzbekistan but isn't. It's run, if you could call it that, by the Uzbek government. It's hot, ugly, polluted—used to be the location of a secret Soviet chemical weapons factory, which for all we know is still toxic. They got dazed camels wandering around wild on the outskirts of town. The best hotel looks like a rundown Ramada in Utah and has running water only six hours a day. The only place to eat is a Korean noodle restaurant where you got about a fifty-fifty chance of not getting ptomaine poisoning, and the whole town smells from rotting cotton and chemicals."

"Sounds great."

"You don't find warlords in places with five-star hotels."

Charlie looked back down at the room service menu and said, "So what do you think about the mutton kebab?"

"You'll probably survive it."

EIGHT

Bada Bink

Fenster's description of Nukus was, if anything, charitable. As the Uzbekistan Airways DC9 dropped altitude over the western edge of the Kyzyl Kum desert, the city emerged on the horizon like a deconstructed Stalinist version of Tuscaloosa. Haphazardly planted cotton fields came right up to the edge of the city. A thin haze of pollution floated from the nitrates plant to the north. To the west, what was left of the Amu Dayra lay like a sprawling puddle.

They took a battered Peugeot taxi into the city, which was even uglier close up than from the air. There were wide, empty avenues without traffic or traffic lights. They drove past the Karakalpakstan Academy of Sciences, a building with a bronze boiled egg on top; the National Bank of Uzbekistan; the State Museum.

The lobby of the Hotel Nukus was cavernous and empty, with false marble and fluorescent lighting. There was nobody at the registration desk. Fenster banged on a bell until a woman in a moth-eaten sweater and pleated skirt, smoking a foul-smelling cigarette, shuffled out and sullenly presented a registration ledger.

Fenster signed in as Tuc Watson from Kansas City, Missouri. Charlie, as usual, gave his real name. If the Vietnamese debt consolidator could track him down in this godforsaken place, he deserved to get his money.

As they were heading across the lobby toward the stairs, beside the out-of-order elevator, a group of European-looking people descended carrying film equipment and speaking a language that sounded to Charlie like Swedish spoken by drunks.

"Swedes?" Charlie asked Fenster.

"Poles."

"They got camera equipment. They couldn't be making a movie here, could they?"

"They must be doing something. Because you would be crazy to spend any more time here than you have to."

"A Polish movie in Karakalpakstan?"

"Fuck do I know. Anyway, we got a couple of hours to kill before the eight o'clock meeting."

"I thought you said he wasn't going to show up at the meeting."

"He won't."

"So why do we have to wait around for this meeting at eight o'clock if the guy's not going to show?"

"What else you want to do?"

"Get something to eat."

"There's no place to eat in this town."

"What about the Korean noodle restaurant?"

"It's the worst fucking restaurant on the face of the earth."

"Where else can we go?"

"No place."

* * *

The Koreaniya Chuchvara Ristaran was located on the eastern end of Gharezsizlik Street near the road to the airport, huddled between empty buildings, its windows steamed up from the chilly desert night.

As soon as you entered, you were assaulted by the odor of boiled cabbage and sesame oil. People sat with their overcoats on, eating large plates of noodles and drinking tea from dirty glasses. There was no conversation, just the sound of people sucking in food and grunting.

The only lighting came from two fluorescent fixtures hanging on the concrete walls, completely devoid of decoration. Charlie sat down and opened the plastic-covered menu. It was in Karakalpak and Russian. He hadn't a clue.

"You want to stay away from the dried carp," Fenster warned and ordered them two Oblomovs and a noodle and mutton dish.

"So let me get this straight," Charlie said. "Tomorrow we check out, head for the airport, and then Izbul shows up."

"Maybe, maybe not."

"Don't tell me we came all the way out here for nothing."

"You want a warlord, this is the game you have to play."

"If we make a deal with this guy, he's going to have to be reliable. We're going to have a crew following him around filming his life. The guy needs to be where he says he's going to be."

"Don't worry. You're going to like Izbul. He even speaks English. He learned it from watching television. The guy never misses *Jeopardy*."

The noodles arrived in one large tureen with a ladle and two plates. There were three or four overcooked pieces of meat floating on the top and some indeterminate vegetables. Fenster dished them each out a plate. Charlie felt a knot start to form in his intestines. He took a long sip of the Russian beer.

"Whoever we choose, I'm going to have to sell him to the network."

"That's your job."

"They're going to want to see some tape on him."

"So we'll put him on tape."

"We don't have a camera crew."

"We'll get one."

"Where?'

"For chrissakes, Charlie, will you stop worrying about everything."

They ate in silence for a few minutes. Then Fenster said, "Want to get laid tonight?"

"In this town?"

"I know a couple of Kazakh hookers for ten bucks'll give you a rim job like you never had before."

* * *

Charlie passed on the ten-dollar rim job and decided to check out the bar at the hotel, such that it was. Since Uzbekistan was nominally a Moslem country, you had to go through a solid metal door that simply had the word *Kafé* lettered on it to gain access to the bar. It was dark inside, with blue lights and a choking amount of cigarette smoke. There was a jukebox playing Russian jazz from records that rotated a few RPMs slower than they were supposed to.

Sitting at a table drinking beer were the Poles he had seen in the lobby. Charlie went over and introduced himself. The Poles invited him to sit down at their table and passed a beer bottle over to him. Charlie asked them if they were making a film in Nukus.

A thin, bearded, older man, who introduced himself as Szczedrzyk explained that they were making a documentary for Polish National Television on the Aral Sea ecological disaster.

"That must be depressing," Charlie said.

Szczedrzyk shrugged. "It's a job. We work. We make film."

A tall, thin, very blond young woman in a Nine Inch Nails tee shirt said, "What else is there to do?"

Her voice was coated with despair; her eyes dripped with weltschmerz.

"Soon there will be no more Aral Sea to film. It disappears—sixty square kilometers every year. Then what?"

"Is there anything they can do to stop it?"

"Stop producing cotton. It's the water from the irrigation that is draining the sea. But Uzbekistan needs the cotton, so they don't give shit."

"How long is the film going to take?"

"Who knows?" The woman shrugged.

"Two months, three months, six, maybe a year," Szczedrzyk elaborated, as if he were describing a prison sentence.

"You have to live in Nukus for *six months*?"

"It's the job. We do it."

"Where do you edit?"

"In Tashkent. At Uzbekfilmlabaya."

"They have good equipment?"

The Polish filmmaker shrugged and then asked the obvious question you would ask any foreigner you met in a bar in Nukus, "You do what here?"

Charlie thought about Fenster's paranoid hectoring about not revealing anything to anybody who didn't have a need to know. And this Polish documentary filmmaker certainly didn't need to know that Charlie was there to audition warlords for a TV reality show.

On the other hand, they were in an underground bar in a rundown hotel in a rotting city near an ecological disaster. What difference could it possibly make?

"I'm a television producer."

"In Nukus?" Szczedrzyk's eyes widened.

"We're scouting locations for a TV series."

"Here? This place is toxic waste dump," said the young woman, whose name was Justyna.

"It kind of works for the concept."

Charlie said nothing more to the Poles that night in the basement bar of the Hotel Tashkent in Nukus, but filed the information away for future use.

Waiting for the Aral Sea to dissolve seemed like the kind of job that left you with a fair amount of downtime. If he wasn't mistaken, Poland had recently entered the euro zone.

* * *

Charlie spent an uncomfortable night in his drab and chilly room at the Hotel Nakus. He managed to grab a quick shower in a tepid trickle before they turned the water off at midnight. In the morning he brushed his teeth with his finger and rinsed with a small bottle of Listerine he had bought at the airport store at LAX.

Breakfast was green tea and pumpernickel bread at a *choyhona* on Turtkulsky Prospekt. The tea house was mostly empty except for a few Mongol-looking men, whom Fenster identified as Karakalpak mafia.

"You got all sorts of mafias in the Stans. You got your local mafia, who, between you and me, can't get arrested. They try to shake you down, you just tell them to fuck off. You got your Uzbek mafia, who aren't a whole let better. Then you got your Russians, and these guys you don't want to fuck with. Unless you're Izbul. He fucks with them all."

By 9:30 they had checked out of the hotel and were back in the battered Peugeot. They drove out Dosnazarov Street north toward the airport, passing abandoned concrete apartment houses with the odd stray camel wandering aimlessly through the weeds.

They were a few miles into the cotton fields when a car approached them from the rear and honked its horn to pass. The taxi driver, being a taxi driver, merely kept to the center of the road. The car behind them, now dangerously tailgating, honked louder.

Through the rear window Charlie saw a dirty BMW with metal plates on the sides about ten feet behind them. The taxi driver put the pedal of the Peugeot to the floor, but the strange-looking BMW stayed right on its ass.

"What the fuck are they going to do?"

"Run us off the road, probably."

Charlie glanced at the speedometer. The needle was hovering at 110 kilometers per hour. The BMW rammed the Peugeot, slowing the old taxi enough so that the bigger, faster car was able to open a narrow passing lane on the left. If a car came the other way, they'd all be dead.

The driver cursed and spat out the window as the BMW pulled ahead, and then started to slow down by degrees, forcing the taxi to slow down accordingly until it ground to a halt on its pancake-thin brake linings, squealing like a pig.

The armored doors of the BMW opened on either side, and two men wearing sunglasses and carrying weapons emerged. Charlie's tattered life began to flash before his eyes. It wasn't, he thought, a totally unfitting way to buy the ranch: gunned down by a couple of goons with road rage on the outskirts of Nukus in an old Peugeot taxi on an abortive mission to find a warlord for a reality TV program.

The taxi driver slouched down in his seat, but one of the thugs ripped the front door open, lifted him out and proceeded to pistol-whip him. The man went down like a sack of melons. They kicked him to the side of the road and then walked around so that there was one of them on either side of the taxi.

Charlie looked over and saw that Fenster was perfectly calm.

"Okay, Kermit, what do you know that I don't?"

Fenster rolled down the window and said to the goons, *"Assalom aleikum."*

"Aleikum salam."

* * *

Ten minutes later they were in the backseat of the armored 750i heading south toward the Turkmenistan border to meet with the warlord. Fenster gave Charlie his customary just-before-he-needed-to-know briefing.

"Izbul's headquarters are across the border in Turkmenistan so he can avoid dealing with Karimov's secret police. He's got a place in the hills outside of Dashoguz, a town that makes Nukus look like Paris. You think Uzbekistan is fucked, you'll really love Turkmenistan. It's run by a psychotic named Saparmurat Niyazov, who rides around in a fleet of Mercedes, regularly pilfering the treasury to build monuments to himself and threatening to declare war on Uzbekistan. He's renamed several days of the week after people in his family."

An hour later they arrived at the Turkmenistan border. Trucks were lined up on the side of the road, with soldiers inspecting them. The BMW cruised through with a wave from the driver to the border guard.

Charlie looked out the window at the cotton fields and desert. As far as he could tell, there was no difference between Turkmenistan and western Uzbekistan, except that there were lots of gas stations along the road.

"What's with all the gas stations?"

"Gas is free in this country. It's one of the ways that Niyazov tries to buy the affection of the people. There's a new coup attempt every six months, but the guy survives. He just whacks everybody."

They entered the city of Dashoguz, which, as Fenster had said, looked like a down-market version of Nukus. It had the same tacky Soviet architecture superimposed on a dry, dusty Moslem oasis. They stopped at a gas station on the Utilitsa Karla Marxa, got a tankful of free gas, stopped at a roadside melon stand, where the pistol-whippers helped themselves to a half dozen melons before heading up into the foothills west of the town.

Twenty minutes up a tortuous dirt road was a roadblock with armed guards in quilted coats and sunglasses. They opened the barrier for the BMW and waved it through. They drove for another mile until Charlie saw a rambling long-slung house with an enormous satellite dish attached to the roof.

The house resembled the Black Sea dacha of an out-of-favor member of Brezhnev's politburo. There were more men in skullcaps and sunglasses, Kalashnikovs strung over their shoulders, hanging around the gate to the compound. They stared at Charlie and Fenster as they were driven into the courtyard. They got out of the car and followed their escorts through a door and into the dark interior, which smelled of black tobacco, onions and gun polish.

They were ushered into a small room with a half dozen high-backed upholstered chairs and a samovar. They sat down in the uncomfortable chairs. Fenster looked at his watch and said, "It's probably time for *Jeopardy*. The fucking world could be falling apart, and Izbul's got to watch that program. He never misses it or *The Sopranos*. Guy thinks that everybody in America talks like Tony and looks like Vanna White."

An old woman in a babushka came in with two cans of Diet Pepsi on a tray. Almost an hour later, just as Charlie was nodding off into his armchair, one of the pistol-whippers entered and beckoned for them to follow him. They walked down a couple of empty hallways with closed doors on either side, through a large room that had nothing in it but a dozen slot machines scattered haphazardly, and finally into an even larger room, where a man sat at a desk watching a large-screen color TV along one wall.

He waved at them and said in an indefinable accent, "Fuckink A."

"Hello, Izbul."

"Fuckink you, Fensterman."

"This is Charlie Berns. From Hollywood."

"Take a load."

Izbul gestured to two stuffed armchairs opposite his desk. The TV was tuned to *America's Most Harrowing Police Chases*.

The warlord was wearing a fleece vest over a flannel shirt, leather pants, cowboy boots and an embroidered skullcap and was smoking a cigarette through an inlaid pearl cigarette holder. He was not a big man, maybe five-eight, but solidly built with piercing dark eyes and a coarse stubble of beard.

"So, Charlie Berns from Hollywood, you want to make television program?"

"Perhaps . . ."

"Fensterman tell me it's dunk slam."

Charlie flashed Fenster a look.

"It is, Izbul," said Fenster. "We just want to check the place out for filming, meet your family."

"My family? You meet them. Fuckink A."

A loud car squeal and the sound of sirens pierced the room, as Izbul turned back to the TV screen and laughed. "Code nine. Sirens, lights. They get that fucker. He does time. Up the ass."

"See, Izbul, the idea is to have a film crew in here twenty-four/ seven, film everything you do."

"Everythink?"

"We would respect you and your family's privacy as much as we can."

"My family? They do what I say. More less. My wife, beggink your pardon, is bitch on wheel. And I got problem with elder son. Wants to join fuckink Taliban. I tell him, the Taliban got ass handed in Afghanistan, but he don't listen. Reads Koran all day long. I got mullah for son."

"I see," said Charlie, nodding sympathetically.

"Younger son smart kid, no balls. Like Tony's son. And daughter like pussy."

"I'm sorry."

"And bada bink."

* * *

They had dinner en famille at a huge wooden table in a cavernous dining room with nonfunctioning chandeliers and a TV set going in the background. The wife didn't show up, but the three kids were there. The elder son's name was Utkur but he had changed it to Ali Mohammed when he became a serious Moslem. He was dressed in black robes with a skullcap and carried a copy of the Koran. The other son, Akbar, was pudgy with glasses, shoveled in his food and washed it down with two cans of Diet Pepsi during dinner. The daughter, Ferghana, was attractive but severe looking. She had studied animal husbandry at the agricultural college in Tashkent and spoke decent English.

"Welcoming you to our home," she said.

"Thank you," said Charlie.

"Do you know Madonna?"

"Afraid not."

"What about Ellen Degeneres?"

"Not really."

She sat beside her father and dished out the food as conversation lurched forward in Uzbek, English and Russian. Ali Mohammed said nothing.

The younger son, like his father, had a smattering of TV English, which he got from watching MTV Europe. His hair was spiked with gel. "Eminem," he said.

"Beg your pardon?" Charlie asked.

"Eminem," the fifteen-year-old repeated.

"Who's fuckink M&M?" Izbul asked.

"American rock singer."

"Eat dick, cocksucker," the teenage boy said, by way of explanation.

Dinner consisted of cabbage soup and mutton kabobs. Everybody drank Diet Pepsi. Izbul kept an eye on the TV set, which was playing a syndicated episode of *Seinfeld*.

"Fuckink Kramer," he guffawed, after Seinfeld's tall geeky neighbor came sliding into the apartment. "Jerry goink to cut him new one."

After dinner, they visited the room with the slot machines.

"Machines goink to Odessa. Big casino for Russian mob guys. I got lots business. Up the wigwam. Tomorrow. You see business. Tonight? We play blackjack."

They followed Izbul to another room, which featured pillows on the floor, a samovar, a Ping-Pong table, jukebox and a couple of framed velvet paintings of the kind you could buy in the lobby of Caesars Palace.

"Whatever you do," Fenster said to Charlie, when Izbul went to fetch the cards and chips, "don't win."

For the next two hours, Fenster and Charlie systematically lost money to the house. They were into Izbul for 275 euros by the time they were allowed to quit. They were escorted to the guest quarters for the night by one of the pistol-whippers. Their room had one double bed in it.

"Are we both supposed to sleep in this one bed?" Charlie complained.

"You can sleep on the floor if you want."

Fenster took off his boots, his corduroy shirt and his leather pants and got into bed in a pair of black Calvin Klein briefs.

"Fenster, I'm not sure this guy's going to work out."

"Why not?"

"He's weird. And he's not particularly telegenic."

"He's our guy."

"What do you mean, he's our guy? I thought we were going to see a bunch of these guys and pick the best one."

"He's the best one."

"How do you know that?"

"Because he's the only one."

Fenster switched off the bedside lamp, turned toward the wall and was soon snoring like a table saw.

* * *

Charlie was too wired from the events of the day to sleep. Not that sleep would have been easy, in any event, given the decibel level in the room from Fenster's snoring.

He lay on the bed, eyes wide open, furious. His "technical consultant" had jerked him around yet again. They were in Turkmenistan, a country that was not even on their itinerary, at the home of a goofball who watched TV nonstop and spoke some sort of bizarre patois mix of New Jersey mafioso English, Uzbek and Russian and who turned out to be the only warlord in town. Charlie would have to call Norman Hudris and explain that there would be no auditions. Here's your guy, like him or not. Izbul Kharkov. The Tony Soprano of Turkmenistan.

He would never work. The network's Standards and Practices Department would have a big problem with his profanity. And then there was the sullen fundamentalist son and the gay daughter. ABC was in enough trouble these days without having the Moslem world after them. The mullahs would declare a *fatwa* against the network, and they'd have to start strip-searching visitors to the lot in addition to looking under their cars with mirrors.

Charlie had gone along with the whole cockamamie business, the multiple names, the different phone numbers, the euros, the trip to Bishkek, the charade in Nukus . . . And now there he was, stuck somewhere in the hills of Turkmenistan, a country that, if he remembered correctly, had a tick-borne encephalitis problem, at the home of a TV-addicted warlord with a serious Diet Pepsi problem.

Tomorrow morning he would wake up, if he ever fell asleep, demand half the money from Fenster, hire a taxi to take him to wherever he could get a train to Tashkent and then take the first plane out of central Asia. He'd call Norman Hudris, explain that the money was ripped off by gun-bearing Turkmen thugs, and retire to a trailer park in Yuma.

* * *

All this might have happened if some time around 4:00 a.m. that morning, just as Charlie was drifting into an agitated sleep, someone hadn't tossed a live grenade into the courtyard of Izbul Kharkov's compound. The explosion rocked the entire house.

This event scared the shit out of Charlie. But it also altered his thinking about the feasibility of building a reality show around Izbul Kharkov. And, *a fortiori*, about his own chances of survival in the Darwinian cauldron of the television business.

NINE

Droppink Trow

Norman Hudris sat at his desk at ABCD staring ruefully at the demos that Tom Soaring Hawk had left on his desk along with a memo about cutbacks on soft drinks and messenger service runs. It was February sweeps, and they were desperately trying to goose the ratings, which were heading south precipitously. After Tierra del Fuego there was only Antarctica.

The network had thrown just about everything against the wall— from an interview with Janet Jackson's gynecologist to a sitcom starring M.C. Hammer and Linda Tripp to a show called *Microbe Squad* about a group of young and fearless biochemists who rooted out terrorist plots to poison the American ecosystem. But nothing stuck. They were getting killed seven nights a week.

None of ABCD's other shows had gotten off the ground. Between budget and legal problems, they were dead in the water before they could even test market them. It was becoming more and more apparent to Norman that his survival at the division, if not in the television business itself, rested with the Central Asian mafioso-warlord show.

Several times he had tried to get in touch with Charlie Berns, but the itinerary that the agent had given him turned out to be inaccurate. He had called various hotels in Uzbekistan and Kyrgyzstan and been told that Mr. Berns had already checked out. The agent claimed that he had no word from his own client either.

"Charlie's an independent kind of guy. Sort of like Roman Polanski, you know what I mean?"

"No. I don't know what you mean. How can a producer who is in development with network funds be incommunicado?"

"Don't worry," Brad Emprin assured him, "he'll turn up."

So when Charlie Berns did turn up, on a Tuesday afternoon in February, at the beginning of the second week of sweeps, Norman grabbed the phone as soon as Tom Soaring Hawk told him who was calling.

"Where are you?" Norman said.

"Turkmenistan," Charlie replied, from Fenster's cell phone.

"I thought you were going to Uzbekistan."

"Next door."

"You got tapes for me to look at?"

"No."

"What do you mean, *no*?"

"Forget the tapes. I found the warlord. His name is Izbul Kharkov."

"You want me to cast the lead in a series that I've never seen?"

"Norman, last night someone threw a hand grenade into the warlord's compound."

"Somebody tried to *kill* the warlord?"

"Uh-huh."

"Who?"

"Fenster said it was the Turkmen mob out of Dashoguz. But it could've been the Russians from Nukus, or maybe even the Uzbek security guys from Tashkent. Norman, these guys don't fuck around. Izbul's men pistol-whipped our cab driver."

"Pistol-whipped?"

"Uh-huh. Fifty feet from us."

Norman took the phone away from his ear and looked back down at the numbers. The 18-34 demos were touching bottom.

"Did . . . anybody get hurt last night?" Norman asked in a small, aspirated voice.

"I don't know."

There was a protracted silence as Charlie's words bounced off the communications satellite somewhere over Central Asia and went careening downward toward Manhattan Beach, California.

Underneath the demos were the nationals. The network hadn't

cracked the top twenty in any of the major markets. In New York and L.A., the local news lead-outs were hitting historical lows, getting beaten by reruns of *Home Improvement*. The iceberg was looming larger in the distance.

There was an old adage in the casting business: you start out looking for Tracy and Hepburn and wind up settling for two white people who can walk. Given the proximity of the iceberg, perhaps auditions were a luxury they could no longer afford.

"What's it going to cost to make a deal with this guy?"

"Don't know yet. I have to make a rights deal with the guy, line up a crew, price out lab costs in Tashkent—"

"Where the hell are you going to find a crew?"

"I may have actually found one."

"Union?"

"I don't think so. They're Poles."

"You found a Polish crew in—where the hell are you again?"

"Turkmenistan. The crew's in Uzbekistan, actually they're in Karakalpakstan. They're filming the Aral Sea dissolving."

"Charlie, get back to me with numbers. As soon as you can."

* * *

This phone conversation occurred at 5:00 a.m. Turkmenistan time, 6:00 p.m. the previous day Pacific Time, and an hour after the grenade attack on Izbul's compound. At the sound of the explosion Fenster had jumped into his boots and taken off on the run for Izbul's office, while Charlie had crawled under the bed and begun to rethink his decision to leave Central Asia and abandon *Warlord*.

During the grenade attack and counterattack, as he lay there in the dust listening to the sound of automatic weapons fire outside in the courtyard, he managed to project his life into the near future. Once he got past the prospect of his own death—which, given the state of his fortunes, wouldn't be entirely tragic—he had the realization that he was living through an experience that people actually might be interested in watching from the safety of their own living rooms. You could sit on your couch with a bag of chips and watch real hand grenades explode in the real courtyards of the real houses of real people.

Was there anything on television like that these days?

They could use the house as a studio, rig permanent lights and cameras in the main rooms. They'd save money on wardrobe and props. They'd use real things. Live off the fat of the land. They'd eat kebabs and drink Diet Pepsi . . .

He would make a product placement deal with Pepsico. That alone could pay for a nice chunk of the filming. They could amortize it over fifteen episodes. Right off the top.

* * *

At breakfast nobody mentioned the grenade attack earlier that morning. Izbul had the TV tuned to Road Runner cartoons off of German television. Ali Mohammed was not present, off to the mosque in Dashoguz for morning prayers, his sister explained. The mother had still not made an appearance.

Izbul prattled about Lisa Marie Presley and whether or not she was fucking Nicolas Cage. Charlie explained that the marriage was over, but that didn't stop Izbul.

"Fuckink Nicolas KGB. Big ugly guy. Make lot of bang-bang movies. Now he fuck Elvis daughter. Big dick, no? You ever see Nicolas KGB's dick, Charlie Berns from Hollywood?"

Charlie confessed that he hadn't.

"Tony got big dick, right?"

Charlie nodded. There didn't seem to be any point in contradicting his host over breakfast.

"How big you think my dick?"

"Big," Charlie said.

"How many centimeter?"

"A lot."

"Twenty-one centimeter."

"That's very impressive."

"You want to see it?"

At this point, Ferghana excused herself and headed for the kitchen.

"I'll take your word for it," Charlie said.

"Droppink trow," the warlord announced as he opened his robe, dropped his drawers and revealed what to Charlie looked like an average-sized penis.

"Wow," said Charlie, as if he were looking at the eighth wonder of the world.

"Nicolas KGB eatink heart out."

* * *

After breakfast, Charlie got a tour of the compound, personally conducted by the warlord himself. The place was an unwieldy agglomeration of large rooms, some empty, some cluttered with packing crates full of TVs, VCRs, computers. One entire wing of the house was a sort of paramilitary barracks, where the fifty or so men who comprised Izbul's private army lived. There were mattresses on the floor, TV sets, hibachi grills, card tables, weapons everywhere, clothes hanging to dry on indoor clotheslines, and the pervasive odor of alfalfa oil and mutton.

The men were dressed in variations of the traditional Uzbek quilted coat and skullcap, boots and gaudy gold neck chains. They treated Izbul with deference but not with servility. There was a sense of rough camaraderie among them.

The family quarters were a hodgepodge of rooms, each one very different from the other. Ferghana's looked like a dormitory room of a neat college sophomore—books and old eclectic furniture. There were framed photographs of Madonna and Virginia Woolf on the wall.

Akbar's room was full of CD equipment, rock posters, Playmates of the Month, computers. A TV was turned to MTV Turkey, even though Akbar was not in the room at the time.

"Is Akbar at school?" Charlie asked.

"Why not?"

"Where does he go to school?"

"Dashoguz. Learn Russian. English. Koran. Chemistry. Pullink pud a lot."

As he examined this typical teenager's room, Charlie conceptualized. They could follow Akbar to school, watch him hang out in the hallways, pick up girls, go out for the soccer team. At home, they'd shoot him in his room, on the phone talking to his buds, like Tony Soprano's kid, listening to Eminem. They could edit out the pud pulling.

Ali Mohammed's room resembled a monk's cell—nothing but a

low cot, a table, a collection of religious books, a prayer rug, and the cloying smell of incense.

"Utkur don't pullink pud," Izbul informed Charlie.

Beyond Utkur's room was a long hallway, with one room off to the side. The door was closed to this room.

"Wife's room," Izbul explained.

"What's her name?" Charlie asked.

"Suck me."

"Her name is . . . *suck me?*"

"Name is Ishrat Khana, means house of joy. But no joy. Only suck me."

They did not visit Ishrat Khana's room but proceeded to the master bedroom suite at the end of the hall.

It looked like a high roller's suite in Vegas. At the center of the huge room was a circular bed, the kind that Hugh Hefner made popular in the '70s, with pastel throw pillows that had sex jokes stitched on them. There was a deep-pile flokati throw rug, faded from its original pink, an Exercycle beside it. The walls were decorated with velvet nudes and LeRoy Neiman posters.

But the main attraction, the focal point of the room, was a large-screen TV with sophisticated-looking sound equipment, attached to a VCR and a DVD player.

"Wrappink around quad," Izbul boasted, grabbing a remote from the bed and switching the TV on. Instantly the room was flooded with the tinned music of an American network soap. There was a push in on some overemoting actress tearfully saying something sublimely banal.

"Melanie leavink Paul," Izbul said. "Paul fuckink around on side."

As Charlie was checking out the room for the best places to put cameras, a woman emerged from the adjoining bathroom. She was dark-haired, busty, with a lot of lipstick and wearing a shortie bathrobe, heels, and carrying a Danielle Steel novel in Russian.

Izbul introduced her as Grushenka, a Ukrainian movie actress who was visiting for a while. Grushenka seemed nonplussed by the fact that Izbul had invited strange people into the bedroom, but her interest perked up when Izbul explained to her that the people in the room were producing a movie about him.

"Speaking exemplary English," Grushenka said, turning away from Charlie in order to flash him a profile. "Much experience in movies. Mostly in Russian, but also Bulgaria and Sweden," she expanded, trotting out her résumé.

"Great," Charlie said.

Izbul turned to Charlie and said, sotto voce, "Nice tit."

*　*　*

Later, when Charlie was alone with Fenster, he told him about his phone conversation with Norman Hudris at ABC.

"What's he offering?"

"He wants us to come to them with numbers."

"Charlie, you've been in this business a long time. You don't want to come to them with numbers. You want them to come to us with numbers."

Fenster was right. Rule number one in negotiation was to make the other party put numbers on the table first. You never knew—their numbers could be higher than the ones you were going to put on the table.

"We need rights not just for Izbul but for his whole family and his private army. And we don't want to negotiate with them individually or we'll be here forever."

"Izbul will deliver the whole package for one price."

"We need to make a budget, cost this thing out."

"We do that after we make the deal."

Once again Charlie had to admit that Fenster was right. The strategy of molding the budget to fit the above-the-line costs of the project was a time-honored one. Get the star, find out what his money was, then figure out how to afford it.

"You get Izbul to name a number for the whole package. Him, his family, his army, location rights to film here and everywhere else he goes. Try to keep the up-front money as low as possible. Sell him some back-end participation, which he'll never see . . ."

"Charlie, you trying to tell me how to make a deal with a warlord?"

"Okay, fine," Charlie conceded, "just make a deal fast. I'll go to Nukus today and see if I can line up a crew. Can I get someone to drive me?"

"Izbul's boys are going to be busy kicking ass in Dashoguz today. He's got to respond to the grenade attack."

"Is there a bus?"

"Yeah. It'll take you a day and a half. Ask Ferghana to drive you. It'll take you forty-five minutes. If you survive."

*　*　*

Ferghana Kharkov drove the midnight blue Mercedes 500 SLC on the windy road as if she were on a test track in Stuttgart. The top was down and the wind was blowing loudly, making conversation virtually impossible. The speedometer on the Benz got up to 140 kilometers an hour on the straightaways. Charlie sat back, nailed to his seat, and tried to relax. He had survived the grenade attack. Why shouldn't he live through this?

She was wearing military fatigues, her hair tied back under a baseball cap. Her face had finely chiseled features, her eyes dark and moody, accented by eyeliner. There was a pretty girl there, under the attitude. She'd have to be lit well.

The women in the audience would have to like her. They couldn't build this series entirely around a male demographic. He'd wardrobe her better, more feminine, get a makeup person to do justice to her eyes, put her in low platform boots, loose slacks . . .

By half-past eleven that morning they were at the Hotel Nukus, where they learned that the Poles had gone to Muynak for the day. He asked Ferghana where Muynak was.

"Two hundred ten kilometers north."

The way Ferghana drove, Charlie calculated, that was only another hour and a half. So they got back into the car and roared out of town, heading north toward what was left of the Aral Sea. The road passed through abandoned cotton fields, slimy from overirrigation, marshes and desert.

It was just after one o'clock when they arrived at the outskirts of Muynak. It was one of the most surreal sights Charlie had ever seen, an entire town of corrosive pools and deserted fish oil factories. Where the sea used to be were hundreds of beached fishing boats rotting in the sand like petrified whales.

They found the Poles having lunch on a sand dune north of the city, among the ghost boats. Charlie introduced Ferghana to Szczedrzyk and Justyna, who greeted them in their dour Eastern European manner.

They drank warm beer and ate sardines and bread in the meager late-winter sunlight.

"So, how's the film coming along?" Charlie asked Szczedrzyk.

"It comes along."

"We are filming slow death. Filming slow death is slow," Justyna elaborated with her despairing blue eyes.

"Death can be beautiful," Ferghana suggested, looking out over the surreal landscape.

Justyna took a lingering look at the dark young Uzbek woman. The Polish blonde didn't smile so much as radiate a kind of pained interest in the grim metaphysics of death—as well as, Charlie couldn't help noticing, in Ferghana Kharkov.

It looked to Charlie like love at first sight. Talk about meeting cute. On a sand dune beside an ecological disaster.

"I would imagine," Charlie said, edging around to the point, "that you must have a lot of time on your hands."

"Depends on weather," Szczedrzyk said. "Weather good, we film. Weather bad, we stay in Nukus and drink beer."

"Probably a little boring, huh?"

Justyna helped herself to another sardine, splayed it on the bread with a dull knife, spread some date paste on top and took a bite.

"Have you ever been to Poznań?"

Charlie shook his head. Justyna left the sentence hanging in the air for emphasis. Poznań was apparently the mecca of boredom.

Charlie finished what was left of his warm beer and asked Szczedrzyk if they could have a little talk, just the two of them.

When they were out of earshot , Charlie cut to the chase.

"Szczedrzyk, how'd you like a job that won't be boring?"

The Pole said nothing, continued to walk, his eyes scanning the birdless horizon.

"I need a film crew to shoot a reality program for American television. It's a kind of cinema verité treatment of the life of a Uzbek man and his family. We shoot across the border in Dashoguz and anywhere else this man or his family go. We shoot as much film as we can, then create the story in the editing room, wind up with a sort of dramatic documentary of his life . . . which is kind of exciting and frankly a little bit . . . dangerous . . ."

"Dangerous?"

"The man's a warlord. Has a private army. Extorts money from people, sells hot VCRs, slot machines and God knows what else. People toss grenades at his house."

Charlie had read the tell on the word *dangerous*. But Szczedrzyk, being a Pole, wasn't going to jump up and down. So Charlie played his other trump card.

"What's Telewizja Polska paying you for this job?"

"Okay."

"They paying five thousand a day for you and the crew?"

Szczedrzyk used his tongue to brush errant bits of sardine from his teeth, belched discreetly.

"Five thousand *dollars*?"

"Five thousand *euros*."

"What about Aral Sea?"

"Couple of months from now it'll still be disappearing, won't it?"

* * *

On the way back to Dashoguz, Charlie and Ferghana stopped at the Korean noodle restaurant in Nukus for a late lunch. They sat in a corner of the deserted place and had dumpling soup with barley and tea served by a comatose Korean wearing corduroy trousers several sizes too big for him and a silk turban.

Charlie told her about the television show. She listened intently as he explained how the whole family would become rich and famous. The Kharkovs would be seen on American television. They would get offers to appear on talk shows, have TV pilots written for them, spreads in international magazines.

"You could travel to Hollywood, be on the Jay Leno show, get comped at Disneyland."

"Has my father agreed to do this?" she asked, when Charlie had finished laying out all the goodies.

"We're in negotiation."

"Then it is done."

She didn't seem very happy about it. Charlie tried to cheer her up. "It's going to be great. The Poles'll be around shooting every-thing. They're a lot of fun."

Ferghana put down her spoon and sat without saying anything for a long moment. Then she looked at Charlie and asked, "That Polish girl, blond girl, she going to be there?"

"Sure."

She didn't say anything else, but she didn't have to. Charlie had read the tell back on the dunes in Muynak. Ferghana Kharkov was already in makeup.

TEN

The Warlord Package

"A million *dollars*?"

"Euros. A million *euros*. You get him, his family, his army, the house, the whole enchilada. It's one-stop shopping."

Charlie sat in bed with Fenster in the guest room of Izbul's armed villa and played with the number. And the more he played with it, the less outrageous it began to seem. For one thing, they would amortize it over thirteen episodes, so that what they were really talking about was seventy-five grand per show for cast, extras and locations.

He began to eyeball a budget for each hour. Seventy-five for Izbul's package, twenty-five for the crew. There was fifty in the ABC deal for Fenster and him to split as executive producers. There was a line producer; there were caterers, drivers, honey wagons, camel wranglers, editors, lab costs, office and shipping expenses. . . . Still, if he brought all the rest in for a hundred per show, they'd be at a quarter of a mil, two point seven-five max . . .

Was there anything on American network TV costing less than three hundred grand an hour? With the product placement, they could bring it down to two and a half, maybe lower if they could get Pepsi to buy out the show . . .

"What if we paid Izbul out at seventy-five grand a week for thirteen weeks? It adds up to the same million."

"He wants the million up front."

"How am I going to get ABC to give this guy a million dollars— worse, euros—up front?"

"Charlie, how much was NBC paying for that show with the kids?"

"*Friends*? I don't know . . . six, seven million an episode . . ."

"I rest my case."

* * *

Norman took Charlie's call from his car on the 405 going through the Sepulveda Pass. The reception was spotty, and Norman was pretty sure that Charlie Berns had not asked for a million plus up front to do the show.

"You mean a hundred *grand*, right?"

"No . . . Norman, I need a million two to get it off the ground."

"One million two hundred thousand *dollars*?"

"That's a million euros."

"Are you crazy?"

"Norman, you can amortize it over thirteen. I can bring this show in for less than three hundred an episode."

It was a little after 8:00 a.m. Turkmenistan time, and Charlie was sitting in the bathroom of the guest quarters talking on Fenster's Nokia. Norman's voice was receding into the ambient noise of the freeway traffic.

"How am I going to sell that to Howard?"

"Tell him it's less than five percent of what NBC paid per episode for *Friends*."

There was more crackling over the line to the San Fernando Valley. Charlie thought they had lost the connection when, after a long moment, Norman said, "I'm going to have to get back to you."

Norman clicked off his phone and edged forward with the rush-hour traffic. A million per. Jesus. That was serious change. He'd have to present the number to Howard, who would have to sell it around the corner, where it wouldn't go over big. Those guys didn't like to pay anybody seven figures, least of all producers. The up-front money would max out the division's development budget. They would be putting all their eggs in one basket. A basket held by an out-of-work movie producer, a guy who may or may not be a former CIA agent, and some Uzbek warlord who had just survived a grenade attack.

Norman speed-dialed Howard's home number and left a message on his voice mail proposing breakfast at eight tomorrow morning at the International House of Pancakes in Tarzana.

* * *

That afternoon, Charlie was on a plane out of Nukus heading for Tashkent. He had two thousand euros from Fenster for his flight, his hotel and a deposit to book equipment at the film lab the Poles had recommended. While in the capital, Charlie would open a bank account to handle funds for the production and see if he could find a line producer, though he had no idea where he would find one, if there even *was* one in Uzbekistan.

Charlie checked into a room at the Intercontinental, took a shower, grabbed an Oblomov from the minibar, and dialed the phone number he had gotten for the Uzbekfilmlabaya from Szczedrzyk. It rang seventeen times.

"They are always not answering the telephone," the Pole had warned him.

He took a cab to the address Szczedrzyk had given him on Pushkin Prospekt, a narrow street east of Amir Timur Square dotted with shops and tea houses.

Beside the heavy wooden street door were several plaques with the names of businesses. Charlie rang the buzzer beside Uzbekfilmlabaya and waited for a response. After a few more rings he pushed open the door and entered a dark courtyard with a dying fig tree at the center.

There was a narrow staircase at the rear of the courtyard. He walked up the stairs peering in the darkness at the names on various doors until he located the Uzbekfilmlabaya at the end of the unlit hallway.

He knocked on the metal door several times before a man in a threadbare cardigan sweater and a millimeter of cigarette dangling from his mouth appeared.

"Hello," Charlie said, "is this the film lab?"

The man shot him a look that seemed to say, "That's what it says on the door, schmuck."

"I got your address from Szczedrzyk Klimaszewski. From

Telewizja Polska. I'm looking for a film lab for an American television production."

The man continued to look at him without acknowledgment.

"Do you speak English?"

The man shrugged, as if the question had no importance.

"I'm interested in using your facilities to edit film."

"Hard currency?"

"Euros."

"Khabib Ghofur. At your service."

* * *

Norman Hudris was twenty minutes late to the IHOP on Ventura Boulevard in Tarzana.

"Sorry. There was some kind of sig alert on the 101. They were backed up all the way to Coldwater," he said, as he swung his Bill Blass beige knit suit, drastically reduced at the Three Day Suit Broker After Christmas Sale, into the booth. "They have Fiber One here?"

"I don't know. I've never eaten here before," Howard Draper said, dismayed that Norman Hudris would think that the president of ABCD would actually have breakfast at a pancake house in Tarzana.

"My colorectal guy tells me I need more fiber. I had a colonoscopy in December. He found a few polyps, nothing serious, but he wasn't thrilled with my colon wall."

Howard Draper, who did not consider the state of one's colon appropriate breakfast conversation, said, with manifest impatience, "Norman, you said there was a development with *Souvlaki*."

"We've got a guy."

"You have him on tape?"

"Actually, I don't."

"Good. I don't want to see it."

"I think he could work out . . ." Norman looked around, then lowered his voice and said, "His men pistol-whipped our producer's taxi driver."

"Jesus Christ . . ." Howard took a sip of his Earl Grey breakfast tea and exhaled loudly. "What does he look like?"

"I don't know."

"Good. So you've never seen him?"

"No. Charlie Berns is the only one who's seen him."

"This guy Berns, he doesn't work directly for us, does he?"

"He's an independent contractor."

"Good. So we give Berns the money, and Berns pays the guy, and there's no paper trail . . ."

"Well, strictly speaking, they could possibly trace the money back to us."

"How do they do that?"

"We buried the location and casting trip in the office supply budget. But now we're into preproduction. We can't write off a million two worth of copier paper."

"One point two million? Is that for the entire series?"

"No. That's just the warlord package."

"What is this guy—a fucking gangster?"

Howard took a napkin to his lip, dabbed an errant bran muffin crumb and said, "Of course. That's what we want. Don't we?"

"That's the name of the game."

"We need one point two up front and how much for thirteen?"

"Charlie thinks he can bring it in for three hundred grand an episode."

"So we're looking at four million for thirteen."

"That's what it looks like."

"Out the door?"

"Let's hope so."

The waiter came over and Norman ordered All-Bran, skim milk and a cup of decaf. When the waiter was gone, Howard said, "I'm going to have to go around the corner for this. They're not going to be happy about it."

"Tell him about the grenade attack."

"The grenade attack?"

"In the middle of the night some rival warlord tossed a half dozen grenades into our guy's compound. Our guy's going to take care of business. Probably whack the guy who tried to whack him."

Norman waited a moment to let that sink in. Then he added, "Remember when Tony took care of Joey Pants. Then cut the body up into pieces and hauled it away in garbage bags?"

Howard nodded.

"What if the body had been real?"

* * *

Uzbekfilmlabaya consisted of an editing bay and an Avid, which looked to Charlie as if it had been jerry-rigged with spare parts from several IBM clones. Khabib Ghofur assured him that it was in good condition.

"Top tip," he insisted.

"What about an editor?"

"No problem."

"You know a good film editor in Tashkent?"

"Truly yours."

"You cut film?"

"Like Jew."

To amplify his point, Ghofur did a crude charade of a circumcision.

Charlie closed the deal at five hundred euros a week, for both the Avid and for Ghofur, bargaining down from Ghofur's initial demand of five thousand euros a day.

He took a cab back to the hotel, where he called Szczedrzyk in Nukus to confirm that Ghofur actually cut film. Szczedrzyk told him that Khabib Ghofur cut film like a Latvian cutting sausage with a dull knife, but that if you sat with him and told him what you wanted, he could operate the Avid.

"Don't make hourly deal with him," Szczedrzyk warned Charlie. "The Avid is breaking down all the time. Better you pay him by meters of film cut."

Charlie hung up with Szczedrzyk and was raiding the minibar for cashews when the phone rang.

"Mr. Bernstein?" a voice inquired in a Russian accent.

"Who is this?"

"I am calling to offer some services to you."

"Excuse me?"

"You want a producer for movie?"

"Who is this?"

"Meet me in bar in half hour."

"What is your name?"

"Josef Djugashvili. I am wearing gardenia in lapel."

* * *

The bar at the Intercontinental was located off the Dome restaurant on the top floor of the hotel. It had a view of the TV tower and the botanical gardens to the north. It looked like a hotel bar in Warsaw or in Bucharest, the clientele made up primarily of foreign businessmen and well-dressed hookers.

Charlie saw a short, pudgy man in a cheap suit with an orchid in his lapel sitting alone at a table, his back to the wall, and went over and introduced himself.

"Sit down. Have drink."

Charlie sat down, ordered a Stoli on the rocks from a hovering waiter.

"So, Mr. Djugashvili," he said, "did Mr. Ghofur talk to you?"

"I am not acquainted with Mr. Ghofur."

"So how did you know I was looking for a producer?"

"Mr. Bernstein, Tashkent is small place. Movie business, small business. Whatever you need I have."

Djugashvili offered him a Marlboro Light. Charlie had stopped smoking seventeen years ago after his doctor showed him an X-ray of his lungs, but for some reason a cigarette seemed appropriate at the moment—sitting in a hotel bar in Tashkent across a small table from an unsavory-looking man in shaded glasses and a very ugly tie.

"You are in the film business?" Charlie asked.

"I am in business of providing what you need."

"Well, I'm looking for a line producer, someone who can get me vehicles and equipment for the shoot."

"Mr. Bernstein, if you are going to make movie in Uzbekistan, you will need our help."

"You have a production company?"

"We have whatever you need. You will find it advantageous to do business with us."

The vodka arrived, and Charlie took a long sip from it.

"Well, I appreciate that, Mr. Djugashvili. Why don't you leave me a card and I'll get back to you."

"*I* will get back to *you*. Do not worry. *Dasvidanya.*"

And the pudgy little man downed the vodka and left the table. Charlie watched him walk out the door and inhaled, feeling giddy from the cigarette smoke he was no longer accustomed to. As he took another puff of his cigarette and felt the nostalgic surge of a nicotine rush, he realized he had just been shaken down.

Fenster confirmed his suspicions when a few minutes later Charlie called him from the room and told him about his meeting in the bar of the Intercontinental.

"His name is Josef *Djugashvili?*"

"That's what he said."

"You know who was born with that name? Stalin."

"Joseph Stalin?"

"He changed it when he was sent to Siberia in 1913. This guy must be out of Tbilisi. Shit, that means we're going to have to pay off the fucking Georgians."

"How much?"

"Stick five grand into the budget for them."

"Why do we have to pay off Georgian mobsters to make a movie in Uzbekistan?"

"Because we want our vehicles to show up."

"It's like dealing with the Teamsters," Charlie muttered.

"Worse. The Teamsters don't dice and slice you."

"Great, so they're on the payroll for five thousand."

"Let's just hope we're below the radar for the Russians. You really don't want to fuck with *those* guys."

* * *

At the bank the next morning, Charlie learned that the Uzbek government was going to be on the payroll, as well as Izbul, the Poles and the Georgian mafia. Dr. Rustram Mazinev was the chairman of the National Bank for Foreign Economic Opportunity, a cavernous Soviet-era building on Sharaf Rashidov Street across from the Hotel Tashkent and the history museum.

The amiable Dr. Mazinev explained to Charlie the abstruse Uzbek banking regulations with respect to currency exchange, taxation and repatriation of capital. As a legacy, the Soviets had left a profusion of bureaucratic barriers to profit. It was virtually impossible for a foreigner to make money and take it out of Uzbekistan without the government taking its cut off the top.

Charlie sat in the overly furnished office of the bank chairman and filled out a profusion of forms, making up the details as he went along. What did he care? They would be wrapped and long gone before the government tax authorities could unravel the money trail.

Dr. Mazinev told him that he was a big fan of American television. Like anyone with resources in the Stans, he had a dish that picked up reruns of American programs on European satellite stations. At home he had a signed glossy of Drew Carey, which he had gotten on eBay.

Charlie left the bank with a file folder full of regulations in badly translated English, which he would turn over to the line producer, should he ever find one, and returned to his hotel and called his agent, Brad Emprin, in L.A.

"Charlie, how's it going?" the agent said, his pathologically upbeat voice bubbling up through the phone receiver.

"Fine. We're waiting for the green light from Norman."

"I'm staying on the guy, Charlie. I call him three times a day."

"Listen, I want you to arrange to have my checks sent directly to you."

"No problem. How much is it?"

"You made the deal, Brad. Don't you remember?"

"Sure, I remember. I backed up a truck." Brad Emprin had his phone headset on, and so while he scampered to the file cabinet to look for Charlie Berns's contract he vamped.

"So how's the weather over there?"

"Shitty. Brad, I want you to keep this money in your safe for me."

"You don't want me to direct deposit it in your bank account?"

"I don't have a bank account."

"All your money's under the mattress." He laughed, his hyena laugh continuing longer than usual as he fumbled through the drawer for the contract. Tamara Berkowitz filed about as well as she gave head.

"Just keep the checks for me in your office. I'll get them when I'm back there."

Charlie Berns's contract was filed under *Warlord* instead of under the client's name, as it was supposed to be, and Brad Emprin finally unearthed it and scanned it quickly.

"Twenty-five per." He whistled appreciatively. "Not bad."

"Call me when the first check arrives."

"Sure. Where? I don't have a number for you—"

But Charlie had already hung up and was about to lie down for a snooze when his phone rang. An accented voice introduced himself as Zholov Dostyk and said that he was calling on behalf of Khabib Ghofur.

"I produce line."

"You're a line producer?"

"The best."

"Can we meet?"

"Tonight. Nine o'clock. The Aladdin nightclub off Mustakillik Square. You know where it is?"

"I'll find it."

* * *

The Aladdin Nightclub turned out to be a garish strip club with ear-splitting music. And Zholov Dostyk turned out to be a Kazakh from Almaty, who said that he had produced twenty-three films all over the Stans.

"I shoot Almaty. I shoot Osh. I shoot Dushanbe. You name it. I shoot there," Dostyk told him, shouting to be heard over the music.

Charlie drank beer and tried not to watch the busty strippers, wearing costumes that looked like they were from 1950s bump-and-grind houses in Kansas City, peel off their clothes down to pasties, spangled panties and high heels, as the line producer proceeded to rattle off the titles of movies that Charlie had never heard of.

"You see *Bride of Bishkek*?"

Charlie shook his head.

"You see *Tales of Timur Amir*?"

"Afraid not."

"No matter. Where you shoot?"

"In the west. Nukus, Dashoguz, the Aral Sea."

Dostyk's face darkened and he chewed his lip. "Very difficult there. Big warlords. You get shaken down bad. Need lots of protection."

"I've got protection."

"Who?"

"Izbul Kharkov."

The line producer's face got even darker. "Izbul shake you down already?"

"No. He's starring."

"You make movie about Izbul Kharkov?"

"It's a TV show."

A light was slowly illuminated behind Dostyk's eyes. "Like . . . *Sopranos*?"

"Meets *The Osbournes*."

"No shits?"

"No shits."

ELEVEN

The Search for Genghis Khan's Grave

It's two tenths of a mile from the gate of the ABC lot in Burbank to the gate of the Mouse House. You make a right for one tenth of a mile, then make another right onto South Buena Vista Street for another tenth of a mile. Five minutes on foot. But it could easily be five times that, or more, in a car. First you have to retrieve your car from the underground parking lot, then drive the two tenths of a mile, present yourself at the gate, where you could find yourself in a lineup of cars whose occupants do not have drive-on passes left for them and have to be cleared by a phone call from the guard gate to the office, where the phone may be answered by a temp who has no idea who the visitor is and whom to call to check with, and then when you finally approach the guard house, you have to pop your trunk, present your photo ID, have a mirror passed underneath the chassis of your car to check for bombs, and, then, after all that, you may be exiled to a parking area farther away from where you were headed than the place you started out from around the corner.

In spite of these obstacles, Howard Draper drove to his meeting around the corner from his Burbank office, where he had made one of his infrequent appearances that morning to go through the mail he didn't receive and check out his empty call sheet. He had allowed a half hour for the two-minute drive, and, as irony would have it, he confronted none of the usual obstacles and found himself in a VIP parking space with twenty-five minutes to kill before his 3:00 p.m. meeting.

Howard knew that he couldn't just sit in his car, not even in a VIP space, for twenty-five minutes without attracting the attention of the roving security force, so he got out and took a walk around the lot. Even with the new buildings that had gone up in the last ten years, the place still had the look of a junior college campus, with its trimmed lawns and academic-style buildings. The animation building looked like it belonged on a Cal State campus in Rancho Cucamonga. You expected bells to ring every quarter hour.

Howard had made his third trip past the commissary when he was confronted by a plainclothes security guard in an unmarked golf cart and asked to state his business. Howard produced his drive-on pass. The security guard informed him that he was fifteen minutes early for his meeting and he could wait in the office he was visiting.

If you're taking an important meeting, however, you do not want to show up fifteen minutes early and sit and read copies of the trades while the receptionist gives you the look she reserves for messengers and agents. It was bad power judo to arrive early; it reeked of being hungry, as if the meeting was much more important to you than it was to the person you were meeting with.

Nevertheless Howard went directly to the Team Disney Building, passing beneath the Maurice Sendakesque statues of Goofy and Mickey, and produced his drive-on pass and his photo ID for the guard at the desk, who gave him clearance to ride the elevator. He rode to the fifth floor, the power floor, walked down the empty, silent hallway past a men's room, which he tried to enter to kill some time but found the door locked, and so he had no alternative but to continue to the suite that housed the offices of Poindexter and North.

Poindexter and North were not the real names of the two men whom Mikey used to insulate himself from anything that might be difficult to explain to the board and the stockholders. Their names were Greg Patowsky and Andy Mack, but Howard and Norman always referred to them behind their backs by the names of Reagan's buffers. They seemed to be apt sobriquets for two men whose raisons d'être were to make sure that the CEO would never have to know more than he had to know.

Their office suite was commodious and deadly quiet. Two well-dressed, middle-aged secretaries sat at their respective computers. Howard went up to one of them and said hello.

"I'm a little early for my three o'clock with Greg and Andy."

She looked back at her screen, hit a few keys to bring up the computerized appointment book and simply nodded. She did not invite him to have a seat or ask if he would like something to drink.

Howard sat down on the cold leather couch, sank into the upholstery, picked up a copy of *The Hollywood Reporter* and was confronted with the headline: "Alphabet Ratings Nosedive."

He should take it into the meeting with him and, as a preamble, put it on the coffee table. See how far in the toilet this network is? Any further and you're going to need a plunger to get it out.

Howard needed not only to get the budget for *Warlord* approved but to get it up and running while his division was still functioning. The corporate hatchet guys were no doubt already hovering with their red pencils. The division could be dissolved and their records shredded in a matter of days, if not hours.

Poindexter and North received him in the small conference room between their offices. It was a featureless, undecorated room, which, Howard was convinced, had been bug-proofed. They too didn't offer him anything to drink. Nor was there a fruit bowl in the middle of the table, the kind you saw in the big agencies that contained fruit that was not designed to be eaten, only admired. The bigger the fruit bowl, the more important the client. If your last picture grossed more than a hundred million, they broke out the kiwis.

The two executive vice presidents looked immaculate in their almost matching Ralph Lauren suits and off-white shirts. Poindexter had a scrupulously groomed beard, which he dyed, and North had a Marine Corps brush cut. They both looked like they spent three hours a day on a Stairmaster.

Since time was beyond pressing and these guys weren't big on small talk anyway, Howard jumped right in.

"There's a project in my division that's ready to be funded. I need one point two right away against a thirteen-episode budget at four all in."

Poindexter and North exchanged a look, pregnant with indifference, and then proceeded contrapuntally.

"Log line?"

"*The Sopranos* meets *The Osbournes* in Central Asia."

"Time frame?"

"We can be testing six weeks from funding, on the air in three months."

"Upside?"

"Watercooler show at three hundred per hour."

"Downside?"

"Inexperienced producers, unpredictable talent."

"Exposure?"

"Most of the exposure is out of the country."

"Attackability?"

"Questionable taste."

"Sex?"

"No."

"Language?"

"Controllable in the editing room."

"Violence?"

"Big time."

"Real?"

"Very."

"Victims?"

"Foreign nationals."

"Women or children?"

"Collaterally."

"Moslems?"

"Nominally."

Poindexter and North shared another one of their coded looks. The buzzer had sounded on the word *Moslem.*

"What's a nominal Moslem?"

"Someone who lives in Uzbekistan and makes his living as a warlord."

"Guy pray to Mecca and wear a robe?"

"Not as far as I know."

"Cover?"

"Some sort of natural history documentary for the Archaeology Channel."

"Exit strategy?"

"Pack up and leave in twenty-four hours."

"Press release?"

Damage control was North's area. He was a vacuum cleaner, his job to suck up anything embarrassing to the company and dump the ashes in a toxic waste dump in Nevada.

Howard improvised: "Ecological concerns for the local flora and fauna."

Poindexter stroked his chin. Rigorous cost-benefit accounting was his strong suit.

"What's the drop-dead date on this?"

"Yesterday."

* * *

North immediately assigned the project to one of his game players, a bright young USC graduate in Media Relations, who by five o'clock that afternoon came up with a sexy title for the documentary that they would be funding in western Uzbekistan: *The Search for Genghis Khan's Grave.*

Poindexter ran the idea by an old fraternity brother who had majored in archaeology. The Psi U buddy informed him that Genghis Khan had died in Mongolia, about a thousand miles from the Western Uzbekistan desert.

"Anybody know that who's not a Ph.D. in archaeology?" North asked.

"Probably not."

By noon the next day, *The Search for Genghis Khan's Grave* was funded by ABCD as a documentary for the newly acquired Archaeology Channel.

Howard gave the news to Norman at a Taco Bell on Magnolia.

"Not bad," Norman responded.

"North came up with it himself."

"I bet you he called Howard Hunt."

"*Souvlaki* is no longer operative. We're calling it *Genghis Khan.*"

"Fine with me. Is the check in the mail?"

"As soon as I tell them where to mail it."

There was a moment of reflection as both men realized that from this point on, they were committed to the project; their fingerprints were on it, or at least Norman's.

"So I guess this is it," Norman said, a little wistfully.

"That's up to you," Howard replied, already distancing himself. "It's your baby, Norman."

Right, Norman thought. Until it gets into Yale.

* * *

Back from Tashkent, Charlie was sitting with Fenster and Izbul watching *Jeopardy* when Fenster's Nokia sounded. Fenster handed the cell to Charlie. "It's Burbank calling. Tell them to get the fuck on the stick."

Charlie heard Norman's anxiety-coated voice tell him that the money had been cleared. The phone to his ear, Charlie walked out of Izbul's office and into the slot machine room.

"You're making a documentary called *The Search for Genghis Khan's Grave*," Norman informed him. "It's for the Archaeology Channel."

Still a little dazed from his whirlwind trip to Tashkent, Charlie didn't get the damage control strategy on the first take.

"It's going to cost *four million* to make *thirteen episodes*," Norman said, slowly and distinctly, hitting the high notes with a sledgehammer.

"Got it."

"I need bank routing and account numbers to get the money to you."

Charlie walked to the guest quarters, as Norman explained to him that everything was going to be written against the putative documentary and that all the paperwork needed to go under that name.

"The dailies, the cut film, even the canisters—everything has to have that name on it."

"I'm not going to be able to send you dailies."

"Why not?"

"The lab's in Tashkent, an hour-and-a-half plane ride from here. Besides, Norman, do you really want to see dailies?"

"All right. Just send me the rough cut episodes."

"You really want to see rough cuts?"

"What if I have Standards and Practices concerns?"

"You *will* have Standards and Practices concerns. I thought that was the point."

"All right. Just send me the cut episodes."

Charlie took the bank account numbers from his wallet and read them to Norman.

"When can I see a budget?"

"You really want to see a budget?"

It took Norman a moment to realize he didn't want to see a budget. "Charlie, I can't tell you how important this project is to us."

"Don't worry—it's going to be great."

"This doesn't work, we might all be out of business."

"It's going to work."

"Worst-case scenario we throw together a documentary about Genghis Khan's grave."

"Sure."

"We'll put it on opposite the Super Bowl. No one will ever see it."

* * *

Charlie returned to Izbul's office, where the warlord and Fenster were now watching *Wheel of Fortune*. He announced that they were going to be starting production very soon.

"Money, Charlie Berns from Hollywood?" Izbul asked, his eyes still on the screen.

"On its way."

"Money come, you produce. Money don't come, you stay here till it come. Fuckink A."

"The money's coming, Izbul," Fenster reassured him.

"You know what Tony do when asshole not payink him? Back of neck with gun, boom."

Izbul demonstrated what he meant by firing a pretend gun into his own neck. "Guy goes to bottom of river. Bada boom."

"I'm sure that won't be necessary."

"You know what happen you put Kalashnikov up guy's ass? You cut him new asshole."

Later as they lay in bed together, Charlie said to Fenster, "Let me ask you a question—does anybody know you're here?"

"What're you talking about?"

"What if Izbul decided to take the money and put a Kalashnikov up both our asses?"

"He's not going to do that."

"Why not? As far as I can gather, this guy doesn't answer to anybody."

"He knows there's more money involved. He does us now, he doesn't get any more."

"You still didn't answer my question."

"What question?"

"Does anybody know you're here?"

"Yeah."

"Who?"

"You."

TWELVE

Preproduction

Two days after his phone conversation with Norman Hudris, Charlie and Fenster went to Tashkent and withdrew cash from the account that Charlie had opened at the National Bank for Foreign Economic Opportunity on U Akhumbabaev Street and that had been funded by wire transfer from the San Fernando Valley National Bank and Trust on Bob Hope Drive in Burbank.

Afterwards they met with Zholov Dostyk. Charlie gave the Kazakh line producer a laundry list of what he was going to need for the location. They sat at the Sharshara *chaikhana*, a tea house on the Burdzhar Canal at the end of Rakatboshi Street, and went over the production needs.

It was going to be a lean and mean crew. Szczedrzyk and the Poles were low-tech and mobile, using natural light and small portable cameras to capture the deteriorating ecosystem of the Aral Sea. They would use a similar run-and-gun technique when they traveled with Izbul. The real challenge was filming what went on inside the compound. They would have to use enough artificial lighting to ensure that the picture quality was up to the standards of American television.

Besides lights and cameras, they would need trailers to use as production offices, to house grip, electric and sound equipment and generators to air-condition them. They would need a mobile catering kitchen, vehicles to move around with, portajohns, a number of things difficult to obtain in northern Turkmenistan.

Dostyk listened patiently and said "No problem" to everything on Charlie's list.

"Don't worry. I shoot Russian revolution in Riga. Three thousand extras. Tanks, cannon, artillery, whatever you want. You want Stukas? I got Stukas. You want Winter Palace? I build it."

Charlie doled out some money to his line producer to begin assembling equipment and transporting it to Dashoguz. If it actually showed up, he would give him more.

Later that afternoon, at the Intercontinental, they were contacted by their silent partner, Josef Djugashvili from Tbilisi. Fenster accompanied Charlie to the bar to meet the new man on the payroll. Stalin was wearing the same ill-fitting suit and smoking the same cigarettes. Charlie took another one, his second in seventeen years.

They drank screwdrivers, heavy on the vodka, and after minimal amenities in a patois of Russian and English, Fenster established the parameters of the protection money they would be paying the Georgians. Charlie marveled at the skill with which both men danced around the transaction without either of them being specific.

Later, in their room, Fenster explained his decision to do business with the Georgians. "Better them than the Uzbeks or the Russians. The Uzbeks are incompetent, and the Russians would want too big a cut. They get involved, they'll want thirty percent of the cash profit and future equity."

"What future equity?"

"The Russians aren't just off the tractor anymore. They read the *Wall Street Journal.* They know about syndication deals, DVDs, foreign territories. They'll want distribution rights in the Baltic."

"You think the studio is going to give distribution rights to the Russian mafia?"

"No. That's why we're doing business with the Georgians. Strictly cash on the barrelhead."

"How much?"

"I got them down to forty-five hundred a show. They wanted five grand."

"Do we get anything at all for that money?"

"Yeah. Our equipment shows up."

* * *

That night they met another person who would become an important member of the production team of *The Search for Genghis Khan's Grave.*

Fenster had taken him to the New World Pizza and Bakery on Bukhara Street, opposite the Navoi Theater. They sat outside in the cool early March evening, drank beer and ate a Central Asian version of an anchovy pizza. Sitting at the next table reading a battered paperback copy of *The Dharma Bums* was a young American with long hair, wearing a baseball cap, grease-stained tennis shoes and a Grateful Dead crew jacket.

The young man, a Peace Corps volunteer from Boulder, Colorado, was named Barrett "Buzz" Bowden. Buzz was AWOL from his post and living a fly-by-night existence in Tashkent until they caught up with him.

"How long have you been in Uzbekistan?" Charlie asked him.

"Fourteen months."

"Doing what?"

"Teaching the Uzbeks how to build septic tanks in Samarkand. You ever build a septic tank?"

"Not that I know of."

"It's basically redistributing shit. It goes in one end and comes out the other end as fertilizer. I decided there's got to be better things to do here, so I split."

"So what are you doing in Tashkent?"

"I'm an independent businessman."

"In what line of business?"

Buzz took a closer look at Charlie, trying to read this guy in the nondescript sport jacket over a sweater, sitting beside a man with the fleece-lined aviator's jacket and cowboy boots. Neither one looked like a Uzbek narc or a CIA agent trawling for assets, so he told them the truth.

"I'm in the exotic pharmaceutical business."

"How's it going?"

"A little slow. You got to grease so many people that the profit margin's pretty slim."

"Same thing in my business," said Charlie, wondering which mafia this kid had to pay off.

"Interested in a few grams of quality Tibetan Tan?"

"Not my thing."

"Sure? One toke of this and you'll be in the stratosphere."

"I can't afford to be in the stratosphere. I'm producing a TV show."

"No shit. What kind of show?"

Charlie told him about *The Search for Genghis Khan's Grave.*

"Funny title for a reality show about a warlord."

"That's just for bookkeeping purposes."

"Any openings on your crew?"

This time it was Charlie who took a good look at Buzz Bowden. Blond, blue-eyed, square jawed. He'd fit right in with the Poles.

"How well do you speak Uzbek?"

"Like fucking Tamerlane."

"I need a translator."

"I'm your guy."

"What about the pharmaceutical business?"

"It's something to fall back on. What's the money?"

"Negotiable."

"How about five hundred bucks a week?"

"How about five hundred euros?"

"Cool. When are you starting?"

"Next week."

"Where are you shooting?"

"In the west. Around Nukus."

"Nukus is the pits."

"Worse."

"I'll bring the hash."

* * *

Charlie booked rooms in the Turkish-owned Hotel Diyabekir in Dashoguz for the crew and him, converting two adjoining rooms into a suite for himself, and booking the rest of the floor for the Poles, who, judging from their tenure at the Hotel Nukus, were not fussy about accommodations. It was a moderately clean hotel with alleged air-conditioning, functional bathrooms and satellite TV.

He brought Buzz Bowden with him to negotiate group rates, but since the owner of the hotel spoke only Turkmen, Charlie had to draft their driver, one of the pistol-whippers, a native Turkmen named Murv, to handle the translating. They wound up getting the rooms for next to nothing.

Heading back to the compound, on the outskirts of Dashoguz, just beyond the bazaar, the pistol-whipper/translator pulled over and got out of the car. At a small roadside stand an old man was selling onions. Murv went up to the guy and shouted some nasty-sounding words at him. When the old man did not respond, Murv kicked over the stand and sent the onions flying in all directions. Then he kicked over the old man.

Murv got back in the car and said something to Buzz in Uzbek.

"What did he say?" Charlie asked Buzz.

"The guy owed him five hundred manats."

"How much is five hundred manats?"

"About a quarter."

* * *

The portajohns were the first equipment to arrive. They came on a flatbed truck, six vintage models from Tbilisi transshipped through Kazakhstan. The trailers showed up two days later in caravan from Ashgabat, dusty from their voyage across the Kara Kum steppe. A production office was set up in the largest trailer, a desk for Dostyk and a desk for Charlie, and a couple of computers with erratic Internet connections.

When the lights and cameras arrived, Charlie took Szczedrzyk and his crew on a location scout through the compound to determine where to rig the equipment. There were lengthy discussions among the Poles about lighting and angles. The cameras would be installed everywhere except in Izbul's wife's room. Fenster had told Charlie that Izbul's wife's room was off limits. Charlie asked Izbul if he could at least meet Ishrat Khana.

"Suck dick."

"I beg your pardon?"

"She not beink here."

"Your wife doesn't live here?"

"I see her. I cut her new one."

And that was that. Fenster explained that Izbul and Ishrat Khana hadn't spoken to each other in years. The woman lived in her bedroom, took her meals there and, as far as anyone knew, never went out.

"What does she do?"

"The fuck do I know. Put the Ukrainian bimbo on TV. They'll love her."

Charlie discussed the problem with Buzz, who, besides being useful in dealing with the finicky portajohns and translating, was beginning to develop a creative interest in the project. Buzz, it turned out, was a reality show junkie. Before joining the Peace Corps he had auditioned for *Survivor* and had gotten all the way to the final cut before his background check turned up a high school marijuana possession arrest.

"What if it's like the inner sanctum?" Buzz suggested. "We don't go in there for a couple of weeks, build up the audience's curiosity, then promo it big on an upcoming episode—'next week we enter Ishrat Khana's room.' "

Dostyk's gaffers had rigged a control board in the production trailer. It was a series of closed-circuit TV monitors that showed the action in all the rooms simultaneously. You could see everything that was going on in the compound as it was happening. The cameras were attached to digital recording devices that, when activated, would transfer all this activity on to computer disks.

Gradually the fields around Izbul's compound began to resemble a high-tech trailer park, with the large generators and portajohns hovering around the trailers. The crew went about their work with the singlemindedness of an oddly configured team with a common purpose, if not a common language. Though the Poles all spoke decent English, most of the Uzbek crew, as well as Izbul's men, didn't. They spoke a mixture of Uzbek, Turkmen and Kazakh, with Russian as the trading language they had all been compelled to study in school under the Soviets but hated to speak.

Before they could begin shooting, they had to wait for some bugs to be worked out in the sound recording. Szczedrzyk's soundman Jacek was having difficulty getting ambient noise filters working so that they could hear what people were saying clearly. Since they were going to subtitle the program anyway, it didn't seem to Charlie to be critical, but Jacek was a perfectionist. There was no point in doing sound if it wasn't authentic, insisted the man who had spent the last few months of his life listening to the Aral Sea evaporate.

As they were ironing out last-minute production problems, Charlie sat at the console and watched the warlord's life through the monitors. Everybody in the compound seemed to be self-consciously aware of the cameras. Buzz explained to Charlie that this was a normal phenomenon with reality television shows but that it wouldn't take long before they forgot about the cameras.

"Pretty soon they don't even see them. Next thing you know, they're picking their noses and screwing on camera."

Meanwhile, Norman Hudris was growing impatient. He called Charlie wanting to know how things were progressing.

"When do the cameras roll?"

"As soon as we fix the sound problem."

"When do you think you'll have something cut together?"

"Soon."

"Any more grenades?"

"Not yet."

"What about this guy's sex life?"

"He's got a Ukrainian actress girlfriend."

"What's she look like?"

"Not bad."

"So he's screwing around on his wife?"

"Apparently."

"What's the wife look like?"

"Haven't met her yet."

"How come?"

"She never comes out of her room."

"We could use a Carmella character. Female demo."

"I'll see what I can do."

When Jacek finally fixed the sound problem to his satisfaction, the computer disks started recording life at the Kharkov compound, which for the first few days followed the same uneventful pattern as it had during preproduction. There was endless footage of Ali Mohammed reading his Koran, Akbar watching MTV, Ferghana drying her hair and talking on the phone, and Izbul playing cards with his men and taking potshots at rabbits with assault rifles.

Charlie sent the mobile crew to school with Akbar, but they wouldn't allow them to enter the school grounds. Izbul got into the BMW with Murv and drove to Dashoguz to have a conversation with the headmaster, which they filmed.

Buzz translated it for Charlie. "Basically, Izbul told him to let the crew in or he would torch the school, the principal's house and the houses of his entire family."

While they were in Dashoguz, the crew followed Izbul into the bazaar and filmed him collecting money from various vendors. On the way back, he stuck his head out of the sunroof and shot a camel that was wandering aimlessly in a field.

The camel shoot would make a colorful opening credit sequence, Charlie thought, as he replayed the tape. They could run it under credits with some upbeat music. With any luck the animal rights people would come after them. You couldn't buy that type of publicity.

*   *   *

Eventually things started to pick up. Grushenka and Ferghana had a nasty fight. Buzz gave Charlie a running translation as they sat in the production trailer and watched the two women go at each other.

"Ferghana's calling Grushenka a home wrecker. Grushenka's calling Ferghana a dyke."

Grushenka stormed into Izbul's office and threatened to leave if his family didn't respect her. Izbul told her to get the fuck out. She said she was going as soon as she packed up, and she stormed out and marched off to the bedroom suite, where she began to stuff her lingerie into a suitcase.

Izbul entered and screamed some more. She screamed back. Thirty seconds later they were having intense sex on the circular bed.

Charlie sat at the console and watched all this unwind with growing interest. Human drama, emotion, anger and forgiveness. He could cut around the hard-core sex, finesse the nudity, tone down the language.

As Izbul and Grushenka collapsed into postcoital bliss, Charlie's eye wandered to the other monitors. Ferghana was in her room talking animatedly on her cell phone. Ali Mohammed was on his prayer rug praying to Mecca. Akbar was pulling his pud.

In the barracks, Murv was throwing a mutton kebab on the hibachi. Outside someone was installing a new quadraphonic CD deck into one of the armored BMWs. Out near the septic tank that Buzz had inspected and pronounced operational, one of the other soldiers was beating the shit out of some poor guy in a turban who hadn't paid his protection money. In the storeroom, they were crating slot machines for shipment to the Caspian Sea.

Charlie edited it all together in his head. Life at home with the Kharkovs. Episode 1. Ferghana and Grushenka fight. Grushenka and Izbul fight and make up. Murv beats up a deadbeat behind on his payments. Ali Mohammed prepares to join the Taliban. Hot slots get sent west.

Bada bink.

THIRTEEN

The Uzbek Demographic

The comptroller at DBA—Fred Fortrain, a fortyish former CPA with a cut-rate hairpiece—was riding up in the elevator with Jodie Jacobian—a thirtyish agent with a $250 Cameron Diaz cut and gym-honed thighs—when, in an effort to make conversation, he happened to mention *The Search for Genghis Khan's Grave*. Charlie Berns's first check had just passed through his office, and the title of the project was on his mind as he was foraging for something to say to the young agent with the great bod.

"The Search for *Whose* Grave?" responded Jodie Jacobian, still waiting for the caffeine from her mochaccino to kick in.

"Genghis Khan's."

"A series about Genghis Khan?"

"Apparently. They're paying the exec producer twenty-five per."

"Who's the EP?"

"Charlie Berns?"

"Charlie *who*?"

"Berns. He's a client of this agency."

"Where's it set up?"

"ABC. It's Brad's deal. So . . . you work out a lot?"

But Jodie was already off the elevator, and—her mochaccino in her hand, her Coach leather book bag of full scripts over her shoulder—on her way down the hall to Brad Emprin's office. She walked right past Tamara Berkowitz and through the open door.

Brad, on the telephone, waved her in.

"Don't worry. They love you over there," he said to whomever he was talking. "You're on a very short list." He hung up and said to

Jodie, "Gloria Garlington. She couldn't get arrested if she walked into the White House with a bomb strapped to her boobs. How're you doing?"

"ABC has a Genghis Khan's grave project?"

"You bet. Charlie Berns. Very hot client."

"That's weird because I pitched Kara an Archaeology show in October, and she said that they weren't interested in the area. I went in with Joel Drucker. They're dying to be in business with him. It was a fabulous idea—*Archo Squad,* a group of sexy, young archaeologists on international digs—you know, *CSI* in the Holy Land–type thing."

"You didn't sell that?"

"Didn't even get a nibble. How did this Charlie Berns—who the fuck is he?—sell her Genghis Khan?"

"Sold it in the room. Thirteen on the air."

"You got thirteen *on the air*?"

"With an option for twenty-two."

"Jesus. Do we have a packaging position?"

"Couldn't get it. Charlie's got a partner, some guy named Fenster. I Googled him and came up blank."

Jodie Jacobian kicked into creative mode. "What if we tried to sell Charlie Berns Joel Drucker as co-EP?"

"Joel willing to go over to Tashkent?"

"Tashkent? That's where they're shooting?"

"Yeah. I put Charlie into the Intercontinental."

"Isn't that like in . . . Pakistan?"

"Uzbekistan."

"They paying per diem?"

"Big time. I got Charlie fifty grand upfront."

"Let me talk to Joel."

Joel Drucker told Jodie Jacobian that there was no way he would go to Uzbekistan to be co-EP under someone else, not even for thirty-five per, a suite at the Intercontinental, a big per diem and a play-or-pay pilot commitment. And so for the moment, at least, the security of the ABCD *Warlord* project was not compromised. But Jodie Jacobian made a mental note to ask Kara Kotch about it next time they talked. She'd drop it into some conversation in a casual, completely nonconfrontational tone of voice, and maybe she'd get a guilt point or two in her favor for the next pilot she brought in.

There was no point calling Floyd directly to ask him about the show. You didn't waste a shot with the head of the network just to satisfy your curiosity. Floyd had obviously signed off on the Charlie Berns—whoever the fuck he was—project. Kara could put a pilot script in development without running it by Floyd, but there was no way she could make a pilot, let alone give someone thirteen on the air, without Floyd signing off.

What Jodie Jacobian did not know was that Floyd was not in the loop. The network president had no idea what ABCD's real mission was beyond the vague rubric of exploring alternative media. Of course, sooner or later Floyd would have to be told about the project, if not about the real purpose of the whole division. There was only so long you could let the head of programming of one of the big three networks stand there with his thumb up his ass. But not until, as Kermit Fenster would say, he had a need to know. And, at the moment, he didn't.

* * *

Now that Charlie had his own cell phone, Norman no longer had to go through Fenster to talk to him. Which meant that Charlie was reachable 24/7. And Norman took advantage of this fact to call him at all hours and nudge him to move faster.

The thirteen-hour time difference between California and Turkmenistan meant that there were few mutually convenient hours to talk without one of them being asleep. Usually it was Charlie who was woken in the morning, early evening Pacific time, by Norman on his cell going home over the Sepulveda Pass after a day in the office. Since life in the compound rarely started early in the morning, Charlie caught up on his sleep during the hours of three to nine in the morning, and he was never entirely awake during these phone calls.

"What happened yesterday?" Norman opened, with no introduction.

"Yesterday?"

"Any action?"

Charlie fumbled for his glasses, as if this would make him somewhat more alert. "Let's see . . . Izbul went to Nukus to collect some money, but he was tipped off at the border that there was an Uzbek intelligence agent waiting for him with twenty armed men at the Korean noodle restaurant. So he headed back to the compound and watched television all day."

"That's all?"

"He had a dick-measuring contest with his men."

"A *what*?"

"That's when he makes everyone in the room pull his pants down to see how big his dick is. He even makes the crew do it."

"We can't air that."

"We'll pixelate it."

"Charlie, are you out of your mind? You *do* know who owns this studio—"

"You wanted ratings."

"When am I going to see something?"

"I'm going to Tashkent this weekend to start cutting some stuff together."

"I need to arrange the test marketing. Send me what you have on Monday."

"All right."

"Address it to Tom Soaring Hawk."

"That your *nom de guerre*, Norman?"

"He's my assistant. And I don't want to see any penises."

*　*　*

After briefing Szczedrzyk and Dostyk to call him immediately if anything out of the ordinary happened at the compound, Charlie caught a plane out of Nukus for Tashkent. He brought Buzz along with him to translate, as well as a briefcase full of diskettes downloaded from the cameras.

They took a cab directly to the Uzbekfilmlabaya and went right to work. It was slow going. Szczedrzyk was right: Ghofur cut film like a Latvian cutting sausages. His unfamiliarity with English made the laying in of the subtitles painstaking.

It took them six hours to cut just the Grushenka-Ferghana blowout. The screaming was mostly in Russian, which Buzz didn't know beyond several words for *septic tank* and *hashish,* and they had to rely on Ghofur's translation, which was spotty because Grushenka's tirade turned out to be in Ukrainian.

At nine o'clock they took a break to get something to eat. Charlie and Buzz found a kebab stand not far from the film lab and ate vegetable kebabs heavy on the cumin.

It was over this modest dinner that Buzz made the first of his valuable creative suggestions for *The Search for Genghis Khan's Grave*.

Charlie was bemoaning the time-consuming nature of the subtitling process. "It's going to take us forever. We're going to need Russian, Turkmen, even Ukrainian translators . . ."

"Why?"

"To get it right."

"Why do you have to get it right?"

"People are going to be watching this stuff on TV."

"Charlie, let me ask you something. How many Americans you think understand Uzbek?"

"Not a whole lot."

"How many of them are eighteen to thirty-four with disposable income?"

"Even fewer."

"And how many of *them* have a Nielsen box?"

* * *

Charlie and Buzz spent the next seventy-two hours, with only a few hours off for sleeping, recutting the footage and writing new subtitles. Khabib Ghofur knew enough English to know that the subtitles he was laying over the footage had nothing to do with what people were actually saying on camera.

Buzz explained to him about the microscopic size of the Uzbek demographic, but the Latvian sausage maker had other concerns.

"People see this, think I'm butcher," he complained.

"Don't worry," Charlie assured him, "no one you know is going to see this."

Without the constraint of using actual dialogue, Charlie and Buzz were able to construct their own version of what was happening in the lives of the warlord, his family and soldiers, thereby transforming the show into a scripted fictional show masquerading as a reality show. And the only ones who would ever know about this were

Uzbek-speaking people who happened to be watching ABC at the time the show aired. Given the state of the network's ratings, they weren't looking at many people. The network could handle three people writing letters to some Viewer Relations person sitting in an office on Riverside Drive fielding complaints about naked butts on *NYPD Blue.*

The Ferghana-Grushenka fight was now about Murv. Ferghana accused the Ukrainian bombshell of cheating on her father with the Turkmen enforcer, and Grushenka accused Ferghana of siding with her mother, who was secretly plotting revenge against Grushenka for stealing her husband by allying herself with a rival warlord in Dashoguz.

Murv, meanwhile, had been bought by the same rival warlord who was having an affair with Ishrat Khana and was biding his time waiting to make his move on Izbul. His dalliances with both Ferghana and Grushenka were strategic more than amorous, given the fact that Murv had lost his testicles in a camel-hunting accident.

What Ali Mohammed was reading in his room was in actuality a coded version of the Koran, slipped to him by Russian agents trying to recruit the warlord's son to turn against his father and help them reassert their power in Uzbekistan and deplete the soil further by planting more cotton.

Akbar was going through a difficult adolescence caused by his being the son of the most feared warlord in western Uzbekistan and northern Turkmenistan. Nobody wanted to hang out with him in school. He was sullen and alienated, a powder keg of emotions, who could implode at any minute and be sent to a therapist in Nukus to deal with his feelings toward his powerful father and invisible mother.

Izbul was trying to divorce the unseen Ishrat Khana, while trying to consolidate his position in Nukus by shaking down the owner of the Korean noodle restaurant, who was himself being shaken down by the Uzbek mafia and who may or may not be a double agent for the government in Tashkent and/or the CIA.

The *pièce de résistance* of Charlie and Buzz's rewriting the subtitles, however, was the explanation for the pixelated version of the dick-measuring contest. A third-person voice-over narrator, a reluctant

Khabib Ghofur, explained it as a ritual loyalty oath that Izbul demanded from his minions. Every soldier joining the warlord's private army had to pledge that his future offspring, represented symbolically by his grabbing and waving his generative organ, would follow in his footsteps and join Izbul's army.

They put the finishing touches on the credit sequence at 8:00 a.m. on Thursday morning, punchy and exhilarated, propped up by Khabib Ghofur's coffee, which made up in caffeine for what it lacked in taste. They put a blood-dripping title graphic on the screen over footage of the camel hunt and laid it over some canned Central Asian rap music that their editor stole off a bootlegged CD.

Charlie and Buzz staggered out into the foggy Tashkent morning feeling as if they had just repainted the Sistine Chapel.

"Out of sight," Buzz yawned.

"Well, it's either the best or the worst thing I've ever done."

"It's gonna be a big hit. I mean, think of the dick-measuring contest . . ." And Buzz broke into a fit of giddy laugher. "Jesus, I'm not even stoned."

They walked to the DHL office on Shara Rashidov Street, where Charlie sent off Episode 1 of *The Search for Genghis Khan's Grave* overnight to Norman Hudris.

Then they went back to the Intercontinental and slept for twelve hours.

FOURTEEN

Izbul's Character Arc

At ten o'clock on Tuesday morning the cassette from Tashkent arrived on Tom Soaring Hawk's desk, after being run through the metal detector in the ABCD mailroom along with audition tapes from actors' and directors' agents eager to find work for their underemployed clients at the network's Alternative Media Division. Following his boss's instructions, Tom Soaring Hawk threw all the cassettes into the wastepaper basket and went back to filling out a medical claim form for Norman's health insurance.

Four hours later Norman arrived at the office. He had spent the morning undergoing an MRI at Cedars-Sinai to determine the cause of the persistent headaches he had been experiencing. When the doctor told him that there was no sign of a brain tumor, Norman thought the man was being a little cavalier. There were incipient tumors that didn't show up on an MRI. Three months later you suddenly keeled over into your Chinese chicken salad.

"A DHL come in from Uzbekistan?" he asked his assistant as soon as he was in the door.

"Yes," Tom Soaring Hawk replied in his inflectionless tone of voice.

"You put it on my desk?"

"No."

"Where is it?"

"I threw it out."

"You *threw it out*?"

"You told me to throw everything out that came in the mail."

"Where? Did? You? Throw? It?"

Norman spoke very slowly, the way one speaks to a toddler who has just thrown the car keys out the window.

"In the wastepaper basket."

His eyes went directly to the empty wastepaper basket beside the assistant's desk.

"What happened to it?"

"They collected the trash."

"When?"

Tom Soaring Hawk consulted his digital Mickey Mouse watch, a Christmas gift from the parent company, and said, with his usual excruciating literalness, "An hour and thirteen minutes ago."

It took great effort for Norman to speak without shrieking. "What happens to the trash after they collect it here?"

"They take it to the trash collection room."

"And what do they do with it there?"

"They recycle the paper and collect the audition cassettes to reuse for dailies and rough cuts."

"They tape over the cassettes?"

"It's an economy measure."

"Get me the person who is in charge of the trash room. Right away."

"I don't know who that is."

"Jesus, what *do* you know?"

"I'm sorry. I was just following orders."

"So was Adolf Eichmann."

Norman hurried into his office and dialed Howard Draper on his private line. When Howard didn't pick up, Norman called Howard's assistant, Carol, who told him that Howard had stepped away from his desk.

Minutes later, Norman entered the men's room closest to Howard's office and found his boss washing his hands meticulously with antibacterial hand soap.

"We've got a security problem," Norman announced, breathlessly. "My assistant threw out the *Warlord* cassette."

"Keep your voice down." Howard kept the sink water running, then approached Norman and whispered, "Why did he do that?"

"He thought it was an actor's audition tape."

"Has your assistant gone through a security check?"

"When I first hired him—Howard, do you know where they put the trash?"

"Why would I know that?"

"Well, who *would* know?"

Howard took out a cell phone and dialed his own office extension. "Carol, it's me . . . Yes, I know Norman's looking for me. Listen, can you find out who's in charge of trash collection for the building and call me back on my cell?"

He clicked off and looked balefully at Norman. "This was the first episode?"

"Yes. Howard, do you know what they do with audition cassettes?"

"Why would I know that?"

"They tape over them for dailies and rough cuts."

"Well, then we're okay. If they tape over the episode . . ."

"What if they look at it first?"

Howard's cell phone rang. He switched it on and listened. After a moment, he said, "Thank you," and turned it back off.

"Milt Karamides, extension 2326," Howard whispered and walked out of the men's room.

Twenty minutes later a cassette marked *The Search for Genghis Khan's Grave, Episode 1, 44:45,* arrived on Norman's desk. He held it with trembling fingers. Those forty-four minutes and forty-five seconds held the key to his future in the television business.

Norman decided that he wasn't up to watching the first episode of *Warlord* right then on his office VCR. He would go home, open a bottle of White Zinfandel and watch the cassette with a little buzz.

By that time it would be daylight in Central Asia and he could get Charlie Berns on the line and fire him. Or send him a fruit basket.

* * *

Jodie Jacobian ran into Kara Kotch at a Women in Film luncheon at the Century Plaza honoring Halle Berry. They were several tables away from each other, but by swiveling her chair forty-five degrees Jodie Jacobian managed to get in the vice president of ABC Series Development's eye line.

They exchanged smiles as they listened to Halle Berry describe the bliss she had experienced by being A Woman in Film. It was all somehow connected to The Man Upstairs, who inspired her every day, and to her agents, who had believed in her even before she'd won an Oscar.

Timing her exit just right, the DBA agent found herself next to the ABC executive on the valet parking line.

"Kara, how *are* you?"

"I'm fine, Jodie. Good to see you."

"How'd you like Halle?"

"I think it's criminal that anyone should be that gorgeous."

"So . . . I hear you have an archaeology project in development."

"Archaeology?"

"Brad told me he set up something with Charlie Berns at ABC."

"Charlie who?"

"Berns."

"Never heard of him."

"You don't have anything about Genghis Khan in the works?"

"Jodie, if I can't sell Al Capone, how am I going to sell Genghis Khan? Now, you want to bring me something about a crime scene investigation team in ancient Mongolia, we would listen. But, between you, me and the lamppost, archaeology's a nonstarter. Whoops, there's my car . . ."

Jodie Jacobian watched Kara Kotch get into her Porsche Cayenne with the vanity plate NETVEEP8 and drive off.

She'd always known that Brad Emprin was a bullshit artist. But what about Fred Fortrain? The guy was an accountant. Accountants didn't invent this kind of shit. Sure, they cooked the numbers, but they generally didn't make up imaginary deals with imaginary clients. When she got back to the office, she'd Google Charlie Berns and see what she came up with.

As she got into her four-year-old Acura Legend and stiffed the valet, she thought about Halle Berry's speech. The person the actress forgot to thank was Billy Bob Thornton, who fucked her on camera. You have an orgasm and lose your kid in the same film, no way you don't win an Oscar.

* * *

At 8:30 that evening, Norman Hudris, a half bottle of White Zinfandel to the wind, sat in the den of his precariously leveraged Mediterranean in Coldwater Canyon and watched the cassette that Charlie Berns had DHL-ed him from Uzbekistan. Forty-four minutes and forty-five seconds later he got up, walked around the room, belching up remnants of the microwave pizza he had chased with the $3.99 wine, and considered using the other half of the bottle to wash down an industrial-size jar of extra-strength Vicodin.

He couldn't believe what he had just watched. It was the kind of thing you expected to see at the Kabul Film Festival. What the hell had he been thinking when he bought this idea? This show would go down in the annals of ridiculed shows, alongside *My Mother the Car* and *The Secret Diary of Desmond Pfeiffer*. Leno and Letterman would take no prisoners. And *Saturday Night Live* . . . He couldn't even bear to think about it.

Howard, of course, would deny any knowledge that the project had even been in development. The money trail would lead straight to Norman. After they fired him, they'd prosecute. Malfeasance, fraud, misappropriation of funds. He had given the money in cash to the agent. What would have stopped him from pocketing a few thousand euros?

After working himself into an anxious stupor, it took a Halcion on top of the rest of the bottle of White Zinfandel to put him to sleep. He fell into a deep, narcotic sleep, only to be jolted wide awake at 3:00 a.m. by paroxysms of fear.

He lay in bed staring at the ceiling and previewed his new life in a $400-a-month apartment in Van Nuys with noisy neighbors who gave Cinco de Mayo parties and listened to salsa music all day. He'd have to walk out on the Lexus lease. That would fuck up his credit rating, which would prevent him from leasing even a bottom-of-the-line Toyota. He'd wind up paying cash for a used Mitsubishi, whose drivetrain would go right after the thirty-day warranty expired . . .

He got out of bed and started to pace around his bedroom, plotting how to take Howard down with him. He would wire himself and get Howard on tape, and then cop a plea, rolling over on him in exchange for a lesser charge . . .

And it was as he was having these vindictive thoughts that a question popped into his head. There in his bedroom, at 4:10 in the morning, he found himself wondering just who Murv *was* schtupping—the daughter or the mistress?

And why didn't Ishrat Khana leave her room? Was she having an affair with the rival warlord in Dashoguz? Would Grushenka or Ferghana wind up getting Murv? Would Akbar make the school soccer team? Would Ali Mohammed turn his back on his father and become a Russian mole?

If *he* wanted to know the answers to these questions, he suddenly realized, why wouldn't a demographically desirable segment of the TV audience want to know? And if there had been another cassette, a second episode, he would have wanted to watch it. And if he wanted to watch it, why wouldn't a demographically desirable segment of the TV audience want to watch it too?

He began to think in a more constructive manner. The dick-measuring loyalty oath was already on the floor. No way they'd show that, not even pixelated, not even at 11:00 p.m. on the Extreme Archaeology Channel. They'd be deluged with letters, e-mails, faxes . . .

But there was one thing worse than getting deluged with letters, e-mails and faxes, wasn't there? *Not* getting deluged with letters, e-mails and faxes.

He went into his office, grabbed a yellow legal pad from the briefcase on his desk, sat down and started to compose his notes.

* * *

It was a little past 5:30 in the afternoon Turkmenistan time when Charlie was awakened by "The Volga Boatmen." His new cell phone was from a telecom in Tashkent and had a limited choice of rings. There were "The Volga Boatmen," "On the Steppes of Central Asia" and "Moon River."

He had been taking a nap in his room after being up very early with the crew filming Izbul kicking ass in Nukus. They had some great footage of the warlord and his men beating a low-level Uzbek mafioso to a pulp over five cases of vodka that the man had tried to skim from a truckload that had come in earlier that week from Azerbaijan.

144

"I got some notes," he heard Norman Hudris's anxiety-coated voice saying, without any preamble.

"Norman?"

"I have concerns about Izbul's character arc. And we're going to have to cut around the violence. I hope you have some coverage—"

"Did you like it?"

"We have to fix it."

"I thought the violence was what you wanted," Charlie said, trying to emerge from the miasma of his heavy afternoon nap.

"There's good violence and there's bad violence. A close-up of blood spurting out of a camel's neck is not good violence. And what about the wife? When are we going to see her?"

"When she comes out of her room."

"Get her out of her room. And get the older kid's nose out of the Koran. There's no sympathy in this country these days for anybody who reads the Koran. Have him reading *Playboy* or, I don't know, watching a video. Better. Have him watching an ABC show. What about *According to Jim?*"

"Norman, this is a reality show. We don't choreograph the action. We record it."

"When can I see the second hour?"

Fifteen minutes later Norman finally hung up after having given Charlie ten pages of notes. What is Izbul's journey? Can we make Ferghana a little more likable? Why does Akbar want to make the soccer team? Do something with Murv's wardrobe. The lighting in the Korean noodle restaurant is too hot. And so forth.

The notes weren't a problem. Charlie could finesse them. But the headline was that Norman wanted to see more film. He hadn't pulled the plug. He hadn't even threatened to pull it. He wanted Episode 2 as soon as possible. They were still in business.

Charlie lay in bed and thought about Episode 2. He had no idea what was going to happen in the next few days that would "inform Izbul's character arc." The warlord's character didn't have an arc. If anything, it was a straight line. The shortest path to money and power.

How could Charlie impose dramatic structure on his chaotic life?

How could he make Ferghana more likable? How could he get Szczedrzyk to pre-rig the lighting in the Korean noodle restaurant?

Charlie was wrestling with these concerns when "The Volga Boatmen" sounded again. This time it was Buzz calling from the compound.

"The kid's gone."

"What?"

"Ali Mohammed's taken off. He's gone to join the Taliban in the mountains."

"Oh shit, really?"

"He left a note saying he was never coming back."

"Izbul going ballistic?"

"Big time. He's threatening to cut the Taliban a new one. Looks like we're going to have to rework the story."

Charlie rubbed his eyes and had a sudden inspiration. "Maybe not."

"What do you mean?"

"Does he have to join the Taliban?"

"Ali Mohammed?"

"What if he ran away to go to law school instead of joining the Taliban?"

"The good son, like Pacino at the beginning of *Godfather One*? The son that was supposed to go straight and become a U.S. senator?"

"Uh-huh."

"Works for me."

* * *

Things were more than usually chaotic at the compound when Charlie arrived an hour later. Buzz and Dostyk told him that Izbul had been wandering around firing his Kalashnikov into the air in an effort to exhort his men to undertake an immediate attack on the Taliban cell that, according to the warlord, had abducted his son. Murv didn't want to go to the mattresses while they were trying to cut a deal with another Uzbek warlord. There was a lot of loud arguing between Izbul and Murv.

"We could have a *coup d'état*," said Buzz.

Dostyk, who was watching the monitors, turned to them and said, "We have other big problem on hands. Take look."

146

Charlie and Buzz watched the monitor in Ferghana's bathroom as Justyna followed Izbul's daughter into the shower. You could see pretty much everything that was going on through the thin plastic shower curtain.

"Wow," whistled Buzz. "We can sell outtakes to the Playboy Channel."

Charlie had seen that one coming. From the very first day the two women had met on the sand dunes in Muynak. The challenge now was to write it into the story line. And to keep it from Izbul, who, if he found out, would cut Justyna, at the very least, a new one, if not the entire crew.

Charlie found the documentary film director shooting B roll of the compound at night. "Szczedrzyk, can I talk to you for a minute?"

The Pole nodded and grunted, and they walked out of earshot of the rest of the crew.

"This is kind of delicate," Charlie began. "Uh, you see, Izbul's a little on the old-fashioned side. You know what I mean?"

If he did, Szczedrzyk didn't nod. Or shake his head. The man was a very hard read.

"Anyway, there seems to be a relationship developing between Justyna and Ferghana. And . . . well, frankly, that kind of thing doesn't play too well over here in Central Asia. Izbul finds out, he's not going to be happy, and you know what happens when he's not happy . . . So . . ."

Charlie was just about to drive the point home with a specific request that Justyna stay away from Ferghana when a truck approached the gate and, instead of stopping, crashed right through it and exploded. There was a flash of blinding light and then a thick blanket of smoke.

At the sound of automatic gunfire Charlie hit the ground and rolled toward the shelter of the production trailer. He heard shouts in Uzbek, hoarse commands issued by Izbul's men, and the roar of car engines coming to life as the armored BMWs sprung into action.

"I'm getting shot," Szczedrzyk muttered, and Charlie looked at him expecting to see blood spurting from the director, but instead he saw him running back to his camera, shouting directions in Polish to the crew.

Szczedrzyk got the shot. And then some. They got it all—the counterattack and the fleeing of the rival warlord's gang into the night as Murv and the men went after them in the BMWs, guns blazing out the windows.

Charlie lay there trying not to tremble. He wasn't in Brentwood anymore. That was for sure. But if he managed to live through this experience, he just might have a hit show on his hands. It was a terrific action sequence. He'd cut it together with the business about Ali Mohammed running away, changing the Taliban to the University of Tashkent Law School, and ship it.

Episode 2 was in the can.

FIFTEEN

Sensitivity Training

Like all efficient covert operations, ABCD was rigidly compartmentalized. Each department within the division knew only what it had to know about the other departments. This insulation provided deniability up and down the line by creating a series of fire breaks to control the spread of potentially incriminating information.

So when Norman received Episode 2 of *The Search for Genghis Khan's Grave* and decided it was time to begin the testing phase, he had the name of only one person in Research and Testing. Norman dialed the extension of his ABCDRT liaison and asked to stop by his office at 2:30 that afternoon.

Dale Yarmouth suggested 2:00 instead of 2:30 and at Norman's office instead of his. In order to limit their exposure, ABCD personnel preferred meeting in other people's offices rather than in their own, especially when they crossed departmental lines.

Norman agreed reluctantly, then e-mailed Howard that "the souvlaki was ready to go in the oven." While he was waiting for a reply—a reply he was hoping not to get—Tom Soaring Hawk buzzed him that the head of Human Resources, Jasmine Liu, was on the phone.

"What does *she* want?"

"I wouldn't know," his assistant replied disingenuously.

"Does she know I'm here?"

"Yes."

"Haven't we talked about this before, Tom? You never say I'm here until I know who's calling."

"Be that as it may, do you want to take the call or not?"

"Do I have a choice?" Norman sighed. You couldn't blow off the head of ABCDHR that easily.

He picked up the blinking light and said, "Jasmine, what can I do for you?"

Jasmine Liu requested a meeting in his office at 2:30 that afternoon. When Norman asked her what it was regarding, she said it had to do with "company policy." He explained that he had a meeting already scheduled for 2:00 that might go longer than a half hour. She told him she would wait in his outer office for that meeting to be over.

What the fuck did *they* want? He had hired a Native American assistant, hadn't he? One of his managers was half African-American, though frankly he wasn't sure which half.

While Norman was wrestling with the politics of this confluence of appointments, he got a phone call from Howard's assistant requesting that he meet Howard for lunch in Glendale at 12:30.

Since Howard was his boss, correct protocol dictated that he should rearrange the other appointments in order to make lunch in Glendale, but Norman was not anxious to have one of their oblique Greek lunches with Howard badgering him for information he didn't want to hear.

Norman e-mailed Howard and asked if they could lunch tomorrow. Howard sent a one-word reply: "Negative." Norman then called Dale Yarmouth and asked to push that meeting till 3:30. The head of ABCDRT told him he had a staff meeting at three. Norman suggested 4:30.

"Staff meetings in my department are at least two hours. How about tomorrow morning first thing?"

"Time is of the essence," Norman said.

"All right. I'll be there at 5:30."

Then he told Tom Soaring Hawk to call Jasmine Liu and explain that he had been summoned to jury duty and would call her as soon as he was dismissed.

"That's not a very effective lie," Tom Soaring Hawk pointed out.

"Why not?"

"When you're summoned to jury duty you know the night before. You've already spoken to her today."

What he disliked most about his assistant, even more than his flat nasal voice and neo–Explorer Scout wardrobe, was that he was always right. Especially about these kinds of logic issues.

"Okay. Tell her the truth. I have lunch with Howard at twelve-thirty."

"You'll be back by two-thirty."

"How do *you* know?"

"You always are when you have lunch with Howard."

Once again, Tom Soaring Hawk was right. They were generally in and out of the Hercules Taverna in under an hour, and with an hour back and forth from Manhattan Beach to Glendale, he'd be back in his office by 2:30.

There ought to be some company policy prohibiting assistants from being right all the time. It was harmful to a good working environment and should be punished. He would make that suggestion when he spoke to Jasmine Liu. They'd let Tom Soaring Hawk off with a warning this time, but the next time he correctly corrected his boss they'd terminate him.

*　*　*

At approximately the same time, another meeting was wrapping up in Burbank. In a large conference room, around a large table with a large fruit bowl containing a large selection of ripening kiwi, the network's de jure development department was discussing the pilots that were beginning to shoot the following week.

Though as vice president of Development, Kara Kotch was presiding at this meeting, she was not seated at the head of the table. Sitting at the head of the twenty-foot conference table, nearest to the kiwi, was her boss, Floyd, to whom she reported.

It was, nonetheless, Kara Kotch's meeting. She was the one who was in fact *reporting to* Floyd. Her boss listened to her describe casting developments and director choices for the scripts that they had chosen to film as prototypes for the fall season. Occasionally, he would ask a question, and Kara Kotch would reply to it or delegate the response to one of her staff.

She was clearly on the line here, expected to justify the choices made and the amount of money spent. The trick was to be upbeat, but to leave yourself an escape hatch in the event that anything you were upbeat about crashed and burned on the runway.

There were a number of all-purpose caveats that could be attached as a hedge against any overly optimistic assessment. This piece of talent was a little unpredictable; this director was known to go over budget; the chemistry between this actor and that actor was untested.

By the time Kara Kotch was finished with her presentation, she felt as if she had just testified in front of a congressional committee. There were several more questions, and then Floyd uttered a few phrases of ambiguous optimism and rose. Everyone else got up at the same time and collected their script bags and water bottles.

On the way out of the conference room, she found herself in the hallway next to Floyd and thought about the archaeology project that Jodie Jacobian had referenced on the valet parking line at the Women in Film luncheon.

"Floyd," she said, impulsively, "we don't have any development that I don't know about, do we?"

"What do you mean, Kara?"

"Someone was telling me at the Women in Film luncheon that they heard we had bought an archaeology project."

"An *archaeology* project?"

At the tone of his voice, she immediately began to back and fill.

"Ridiculous, isn't it? It was some agent at DBA, probably overheard some other agent bullshitting over breakfast at Hugo's."

"What was the project called?"

Floyd had a tendency not to let a subject drop until every drop of water was squeezed out of it.

"I don't know—something about Genghis Khan."

"The Mongol warlord?"

"Yes. I mean, who would want to watch that?"

Floyd walked in silence for a few moments, carefully considering the answer to what Kara Kotch had meant as a totally rhetorical question, and then said, "You know, there may be something in Genghis Khan."

"Really?"

"I don't know—there's an exotic quality to the life of a warlord. He's a guy with some interesting life options. The audience wants to be taken into worlds they haven't experienced. Ancient Mongolia's a pretty exotic world. Of course, we'd have to deal with the Asian racial sensitivity issue, but if we presented him as a dimensionalized character, a man with a family and children . . . Did Genghis Khan have a family?"

"I'm not sure."

"Why don't you take a couple of pitches, see where it goes?"

"Sure," mumbled Kara Kotch.

"Warlord with a heart of gold type thing."

"Sounds promising . . ."

"Jimmy Smits is looking for a series."

* * *

"Can we get some footage of the kid in school? You know, at the law library, or maybe studying in his room. How about he tries out for the football team? Meets a cheerleader. What if he met an American girl? They have Americans in Tashkent, right?"

Charlie Berns sat in the production trailer in Dashoguz listening to Norman Hudris talk to himself on the phone. When Norman came up for air, Charlie explained, "Ali Mohammed's at law school in Kazakhstan. They don't have a football team. The school's a thousand miles from here. We'd have to fly a second-unit there, put them up, per diem them . . . it'll blow our budget."

"So he e-mails his sister about life at the university. We can run some sort of voice-over . . ."

"Listen, I've got to run. I'm late for casting."

"See if you can find a couple of attractive women. Preferably without mustaches . . ."

Charlie hung up and was exhaling deeply when Fenster entered the trailer with Izbul.

"How they hangink, Charlie Berns from Hollywood?" the warlord greeted him.

"Fine."

"Droppink trow, okay?"

"What?"

153

"We measurink dicks?"

There were very few things that Charlie Berns was not prepared to do in order to get *Warlord* on the air, and participating in a dick-measuring contest with the warlord was one of them.

Fortunately, Izbul was distracted by one of the monitors that showed Ferghana talking to Justyna in the kitchen. They were having a conversation in English about hair conditioner. Izbul was watching the monitor screen with interest.

Concerned that the two women's body language would tip Izbul off to the nature of their attraction to each other, Charlie asked the warlord, "So what are you going to do about the truck full of explosives that crashed into the compound the other night?"

"We go to Urgench, cut new one. Big time."

"What time?"

Izbul shrugged and left the trailer.

"Which one of these monitors covers the game room?" Fenster asked as soon as the warlord was gone.

Charlie pointed to one of the monitors on the far side of the trailer, dark at the moment since the game room was empty and Charlie was trying not to overtax the generators.

"We're going to have to pull that camera."

"Why?"

Fenster gave him the you-don't-need-to-know look and said, "Haven't we been through this already?"

"Fenster, we get a lot of good footage there. It's a place where people congregate, and we get interaction. The network's already growling about the lack of interaction among the main characters."

"They want interaction, wait till they see Izbul kick ass in Urgench today. The fucking Uzbeks won't know what hit them."

"You think we can get in before to pre-light?"

"Why not? The Uzbek mafia is so stupid, you go in there and ask for permission to film them getting whacked, they'll probably say yes and make you lunch while they're at it."

"What happens if the hit goes bad?"

"You kidding? With those clowns? You could send the fucking Canadians in there and kick ass. What's with the Polish dyke?"

"You mean Justyna?"

"Yeah. She got in the shower with the daughter the other day. If Izbul finds out about this, he'll go ballistic."

"I'm working on the problem."

"Fucking shame. The only piece of ass within a hundred kilometers, and she turns out to be a muff diver."

Buzz entered the trailer. "We should get the crew out in the courtyard. Akbar and Grushenka are going at it."

Charlie picked up his walkie-talkie and broadcast. "Szczedrzyk, you there?"

After a moment, a crackling voice responded, "What's up?"

"Crew to the courtyard."

"Ten-forty."

Charlie told Buzz about Fenster's blacking out the game room.

"Figures," Buzz said.

"Drugs?"

"Probably. This used to be called the silk route. Now it's the dope route. They grow the poppies in Pakistan, ship them to China where they're processed into heroin and transshipped through Uzbekistan and across the Caspian to Azerbaijan. From there it goes all over Europe. Izbul must be taking his cut in product to allow it across his territory."

"We got a game room full of heroin?"

"If not something worse."

"Like what?"

"Like weapons-grade plutonium."

* * *

Norman's lunch with Howard at the Hercules Taverna was more excruciatingly inexplicit than usual. They dispensed with the Retsina aperitif and went directly to the *htapothi vrasto*.

"So . . . the product is good?" Howard asked.

"Excellent."

"Anything unexpected?"

"Meaning?"

"Something you weren't expecting."

Norman let this tautology go unchallenged and said, in an effort to comfort his boss, "It's everything we wanted it to be."

"So . . . what's the next step?"

"Testing."

"Do we outsource that?"

"No. We have someone in the division—"

"Right. Of course. Someone I've never met, by the way."

"I'm meeting with him at five-thirty this afternoon."

"I can't make it. What's the time frame?"

"He'll tell me."

"I don't want to see the results."

"I'll make sure you don't."

"I'll just need the high points. For Poindexter and North."

"Don't you think someone should go to Floyd on this? Sooner or later he needs to know he's putting a program on his network that he's never seen."

"That's not our problem."

"I hear he's got feelers out at ESPN."

"You heard that?"

"Not from you."

* * *

At 2:30 on the nose Norman Hudris returned from his lunch with Howard Draper to find ABCD's head of Human Resources waiting for him. Jasmine Liu, an indeterminate Asian, was sitting on a chair in a short skirt, a skirt that Norman thought she had no business wearing considering that her job encompassed sexual harassment. The skirt seemed to be saying, "Harass me. Go ahead, make my day."

Norman ushered her into his office and closed the door behind them. Whatever this was about, it couldn't be good. At best, Norman would have to reprimand someone on his staff for an inappropriate remark; at worst, he'd have to fire someone and go through the whole security background business entailed in replacing them.

When Norman had first arrived at ABCD, he, as all new employees, was given a twenty-page printout, authored by Jasmine Liu, explaining the network's position on sexual harassment. The material featured a schematic diagram showing the appropriate insulating distance to maintain with any potential sexual partner. Bottom line: you couldn't even think about fucking anybody who knew anybody who knew anybody with whom you were or might someday be in business. Nor could you do or say anything to any coworker that was not demonstrably related to business.

"So, what's the problem, Jasmine?" Norman folded his hands in front of him and did his best to look concerned.

"There's been an incident reported to me that took place in your department."

"I'm sorry to hear that."

"Someone made an inappropriate remark."

"Who?"

"You."

"*Me? I* made an inappropriate remark?"

"I'm afraid so, Norman."

"What did I say?"

"You said . . ." She removed a PalmPilot from her voluminous pocketbook, dialed it up and read, " 'So did Adolf Eichmann.' "

"I said that?"

"Do you deny saying it?"

He could deny saying it, and it would be his word against Tom Soaring Hawk's. But he wasn't altogether convinced that his assistant didn't have some sort of tape-recording device running in the office, trawling for these types of remarks.

"Okay, I said it," he admitted. What could they do to him? Tom Soaring Hawk was not a Holocaust survivor. He wasn't even Jewish, as far as Norman knew, unless he was one of those latter-day Jews who had signed up to convert at some radical orthodox holy roller held on a reservation.

"Are you aware that that's a racially insensitive remark?"

"Look, if I was making the remark to a guy who survived Auschwitz, maybe it would be, but my assistant is a Native American."

"Are you aware of the genocide committed against Native Americans?"

"Yes. Are *you* aware of Custer's Last Stand? You want to talk about genocide—let's talk about Sitting Bull. Anybody haul *him* in front of a war crimes tribunal?"

The head of ABCDHR simply plowed right over that argument

and continued. "It is the responsibility of a supervisor to create a racially salubrious atmosphere in his or her department. Comparing an employee to a well-known Nazi war criminal is not salubrious."

"I was just making an analogy. He did something wrong and his excuse was that he was just following orders. I was merely pointing out that following orders was not an acceptable excuse, and I used Eichmann as an example."

"Whatever your motivation, Norman, the remark, on its face, compares a Native American with a Nazi. And that's unacceptable in this company."

"All right, fine. I'm sorry, okay? I'll apologize to Tom."

"I'm afraid, Norman, that a simple apology is not sufficient here."

"What would you like me to do, Jasmine, wear a hair shirt?"

"It's not a question of what *I'd* like you to do. I merely implement company policy."

"Oh, you're just following orders . . ."

She didn't even blink. "Company policy calls for sensitivity re-training. You are required to attend a series of seminars. I have a list of them in my office. If you like, I'll help you find one convenient to your home. These seminars are very valuable in getting you to look at your own behavior. If I were you, Norman, I wouldn't just phone this in. There could be a serious problem here."

She got up, barely bothering to pull her skirt back down to mid-thigh. "I'll e-mail you the location of the seminars. You can e-mail me back your choice."

"I assume this is paid for by the company . . ."

"No. It's three hundred for four seminars. If you miss one, you can make it up, but they'll charge you for it. Seventy-five a pop, so you might as well do all four and get them out of the way."

* * *

For the next couple of hours, as he waited for his 5:30 meeting with Dale Yarmouth, Norman Hudris sat at his desk and plotted revenge on the assistant who was responsible for his having to spend four Saturdays and three hundred dollars getting his sensitivity up-graded. Firing Tom Soaring Hawk was no longer an option: it would be a clear case of vindictive action and expose Norman to more serious charges than he was already facing.

Besides, he would have to fire him for cause, and he couldn't point to any one particular cause that would pass muster at Human Resources. The Boy Scout belts and the nasal voice wouldn't cut it, nor would his assistant's annoying habit of pointing out the logical flaws in many of Norman's ideas.

Moral turpitude didn't seem to be a promising area. The man didn't take drugs or screw around, not at the office at least. Tom Soaring Hawk's idea of a good time, as far as Norman could tell, was rearranging the filing cabinets.

What was left to him, he concluded, were guerrilla tactics, small acts that were not, in themselves, demonstrably vindictive but would eat around the edges of Tom Soaring Hawk's quality of life. If he made things unpleasant enough for the man, maybe he would just quit.

So when his assistant announced that Dale Yarmouth had arrived and asked if Norman needed him any more that day, Norman said that he did.

"What would you like me to do?"

"Answer the phones."

"You never get any calls after five," Tom Soaring Hawk pointed out, correctly.

"Be that as it may," Norman replied, echoing the phrase his assistant had used with him that morning. "I'd like you to stay. Just in case."

"I could switch the phones to voice mail. You wouldn't miss a call."

"If Howard calls, I'll need to be interrupted."

"Howard's gone for the day."

"He may call from his car."

Norman held his assistant's impassive glare for a full five seconds. Then Tom Soaring Hawk retreated into the outer office and returned a few seconds later with Dale Yarmouth.

"I'll be outside. If you need me," the assistant said, firing a pointed dart into the office.

Norman offered ABCD's head of Research and Testing the same chair on which Jasmine Liu had sat exposing her workout-hewn thighs. Dale Yarmouth, on the other hand, did not look like he had ever been anywhere near a gym. He was a soft, pasty man with a sallow complexion and bad posture. His eyes kept blinking as if his contact lenses didn't fit right. The ABCDRT guy was not big on banter so Norman got right to it.

"We've got a program ready for testing. We have the first two hours, with hour three expected Wednesday. It's an hour-length reality-documentary hybrid that we need a quick read on. Howard wants numbers ASAP."

"Okay."

"Are you going to focus group it?"

"We may."

"Where you're going to test it?"

"It'll all be in my report."

"The reason I'm asking is that I'd like to watch it myself, see how it plays on air."

"Your cable package doesn't have this channel. It's a closed circuit by subscription arrangement. You have the cassettes?"

Norman unlocked the bottom right drawer of his desk. He extracted the two cassettes that Charlie Berns had DHL-ed him from Tashkent and handed them to Dale Yarmouth.

"What's your time frame on this, Dale?"

"The longer the time frame, the better the data."

"We're looking at sweeps."

Dale Yarmouth exhaled deeply and squinted, as the variables bounced around inside his mind. Ten seconds later a date emerged.

"April seventeenth."

"That's the earliest?"

"When you're dealing with computer-generated statistical models, the value of what you get out is only as good as the value of what you put in the system."

"It'll give me only two weeks to promo the show, less after I clear it upstairs and around the corner."

"You want decent numbers, or do you just want me to make them up?"

"All right, look, just get them to me as soon as you can, okay? There's a lot riding on this."

"There always is."

He walked out with Dale, past Tom Soaring Hawk, who was sitting at his desk doing a double crostic. Doing puzzles at your desk on company time clearly amounted to dereliction of duty.

Norman returned to his office, closed the door and started a new file. He wrote down the date and time of the infraction and then locked the file away in the same drawer he had kept the *Warlord* cassettes. When the time came, he would have a documented case for Tom Soaring Hawk's incompetence and lack of professional attitude in performing his job.

SIXTEEN

The Zavodni Curve

ABCDRT's testing process was both covert and unconventional. It involved broadcasting product over a closed-circuit network that reached a series of homes chosen with painstaking attention to the demographic distribution of the U.S. population. The model used was more rigorous than that used by Nielsen, according to Dale Yarmouth, who held a master's degree from MIT in advanced statistical analysis. It so accurately mirrored the television viewing audience that, he claimed, the margin of error did not exceed plus or minus 1.435 percentage points.

"Even when we're wrong," Dale Yarmouth was fond of saying, "we're right."

And so episodes 1 and 2 of *Warlord* were sent out to the white mice in Dale Yarmouth's system. However this group of respondents felt, that was how America felt. Except, of course, for the 1.435 percent of people who acted in a manner that was atypical of their group.

In exchange for allowing the network to wire their TV sets and pipe in the testing channel, these demographically correct people received a package of benefits that included free cable, DVDs of the network's hit shows, both of them, and passes to Disneyland, Disney World and Euro Disney.

So while the adventures of Izbul Kharkov, his family and private army, his girlfriend and his enemies, were being viewed by this privileged group, life at the compound outside of Dashoguz continued in its erratic yet growingly familiar manner.

The principal drama in the warlord's life at the moment continued to be his son Ali Mohammed's defection to the Taliban. Furious as he was about this, Izbul was unable to take direct action because no one knew where this particular cell of the Taliban was at the moment. There was speculation that it was in Afghanistan, Pakistan, Tajikistan and a couple of other Stans. Izbul could not cut anybody a new one if he couldn't find them.

As far as Charlie Berns was concerned, however, Ali Mohammed's absence was an opportunity to inject some local color into the series. He and Buzz had started to write voice-over narration of his correspondence to his sister back in Dashoguz. Life at Tashkent University Law School was going well. He had made Law Review and was top of his class in torts and contracts. He was captain of the tennis team and had been accepted into UA, Ustyurt Akkafa, an Uzbek fraternity. Recently he had met a young American woman, a fellow law student at TU, and they had gone out on a few dates. He confided in his sister that he didn't know how his father would accept a non-Moslem woman in his life.

Back at the family compound meanwhile, Grushenka's feud with Ferghana had escalated. She was threatening Izbul that it was either his daughter or her. The warlord was caught in a vise between the two women he loved.

His real wife, meanwhile, was, presumably, still locked away in her room. Buzz and Charlie had fudged with the dialogue to suggest that Ishrat Khana was off getting a face-lift in Odessa. The expectation of the audience, they calculated, would be to see the shit hit the fan when the newly remodeled wife returned home to confront the Ukrainian home wrecker.

Akbar's pud pulling had graduated to heavy petting sessions with a fifteen-year-old girl after school in the back of the armored BMW, which one of the pistol-whippers obligingly drove around aimlessly in the desert. They could use an edited version of Akbar's exploits, though the kid was so inept it took him four sessions before he could figure out how to unhook the girl's brassiere.

Murv spent a lot of time talking in Turkmen on his cell phone, and even though Buzz couldn't translate what he said, he sensed there was something fishy going on. His theory was that the head of the Uzbek mafia family in Nukus had offered Murv serious change to whack Izbul.

The Ferghana-Justyna romance had progressed to a hot make-out session in back of the wardrobe trailer one night. One of the exterior cameras that swept the compound haphazardly had picked it up. Charlie knew he had to deal with this problem before Izbul found out. So after dinner one night he approached the Polish camera operator and asked if they could have a talk. She nodded in her world-weary, Eastern European manner and walked out to the edge of the field outside the compound.

Charlie offered her a cigarette. He had taken to smoking again. After being shaken down by Stalin in the bar of the Intercontinental in Tashkent, Charlie had started having one or two smokes a day. The one or two had grown to three or four and then to five or six. He was now up to a half pack.

She took the cigarette and his proffered light, inhaled and blew the smoke out her finely chiseled nostrils.

"Justyna," Charlie said, searching for just the right tone, "we have a problem."

She looked at him bleakly, as if to say, "What do you expect? The world is a disappointing place. We all have problems. Nothing goes smoothly."

"I want you to know that I'm just trying to protect the show. I have no particular desire to supervise anybody's personal behavior. We're all adults here. But we're here as guests of Izbul, and we have to conduct ourselves in a manner that is not offensive to him or, in a larger sense, to the Central Asian sensibility."

"Central Asian sensibility? What is that?"

"Well, let's just say that it's a trifle more conservative than, say, Warsaw."

"Warsaw? Have you ever been there?"

"No."

"It's full of old apparatchiks."

"Be that as it may—"

"Catholic ex-communists. Who are drinking at seven in the morning. The whole city is drunk half the time. You take streetcar, driver has four glasses of vodka for lunch. Prostitution all over the place. You can get a girl for fifty zlotys. Heroin for one hundred. The Baltic

Sea is polluted. You can't eat the fish. You eat dumplings. They make you constipated. Kwasniewski is big asshole—"

"So," interjected Charlie, when she came up for air, "the thing is, could you be a little more discreet with Ferghana?"

"Discreet? You want me to be discreet?"

"I'd appreciate it."

"Izbul displays his organ and fucks that Ukrainian whore right in the courtyard, and you want *me* to be discreet?"

"It would make things easier . . ."

Justyna merely snorted and walked away. And that apparently was that. Charlie walked back to the trailer, where he found Grushenka waiting for him.

"You, *produttore* . . ."

Grushenka had done some films in Italy, and she gave crew members titles in Italian. Szczedrzyk was her *direttore*.

"What can I do for you, Grushenka?"

"I want better role."

"A better role? What do you mean?"

"I'm trained actress. I do theater in Kiev. *Hedda Gabler, Streetcar of Desire, Katz.* You write better script for me, all right?"

With four episodes already in the can, there was no point in explaining reality television to Grushenka. That particular train had left the station weeks ago. So Charlie just nodded as she barreled ahead.

"I am only actress on set knowing what she is doing. The daughter is big dyke. Can't act. I want scene where I tell Izbul I am dying. Consumption. I am coughing up blood into handkerchief. Like Camille. I play Camille in Minsk. Bring down house. Eleven curtain calls."

"I'll talk to the writers."

"Tell them to write me soliloquy. On my deathbed. Dusk. Twilight coming in through window. We light with candle. Then priest giving me last rites, I closing eyes . . . but I don't die. No. I survive. I live on, with inner strength, winning back my warlord against all odd. Good, *non è verro?*"

"Terrific."

"Grazie tanto, produttore . . ."

She smiled at him, a smile revealing some cheap dental work, and walked out of the trailer. He should get her teeth bleached. Maybe implants. If he could find a dentist within five hundred miles, let alone one who did implants.

The soliloquy idea wasn't bad, he had to admit. He could shoot her doing it directly into camera. He'd have to convince her to speak Ukrainian, so that they could rewrite it in the subtitles. Or better, in Italian. He'd lay in an opera score underneath. *La Traviata* on the steppes of Central Asia. They'd switch consumption to AIDS. It would make the story line more contemporary.

Charlie's eyes wandered to the monitors. The last one in the line—the one that covered the game room, the one that Fenster had told him to pull—was dark. Whether there was heroin or weapons of mass destruction in there, Charlie didn't want to know. They'd tease the game room, build up a story line around it—maybe they had Bin Laden in there. Izbul had him stashed away and was planning on trading him to the Taliban in return for his son.

On the monitor to the left of the dark one, the one covering Ferghana's room, he saw Justyna walk in and close the door behind her. Not one word passed between the two women. Justyna grabbed Ferghana, kissed her, slid her hand between her thighs. They fell onto the bed and started going at it with such fervor that they fell off the bed. And, fortunately, out of camera range.

Charlie would sell it as calisthenics. Ferghana doing push-ups beside her bed. They'd match it with other footage they had of Ferghana and see if it would fly.

His attention was caught by the monitor in Akbar's bedroom. It was pud-pulling time again. The counterpoint couldn't have been better.

Just another day at the Kharkovs'. Grushenka takes protease inhibitors. Ferghana does her calisthenics. Akbar does his homework.

* * *

Stalin visited the set the next morning. His arrival caused a tense moment at the gate, until Fenster convinced Izbul to have his men let him in. Murv insisted, nevertheless, on patting Stalin down. Things got a little testy as the sullen Georgian took his piece out of his jacket pocket, put it on the ground and said that if anybody so much as breathed on it he'd make sure that was the last breath they ever took.

They all went into Izbul's office. The conversation was heated and in Russian. Charlie and Buzz watched the meeting on the office monitor.

"He looks like some sort of Russian mafioso," Buzz remarked.

"He is."

"What do you mean, he is?"

"He *is* a Russian mafioso. Actually, Georgian. He approached me in Tashkent, before we started shooting, leaned on me for protection."

"So this guy's getting a piece of the show?"

"We're paying him a flat rate. It's already in the budget."

"How much?"

"Forty-five hundred a show."

"Rubles?"

"No. Euros."

"Jesus. That's serious change."

"The cost of doing business."

Buzz stared at the monitor for a moment, and then was seized by one of his out-of-the box ideas. "What if we used it?"

"Used what?"

"The shakedown. Introduce this guy as a recurring character. He's moving in on Izbul's operation. Maybe he's allying himself with Murv. They're planning some sort of power play—get rid of Izbul, run western Uzbekistan out of Moscow. This guy could be like Tony's uncle, what's his name?"

"Stalin."

"No, I mean Tony's uncle."

"Junior."

"The guy's name is really Stalin?"

"Actually, it's Josef Djugashvili. Stalin's his nickname."

"We could build a whole story line around this guy. Izbul's getting leaned on from all directions—not just from the Uzbek government, and the Turkmen mafia, but from the Russians. He's a guy with a lot of problems. We'll put him into therapy. Like Tony."

"With whom?"

"With Ishrat Khana."

"The wife? She's never come out of her room."

"Izbul goes in there, but we don't see what goes on. It's confidential, patient-doctor shit. So we imagine it. Where did we send the wife, by the way?"

"She's in Odessa having a face-lift."

"So when she comes back she looks different. She could be the therapist."

"Buzz, she really *isn't* in Odessa."

Buzz had become so wrapped up in the fictional *Warlord* that they had been creating that he occasionally forgot that they were making the whole thing up in the subtitles.

"Fuck, right . . ." he muttered. "She's not really in Odessa."

Buzz exhaled deeply, leaned back in his seat, shook his head. "I haven't been this fucked up since I was smoking three pipes of hash a day. I think I need a little sleep."

And Buzz got up and dragged himself out of the trailer. Charlie turned back to the monitor just in time to see Izbul droppink trow for Stalin.

* * *

In order to keep its data as pure as possible, ABCD's research and testing department outsourced its focus groups. One of Dale Yarmouth's principles of statistical analysis, as he had maintained in his MIT Ph.D. thesis entitled "Preserving a Sterile Statistical Laboratory," was to deal exclusively with raw data. Any interaction between tester and testee polluted the results by filtering them through the subjective lens of the tester.

So although Dale Yarmouth had devised the questions to be put to the focus group, he didn't administer the test, nor did he even observe the group from behind a two-way mirror. He compared this precaution to a surgeon's wearing rubber gloves and a surgical mask.

As Dale Yarmouth scanned the focus group data that had just arrived on his desk, he realized that he was dealing with an unusual statistical phenomenon. The bell-curve that generally described audience response to new television programs was inverted. Usually the two extreme response options—"would watch this every week" and "would never watch this" would be significantly lower than the three middle-range response options—"would watch this somewhat more often than other programs," "about as often as other programs," and "somewhat less often than other programs."

With *Warlord,* however, the curve was an upside-down bell curve, higher on both ends. What this meant to the statistician was that there was strong feeling about the product on both the positive and negative poles and less than usual in the middle. There weren't a lot of people on the fence about this show. One of the focus group subjects had handwritten on the form, next to the "would never watch this" choice, "I wouldn't watch this even if I had just spent two years in a sensory deprivation chamber." But there were an equal number of very positive results indicating that there was a strong desire to see more episodes.

The focus group's favorite character was Ferghana. The story line that most intrigued them was Ali Mohammed's break with his father's business to attend law school, closely followed by Murv's power play to gain control of Izbul's empire. In response to the question, "What would you like to see happen?" there were a number of variations on the theme of seeing Ishrat Khana finally appear with her new face to confront Grushenka.

In terms of sex and violence, the group divided predictably along male and female lines. The men loved the pistol-whipping and the truck bomb, Grushenka and Izbul going at it, Akbar making out with his girlfriend in the car; the women thought that Izbul should be more sensitive to his son's true nature, stick by his wife and get rid of his mistress, and that Ferghana should find a good man to marry and settle down with. Both groups thought that Murv was up to no good and wanted to know what was going to happen. And, strangely enough, both groups, apparently for different reasons, were intrigued by the pixelated loyalty oath sequences.

When Dale Yarmouth stopped by Norman Hudris's office to go over the focus group results with the ABCD development vice president, he found Tom Soaring Hawk at his desk reading *Bury My Heart at Wounded Knee.* Norman's assistant buzzed his boss to tell him that the head of ABCDRT wanted to see him.

Norman, on hold with his endocrinologist's office, was reading the trades, scanning the production rosters of TV programs to see who had gotten fired that week.

"What is it, Tom?"

"Dale Yarmouth is here to see you."

"Did you tell him I was in?"

"He knows you're in."

"How does he know that?"

"Because there's a line lit up on my phone console."

Norman opened his Tom Soaring Hawk Dereliction of Duty folder, made another note and dated it. As he was doing this, the door to his office opened and Dale Yarmouth entered with a large envelope. Tom Soaring Hawk, without having been told by his employer to usher Dale Yarmouth in, had done just that. To make matters worse, Norman Hudris's Chilean endocrinologist finally picked up the line at that moment.

"Dr. Estenssoro?" Norman responded

"Who's this?" the doctor inquired, as if he had no idea to whom he was talking.

"This is Norman Hudris."

"Who?"

"Norman Hudris. Thyroid problem," he whispered, trying to keep this information out of earshot of Dale Yarmouth, who was standing just inside the door waiting for Norman to acknowledge his presence.

"What?"

"Overactive thyroid." Norman raised his voice a few decibels while motioning for Dale Yarmouth to give him a minute. The research man took this gesture to mean that Norman was offering him a seat and approached the desk, sitting down across from Norman, now only about six feet away.

There were a few moments of silence on the other end of the line, accompanied by the rustling of papers, then the doctor said, "I picked up some hot nodules on your radionucleide scan."

"Hot nodules?" Norman whispered intensely.

"Yes. They could be benign."

"Uh . . . good . . ."

"But they also could be malignant."

"So . . . what does that mean?" Norman asked in a very small voice.

"I want to biopsy you."

"Bi . . . op . . . sy?"

"Yes. Make an appointment with my nurse for a thyroid biopsy."

And the line went dead. Just like that. The man tells you you might have cancer and then just hangs up the phone. What kind of bedside manner was this?

When Norman looked back up, he saw that Dale Yarmouth was sitting across the desk from him. For a moment he wasn't sure who this man was, his mind immersed in thoughts of hot nodules and biopsies. He was already undergoing chemo. He saw himself show-ing up at the office bald-headed—a shorter, thinner, white version of Shaq. He'd leave the office early, his strength ebbing. People would cut him a lot of slack, offer him overwhelming sympathy . . .

"Are you all right, Norman?"

"Yes, sorry . . ." Norman recovered.

"Would you like me to come back another time?"

"No, no . . . it's just a couple of hot spots on my radionucleide scan. We'll do a biopsy and if it's it, then we'll do some chemo and deal with it. Life is a gift, Dale. No matter how short it is. Seize the day. So . . . how did the focus group go?"

Dale Yarmouth told him that, judging from the responses, *Warlord* would be either a colossal bomb or a runaway hit. "There's not a lot of indifference here, one way or the other."

"So . . . is that good?"

"Could be. Or it couldn't be."

"What do you mean?"

"I could make a statistics-based case for either scenario."

"We've got to sell this in Burbank."

"Well, let's see what the ratings are. Those numbers only go one way. Unless you want to put something on the air that you don't want anybody to see."

Norman flashed him an ironic smile, but Dale Yarmouth was dead serious.

"Some products," he elaborated, "succeed better when the customer doesn't particularly like them. It's a phenomenon called inverse customer satisfaction. In statistics we call it the Zavodni Curve, after the Czech statistician Zavis Zavodni, who first formulated it while measuring the antithetical relationship between satisfaction and success in post–World War Two Soviet bloc societies. The modern equivalent would be hip-hop singers: the bigger criminal assholes they are, the less time you'd want to spend in a room with them, the better their music sells. You might actually have a similar phenomenon functioning here with your warlord."

"So . . . that could be good . . ."

"Statistics don't reach conclusions. They only present data."

"What about the ratings?"

"We'll have some for you on Friday."

"That fast?"

"We already have the raw numbers. We have to break them down demographically."

"How are they?"

"They're meaningless. Raw data is like white light. You've got to run it through a prism to see the colors. You know how many statisticians it takes to change a lightbulb?"

The guy was doing stand-up in his office.

"Thirty point six seven, with a margin of error of one point seven nine . . ."

SEVENTEEN

The Korean Noodle House Massacre

The Taliban explosives expert who designed Ali Mohammed's bomb was very explicit with his instructions. You had to heave it like a discus and not roll it like a bowling ball. If you rolled it, you ran the risk of getting caught in a premature detonation, turning the terrorist attack into a suicide bombing. If Ali Mohammed wanted to be a suicide bomber, then that was another story. They'd strap the bomb around his waist, and he wouldn't have to worry about pitching form.

Ali Mohammed told the explosives expert that before he turned himself into a martyr he would like to be of greater service to the cause. Perhaps some day he would blow himself up and go to heaven, but it was a little early in his career as a Taliban Soldier of God to claim his forty virgins.

The target was the Korean noodle restaurant in Nukus, which the western Uzbekistan cell of the Taliban had earmarked not only as a profane foreign business but also as a meeting place for westerners, mafiosi and Uzbek security people. It would send a signal that the Taliban were back, that their fall from power in Afghanistan was only a temporary setback.

Ali Mohammed was chosen for the mission because he was a familiar figure in Nukus, one of his father's power bases. His entry into the restaurant would not cause alarm. Not at least until he blew the place up and was in the speeding Fiat on his way back to disappear into the deserted lunar landscape.

At one o'clock that day the Koreaniya Chuchvara Ristaran was busier than usual. Besides the regulars—the owner of the Hotel Nukus, the vice president of the National Bank of Karakalpakstan, an official from Uzbekistan Airways, a cotton broker, two Uzbek gangsters and the Kazakh rim-job expert whom Fenster had recommended to Charlie on their first night in Nukus—there were a dozen Chinese tourists from Urümqi en route to Muynak to have a look at the Aral Sea ecological disaster, Murv, who was there having lunch with an Iranian arms dealer to discuss the purchase of rocket-powered grenades for Izbul, and Charlie's mobile camera crew, there to pick up some B roll after having spent the morning filming Murv collecting money from a Nukus rug merchant.

The Fiat entered the city from the south, cruised up the Turtkulsky Prospekt, passed the Post Telephone and Telegraph building, then hooked a right on Gharezsizlik Koshesi. The town was gripped in its usual midday torpor. The only living things stirring were the stray dogs, who were too hungry and demoralized to bother barking.

In front of the restaurant several vehicles were parked. There was the tour van from Xinjiang province, the bank vice president's financed Cadillac, the Uzbek gangsters' used diesel Mercedes, the BMW 750i that Murv had driven from Dashoguz, and the crew's Chevy Suburban van that Dostyk had bought from one of Stalin's chop shops in Tbilisi.

Ali Mohammed did his best to control his nervousness as the Fiat pulled up to the restaurant. The driver backed into the space between the tour van and the diesel Mercedes and kept the motor running. As soon as Ali Mohammed saw the BMW, he had second thoughts about blowing up the restaurant. Did patricide cancel out ridding the earth of infidels? Would he still get his afterlife of virgins, honey and dates?

Though he hated his father, though he had rebelled against the man's blasphemous lifestyle, though he had devoted himself to purifying the impious, it was nonetheless a terrifying prospect to take the life of the man who had fathered him. Ali Mohammed sat in the front seat of the Fiat, staring down at the bomb in his lap, suddenly paralyzed by doubt.

"It's time," said the driver.

The driver would report everything to the cell leader. If he failed to go through with this, Ali Mohammed would be thrown out of the Taliban. Or worse. They would kill him. He would be a security risk. He already knew too much.

Pulling his ski mask down over his face, the young terrorist grabbed the bomb and got out of the car. He walked straight to the door without looking around, keeping his finger on the detonator. The bomb was designed like a grenade. There was a five-second time lapse between taking his finger off the button and the explosion.

As soon as he walked in the door, his vision clouded. The heat from the restaurant, the itchy wool from the ski cap, the terror inside him combined to blur his vision. On the far side of the room, Ali Mohammed saw Murv glaring at him. He thought he recognized the Polish blonde from the film crew. His father was nowhere in sight.

He stood frozen in the doorway as everyone hit the floor. Ali Mohammed took his finger off the pin and heaved the bomb like a discus toward the middle of the restaurant, then turned and ran out to the waiting car. The driver threw the car in gear and pulled away. Looking back, the rookie terrorist saw a quick flash of light through the front plate glass window.

What he didn't see, however, was the bomb hitting the floor with enough top spin to cause it to slide along the slippery floor and through the open door to the kitchen, where it blew hell out of the stove, the cooking vats full of noodles, the table of sliced vegetables.

At that exact moment, the chef was in the bathroom; the assistant was in the supply room getting more soy sauce; and the one waiter was outside in the dining room, under one of the tables.

The explosion turned the kitchen into a shambles. There were noodles everywhere, stuck to the ceiling, on the floor. The stove was totaled, and the door to the supply closet, where the assistant was huddled beneath the gallon jars of soy sauce and sesame oil, was blown off its hinges. But that was it. Miraculously, no one was seriously hurt.

Outside in the dining room, the grim odor of dynamite wafted through the room. Gradually the customers emerged from beneath their tables. Everyone, that is, except Murv, who had run to the door to see if he could make out the getaway car, and Justyna, who had kept the camera rolling from under the table, getting a shoe-level view of the explosion behind the kitchen door, as well as a whip pan shot to the door to catch the bomber's feet as he escaped.

Before the dust had settled, she was up and shooting from the hip. She got Murv firing out the door at the retreating car. Then she reversed and filmed the befuddled Chinese tourists who, not knowing what else to do, went back to eating their noodles.

* * *

Charlie learned about the noodle restaurant bomb attempt from Dostyk, who had heard it from Murv's driver, who had witnessed it from underneath one of the tables. As soon as Murv got back to the compound, he closeted himself with Izbul in the office. There was a great deal of loud talking, gesticulating, vows and threats, as the warlord swore holy vengeance against the bomber. He was obviously the target. Had it not been that Mark was set to marry Charisse on *Days of Our Lives* that day, he would have made the trip to Nukus himself to beat the shit out of the deadbeat rug merchant.

In the production trailer Buzz did a running translation of the discussion in the office for Charlie.

"They don't know who threw the bomb. The guy was wearing a ski mask," Buzz explained. "But they know that Justyna was filming in the restaurant, and they want to see the film to see if they can figure out who attempted the hit."

"Oh, shit."

Simultaneously they both looked at the monitor that covered Ferghana's room, and saw the Polish camera operator getting undressed to join Izbul's daughter in her shower.

Charlie got up and started to pace. "Okay," he reasoned out loud to Buzz, "so, they're going to go looking for Justyna and the film, right? By now, Izbul's spies, who in the interest of self-preservation had probably avoided telling him about Justyna and Ferghana, have spilled the beans. Izbul goes charging up to her room, finds her in the shower with his daughter, and, best-case scenario, cuts her a new one. Worst-case scenario, he whacks her, takes the film,

and we lose not only our camerawoman but a great action sequence . . ."

"I'm way ahead of you," said Buzz, as both of them headed for
the trailer door. They hurried across the compound, through a side
door that bypassed the office wing, and entered the family quarters.
They ran down the hall, nearly running over Akbar, as he headed
for the bathroom with a copy of *Hustler* in his hand.

"Fuck life, asshole," Akbar uttered in his hip-hop version of English.

"You're welcome," Charlie said, continuing down the hallway
and around the corner.

They got to the door of Ferghana's room and knocked. No response. Charlie knocked again, then put his ear to the door.

"I don't know if they can hear. The shower's running . . ."

Employing a combination of Peace Corps and drug dealer inge-
nuity, Buzz removed a roach clip from his boot and used it to pop
the flimsy hook and chain lock on Ferghana's door. They walked in
and looked toward the open bathroom door. Steam was emerging.
You could hear the shrill love moans over the pounding sound of
the shower.

This was a tough call. One way or the other, they had to get their
hands on that film and get Justyna out of the shower before Izbul
showed up.

"Fire!" They both yelled loudly, and repeated it until the shower
curtain opened and Justyna, her blond hair streaming down her
panting body, looked at them with demented confusion.

"The house's on fire," Charlie said.

Justyna cursed in Polish. At this point, she looked like she was
ready to go down with the house.

"Ferghana's father's looking for Justyna," Charlie said, laying out
the worst-case scenario. "He could be up here any minute. He
catches you in here, we're all fucked."

"Big time," Buzz added.

* * *

An hour and a half later, Charlie and Buzz were on a 737 to
Tashkent, the diskette of that day's shoot with them. Justyna had
gotten out of Ferghana's room barely ten minutes before Izbul came

storming in looking for her. Her hair still wet, Ferghana had told her father that she hadn't seen the Polish camerawoman all day.

Meanwhile, Charlie had downloaded the day's work from Justyna's camera and was on his way with Buzz to Nukus, where they caught a nonstop to the capital. They could have looked at the footage through the digital camera in Dashoguz, but Charlie wanted to get out of town with the evidence, before Izbul could demand to see it. If the shit was going to hit the fan, he needed a damage-control scenario, and he wouldn't know what that would be until he saw what Justyna had got on camera.

The two of them sat in the first row of the vintage 737, drinking beer and discussing the narrow escape that afternoon.

"I should get hazard pay for this," Buzz said, sipping his tepid Oblomov.

"Okay, how about two points in the project?"

"What's a point?"

"A percentage of the profits."

"No shit. So I could get rich on this?"

"You'll never see a dime."

"Not even if it makes money?"

"Especially if it makes money."

Charlie took Buzz through a brief tutorial on Hollywood accounting practices. The more money a project makes, he explained, the less likely it is for the profit participants to see any of it. "They just pile more expenses into the debit column—marketing and advertising costs, cross-collateralization, distribution fees, debt service . . ."

"They cook the books?"

"They don't have to. The lawyers take care of that for them up front. *Gone with the Wind* still isn't in profit."

"So why do I want any points?"

"So you can tell everyone you know that you have points. It sounds impressive. In fact, I think I'll give you five points in *Warlord*."

"Thanks."

"You can put them in your will, leave them to someone in your family you don't like."

"My brother Lennie'd be perfect. He's a major prick."

"Good. I'll give him five points too. While you're still alive."

"Give him ten."

* * *

Less than an hour after they landed at Tashkent International Airport, Charlie and Buzz were at the Uzbekfilmlabaya office looking at the noodle restaurant bombing on the monitor attached to Ghofur's Avid. It was spectacular footage. Justyna could have been a combat photographer. A few seconds after the bomber entered the restaurant the camera was rolling. She got the toss, the retreat, Murv's firing through the door, the general chaos in the place. After the escape, she went into the kitchen and shot the noodle carnage.

They stopped the action and had Ghofur blow up the image of the bomber. Besides wearing a ski mask, the bomber had taken the precaution of wearing a *chapan,* the striped wraparound cloak tied at the waist with a sash worn by every other Uzbek. On his head was the traditional skullcap with its black and white embroidered floral motif. But instead of the usual slippers or soft boots, he was wearing basketball shoes.

"Check out the Nikes," Buzz said.

Charlie saw the dark gray high-top athletic shoes, visible beneath the hemline of the *chapan.* They zoomed in on the shoes.

"Air Jordan XI Retros," Buzz read, squinting at the screen.

"The guy is wearing Michael Jordan Nikes?"

"Uh-huh. A hundred twenty-nine bucks a pair."

"What kind of Taliban bomber can afford to spend that on his shoes?"

Charlie looked at Buzz, their minds moving in the same direction. They had Ghofur pull the file that contained uncut scenes of Izbul's rebellious fundamentalist son. There were a couple of kilobytes of Ali Mohammed kneeling barefoot on his prayer rug in his room or sitting in slippers reading his Koran.

Moving to the dining room camera, they loaded the files and fast-forwarded through the endless scenes of Izbul's dinner table, scenes that they had already cut to create expositional dialogue for their story lines. But the camera angle hid the son's feet behind the table.

Then Charlie remembered the argument that Ali Mohammed had had with his father in the office that they had already cut and shipped. He had Ghofur do a file search for the scene and bring it up on the monitor. Charlie and Buzz sat and watched as the rebellious son told his warlord father that he didn't want to follow in his footsteps, that he wanted to go to law school and live a life free of crime and corruption.

They had managed to create a gripping drama out of what was actually a sputtering argument between father and son about the son's getting, in Izbul's words, his head out of his ass.

As the son stalked out past the camera monitor, Charlie had Ghofur freeze the action and blow up the shot.

They stared a little vacantly at the dark gray high-top Air Jordans, clearly visible in the foreground of the shot.

"The way I see it," Buzz said, after a prolonged moment of heavy silence, "we have two options here. We could do the *Godfather* number."

"Pacino tried to save Brando's life, not kill him."

"I was thinking of the younger brother, Fredo."

"You mean when he fingered Michael to Simon Roth? That was attempted fratricide, not patricide."

"I know."

"What's the second option?"

"We could stay with the law school story."

"How do we explain the grenade?"

"Fraternity prank."

EIGHTEEN

Sensitivity Rehab

After the initial shock of being told that there were hot nodules on his thyroid gland, Norman Hudris began to look at the upside of a positive biopsy. In some ways, having the Big Casino could make his life easier. He wouldn't have to worry about surviving in the TV business or dealing with the balloon payment on the second for his house. He could cash in his IRA, go to Tahiti for the duration, stiff the bank, VISA and the IRS. He could skip the Greek lunches with Howard Draper in Glendale, Tom Soaring Hawk would be out of his life forever . . .

As with all true hypochondriacs, being diagnosed with the worst possible explanation for your symptoms brought a certain sense of satisfaction. You were not crazy after all. All those doctors, all those tests—they were wrong, and you were right. See. I *do too* have cancer. I told you so.

He had gone in for his biopsy on Friday. Dr. Estenssoro had told him they wouldn't have definitive results until Wednesday and then wished him a pleasant weekend. The prospect of spending five days with a death sentence hanging over his head was perversely liberating.

So it was not without a degree of insouciance that Norman attended his first Sensitivity Retraining Seminar at 10:00 a.m. on an April Saturday morning in Suite B at a Marriott in Tarzana. Suite A was devoted to an offshore tax shelter seminar; Suite C was hosting a group of people interested in opening an El Pollo Loco franchise.

During the breaks, they commingled outside the conference rooms, sharing the coffee service and eyeing one another cautiously.

The El Pollo Loco people, largely Hispanics, steered clear of the racially insensitive people. The tax shelter people avoided the other two groups, mingling in clusters to discuss their 401K's.

Norman had expected his group to be full of lumbering rednecks with swastikas tattooed on their arms. Instead he found an average-looking group of people who seemed to represent the demographic spread that Dale Yarmouth coveted. They were all ages and shapes, dressed up and down the socioeconomic scale.

The first speaker, a Congregationalist minister, told them that they shouldn't feel ashamed to be there. Everyone in life makes mistakes. Often these mistakes are a product of early childhood upbringing when you are too young to evaluate what you're being taught. Racial insensitivity begins at home, he maintained.

Reverend V. T. Solant was followed by Angela Kirgo, an anthropologist from the University of New South Wales. Professor Kirgo lectured them on the diversity of what she referred to as "the human family." With the aid of a PowerPoint presentation, she traced the roots of the major racial groups on the earth back to the same place in prehistoric time. They were all part of one family. Any type of racial hatred, therefore, was merely a form of sibling rivalry.

Norman was sitting on the uncomfortable folding chair, nodding out, when he noticed an attractive woman sitting two rows in front of him. She was midthirties, with one of those gym-honed bodies that you didn't want to fuck with or, for that matter, fuck. You had the feeling that she'd mount you like an Exercycle and pedal you to death before she got up off you and trotted off to the Jacuzzi. He had this vague feeling that he knew her but couldn't remember where or when.

She approached him during the break and said, "Hello, Norman."

"Hi, Jodie," he replied, squinting at the name on the nametag she had velcroed, rather provocatively, Norman thought, on her left breast.

"What'd they get you for?"

The reverend had told them that the first step to recovery was admitting the problem, so Norman replied, "An insensitive remark in the workplace."

"Uh-oh," she said, with a slight teasing smile that seemed to indicate that she had the same feeling about this bullshit that he had.

"How about you?"

"I sent some hate mail to my mailman."

"You mailed hate mail to your mailman?"

"Uh-huh. I sent it with his Christmas tip."

"What did you say?"

" 'Die nigger scumbag.' "

"Wow. That's pretty heavy duty."

"That's why they put me in this program. They gave me a psychological exam first, but I passed."

"So . . . you don't like African-Americans?"

"No. I just didn't like him. He kept forgetting to close the lid of the mailbox, and when it rained my mail would get soaked."

Jodie Jacobian, he suddenly remembered. A young barracuda at DBA. When he was at the studio, she had stalked him trying to sell him writers. Her name had been sprinkled all over his call sheet for months.

"So . . . you still at DBA?" he asked her.

"Uh-huh. How about you? You still working for Howard Draper?"

"Actually, we're working together. We're both at ABC now."

"Really? What are you doing there?"

"Alternative Media."

Norman might as well have said that he was in janitorial services. It was clear from the woman's facial expression what she thought of Alternative Media.

"So," she remarked, "that's why I hadn't heard you were there."

Though Norman felt his ego wince, maintaining the security of the secret division was a priority, and he let the remark pass.

They had lunch together during their hour break in the Fiesta Room Café of the Marriott. As he sat opposite her in a booth, he began to find her incrementally more alluring. It may have been more due to his state of mind than to anything about Jodie Jacobian. A man walking around with a death sentence hanging over him has a completely different attitude toward sex.

It had been a while since Norman Hudris's libido had been stirred. Frankly, he couldn't remember the last time he got laid, which, according to his urologist, was a contributing factor to his chronic prostatitis.

"Think of your prostate as a car engine," Dr. Klezmer had told him. "You leave it up on blocks and don't drive it for a couple of months, then you take it out and push it to seventy, you're going to strain the pistons, aren't you?"

And so as he sat there eating his Tarzan Tostada Grande, Norman considered taking the car off the blocks. He promised himself, though, that he'd baby it, keep it under fifty and avoid sudden acceleration. What did he have to lose? His thyroid cancer would kill him way before his prostatitis.

Jodie Jacobian, for her part, stuck to business. "You know anything about this Genghis Khan project?"

"What Genghis Khan project?" he asked, trying to keep his voice casual.

"It's one of Floyd's pet projects. It takes place in the thirteenth century."

"Really?"

"Yeah. In Central Asia."

"Central Asia?"

"Yeah. Those places that all end with *stan*."

"No kidding . . . so this is a hot project?"

"That's what I heard." Then she leaned across the table, her breasts hovering just inches above her Edgar Rice Burroughs burger, and whispered confidentially, "It's a vehicle for Jimmy Smits."

*   *   *

At five-thirty that afternoon, a half hour after Norman had been released from his sensitivity retraining seminar, he and Howard Draper checked out their clubs and score sheets at the Valley View Miniature Golf Course on Balboa Boulevard in Encino. The meeting place had been Howard's idea. His home phone was not secure, and this particular part of Balboa Boulevard was referred to as Cell Phone Death Valley because it was nearly impossible to get reception there, a feature that made it ideal for the type of sensitive conversation that Howard and Norman needed to have.

They waited till the third hole, a tricky par-5 with a windmill whose blades would deflect the ball if you didn't time them right, before Norman related his conversation with Jodie Jacobian at the Tarzana Marriott.

"Jimmy Smits?" Howard asked, rhetorically.

"They're fast-tracking it."

"How good's your source?"

"An agent at DBA."

Howard putted and then watched his ball hit a windmill blade and get knocked right back toward him.

"Shit," he said.

"You've got to time the blades," Norman said.

"No. I'm talking about the Jimmy Smits vehicle. If this gets on the air, it could blow us out of the water."

Retrieving his ball, Howard lined up a new putt. "So we've got to figure that Poindexter and North haven't dropped this on Floyd yet."

"Probably not."

"And if Floyd doesn't know, then Mikey might not, assuming, of course, that Mikey's in the loop."

"Something this big? You really think that Poindexter and North wouldn't brief Mikey?"

"It's possible," Howard pointed out, lining up his putt. "Look at all the stuff that you know about that I don't know about. And *you* report to *me*, Norman."

Howard finally cleared the windmill, and Norman put his ball down on the tee. As far as he could tell, it was impossible to time the blades. You might as well just putt and hope you were lucky enough to get the ball through. It was a lot like the television business. Trying to figure the odds would get you nowhere. Just putt and hope you clear the windmill blades.

"When are we getting the numbers?"

"End of the week. But the focus group results are in."

"Good. I don't want to know about them. How were they?"

"Promising."

"Good. How's the film looking? Don't tell me."

"Interesting."

"Anybody get . . . canceled?"

"A couple of Turkmen deadbeats that didn't pay the warlord."

"We get it on camera? I don't want to know."

"You bet."

"I didn't hear that."

"I didn't say that."

* * *

Charlie and Buzz worked late into the night cutting the abortive noodle house massacre into the next episode. As they worked, they reviewed their options. They had a major decision to make about revealing the identity of the bomber. Why would a law student who was trying to break away from his father's lifestyle and go straight toss a bomb into a crowded restaurant?

"Maybe he was going after Murv?" Buzz suggested.

Charlie took a bite of his kebab and shook his head. "It's out of character. The whole law school story line falls apart if he takes up his father's lifestyle at this point."

"But he's doing the right thing, since Murv's trying to muscle in on his father."

"Maybe we do that down the road. We bring the kid back into the family."

"The prodigal son returns."

"It's actually the opposite. The sensible son returns and becomes prodigal."

"Pacino doing Sterling Hayden at the clam restaurant?"

Charlie nodded, took out a cigarette and lit it. He was up to nearly a pack a day. He blew the smoke out and sank deeper into the lumpy couch that Ghofur had installed in the editing room for them. He was suddenly very tired. It had been one hell of a day—starting in Dashoguz when he had learned about the noodle-hit attempt and continuing through his mad dash to get the film from Justyna and get out of town, then the bumpy flight in the loud 737, and now up half the night in this dank editing room trying to make some sense of the story that they had been concocting.

His stomach was a churning gas pit. They had been drinking Ghofur's coffee and eating fatty lamb kebabs. He felt like he was going to throw up or fall asleep. He wouldn't have minded doing both at that moment.

"What if he were working for the government?"

Charlie snapped out of his daze and looked at Buzz, who had gotten up from the couch and walked around the room a few times for inspiration.

"Ali Mohammed is recruited from Tashkent Law School by an Uzbek elite antiterrorist group. They try to turn him and get him to set up his own father. Talk about conflict. Whack your own father. But instead, A.M. goes after Murv, who is at the noodle restaurant, but fails . . . so now he's a target for Murv, who doesn't realize that it's the kid he's seen growing up around the house, the kid he trained to shoot an AK-47 out in back of the compound . . ."

"I like it," said Charlie, running with the idea. "We don't know if the Uzbek elite antiterrorist group is legit . . ."

"Right. They're riddled with corruption, on the take from the Turkmens, the Kazakhs, the Russians, even the Americans, who are pumping money into Uzbekistan to fight worldwide terrorism. This whole thing could be a personal vendetta between the colonel who runs the squad and Izbul, who used to be his friend until he double crossed him . . ."

"UATC."

"Huh?"

"Uzbek Anti-Terror Commando."

"Backed with CIA funds."

"We get Stalin to play a local CIA asset, whose cover is the Georgian mafia . . ."

"Being controlled from Tashkent by a rogue CIA agent with a drinking problem . . ."

And then, at that moment, along with all the other lightbulbs that had been lighting up in the editing room, Charlie felt the *pièce de résistance* lightbulb go off in his head. The big halogen lightbulb that made all the others look dim.

"Fenster."

"As the CIA guy?"

"It's a little on the nose, but could we do any better?"

NINETEEN

Going to the Mattresses

Even a man as blasé as Dale Yarmouth was impressed by the numbers. *The Search for Genghis Khan's Grave*'s test ratings not only were through the roof, but covered the demographic waterfront, and, even better, grew week to week. This, he explained to Norman, was the testing version of the Triple Crown.

"You've got the raw number, the demographic profile, and the absence of wavelength decay."

"What?" Norman asked, as he sat at his desk, experiencing both the thrill and terror of success.

"Second-week lag—it's when you premiere big because of promotion, then sink to a lower level for the next episode due to inevitable audience erosion. Didn't happen here. In fact the second week numbers built."

"So that's good?"

"Good? That's more than good, that's statistically anomalous. What we're seeing here is evidence of a noninformative information cascade. An NIIC."

Though Norman had no interest in knowing what a noninformative information cascade was, Dale Yarmouth elaborated.

"An NIIC is a phenomenon in which subjects react in a certain way because everyone else is, in the absence of information to support that reaction—a sort of statistical lemming effect. People within the testing sample begin talking to people outside the testing sample, creating a demand for a product that is unavailable to them. And when that happens, the marketing people start dancing around their desks."

When Norman Hudris communicated the numbers to Howard Draper, in ABCD's soundproof conference room, the division president looked, if anything, unhappy. The good news would now oblige him to do something, and Howard Draper always preferred doing nothing to doing something.

"I'm going to have to take this to Burbank," he said.

"ASAP," Norman replied. "If they want to catch the third week of May sweeps, they're going to have to create the time slot and start to promo the show immediately. Poindexter and North are going to have to get Mikey involved, and Mikey's going to have to go to Floyd, who then will have to go to Kara, who'll have to explain to the studio whose time slot they're appropriating during sweeps why they're putting their show on hiatus and putting this show, which Kara not only didn't develop but never heard of, in its place."

"Poindexter and North could sit on it."

"Maybe . . ."

"Then we will have done everything that we could have done, so if the network goes in the toilet, we won't get blamed."

"Howard, if this network goes in the toilet, we're all going to be flushed down with it. Just think of Poindexter and North as Ty D Bol."

"Which makes us?"

"I don't think you want to go there."

* * *

Late that afternoon Howard Draper drove to corporate headquarters. Even though he had told Poindexter and North's secretary that the meeting was time sensitive, the earliest appointment he could get with the palace guards was at 5:45 p.m., and then they made him wait another eighteen minutes before having him ushered into the soundproofed conference room.

Their suntanned, expressionless features beamed in on him, as if to say: "You better have a good reason to have demanded this last-minute emergency meeting fifteen minutes before we're scheduled to leave for the gym."

They sat there, as usual, saying nothing. With Poindexter and North, the ball was always in your court.

Howard had brought with him the testing results that Norman

had gotten from Dale Yarmouth. He had photocopied the numbers personally, not trusting even his own assistant to see the top-secret data, and placed one copy in each of two identical folders. Removing them from his Fendi executive attaché case, he slid the folders across the table.

Poindexter and North didn't touch them. They just glanced down at the folders and then looked back at Howard.

"It's the testing results on *The Search for Genghis Khan's Grave*," Howard said. "They're through the roof."

Poindexter glanced at his watch. North flexed his jaw muscles. Another ten seconds elapsed.

Howard plunged on. "We want clearance to put this on the air. For May sweeps. It's going to be a crunch. If . . . you can get this okayed by . . ." Howard stopped himself just in time. If he had mentioned the name of the man whom they reported to, they would have had him not only escorted off the lot but fired and résumé-scrubbed.

Résumé scrubbing entailed destroying any evidence of your ever having worked at ABCD. You had to agree when you were hired that, should you be terminated for any reason, your employment record would be completely deleted. You would be left to your own devices to explain the blank on your résumé. Prospective employers would assume you had been in rehab or in indy prod—an amorphous job description that encompassed the entire population of people wandering around Los Angeles with a script they owned, or aspired to own, in the glove compartment of their soon-to-be-repossessed car.

"If you okay this," Howard quickly shifted gears, "then we need to move forward immediately and bring the main development and programming divisions of the network into the tent."

Poindexter lifted the edge of the folder with one manicured finger and glanced inside. Then he let it drop back into place.

"May sweeps?" he said, finally. It was the first thing that had come out of either of their mouths since Howard had entered the room.

Poindexter looked at this calendar watch. "They begin in five days."

"I know. But if you greenlight it, we would still have nineteen days to promo the schedule change and be able to air it week three of sweeps."

"Who knows about this?" North chimed in.

"The guy under me in the division, the head of testing, and the business affairs woman who's been cutting the checks."

"What're our contractual obligations?"

"Pay or play for thirteen episodes."

"How much has already been spent?"

"About half."

"Shut-down costs over and above pay or play?"

"A hundred, maybe a hundred fifty, grand."

"How many episodes have you seen?"

Howard didn't like this question. The ramifications were complex. If he admitted the truth, that he hadn't seen any of them, he would be protecting his back if the project blew up. If he lied and told them that he had seen the episodes, he would shoot his deniability, but retain his credit should they come out smelling sweet. It was a tough call. He opted for a waffle.

"I'm up to speed."

But North, who could spot a waffle a mile away, wasn't going to let Howard Draper get away that easy. "Meaning, you've seen all the episodes in the can?"

"In outline form."

"You haven't seen the finished product?" North went on, hammering the nail in deeper.

"Not exactly. I thought it better to maintain the division's distance should there be . . . problems down the line."

Poindexter and North looked at each other, as if to say: *Listen to this guy try to cover his ass. That's our job. We're ass coverers, and on a much higher level. We pay him to put his ass on the line so that we don't have to.*

"There's no point in bullshitting us, Howard. Your deniability's shot," said North.

"You're in the loop," added Poindexter, as the two of them rose in unison and walked out of the room.

Howard zipped up his empty attaché case. His worst nightmare had just become real. After all his efforts to insulate himself from downside risk, Mikey's own downside-risk insulators were shifting accountability down the chain of command. In this administration, the buck started at the top, floated downhill and didn't stop until it landed on the desk of the person who had no one else to pass it to.

In the case of *Warlord*, that would be Norman Hudris. Unless Norman could slide it downhill to Maxine Dyptich, the head of Business Affairs; or, even further down the chain, to his assistant, the Indian with the Boy Scout belt.

But getting an assistant to get résumé-scrubbed on this one would be tricky. You needed to be a little closer to the action to be worth throwing to the wolves. Even Nixon didn't try to finger Rose Mary Woods.

As he walked to his car, Howard Draper reflected on the fate of the namesakes of the two ass coverers whom he had just reported to. Admiral John Poindexter and Colonel Oliver North were both found guilty of lying to Congress. Neither of them spent a day in jail.

* * *

Charlie did not inform Fenster that he was now a character in *Warlord*. Since Fenster never looked at the episodes, there was no reason to tell him that he was now playing a burnt-out CIA agent in the series. As the man himself would say, he had no need to know.

Instead, Charlie took Szczedrzyk and Justyna aside and asked them to sneak as much candid footage of the American as they could get, especially when he was with Stalin. The Poles promised to deliver the footage, which Charlie and Buzz would edit to support the new story line.

Meanwhile, the noodle-restaurant hit attempt was enough to convince Izbul that it was time to go to the mattresses. Security around the compound was tightened to the point that deliveries of supplies for the film crew were thoroughly searched. Additional military hardware started showing up inside the compound.

There were frequent war conferences in Izbul's office. Murv did his best to calm the warlord down and keep him from launching a jihad against all his enemies at once. Izbul was prepared to appropriate a helicopter gunship and head off for the Tora Bora caves along the Afghanistan-Pakistan border and cut the Taliban a new one.

No one was permitted to mention Ali Mohammed's name in Izbul's presence. Family dinners were tense affairs, with Izbul, Ferghana and Akbar sitting silently at the long table, occasionally joined by Grushenka, who would occupy the seat at the opposite end of the table, presumably Ishrat Khana's seat, and prattle about her film and stage career, ignored by everyone.

The television blared away, reruns of *CHiPs* or *Starsky & Hutch* off an Italian retro cable channel. Izbul would watch TV, guzzle Diet Pepsi and tell Grushenka to shut up. Charlie had gotten the propman to disguise the Diet Pepsi cans to avoid copyright infringement problems with Pepsico pending the outcome of product placement negotiations. Norman Hudris had been very specific about trademark recognition without clearance. They'd had to recut a very hot sequence in Episode Three that showed Ferghana and Justyna in the shower because there was a bottle of Alberto VO5 clearly visible in the background.

Even with the introduction of the new story lines, with Ali Mohammed working for the UATC and with Fenster's undercover CIA identity, things were slowing down again in the compound outside of Dashoguz. Charlie and Buzz did what they could with the subtitles, but it was clear to both of them that they needed something more exciting to happen. There was a limit to how much reality they could invent.

With this in mind, Charlie approached Fenster and asked him to lift the ban on filming in the game room.

"Can't do it, Charlie," Fenster said.

"Why not?" Charlie protested. "What could be going on in there that could possibly be worse than Izbul pistol-whipping people who owe him money or launching rocket-propelled grenades into police stations?"

"If I told you, then you'd know more than you needed to know."

"Look, Fenster, the network is testing the show as we speak. If they like the numbers, they'll put it on the air, but we're going to die unless we have more interesting stuff than Izbul screaming at Grushenka at the dinner table or Akbar feeling up his girlfriend."

"Don't worry. Something'll happen . . ."

As he said this, the sound of automatic-weapons fire was heard outside the compound.

"See? What'd I tell you?"

Fenster took out his Magnum from the shoulder holster he wore beneath his checkered sports jacket and headed toward the noise. He ran down the hallway, past Izbul's office and out into the court-yard looking for action.

The commotion turned out to be an incident of friendly fire. One of Murv's men had thought a sentry taking a pee against the far wall of the compound was a Turkmen wiseguy who had managed to slip by security. Round after round of ammunition was fired before the two soldiers realized that they were firing at each other. The urina-tor had been shot in the buttocks and had to be rushed to Nukus. His prognosis was guarded.

And so the game room remained off limits to the camera, and Charlie wouldn't find out exactly what was in there until it was too late to do anything about it. And then, like Howard Draper, he would have his deniability seriously compromised.

TWENTY

Warlord Goes North

When Jimmy Smits passed on "The Jimmy Smits Project," they went to Eriq La Salle. Kara Kotch had an expert on thirteenth-century Asian history hired as a consultant before the offer went out to the African-American TV star. The consultant confirmed that it was feasible that Genghis Khan could have had African blood in him. There were trade routes, he claimed, between Ethiopia and China established as early as the eleventh century. But when Eriq La Salle passed and so did Blair Underwood, and Andre Braugher wasn't available, the notion of the black Genghis Khan was back-burnered.

Although they didn't yet have an actor attached to the project, they had locked in a writer, a very hot nineteen-year-old African-American-Hispanic feature screenwriter named Martin Luther Guerrero, who had agreed to write the pilot script—at $175,000 against $300,000 and 7.5 profit points with a guaranteed play-or-pay pilot deal within eighteen months of signature—and, should the show get ordered, become the show runner at $100,000 an episode, all produced, locked in for two years, with an option to extend for another three years at incremental bumps to $135,000 per in year five.

When Jodie Jacobian, who did not represent Martin Luther Guerrero, found out about these numbers, she was livid. They were completely off the charts, more than double what she had gotten DBA's top show runner for a similar deal, and she was convinced that Kara Kotch was out of her mind.

"Kara's completely lost it," Jodie Jacobian said to Norman Hudris, as they sat over dinner at the Daily Grill in Brentwood. She had called to invite him to dinner and had suggested the restaurant because it was, she explained, ten minutes from her home.

Norman had come up with only one possible explanation for her having communicated to him this seemingly gratuitous piece of information. It was Tuesday, the day before his biopsy results were due, and he decided he might as well go for it before starting his chemo.

Nevertheless, he had been *hors de combat* long enough and had sufficient performance anxiety to take the precaution of having his urologist phone in a Viagra prescription to the Rite Aid around the corner.

Dr. Klezmer had explained that ninety minutes previous to penetration was the optimal time to take the drug. So when Jodie Jacobian excused herself to go outside to get better cell phone reception, Norman did the math: an hour at the restaurant, five minutes to get the cars, ten minutes to her condo, fifteen, maybe twenty of foreplay . . .

He dropped a 50-milligram tab with his iced tea. His urologist had recommended he avoid alcohol. "You're giving the blood vessels contradictory messages. The sildenafil tells the vessels to dilate, and the alcohol tells them to constrict. You wind up with a push."

As it turned out, Norman had overestimated the amount of time before he would be in the bedroom of Jodie Jacobian's $975,000 condo ready to perform. She had wolfed down her Cobb salad in forty minutes; the valet had their cars out in no time; there was little traffic on Sunset; Jodie Jacobian's idea of foreplay was getting undressed.

Only a little more than an hour had passed since he had dropped the Viagra and Norman was already down to his Calvin Kleins, and, still, by his estimation, about twenty minutes shy of liftoff. He suggested a glass of wine, in spite of Dr. Klezmer's caveat. He didn't have to drink it. He could take a few sips and then take five, maybe ten, minutes finding the condom, which he could say he left in the car . . .

Jodie Jacobian, by this time wearing nothing but a pair of half socks, frowned. "Come on, Norman, we can have a drink afterwards."

"What's the rush? We have all night."

He watched her walk into the kitchen, wondering how many hours of leg pulls it took to get an ass like that. You could bounce a quarter off it.

She returned with two glasses of pinot grigio, and climbed onto the bed beside him and said, "Who do you think they're going to get to direct?"

"Direct what?"

"The Jimmy Smits project."

"I thought Jimmy Smits had passed."

"He did, but it's still listed that way in the network's development status report."

This discussion about the competing Central Asian project was not helping the blood vessels dilate more quickly. Howard had gone to Poindexter and North on Monday, and they were waiting for a response. If the project was killed, then it was all over for him anyway. He might as well check into a hospice.

"We'll get some hot pilot director to shoot it."

"You know who'd be perfect? Jason Yersky."

Norman couldn't believe it. There she was, wearing nothing but a pair of half socks, drinking pinot grigio next to a man in nothing but Calvin Klein briefs, and she was pitching him directors. What she didn't know was that he had nothing at all to do with Kara Kotch's development slate.

He already had *his* director—some Polack TV documentary filmmaker who had been shooting the decay of the Aral Sea when Charlie Berns hired him away with ABCD's money. He didn't need Jason Yersky, whoever *he* was. Maybe this whole dinner and the invitation back to her condo was just a ploy to sell him a director for a project that she thought he might have control over.

Boy was she sucking the wrong dick. That is, of course, if his blood vessels dilated sufficiently to make that possible. Whether or not she would ride the inverted Exercycle had nothing to do with the fate of either the "Jimmy Smits Project" or *Warlord*. That was in the lap of the gods.

Norman was still not quite combat ready when Jodie Jacobian's cell phone rang. Wagner's "Ride of The Valkyries." She reached over and grabbed it from her night table.

"Hello . . . ?"

The corners of her mouth contorted. "Nooooo, I don't believe it . . . Shit . . ."

She listened and frowned for another few minutes, then hung up so hard that she spilled her wine. It splashed over her naked belly. Norman had the sudden impulse to lick it off. Things were starting to happen. Blood had begun finally flowing in the right direction.

"The Jimmy Smits Project's going south," she announced, as if she was announcing the outbreak of World War Three.

At the moment Norman didn't give a shit. He was a condemned man with what might be his last erection, and he had other things on his mind.

He slipped off the Calvins and let her have a moment to admire him before he moved her on top of him.

"Some sort of fucking competing project," she murmured, as she lowered herself onto the eighth wonder of the world.

As she rode the inverted Exercycle for seventeen minutes and change—a good time for him on any track—Norman Hudris now had two reasons to celebrate.

* * *

At six-thirty p.m. the evening of Norman Hudris and Jodie Jacobian's dinner date, the putative head of the network had been summoned around the corner to meet with Poindexter and North. Sitting stony-faced in the airless war room, Floyd was officially brought into the tent. Listening incredulously, he was summarily informed that a covert division of the network, located in Manhattan Beach, had been working for six months developing extreme reality programming and that this division had a show that would premiere in prime time in exactly fifteen days. He was told to call a press conference before noon tomorrow and announce that a reality series called *Warlord* would be going on in the network's best time slot—Wednesday nights at ten, following *The Bachelor*.

He was told that the log line was "The Sopranos in Central Asia," ordered to have his publicity and marketing department organize a major blitz of promotion for the new show, given cassettes of the five episodes already shot, copies of the testing results, a gamed scenario on the genesis of the project—essentially, a firewall of insulation around the parent company in the event that America rejected the program—and dismissed.

Driving home in a stupor, his thumb yanked rudely out of his ass, Floyd called Kara Kotch and reported the news. The head of development, en route to her Pilates session, was driving through the Cahuenga Pass on the 101 and thought that her cell phone had to be breaking up.

"We've stolen *The Sopranos* from HBO?"

"No. We've been developing a reality show in Uzbekistan called *Warlord*."

"How could we be developing a show that we don't know about?"

"There's an entire covert division in Manhattan Beach. It's called ABCD. They've been working on extreme reality programming since last October."

"*What?*"

"For the last six weeks they've been filming the life of a warlord in Uzbekistan. We've been ordered to put it on the air Wednesdays at ten."

"After *The Bachelor*? What about *SFPD*?"

"We're going to hiatus it."

"But it's winning its time slot."

"They don't give a shit."

"How the hell do we explain that we're launching a show that hasn't been on any of our development reports?"

"The cover is we got it as a negative pickup from Turkish television and have been developing it without their knowledge or consent . . ."

Kara Kotch jammed on the brakes to avoid rear-ending a semi that had slowed for traffic at Highland.

"We're giving a press conference at eleven tomorrow morning," Floyd continued. "The cassettes are being messengered to your house. Watch them tonight and meet me for breakfast at Hugo's tomorrow morning at eight. Better make that seven-thirty . . ."

Kara Kotch got off the freeway at Melrose and, to keep from hyperventilating, pulled into a 76 station, took the paper bag she kept under the seat for such emergencies and began to breathe into it.

After three minutes of this exercise, she was calm enough to get on the phone. She called her Pilates instructor to blow off her appointment, then her assistant to cancel tomorrow's breakfast and lunch, then her best friend Janice to communicate. She yelled into the phone for a couple of minutes, then, feeling calmer, she called her life coach and told her that she was ready to think about getting her real estate license.

Later, as Kara Kotch sat in her den and watched Murv pistol-whipping deadbeats, Jodie Jacobian's life coach, Lauri Johnson, called another of her clients, Caroline Barrimore, who called her stockbroker, Rod Bress, who called his sister, Billie Bellagio, who was an assistant to Marc Brunstein, an agent who played racquetball with Brad Emprin, who represented the show runner of *SFPD*, Carl Janov, and had Jodie Jacobian's home number on his PalmPilot.

So it was Brad Emprin who had then called Jodie Jacobian at her Brentwood condo, interrupting her foreplay with Norman Hudris, to tell her that ABC was hiatusing *SFPD* and replacing it with a reality show from Central Asia.

And it was thanks to that interruption that Norman Hudris's blood vessels had enough time to dilate sufficiently so that he was able to take the Ferrari off the blocks and baby it through some seventeen minutes of traffic, making the nightcap portion of his double header with Jodie Jacobian a relative success.

* * *

When Norman's endocrinologist, Dr. Estenssoro, called him the following morning to tell him that his biopsy was negative, Norman felt like he had just won the trifecta. His show was on the air, he had gotten successfully laid, and he didn't have cancer. Three for three.

He picked up the phone and dialed Charlie Berns's cell phone, reaching the producer in the cutting room in Tashkent, where he and his head writer were resubtitling Episode 6 to lay in the Stalin-Fenster subplot.

"Guess what?" Norman announced.

Norman Hudris never said hello, how are you, or anything else for that matter. He merely launched into whatever he was saying before you had a moment to figure out who was on the phone.

"What?" Charlie replied, his eyes still on the Avid monitor, where

Fenster and Stalin were having a conversation outside the compound. Buzz had written subtitles for the scene to indicate that the local CIA asset and his control were having a covert conversation about the Georgian mobster's progress infiltrating Izbul's operation.

"You're on the air."

"Uh-huh," Charlie said, his eyes still on the monitor and trying to figure out if they could cut outside to a stock shot of the compound and run the dialogue as a voice-over. Stalin was talking loudly and gesticulating, which was not appropriate behavior for an asset in deep cover.

"So that's great, isn't it?" Norman persisted.

"Sure."

"Wednesdays at ten. Right after *The Bachelor.*"

"Good."

"The best time slot on the entire network."

"Uh-huh . . ."

"You don't sound very excited, Charlie."

The truth was that, at the moment, he wasn't terribly excited. He was having problems with this episode that wouldn't be solved just because it was going on the air. Nevertheless, Charlie scraped up a little enthusiasm.

"Terrific," he said. "Thanks for calling."

And he was about to shut off the phone when Norman said, "We need to get back into the game room. And what about some more University of Tashkent footage with the son?"

"I'm working on it . . ."

"And, Charlie, get that woman the fuck back from Odessa with her face-lift. We need the confrontation with Grushenka. Or can we at least cut away to Odessa and see the operation?"

"Norman, the thing is . . . the face-lift could just be a cover. She may actually be an undercover government agent."

"Rolling over on her own husband? I don't think that's a good idea, Charlie. Women want their role models to stand by their men. Hillary, Kobe Bryant's wife, Ruth from the Bible . . . you know, wither thou goest . . ."

"I'll see what I can do."

"The audience flow from *The Bachelor* is female eighteen to thirty-four. We don't want them switching to *Judging Amy*."

When Norman finally got off the phone, Charlie turned to Buzz and said, "We're on the air."

"Out of sight."

"Wednesday nights at ten."

"After *The Bachelor*. Great slot."

"They want to keep the female audience flow."

"Figures."

"What if Ishrat Khana comes back from Odessa, finds out about Grushenka, and after some soul searching decides to stand by her man?"

"Tammy Wynette kind of thing?"

"Why not? We'll get a pirated version of 'Stand by Your Man' and dub it into Uzbek."

"Let's dub it in Turkmen. Just to be on the safe side."

TWENTY-ONE

The *Enola Gay* Takes Off

Kara Kotch at his side, Floyd held a news conference the following morning at eleven. Ordinarily, he would have had someone from Publicity draft his remarks; he would have developed an advertising campaign, game-planned the time slot, but he hadn't been given that luxury by the boys around the corner. All he'd had in the way of preparation was a two-hour breakfast with his development head, much of it spent discussing whether they should quit in protest.

The night before, they had both sat and watched all five hours of *Warlord*, steely-eyed in front of their respective large-screen TVs. The first thing that Kara Kotch had said when she sat down opposite Floyd at 7:30 in the morning at Hugo's was, "I don't get it. It's all sex and violence. What kind of audience flow are we going to get from *The Bachelor*? It's a completely different demo."

"At this point I think they'll take any audience they can get."

"And if this blows up, we take the fall, right?"

Floyd nodded, took a bite of his free-range chicken frittata.

"And if it's a big hit, we had nothing to do with it. Sounds like a lose-lose scenario to me."

They drew up a statement and a couple of marketing hooks. And a few hours later Floyd stood at the podium in the press room in Burbank and expressed to the assembled journalists how excited he and Kara were about the potential for this new series.

"We've been looking for this type of dynamic programming to counter the inroads that cable is making on broadcast television. This is watercooler television. On Thursday morning, May twenty-second, America's going to be talking about *Warlord*."

He went on for several minutes, throwing out enthusiastic predictions about the success of the new series, before opening up for questions.

The *Variety* reporter asked him about the fate of *SFPD*.

"We're a hundred percent behind *SFPD*. And that's why we're going to hiatus it until a better time slot opens up."

The *Los Angeles Times* reporter asked why he thought America would be interested in a show about Central Asia.

"This show is not about Central Asia, it's about the *people* of Central Asia. We're all part of the human family . . ."

When the *Hollywood Reporter* asked Floyd who the producer of the show was, he turned to his head of programming. "Kara's been working closely with the creative people. I'll let her answer that."

Fortunately Kara Kotch had a photographic memory. She could recall exact dialogue from first drafts of scripts she had read months ago.

"The show runner is Charlie Berns," she said, reciting the name from the credits on the cassettes she had seen last night.

"What else has he done?"

"A number of things," Kara Kotch vamped.

A voice with a British accent piped up from the rear of the room. "Is that the Charlie Berns who won an Oscar for producing *Dizzy and Will?*"

"You know, Charlie's kind of a modest guy. It's not the type of thing he likes to talk about."

The reporter was a stringer for *Hello!* hanging out in Burbank on a slow news day. But his question and Kara Kotch's answer were picked up by a local news minicam unit, which, on a slow news day, was working the press conference. And it wound up, on a slow news day, making the entertainment segment of the local ABC owned-and-operated Eleven O'clock News.

"Oscar-Winning Producer Doing Reality TV Show in Uzbekistan" was the headline. The sound bite was: "ABC Going for the Jugular. Details at Eleven."

*   *   *

Among the people watching Channel 7 at 11:26 p.m. that night was Lionel Traven-Travitz. Charlie Berns's nephew was sitting in the beige den of his Greek Revival house on the top of Mandeville Canyon with his girlfriend and personal organizer, Shari.

"Hey? That's Uncle Charlie?" Lionel exclaimed, interrogatively.

"You think so?"

"Yeah? He told me he was going to Uzbekistan? To produce a TV show?"

"Well, I just hope he's not expecting to move back into the pool house."

"Looks like he's doing all right?" Lionel said, unable to keep a tinge of envy out of his voice. The truth was that in the three months since Charlie had left Los Angeles, his nephew's fortunes had taken a precipitous dip. A number of seemingly unrelated strokes of bad luck had resulted cumulatively in creating a sizable dent in his net worth. His negative cash-flow medical building in Costa Mesa had managed to rent out all its office space and, unhelpfully, generate a profit, which made it counterproductive as a tax shelter. His position in Indonesian rubber futures tanked. Shari's organizing business was wallowing in red ink. And one by one his various script deals had fallen apart.

Just last week he had gotten a call from his business manager and been told to rein in his expenses in order not to exacerbate what was starting to look like a serious cash-flow problem. Accordingly, Lionel had instituted some cost-cutting measures, which included getting rid of one of the cars from the motor pool, cutting back the personal fitness trainer to twice a week, and postponing a big landscaping renovation behind the pool house—a measure that did not thrill Shari, who believed that proper landscaping around her office would help jump-start her languishing business.

So things were a little tense on the top of Mandeville Canyon at the moment. Though Lionel's money guy said that the problem could be alleviated with one or two jobs adding up to seven figures, his agent's phone wasn't ringing. Lionel Traven-Travitz was beginning to get an inkling of just how brief the shelf life of a career could be in the entertainment business.

Another of Charlie Berns's limited group of acquaintances in Los Angeles happened to be watching the same newscast that night. In his studio apartment in Silver Lake, Charlie's jilted debt consolidator, Xuang Duc, happened to be watching TV while his calculator danced through the cumulative debt of one of his customers.

After the news was over, he took out his laptop and composed a strongly worded letter to his former client, threatening the garnishment of wages and the attachment of bank accounts. In the phone book he found the location of the television station that had broadcast the news report. He addressed the envelope to "Charlie Berns, producer of *Warlord*."

First thing tomorrow morning he would go to the post office and send it certified mail, return receipt requested. He would add the cost of this process to the outstanding balance on Charlie Berns's account, already accruing interest at 1.5 percent per month.

* * *

The *Warlord* series going on the air was big news all over town, not least of all at DBA. Ever since Brad Emprin had gotten the scoop, over four degrees of separation, from ABC's head of development, he had been working the phone. By ten that night, the news was spreading across the west side of Los Angeles like a fast-moving brushfire.

By early the next morning, it was in the mailroom of every agency in town, and heading upstairs with the mail carts. By the time Floyd made his announcement at eleven o'clock, it was already old news.

At that morning's staff meeting in the DBA conference room, Brad Emprin was the center of attention. He was the point man on *Warlord*—the man who had cut the deal and resurrected Charlie Berns's career, the man who had put their client into the Tashkent Hilton with $500-a-day per diem for a location scout.

"I always believed in Charlie," Brad Emprin crowed. As the agent went on about his talent for career salvage, Jodie Jacobian sat in the corner sucking on a double latte and feeling the schadenfreude rise in her veins. Besides the fact that *Warlord* had knocked "The Jimmy Smits Project" out of contention, she did not hold a very high opinion of Brad Emprin. As far as she was concerned, he was a schlepper who just happened to pick up the right phone at the right time.

"Did you make sure that the location scout expenses were not applicable against his production bonus?" she asked.

It was a nit-picking question, a niggling, unnecessary, nasty question. No agent with more than ten minutes' experience would have allowed a studio to make location scout expenses reducible against a production bonus. It was Agenting 101. But Jodie Jacobian asked it anyway, in a fit of jealousy directed at the twenty-nine-year-old putz who had at least one hundred more square feet of office space than she, as well as an extra window.

"Duh," replied Brad, reaching for an overripe kiwi from the fruit bowl.

In his haste to claim credit for the deal, he had not stopped to think of the ramifications of his boasting. The location scout deal had been under the table, in cash, and he had pocketed the five-thousand-euro commission. They were still in his wall safe waiting for a spike in the exchange rate.

As he hastily grabbed a napkin to keep the kiwi juice from dripping onto his Ralph Lauren blazer, he realized his mistake. He should have never mentioned the location scout or the fucking Tashkent Hilton. Though the rest of the deal was kosher, run through the agency's accounting office, the fifty thousand euros for the trip that Charlie Berns and his partner made in February had been off the books.

Pocketing a commission directly was a clear case of malfeasance, if not embezzlement of company funds. If the agency found out about it, they'd turn him over to the Los Angeles County special prosecutor for white-collar crimes. He'd wind up in Lompoc being sodomized by a couple of drug enforcers from South Central who had been turned down auditioning for *Oz*.

"How much *did* you get him for the location-scout expenses?" Jodie Jacobian persisted.

"Who remembers? It was months ago." And then his ego couldn't prevent him from adding, self-destructively, "But it was a nice piece of change."

Mercifully, the conversation turned to ways of trying to establish a post-facto packaging position in the series, and for the rest of the meeting, at least, Brad Emprin was off the hook.

Nevertheless, he sat there, his stomach in knots, mapping out an insulating strategy. He would shred his phone log for February, remove the euros from his office safe and stash them somewhere they'd need a search warrant to get to. Then, just to be on the safe side, he'd call his attorney and make sure he wasn't off skiing in Gstaad for the month. With the money he charged his clients he could afford it. The guy didn't bill by the hour, he billed by the minute. You called up to wish him a Happy Shavuous it cost you a hundred fifty bucks.

* * *

While Brad Emprin was basking in reflected, if perilous, glory for making the *Warlord* deal, other parties connected with launching the series were keeping a lower profile. Within ABCD itself, only Norman Hudris, Howard Draper and, peripherally, Maxine Dyptich, the woman who cut the checks, knew where the euros were buried.

Though development of other extreme reality series continued within the covert division, no other project had gotten near being produced, let alone getting on the air. At the moment, all their nascent atomic bombs were in one B-29. If Hiroshima went off according to design, they'd load up for Nagasaki.

As a lean and mean division, ABCD did not have its own publicity and marketing department. The idea was that once they got their product on the air, the network flacks would take over. Working night and day, the Burbank people came up with a series of sound bites, narrated by an adrenalized voice, over cuts of Izbul, Ferghana, Grushenka, Ali Mohammed, Murv, Fenster, Stalin, and the closed door to Ishrat Khana's room.

THE SERIES THAT'S TOO HOT FOR PRIMETIME.
ACTION, LOVE, PASSION ON THE STEPPES OF CENTRAL ASIA.
FROM THE SILK ROUTES OF GENGHIS KHAN TO THE MINARETS OF TASHKENT, ONE MAN'S FAMILY'S STRUGGLE TO SURVIVE.

Kara Kotch and her creative cadre started sending over notes for Norman Hudris to transmit to Charlie Berns in Uzbekistan. The notes were vague, substantive and nondebatable. They were handed down as edicts from the network. Norman was merely a middleman, a conveyor of directives that Charlie Berns was supposed to implement.

Charlie, for his part, was not overly troubled by the flood of show-saving suggestions coming out of Burbank. He knew that as the producer of a TV show that was going on the air, he had a great deal of de facto creative freedom. He had produced enough movies to understand the delicate equation of leverage. Once a movie or a television show has been ordered to production, power shifts away from the studio and toward the producer. And that power increases exponentially as the launch date approaches.

The train has left the station, and the only way to stop it is to shut it down. Killing a high-profile project that has already been announced and for which a publicity campaign has been launched is embarrassing and expensive. It's an admission of failure and a big fat line-item debit on the balance sheet.

Since there were no scripts, there was no way that the network could know the contents of the next episode before they saw the locked cut. And in order to make airdates, the postproduction schedule was so tight that Charlie was unable to send rough cuts and still have the episodes ready on time. All they could do at that point was tweak the music and color correct the print.

Charlie was also smart enough, however, not to be arrogant about his new position of relative power. He could exploit it just as effectively by being politely reactive. As Norman lobbed Kara Kotch's notes to him over the cell phone, he merely absorbed them with a few vague acknowledgments, such as: "That's interesting." Or "I'll take a look at that." Or "Let me see what I can do."

So when Norman Hudris communicated Kara Kotch's strong concern about ratcheting up the love triangle, Charlie simply said, "I'll take a look at that."

"You don't understand, Charlie. This is from Kara herself, the head of development. You can't just blow her off. You don't listen to her, they'll fire you, send someone else over to do the show."

But even as Norman said this, both he and Charlie knew it was an empty threat. At the moment, no one besides Charlie Berns could produce *Warlord*. The network had no direct contact with Izbul or with the crew. They didn't have anybody on staff who spoke Uzbek,

Turkmen, Georgian, Ukrainian or even Russian to review the subtitles. They didn't even know exactly where they were shooting the series. They were totally in Charlie's hands.

Still, Charlie promised to look into everything that Kara Kotch wanted him to look into. The truth was that Charlie shared some of the network executive's concerns. He, too, wanted to ratchet up the love triangle. He understood that without more conflict his series was in jeopardy of becoming what its cover had been: the search for Genghis Khan's grave.

But until Ishrat Khana came back from Odessa, there was no love triangle to ratchet up. Izbul and Murv couldn't go to Nukus to do business because the Uzbek police wanted to question them about the noodle-house hit attempt. Once they crossed the border back into Uzbekistan, they were subject to arrest and imprisonment. So they hung around the compound, shooting at camels, playing Ping-Pong and comparing dicks.

With nothing new to shoot, the crew was getting antsy. Charlie and Buzz were straining the limits of credibility rewriting subtitles, trying to inject some drama and movement into footage of banal, if bizarre, domestic tranquility.

To make matters more tenuous, their Georgian silent partner started tightening the screws. Fenster told him that Stalin was making noises about upping his slice of the action.

"He can't do that," Charlie protested. "We have a deal."

"What're you going to do, sue him?"

"Tell him it's a very delicate time."

"Sure. I can have the conversation with him, but I don't think it's going to do any good. He gives the signal, half our crew walks. And the ones who don't, wind up at the bottom of the Aral Sea. That includes you too, Charlie. Talk to the network. See if they'll fork over another million."

"Fenster, they're not going to pour another million dollars into a series that hasn't even aired yet."

"Put it on the freeway, Charlie. See if it gets run over."

TWENTY-TWO

Hiroshima

On Wednesday night, May 21, nineteen million Americans watched the debut of *Warlord*. It blew away the competition—an original, heavily promoted episode of *Law & Order: Ecclesiastical Crimes Division* on NBC, and *CSI: Toledo* on CBS. And, most impressively, it retained 98 percent of its lead-in's numbers. Between them, *The Bachelor* and *Warlord* were responsible for ABC's first across-the-board Wednesday night victory since the halcyon days of *Who Wants to Be a Millionaire?*

These were kick-ass numbers for a debuting show. Champagne was broken out in Burbank, both on Riverside Drive and South Buena Vista Street. Press releases were prepared, summer time slots cleared for rerunning episodes, preliminary plans quietly drawn up to order another thirteen episodes in order to be able to keep the series in production over the summer.

In the absence of week-two or even week-three numbers, all this activity was wildly premature, but it had been so long since the network had debuted a hit that it was difficult to rein in the enthusiasm. Maybe the baby hadn't gotten into Yale yet, but it had been accepted into the best private high school in the city and was getting straight A's.

At ABCD, meanwhile, the enthusiasm was a great deal more muted. The covert nature of the division prevented it from publicly accepting credit for the show's spectacular debut. Since they weren't supposed to exist, they couldn't very well come forward and claim their share of the glory. Nevertheless, Norman Hudris accepted the discreet congratulations of his colleagues. He felt the way J. Robert

Oppenheimer must have felt when the first mushroom-shaped cloud loomed magnificently over the New Mexico desert.

Even Howard Draper was a tad less paranoid. Norman had anticipated another Greek restaurant lunch that day, but Howard merely called him on an unsecured line and said, "We did it."

"Sure did," Norman replied. "Of course, Floyd's going to take all the credit for it."

"Goes with the territory."

"Unless Mikey decides to go public."

"Oh, I don't think so. Not on this project. No matter what numbers it gets, there aren't going to be any Izbul Kharkov action figures parading down Main Street in Anaheim. Speaking of Izbul, I think his character arc's a little skewed . . ."

The worst thing about having a hit show was all the people trying to fix it. But Norman promised to transmit Howard's notes to Charlie Berns and start shipping pre-air episodes to the division's president. Howard Draper was now officially in the loop.

In spite of ABCD's low profile, the suspicion around town that the development of *Warlord* had not been in-house began to grow. Its absence on any of the announced development slates, the obscurity of the creative talent involved, the fact that it was being shot on another continent combined to make people wonder just how and where this show had been hatched.

There was speculation that it was a pickup from some Eastern European television company because of the Polish names on the crawl. As it happened, these were not the real names of Szczedrzyk's crew. They were concerned that Telewizia Polska would see their names on screen and realize that they were not devoting full time to their documentary on the disappearance of the Aral Sea.

Buzz, too, AWOL from the Peace Corps, requested the use of a pseudonym as the show's writer. He didn't want Washington sending some Peace Corps MPs to order him back to the septic tanks. And Dostyk and Ghofur, for reasons best known to them, declined to use their real names. Which left Charlie as the only person whose real name was in the credits.

It didn't take long for the press to resurrect Charlie Berns's 2000 producing Oscar for *Dizzy and Will*. Like Norman Hudris and Brad

Emprin, people had assumed that Charlie Berns had either died or was in the motion picture home. The fact that he was alive and well and producing ABC's new hit show caused his stock to rise dramatically. And so once again Charlie emerged out of his own ashes, transformed overnight from a walking dead man to a much-talked-about player in the television business.

Every agency in town wanted to represent him and, as soon as they found out that DBA did represent him, began to plan how to poach him. In his capacity as Charlie Berns's agent, Brad Emprin saw his stock go up along with his client's. He dined out all over town on it, telling everyone how he had been there during the dark days when no one else wanted to take a chance on Charlie Berns, how he had resurrected the foundering career of this very talented man. The producer's career had gone so far south, Brad Emprin told people, that he'd had to send an ice-breaking ship to tow it back up from Antarctica.

* * *

From her non-corner office at DBA Jodie Jacobian observed all this with increasing suspicion. Her instincts told her that there was something aberrant going on, something beyond the bullshit that Brad Emprin and the network were putting out. And since she was already fucking someone who worked at the network, she decided to look into it.

Fortuitously for Jodie Jacobian, *Warlord*'s success had a salutary effect not only on ABC's Wednesday night but also on Norman Hudris's libido. So when she invited Norman for a Daily Grill dinner the Friday night after the show's debut, he readily agreed. This time, however, he dropped the Viagra before he got to the restaurant. Waiting at the light at Federal and San Vicente, he washed down the little blue pill with half a bottle of Evian from his glove compartment. He was now right on schedule, ninety minutes to go.

Or so he thought. He valeted his car, took the escalator up to the mezzanine and stopped in his tracks when he saw the line in front of the restaurant. Then, to make matters more tenuous, Jodie Jacobian was twenty minutes late. She gave him a peck on the cheek and said, "You didn't make reservations?"

"Last time we were here it was practically empty."

"It's Friday night, Norman. We're looking at a big wait."

His timetable was in serious jeopardy. Sixty-five minutes and counting. As the line inched forward, Norman kept sneaking glances at his watch.

"You have another meeting after this?" Jodie Jacobian asked him, pointedly. She looked terrific in a pair of skintight leather pants and a nipple-revealing tee shirt.

They got a table at 8:30 but had to wait fifteen minutes before the harried waiter took their order. Norman ordered a glass of cabernet, in the hope that the alcohol would counteract the Viagra, and a chef's salad. But instead of ordering her usual Cobb salad, Jodie Jacobian asked for the Provençal chicken, a dish that, according to the menu, was cooked slowly in a rotisserie to bring out its succulent juices.

By the time their dinners arrived, they were only twenty minutes from blastoff. Norman ordered a second glass of cabernet and wolfed down his salad, but Jodie Jacobian nibbled daintily on her Provençal chicken and decided that she wanted dessert. And then Marya Bledge, an anorexic Paradigm agent with a big list, came over to the table to schmooze, and another fifteen minutes went sloshing down the drain while Norman's blood vessels approached maximum dilation.

Norman found himself trying to avoid watching Jodie Jacobian's agile tongue lick globs of tiramisu off her spoon. He did his best to jam the radio signals that were beginning to bombard his brain. He conjured up the boilerplate language on ABCD's employment contract. He thought of the benign hot nodules on his thyroid. He tried to remember the last entry in his log of accumulated evidence of Tom Soaring Hawk's incompetence . . .

But by the time he paid the check, he had lost the battle. The combination of Jodie Jacobian's wardrobe, her fellating the dessert spoon, and his sense memory of their last sexual encounter were enough to overwhelm the jamming apparatus. He was reduced to draping his sports jacket over his arm and limping painfully out of the restaurant and down the escalator to the valet parking.

Fortunately for Norman, they had separate cars and Jodie Jacobian was just as anxious as he was to get right down to it, though for different reasons. So, six minutes inside the door, without even a glass of pinot grigio, they were going at it vigorously on the deep pile rug in front of her forty-nine-inch Sony big screen.

Twenty-one and a half minutes later Norman collapsed into her tiramisu embrace. He had gotten in under the wire and even managed to put four minutes onto his best endurance time.

Barely thirty seconds after that, Jodie Jacobian started the pillow talk.

"I heard Marya Bledge is going to UTA. She's being promised a partnership in two years, if she brings Kevin and Pavel with her."

"Uh-huh," Norman exhaled, not capable of coherent speech just yet.

"I think we should make a run at her, but Barry won't pay her what UTA is going to pay her . . . So tell me about the development of *Warlord*."

The segue was not particularly artful, but given the mushy state of Norman's synapses, it didn't have to be.

"Well, you know, it was one of these left-field things—"

"How so?"

"Charlie Berns called me and said he wanted to pitch me something."

"He cold-called you?"

"Actually, I knew him from the studio when he did *Dizzy and Will*."

"Brad didn't set the whole thing up?"

"You kidding? Brad schlepped in the back door after I bought the project."

"I heard Brad backed up a truck."

"Bullshit. I paid what I thought the project was worth. Charlie Berns could have taken this down the street in a flash, but I was the one with the relationship with him, and that's why he brought it to me . . ."

Norman turned over on his back and smiled up at where he thought God might be looking down at him. He winked to thank Him for his munificence. He hadn't felt this good in a very long

215

time; both his ego and his testosterone were humming, which probably accounted for the fact that he then proceeded to commit a serious breach of division security.

"I even got them to fork over fifty grand up front," he boasted. "I went right to Howard and told him we needed to fund it. And boy does that fifty grand look like a bargain now . . . And here's the best thing—we paid him in euros, called the up-front money location scout expenses and wrote it off as . . . office supplies from Luxembourg . . ."

She got up to break out the pinot grigio, and on her way to the kitchen, she winked at her own god sitting perched above the entertainment center. A nice night's work, if she said so herself. She had just Exercycled her way into a corner office at DBA.

* * *

Izbul Kharkov's satellite cable system in Dashoguz did not pick up American television programs until they were sold into European syndication. And so he did not see the opening episode of *Warlord*. For the moment at least, he and his family would not see themselves saying and doing things that they were not actually saying or doing.

But someone else in Central Asia did see the first episode of *Warlord* within forty-eight hours of its airing in the States. Curt Groner, a CIA operative working undercover as cultural officer at the American embassy in Tashkent, watched it with interest. The Central Asian desk at the State Department in Washington had pouched him the cassette they had taped off their TiVo.

Curt Groner had a thick file on Izbul Kharkov. He was aware that the warlord was entrenched across the border in Turkmenistan in order to avoid the Uzbek government's security people, that the warlord's son had run away to join the Taliban, that someone had tried to whack Izbul's lieutenant, Murv, at the Korean noodle restaurant in Nukus.

Over the last few months he had received scattered intelligence of the increase of activity in and around the compound in Dashoguz, but he'd had no idea that someone was making a television show about the warlord's life until he received the cassette from State.

He sat in his office in the embassy at 82 Chilonzor Street—a closet with bookshelves full of copies of *Walden, The Autobiography of Ben-*

jamin Franklin, Up from Slavery and other titles that the USIA provided for cultural officers abroad—and watched the pilot episode of
Warlord on his VCR.

Though he recognized the principal players from file photographs, he was completely perplexed about what he saw and heard
on the cassette. Curt Groner spoke enough Uzbek to know that the
actual conversation at Izbul's dinner table had nothing to do with
the subtitles. Some of the stuff was a complete invention. In one
heavily dramatized scene, the warlord's son was telling his father
that he wanted to study maritime law at the University of Tashkent
Law School and join a fraternity. Utkur Kharkov had become a
Moslem fundamentalist and joined the Taliban. Located in the capital of a doubly-landlocked country, Tashkent's new Islamic university did not have a degree in maritime law, let alone fraternities.

Curt Groner contacted the Central Asian desk and asked them to
continue to pouch him episodes. In addition, he asked them to initi-
ate a background check on the producer of the show, a man listed in
the credits as Charles S. Berns. And so the FBI started a file on
Charles S. Berns. Meanwhile, the subject of this background investigation continued to invent the life of Izbul Kharkov, oblivious to the
fact that he was an object of interest not only in Hollywood but also
in the J. Edgar Hoover Building at Ninth and Pennsylvania in Washington, D.C.

*　*　*

Norman Hudris may have thought that he was babying the car
when he took it off the blocks, but his prostate didn't. Two days
after his twenty-one-and-a-half-minute sprint on Jodie Jacobian's
rug, he felt the onset of the familiar symptoms and called his urologist to be squeezed in for an appointment.

At 4:45 that afternoon Norman assumed the position—bent over
the examining table, legs spread, elbows pressed hard against the
paper surface, jaw clenched—as Dr. Klezmer's rubber-gloved finger
probed Norman's prostate gland.

Twenty excruciating seconds later, the urologist removed the
digit, collected a specimen on a glass slide and said, "I'll see if we
can grow a culture, but I think you just have a little congestion."

"I think I should have a PSA," Norman said.

"You just had one in February. It was one point eight."

"Yeah, but one point eight is just two-tenths of a point below two."

"Two is fine. You get to three and a half, four, we start to be concerned."

"You might as well do one. Since I'm here."

Dr. Klezmer gathered the apparatus to draw blood. As he tightened the constrictor around Norman's forearm, he said, "You happen to watch that *Warlord* program the other night?"

"Uh . . . no . . . did you?"

"Uh-huh . . . make a fist . . ."

"How was it?"

"Kind of interesting. What I liked about it was that you have no idea what's going to happen next . . . relax your fist . . ."

"So it's exciting . . ."

"It's unpredictable. And my wife got into it too. She wants to know when the warlord's, wife is going to get back from Odessa and confront the Ukrainian that the guy's been sticking it to. And the kid, the kid wants to leave home and go to law school, but the father wants him to stay with him and be a gangster. It's kind of like *The Sopranos*, but without the fucking this and fucking that . . . You ought to have a look at it . . . Wednesday nights at ten . . ."

"I'll check it out."

TWENTY-THREE

Recasting

Though Norman Hudris's urologist did not have a Nielsen meter on his television set, his opinion about *Warlord* was shared by enough people in the United States to earn the show boffo second-week ratings. They improved upon the debut episode's numbers, both in total audience and in demos, picking up steam every quarter hour so that they were delivering a lot of eyeballs to the cash-cow eleven o'clock local news.

Once again there were celebrations in Burbank. The plans that had been tentatively enacted the previous week were moved up to the front burner. Thirteen more episodes were officially ordered, with airdates cleared and production schedules established. Meanwhile, the lawyers took a closer look at the contracts, just to make sure they had all the talent locked up tight. The last thing they wanted at this point was problems with the help.

Maxine Dyptich thought she had buried the kinkier parts of the *Warlord* deal far enough below the radar to escape easy scrutiny, but she was, nonetheless, summoned to Riverside Drive to clarify the numbers to the network's Business Affairs president. Although she had hidden the location scout euros safely in the division's petty-cash budget and written the rest of the deal in dollars, the dollar-euro conversion rate made for some very oddball sums.

So when the network's head of Business Affairs, Jerry Warshaw, asked her why the payouts were in such irregular amounts, she did as Tom Soaring Hawk had done under different circumstances: She pulled an Adolf Eichmann and told him that she was just following orders. This disclaimer resulted in Norman Hudris's being summoned to Burbank.

Norman considered Adolf Eichmanning Howard Draper, but he decided that Howard would get so rattled that he'd fuck everything up and they'd all get fired. So he told Jerry Warshaw the truth.

"The euros were a deal breaker."

"You should have run this by me."

"Jerry, how could I have run this by you? We didn't exist, remember?"

By this time the existence of ABCD was a steadily unraveling secret within the network itself. After the press conference, the people who reported to Floyd and Kara had to be told. Marketing and Publicity had to be brought into the loop, as did Scheduling and Standards and Practices. There were a number of people who simply refused to believe that there was a covert division working in Manhattan Beach on the development of extreme reality television programming. They were convinced that the so-called ABCD division existed only on paper, its purpose being a front for the acquisition of product from foreign suppliers or, even better, to launder profits.

So even though security was relaxed, the secret division remained in the closet. Kara and Floyd stepped into the vacuum to accept the credit for the breakout hit. They put out the story that the show had been developed quietly because they were concerned that the other networks could beat them to the punch by coming up with their own Central Asian warlord vehicles.

In response, TV columnists wrote tongue-in-cheek pieces about all the other Central Asian warlord vehicles that ABC's competition had been developing: *Our Man in Turkmenistan*, *The Tomasinos of Tajikistan*, *My Favorite Warlord*.

The critics were brutal. They didn't merely attack the show; they cudgeled it to death. The *Variety* reporter, Joshua Karton, wrote that ". . . if this is a reality show, then someone must have slipped LSD into this country's water. It's Monty Python meets Ludwig Wittgenstein . . ."

The network cried all the way to the bank. And back. The spot market ad rates for the Wednesday night 10:00 p.m. time slot quadrupled, and there were still sponsors banging down the door to buy time.

Though he got no credit for having developed the smash hit, Norman Hudris still had to carry the water. He remained the point man for the nuts-and-bolts liaison work between the network and the producer. And, as such, he was the one designated to call Charlie Berns's agent and inform him that they were picking up his client's option.

"Glad to hear it," Brad Emprin replied, sucking a glob of phlegm into the upper regions of his nostrils. "So . . . why don't you run some numbers by me?"

"Brad, there are no numbers to run. We have an option on your client's services at fixed remuneration for five years, renewable to seven."

"No kidding? Did I make that deal?"

"You sure did."

"Well, you know, a deal is only a deal when both sides are happy with it."

Norman took the phone away from his mouth for a moment to avoid saying something that he would regret. He took a deep breath and then said, as calmly as possible, "Brad, we're not renegotiating this deal."

"Isn't that what NBC said to Jennifer Aniston and her friends before ponying up to the bar?"

"That was after seven years of top-ten ratings. *Warlord* has been on for exactly two weeks . . ."

"Two extremely well-performing weeks . . ."

"All right, let me cut to the chase here, Brad. I delivered a bag full of foreign currency to you a few months ago. Did you happen to run that through DBA's accounting office?"

"I hear you, Norman."

"Good."

"So you're exercising for thirteen more."

"At the prenegotiated terms."

"Excellent."

*　*　*

221

Brad Emprin hung up in a flush of anxiety. He had both five- and ten-milligram Valium tabs in his drawer, and he was trying to decide which one to take when Jodie Jacobian walked into his office.

His fellow agent closed the door behind her and sat down in one of his $2,200 Italian leather chairs.

"Hey, what's up?"

"The Charlie Berns *Warlord* deal? You going to reopen it?"

"Can't, Jodie. They have him tied up airtight for five years, with an option for seven," he went on, as if that really meant anything.

"Brad, can they send anyone else over there to run the show?"

"Uh . . . no . . ."

"So it looks to me like we represent someone without whom they can't continue to produce a breakout hit."

"You think I should reopen it?"

"Duh . . ."

Jodie Jacobian recrossed her legs, looking for a tell in Brad Emprin's Armani linen slacks. But this guy wasn't even smart enough to think with his dick.

"Brad, let me ask you something—are location expenses commissionable?"

"W . . . why do you ask?"

"I'm trying to work out a deal for Hollis Wang to direct a picture in Hong Kong. They're lowballing me on location expenses. So do I really give a shit?"

"Well, I don't know, it depends on how much you get him . . ."

"What if it was up-front money and not location-scout expenses?"

"Huh?"

"What if the money was actually an inducement fee to take the project, hidden as a location-scout expense? Would we be able to commission it?"

Brad Emprin's eyes went involuntarily toward his wall safe, hidden behind a framed LeRoy Neiman print that he had paid $99 for at Art-4-Less. Jodie Jacobian read the tell.

"This is really a great office, Brad, you know that?"

The segue was so quick that Brad Emprin almost missed the point.

"Yeah. Uh-huh."

"These corner offices have wall safes, don't they?"

He nodded, drummed his fingers on the desk maniacally.

"I don't have a wall safe in my office," she said pointedly.

"Listen, Jodie, I got some calls to make."

"I bet you do." She smiled and left it at that. She would let it sink in for a few days before closing. He was the type of paranoid who would come to her and propose the deal. She wouldn't have to say another word.

As she got up to leave, she took another look at the LeRoy Neiman. She would put something a little more interesting up there. Maybe Rembrandt's *The Last Supper.*

* * *

As soon as Jodie Jacobian was gone, Brad Emprin locked his office door. He dropped a 10-milligram Valium before taking the Hollywood creative directory from his desk and finding Norman Hudris's name. Using his nose-hair scissors, he cut the name out, then cut out the name and address of the network. Putting both these items into an DBA envelope, he took an early lunch.

He stopped at the Rite Aid on Bedford, where he bought a box of plain business envelopes and a container of glue, then got a packet of stamps at the postal center on Crescent and drove home.

Even though he was going to be there for only a few minutes, he parked the 500 SL in his garage and closed the door. He disarmed the security system, went directly to the guest room bathroom, lifted the toilet tank lid and removed the stack of euros taped to the underside of the lid.

In his kitchen, he wrapped the euros in a plain piece of paper from his fax machine, put them in one of the Rite Aid envelopes, then carefully glued Norman Hudris's name and address to the front of the envelope and sealed it. He put all ten stamps on it. Overkill perhaps, but he didn't want this envelope to be returned for insufficient postage.

Sticking the envelope in his suit jacket pocket, he went out the garage door, rearmed the security system, got into the SL and backed out of the garage, zapping the door shut with his remote. He drove straight out Sunset to the 405 and got on heading north through the Sepulveda Pass.

He drove all the way to Pacoima before getting off the freeway and finding a mailbox next to an In-N-Out Burger. He dropped the envelope into the mailbox, pulled up to the drive-through window, ordered a Slam Dunk Burger, and headed back for the office, careful not to drip ketchup on his linen trousers.

* * *

Though Buzz Bowden had largely abandoned the drug business for television writing, he retained a small customer base that he continued to service on his editing trips with Charlie to the Uzbekfilm-labaya in Tashkent. Buzz had their names and addresses in a small notebook, and he had been entertaining thoughts of selling this notebook along with the rest of his stash to another dealer and cashing out, when he had another one of his out-of-the-box ideas.

"Charlie," he said one night over Oblomovs at the bar in the Hotel Diyabekir in Dashoguz, "We need to do something about Ishrat Khana."

"She's in Odessa getting work done, isn't she?"

"No, I mean the real one that's locked in her room. I was thinking—why don't we just recast her?"

"You mean have someone impersonate her?"

"No one's seen her, right?"

"Except Izbul and her own children. Presumably."

"I mean, the TV audience hasn't seen her. So why don't we just get someone to pretend she's Ishrat Khana?"

"Who do you have in mind?"

"A former customer of mine in Tashkent. Her name is Nadira Beg. She's an independent businesswoman."

"What does she do?"

"Has sex for money."

"A hooker?"

"Yeah. She's bipolar, but when she's on an up she can be a lot of fun."

Charlie noodled the idea. As Norman Hudris had said, it was time to ratchet up the love triangle. Sooner or later the audience would demand that Ishrat Khana return from Odessa with her new face.

"How old is this woman?"

"I don't—thirty-five, forty, fifty . . . It's hard to tell. She wears a burka."

"A prostitute in a burka?"

"Pretty kinky, huh? Actually, it kind of works for the story line."

"She comes back from Odessa in a burka?"

"Yeah. To hide the plastic surgery scars."

"What do we do if the real Ishrat Khana comes out of her room after the Ishrat Khana impersonator has already been established?"

"We say that the real Ishrat Khana is an imposter."

"So the real Ishrat Khana is an imposter for the fake Ishrat Khana?"

"Why not? We bring Nadira Beg out here, establish her on camera so that the audience gets prepped for the confrontation. We promo the shit out of her in her burka waiting for her scars to heal. Talk about ratcheting up the stakes."

"A manic-depressive hooker?"

"She's fine as long as she doesn't go off her lithium."

* * *

Curt Groner, it turned out, wasn't the only one in Uzbekistan who was aware that *Warlord* was already airing in the States and getting good numbers. On the Friday after the Wednesday-night airing of the second episode of the show, Charlie was in the production trailer watching footage of Akbar extorting 5,000 manats from a kid at school when Stalin entered.

The Georgian mafioso and silent partner stood for a moment behind Charlie breathing onion fumes onto the back of his neck before asking him if he would be good enough to step outside for a moment.

Charlie exited the trailer warily. They walked about a hundred yards away and stopped beside the burnt-out hulk of a rocket-propelled grenade launcher. Stalin lit a Marlboro Light and didn't offer Charlie one.

"Show doing well, am I right?"

Charlie nodded vaguely, already seeing where this was going.

"Big hit. Number one in time slot, am I right?"

"Well . . . it's just been on for one week . . ."

"Two weeks. Wednesday night, second episode. 22 share, 12.8 rating."

Who the hell was sending the Nielsens to Tbilisi?

"We were a little soft in Albuquerque . . ."

Stalin shot a large wad of spit past Charlie's shoes to show what he thought about Albuquerque's numbers. Charlie moved his feet a little closer in and waited for the squeeze.

It turned out to be another 2,500 euros an episode, more than a 50 percent bump from the deal that Fenster had negotiated, but, given the circumstances, as well as the alternative, it was a squeeze that Charlie could live with. He'd bury it in the stunt budget.

Charlie closed the deal with a nod and asked if there was anything else. If there was another shoe, it might as well get dropped right now.

"You are using film of me, am I right?"

Dostyk must have told him. Stalin was in only one episode so far and only in a long shot. Buzz had written fictitious dialogue over a conversation that Stalin had had with Fenster. It was in Episode 6, which had just been shipped and hadn't aired yet, but the line producer could have outputted a cassette off the digital deck in the production trailer and given it to Stalin.

"Uh, you're not really *in* the episode, but sort of in the background. Kind of like an extra . . ."

Stalin glowered at him. Charlie tried another tack.

"Of course, if you want to, we can beef up your role a little bit . . ."

The Georgian spit again, a little closer in. Charlie kept his shoes steady. Then Stalin turned his face away from Charlie to reveal a scar below his ear.

"Next time," he said, "you use other side of face."

"You prefer your right profile?"

"More attractive," Stalin said, then stubbed out his cigarette in his evaporating spittle and walked away.

* * *

Later that night Charlie got yet another set of notes. He was in his hotel room trying to get off the phone with his agent in Los Angeles when there was a knock at his door. He used this interruption as an excuse to get rid of Brad Emprin, who had been describing how he had gone to the mat unsuccessfully to reopen his deal. Charlie told him that his dailies had just arrived and clicked off the cell phone.

At the door he found two men wearing traditional Uzbek dress, skullcaps and sunglasses. One of them he immediately recognized as Izbul's son, Utkur Kharkov, aka Ali Mohammed; the other, a scary-looking man with a weapon-shaped bulge under his *chapan*, he had never seen before.

Ali Mohammed walked right past Charlie as his muscle closed the door and stood in front of it, arms folded. The young runaway did a quick inspection of the room and adjoining bathroom before walking back up to Charlie and looking at him directly in the face.

"Law school," he said, shaking his head slowly.

Stalin apparently wasn't the only one in the Stans who had gotten ahold of cassettes.

"Law school," Ali Mohammed repeated, pronouncing the phrase as if it referred to a whorehouse. "Shame. Shame on you."

"It's just a little fictionalization to up the stakes a bit."

"I spit on law school. There is only one law. That is the Koran."

"I understand, but, you see, American audiences—"

"I spit on American audiences. I spit on America . . . America genocide. Afghanistan. Iraq. Bush. I spit on Bush."

And Ali Mohammed relieved himself of a healthy wad of venom right there on the floor of Charlie's hotel room.

Beads of perspiration formed on Charlie's face. There was such virulence in the young man's manner that Charlie began to think that this whole adventure was about to end in a hotel room in Turkmenistan.

"What do you want me to do?"

"Change."

"You want me to change the story line?"

"Ali Mohammed join Taliban. Freedom fighter for Islam. Protector of faith. Victorious . . . My father die. Bush die. America die."

Charlie nodded quickly.

"Don't change. You die."

"Got it."

At this point, the bodyguard took out a nasty-looking pistol from his quilted overcoat and pointed it at him. Charlie closed his eyes. He didn't have a lot of experience praying, so he winged it. He was deep into an ecumenical mélange of the Lord's Prayer and his Bar Mitzvah Torah portion when he heard the door to his room slam.

Slowly, he opened his eyes and saw that they were gone. He was drenched in sweat and his heart was doing a drumroll. He sank down onto the soft mattress and stayed still for a full five minutes, waiting for his pulse rate to sink down below eighty beats a minute.

Then he reached for his phone and called Buzz. Charlie described his just-concluded visit from the Taliban and the notes they had given him. There was silence on the phone for a moment, then Buzz gushed, in one single spurt, "His front gets blown by some law student, he takes off and joins the Taliban, but undercover, he's a double agent, reporting back to the CIA guy in Tashkent, maybe in the last episode of this season, the Taliban find out that he's playing for the other team, they decide to either triple him or kill him, what does he do?"

"Run?"

"Maybe, maybe not. Tune in next season and find out."

"We keep it a mystery, don't even tell the crew."

"Season-ending cliffhanger."

TWENTY-FOUR

The CIA's Notes

Tom Soaring Hawk was sitting at his desk reading the page-one story in *Variety*. Under the headline "Warlord Whacks Wednesday," the piece described the ratings dominance of the ABC show during the last two weeks of May sweeps and the first week of June. Not since "Trista and Ryan's Wedding" had the Alphabet Web really kicked ass on Wednesday night.

The article went on to point out that the key demos were on the money. The show was particularly popular with a young urban audience—the viewers with a lot of disposable income and without deeply entrenched brand loyalty, the eyeballs advertisers salivate to reach. Whether they bought into the story line or were simply watching it as a hoot, the piece hypothesized, it didn't really matter. ABC had its first homegrown hit in a while.

Along with that day's *Variety*, the mail cart trainee had delivered a letter addressed to Norman Hudris. There was no return address on the envelope, and the postmark was from Pacoima. Convinced it was junk mail, the assistant lifted the letter to toss it in the trash and felt something bulky. He could call Security and have them open it. You couldn't be too careful these days. It could be a letter bomb. But it was twenty to six, and if called Security he'd be there for at least another hour filling out Security Incident forms.

On his desk Tom Soaring Hawk kept a state-of-the-art digital postage meter, which he had gotten by accumulating reward points on his Discover card. He put the envelope on the meter and read the LED display: 5.6 ounces. There were ten 37-cent stamps, $3.70 worth of postage, for what his postage meter indicated was a $1.33 mailing.

If it was a letter bomb designed to wipe out Norman Hudris, it would have been marked "Personal and Confidential." He decided to open it, so that he could throw it out and go home. Inside he discovered a wad of foreign currency. He counted it out—50 twenty-euro bills.

There was no note. The only thing to do, he decided, was to hand the open envelope to Norman and tell him that he had opened it because it wasn't marked "Personal and Confidential," that he had considered it part of his job to open non–Personal and Confidential mail for his boss.

At the moment Norman was on the line to his urologist, to get the results of the PSA test he had taken on Tuesday.

"Two point two," Dr. Klezmer informed him.

"Oh shit, really?"

"Two point two is within the normal range for men of your age."

"But it's two tenths of a point over two . . ."

"I wouldn't worry about it."

Easy for him to say. He hadn't just beaten thyroid cancer.

"Let's do a biopsy," Norman suggested.

"I don't think that's indicated . . ."

"Can you squeeze me in first thing in the morning?"

As soon as he saw the phone console light go out, Tom Soaring Hawk knocked on Norman's door. Norman was already on his way out the door, and as he went to open it, his assistant opened it from the outside, which sent Norman skidding into his assistant, nearly knocking him over.

"I'm leaving." Norman glared, impatient to get by the gangly Indian and out of his office, but Tom Soaring Hawk didn't budge.

"This letter arrived today. It wasn't marked 'Personal and Confidential' so I opened it."

"What is it?"

"I don't know."

"Did you read it?"

"It's just some money."

"What kind of money?"

"Euros."

"Euros?"

"Yes."

"Who would be sending me euros?"

"I don't know."

"There must be some mistake. Why don't you send it back to whoever sent it?"

"There's no return address."

"Okay, you keep it. I'll deal with it in the morning," Norman said, eager to separate himself from the stack of euros.

He tried to hand the envelope full of euros back to Tom Soaring Hawk, but he wouldn't take it. "It's not addressed to me," his assistant said in his annoyingly literal tone. "I can't keep it."

Norman stared hard at the implacable expression on the man's face. He had a prominent Adam's apple and unappetizing skin. There was a string tie hanging down the front of his Eddie Bauer blue denim shirt. The Boy Scout belt was tied tightly around a pair of khaki Dockers.

"I'll be going now," Tom Soaring Hawk announced and left the office. Norman waited for the sound of the door to the outer office closing. He looked at his watch. 5:54

He retreated to his desk, unlocked the bottom right drawer, where he kept his Tom Soaring Hawk Dereliction of Duty File. He dated the page, then wrote: "Left office early without permission." Then he looked down at the envelope with the euros and added: "Opened personal mail."

* * *

After spending the afternoon at the Uzbekfilmlabaya recutting the noodle-house hit attempt scene to avoid showing Ali Mohammed's Air Jordans, Buzz took Charlie by taxi to the Chorsu bazaar. This old section of Tashkent was full of narrow dirt streets, low earth houses and mosques. Sitting near the entrance to the Juma Mosque were a number of women, dressed in burkas, hawking dried fruit, moldy kebabs, refrigerator parts, rusted steam irons and a number of other things Charlie couldn't imagine anyone wanting to buy.

"That's her, third from the left selling carpets. Her johns come out of the mosque, go over and pretend to haggle over a carpet. They settle on a price and meet ten minutes later at a ratty hotel two blocks from here."

"How much is she going to cost us?"

"Not much. She only charges two thousand som for a trick."

"Five dollars?"

"That's only if she takes the burka off. She keeps it on, it's a little pricier."

Buzz approached her and pretended to negotiate a price for a rug. Ten minutes later they were sitting in a *chaikhana* on Navoi Street drinking tea. Nadira Beg had hash-brown eyes and a hazy-sounding voice.

Charlie offered his one phrase of Uzbek, *"Assalom aleikum."*

"Waleikum assalom," she replied, lowering her eyes as befitted a woman covered head to toe in a black garment.

Buzz explained to her in Uzbek what the job entailed. There was some back-and-forth conversation, none of which Charlie understood. She spoke for a while in a tone that sounded to Charlie a little peremptory, then stopped abruptly and drank her tea.

"She wants fifty thousand som a day and her own hotel room," Buzz explained.

"No problem."

"Plus two hundred fifty grams of hash and her daily supplement of lithium."

"She's hired."

* * *

So Nadira Beg joined the cast of *Warlord* as Ishrat Khana. Over a fast food dinner at the Ardus FM Burger on Ataturk Street near Amir Timur Square, Charlie and Buzz brainstormed how to write her into the series. They would ease her in gradually. Back from Odessa, she would bide her time in her room. They'd redress Ali Mohammed's empty room to be Ishrat Khana's room, then cheat the doorway to make it look like she was exiting the warlord's wife's room. They'd wait till Izbul was out shooting camels to have her confront Grushenka and see what happened.

Back at the Intercontinental, Charlie was told by the desk clerk that there was a man waiting to see him in the bar. Men waiting to see you in bars in Tashkent generally meant that someone else wanted to squeeze you, and Charlie was about to pass when the desk clerk added that the man was an American, who had said that his business was urgent.

Charlie looked at Buzz, who shrugged and said, "The network's probably sent someone over here with more notes. It's been a long day. I'm going to go run a bath and smoke a pipe."

Standing at the bar in a brown checkered sports jacket and a shirt without a tie drinking scotch was Curt Groner. Charlie spotted the man immediately by his American body language. His countrymen never stood at a bar, they bellied up to it, holding their midsections against the wood and leaning over. The guy looked like an off-duty cop. Down to the sweat socks.

"Nice to know you." Curt Groner offered a pudgy hand. "What're you drinking?"

Charlie ordered an Oblomov and took out a cigarette. He was over a pack a day now.

"I caught your series the other night."

"You just fly in from the States?"

"No. I'm at the embassy here. Cultural officer. The Central Asian desk in Washington TiVo-ed the show and sent it over to me. Thought I'd get a kick out of it."

"Did you?"

"Yeah. It's terrific. Good stuff . . ."

The FBI check on Charlie Berns had come up dry. Except for some judgments against him for unpaid bills, there was nothing particularly hinky about the guy. Groner couldn't understand how a film producer from Los Angeles, who had never been to Central Asia before, let alone to Nukus and Dashoguz, could have put this thing together.

"I'm kind of curious," he said, "how you managed to contact Izbul Kharkov and get him to agree to this."

"I had a few contacts."

"People here?"

Charlie took a long sip of his beer and thought about how much information he wanted to provide to the cultural officer of the U.S.

embassy in Uzbekistan. He used Fenster's criterion: How much did this man need to know? And he decided that he didn't need to know much at all.

"Actually, the network put me in touch with him. They'd had an idea of doing a series like this ever since they did a documentary called *The Search for Genghis Khan's Grave*."

"You know that Kharkov is wanted by the Uzbek government?"

"I'm not really interested in the man's politics. The series is about his family life."

"I'm telling you this, Charlie, for your own good. Islam Karimov would love to put Izbul out of business. As soon as he finds out that you've got access to him, you may wind up getting a visit from his secret police."

"I see," said Charlie, recognizing the squeeze at last.

"You're an American citizen, of course, and we would do our best to protect you under those circumstances, but they have kind of a fuzzy notion of habeas corpus in this country."

"Well, I appreciate the word to the wise."

"I could tell you where the minefields are."

"Thanks."

"I could also help you with the show. Give you some logistical support."

"Sorry, Curt, but we don't have a role for an American in the show. Unless you want to be a visiting professor at the University of Tashkent Law School."

Charlie smiled, and Curt Groner smiled back, but it was an effort. He reached into his pocket, took out a card and handed it to Charlie.

"Hang on to this. You may need it." And with that, he turned and walked out of the bar. Charlie watched him leave, then stubbed out his cigarette.

Upstairs in his room, he called Fenster in Dashoguz and told him about the conversation with Curt Groner at the bar of the Intercontinental.

"What'd he want to know?"

"He wanted to know how I got access to Izbul."

"Jesus, you didn't tell him, did you?"

"No."

"This guy's an imposter. He doesn't work at the embassy. He's a rogue CIA asset who's sold himself to the Russians. He's stealing secrets from our people and sending them to Moscow."

"How come we're not shutting him down?"

"Because we're feeding him disinformation."

"No kidding?"

"I'm not kidding." There was a pause on the line, then Fenster said, in his solemn voice, "Charlie, I just gave you information that you didn't strictly need to know. So now you've got to be very careful."

"About what?"

"Getting captured. They torture you, you can give them information that would compromise the lives of a lot of people."

"Torture?"

"The Uzbeks just keep you in a cell with the light on all night. But the Russians attach electrodes to your testicles."

Charlie felt his scrotum tighten.

"You have any idea what it feels like to get two hundred volts shot through your balls?"

Charlie didn't even want to imagine what that felt like.

"You want, I can arrange to get you a cyanide cap. You tape it to the inside of one of your molars, pop it with your tongue . . ."

TWENTY-FIVE

The Return of Ishrat Khana

Of the 24.7 million viewers in America who tuned in to week four of *Warlord*, only seven of them understood Uzbek. One was drunk, two were in the country illegally, and, of the remaining four Uzbek-phones, only one took the trouble of writing to the network to point out the discrepancy between what the subtitles indicated that people were saying and what they were actually saying. This letter got forwarded to Norman by the network's Public Relations department.

Norman immediately got on the blower to Turkmenistan, Volga Boatmening Charlie in the production trailer, where he and Buzz were trying to write dialogue for one of Grushenka's blood-spitting soliloquies.

"Now and then we tweak a line or two, but essentially that's what the characters are saying," Charlie reassured him.

"That's what I figured. Probably just a crank letter."

"Could have been the guy was from a different region of Uzbekistan. There's a lot of different dialects. . . . By the way, I'm going to need another forty thousand euros," Charlie said, without a segue.

"What?"

"One of my local associate producers found out about the ratings."

"How the hell did he do that?"

"I have no idea. He wants two thousand five per episode extra. We've got three more to shoot in the original order and thirteen for the new one. That's sixteen times twenty-five hundred. Do the math."

"Charlie, they're already making noises about what this show's costing."

"How much are they shelling out for *Alias*?"

"I'll see what I can do . . ."

After Norman hung up, Charlie told Buzz about the Uzbek guy who had called the network to complain about the subtitles.

"Sooner or later someone's going to figure out that we're making them up. Some rival network is going to hire an Uzbek and blow the show out of the water."

"Bummer . . ."

They mulled over the problem, pitching ideas back and forth, until Charlie came up with an interesting solution.

"What if we fuck with the sound?"

"What do you mean?"

"Sort of like pixelating the picture. We get Ghofur to futz the audio track so that no recognizable language can be heard."

"We pixelate the sound instead of the picture?"

"Right."

"And if anybody claims it isn't Uzbek, we can always say that it's Karakalpak."

"Southern Karakalpak . . ."

"South-*eastern* Karakalpak . . ."

"Right. And who the fuck speaks *that* language in America?"

"Who the fuck speaks it in *Tashkent*?"

"Forget Tashkent, who the fuck speaks it in *Nukus* . . . ?"

And the two of them got the giggles, losing it right there in the production trailer. Dostyk looked over at them convulsed with laughter and shook his head, convinced that they were both stoned out of their gourds. Only one of them was. The other might as well have been.

* * *

They stashed Nadira Beg at the hotel in Dashoguz until they had time to transform Ali Mohammed's monastic cell into something more befitting the pampered wife of a powerful warlord. They used

237

photos from books they got at the Mustaqillik International Library in Tashkent and stole money from some of the more padded areas of the budget to buy furniture and artwork.

When they were finished, they had the Central Asian version of Carmella Soprano's boudoir in New Jersey: colorful carpets, damask wall hangings, heavy brass sconces, gossamer mosquito netting, brocade bedspread, throw pillows with Islamic homilies sewn on them.

The idea was to get some establishing footage of Nadira Beg, returned from Odessa to recover from her plastic surgery, in her bedroom, and cut it into the episodes that were not locked. They could tease the audience with the upcoming confrontation, building to the episode where she emerged.

To sneak the bipolar hooker-turned-actress into the compound, they would disguise her as a member of the crew, wearing Justyna's Polish hiking shorts and a Gapski Gdansk tee shirt. As soon as she was safely ensconced in her room, she could change back into the burka.

So late one night, when Izbul and Murv were out behind the soldiers' quarters setting off firecrackers, they slipped Nadira Beg into the compound and up into Ali Mohammed's room with a hamper containing food, her hash pipe and lithium, a cell phone and her burka.

She was told to spend a lot of time on the cell phone. When Nadira Beg asked whom she was supposed to talk to on her cell phone, Buzz told her to talk to her friends. When she said she didn't have any friends, he gave her the number of a phone sex service in Tashkent.

Under no circumstances was she to leave the room until they told her to. And if she needed anything, all she had to do was talk into one of the cameras camouflaged in the room. They told her to lock the door from the inside and returned to the production trailer, where they were trying to figure out the timing for Ishrat Khana's appearance when Norman Hudris made his daily call.

"How's it going, Charlie?"

"Fine, Norman. Listen, we've got some good news on the Ishrat Khana front. She's back from Odessa."

"Great. Fabulous . . ."

"We're going to start cutting footage of her into Episode Eight, teasing the audience with her coming out of her room to confront Izbul and Grushenka."

Then Norman Hudris asked the question that everyone else had been asking. "What's she doing in her room?"

"We're not entirely sure yet. She's spending a lot of time on the phone, so she could be talking to someone."

"Who?"

"My Uzbek translator thinks there's something fishy going on. She could be working for the Ukrainians."

"No shit."

"They might have turned her when she was in Odessa getting her lift. We'll keep you posted."

"What's she look like?"

"Hard to tell. She's wearing a burka."

"A what?"

"A kind of robe that covers her head to toe."

"Really? You can't like see her . . . body?"

"Just her eyes. She's recovering from her face-lift, remember?"

There was a moment of silence on the line, while Norman Hudris digested this information. Then, thinking positively, he said, "Well, I suppose it shrouds her in mystery. Sort of like Scheherazade. "

"Exactly."

"Listen, you need to have her drinking Pepsi."

"I thought you wanted me to mask the labels."

"We just made a product placement deal with Pepsico."

"So now you want to feature the Pepsi cans?"

"We need to see the product at least three times an episode. What type of shampoo does Ferghana use?"

"I don't know."

"They're working on a deal with Clairol. If they close it, we're going to want to see Clairol shampoo in her shower scenes. Okay?"

"How about Kalashnikov?"

"What?"

"You can make a deal with them too. Izbul uses one to shoot camels with."

* * *

When they were told of the preparations being made for Ishrat Khana's reemergence into Izbul Kharkov's life, the network's publicity machine sprung into action. To capitalize on the skewing to a female audience, the head of on-air publicity, Erica Einhoven, suggested putting the warlord's sequestered wife on a satellite feed for the morning news show and sending Barbara Walters over to do a heart-to-heart talk for a prime-time special.

Floyd thought sending Barbara over was a little premature. He wanted to wait until they had some idea what this woman looked like and whether she could carry on an articulate conversation. It was a big gamble devoting an hour of prime-time to an interview with someone nobody had ever seen.

So Erica Einhoven did an end-run around Floyd and confided the idea to Norman, who called Howard Draper on the secure line and asked him if he wanted to pitch it around the corner.

"Barbara Walters in Uzbekistan?"

"Actually, it's Turkmenistan."

"Who knows about this?"

"Just the Publicity department. They pitched it to me."

"Do they know you're talking to me?"

"No."

"Good."

"So will you get me an answer?"

"Affirmative."

Howard hung up and called over for fifteen minutes with Poindexter and North. He was awarded 1:15 to 1:30.

Thinking he would grab a patty melt at the commissary, Howard drove over at 12:15. The guard at the gate checked his drive-on pass in the computer and pulled a 1:15 appointment.

"How come you're here at 12:15 for a 1:15 appointment?" the man asked him, as his partner went through the trunk of Howard's El Dorado, checking for bombs under the spare tire.

"I thought I'd grab a bite in the commissary."

"The commissary's for people who work here."

"I work around the corner," Howard retorted, adding, "at your subsidiary."

"Don't you have eating facilities there?"

"Yes, we do, but I wanted to make sure I was on time."

"In case you got caught in traffic?"

His interview with Poindexter and North was just as disagreeable. Howard laid out the idea of bringing Barbara Walters over to interview Ishrat Khana, explaining that he was coming to them only because Floyd had killed it.

"What's the time window?" Poindexter asked.

"Two weeks, maybe three. Depends upon the scheduling. The idea is to air it right after we broadcast the episode where she emerges."

"Full hour, prime time?"

"Yes. Ten o'clock, the Thursday following the Wednesday when she comes on the show."

"Cost?"

"Round trip first-class airfare, hotel. With hair, makeup, camera crew—we're looking at eight to ten times that."

"It looks like a hundred, a hundred twenty to me," said North, eyeballing the numbers.

"Dead money," said Poindexter.

"It's going to stick out of the amort budget like a sore thumb," grunted his colleague.

"With a red flag coming out of its ass."

* * *

Now that they were sleeping together, if you could call it that, Jodie Jacobian and Norman Hudris spent quality phone time together every day. The fact that *Warlord* was a reality show and did without actors—at least as far as anybody but Charlie Berns and Buzz Bowden knew—did not deter the intrepid agent from pitching talent to the network executive.

"What about Courteney Cox?" she suggested.

"You don't even represent her," Norman pointed out.

"Yeah, but if I come to her with a job, maybe I could."

"Jodie, it's a reality show. We don't use actors."

"But you can stunt cast it—or even better, develop a spin-off, *Celebrity Warlord.* What do you think?"

"I don't know . . ."

241

"Jimmy Smits is looking for a new series. He'd be great. He even looks like one of his parents could have been born in Afghanistan."

"Uzbekistan . . ."

Tom Soaring Hawk buzzed Norman.

"Just a second," Norman said and made a mental note to add "Interrupting important conference call with frivolous demand" to the DOD file. He put Jodie Jacobian on hold and barked into the intercom.

"What?"

"It's six o'clock. If it's all right with you, I'm going to head off."

Norman considered telling him to stay, just to spite him, but then he had a better idea.

"Good night," he said, then returned to Jodie Jacobian.

"I'll think about Jimmy. Got to run."

He hung up and leaned back in his swivel chair, turning the idea over in his mind. He needed something a little bigger before going to Jasmine Liu to demand the head of his assistant. This just might be it.

* * *

At 6:10 that evening, as Norman Hudris was baiting the trap for Tom Soaring Hawk, Jodie Jacobian was laying a large slice of cheese right in the middle of her own trap for Brad Emprin. Sitting at her desk in her one-window office, she composed the following e-mail.

> Brad . . . I've heard your retinitis is aggravated by exposure to excessive sunlight. You'd probably do a lot better without getting it from two sides. My office has only one window. Even swap. No questions asked. I know where the euros are buried.

Then she downloaded it onto a diskette, deleted it from her computer's hard drive and left the office. She drove to an Internet café, uploaded the text, and sent it to *BEmprin@DBA.com* as an attachment to her anonymous e-mail, traceable to the Byte Size Internet Café at the corner of Wilshire and Roxbury.

By Friday she'd be in the corner office. With views of both Santa Monica and Wilshire, a wall safe and an extra hundred square feet.

TWENTY-SIX

At Home with the Kharkovs

Warlord's week five numbers held up across the board, with only a minimum of softening due to some nasty stunting on the part of the other networks. They pulled out all the stops in an effort to slow down the juggernaut that was running away with the Wednesday at ten o'clock time slot. CBS went with a two-hour *CSI: Toledo,* guest-starring Sigourney Weaver as a forensic accountant who murders a client with a poisoned Post-it Note. NBC burned one of their scheduled airings of *The Passion of the Christ.* Fox moved up their premiere of *Lingerie Models at Home.*

Though there were no letters from Uzbek speakers this week, there were complaints from other quarters. The ASPCA was concerned about the violence perpetrated against camels. The Korean Anti-Defamation League was unhappy with the "stereotypical depiction of Koreans" in the Korean noodle restaurant. The U.S. State Department, responding to formal complaints lodged by the government of Uzbekistan, was concerned about the depiction of one of its staunchest allies in Central Asia as a fourth-world country run by warlords.

Feeling that State's public relations people were getting blown off by the network's Viewer Relations people, the undersecretary for Central Asian Affairs called Floyd himself. When Floyd was in a screening and unable to take the call, the complaint moved up a level to the secretary of state himself, who lobbed a phone call into the CEO of the parent company's office.

With Poindexter and North on extension phones, the CEO of the parent company listened to the secretary of state explain his problem. The CEO of the parent company then told the secretary of state that he understood where he was coming from and would do his best to address the issue. The secretary of state thanked him. The CEO of the parent company told him he was welcome and wished him good luck in pacifying Iraq.

When he was off the phone with Washington, the CEO of the parent company asked Poindexter and North for their advice on how to handle the problem.

"Here's the way I see it," said Poindexter. "He doesn't work at the FCC, does he?"

"Right," North agreed. "So fuck him."

* * *

At 5:30 that afternoon, Norman Hudris walked out of his office with his car keys jangling and told Tom Soaring Hawk that he was leaving early and that he could put the phones on voice mail and take off. Then Norman turned left down the hall, past the elevator, and entered the men's room. He spent several minutes in a closed toilet stall, alphabetizing the credit cards in his wallet, then exited and returned to his office to find, as he had expected, his assistant gone.

He sat down at Tom Soaring Hawk's anally neat desk and opened the top drawer, in which he knew from experience he would find his assistant's personal hygiene kit. Norman extracted the 1,000 euros that had arrived in the mail a few days ago from the envelope in his jacket pocket and carefully placed them beneath Tom Soaring Hawk's mouthwash and deodorant.

Then Norman took the phones off voice mail and dialed Jasmine Liu's extension.

"Jasmine, hi. This is Norm Hudris. I wonder if you could stop by my office."

"All right if I come by on my way out at six?"

"Actually, this is kind of time sensitive."

"Fifteen minutes is going to make a difference?"

"Yes."

Seven minutes later, at 5:52, Jasmine Liu entered Norman's office to find Norman sitting at his assistant's desk.

"What is it, Norman?" the ABCD Human Resources chief said irritably, unhappy at being summoned to appear immediately by someone in a parallel position of authority to hers.

"Thank you for coming, Jasmine. Do you know what time it is?"

She looked at the wall clock pointedly and nodded curtly.

"You'll notice that my assistant is not at his desk."

"Where is he?"

"Gone. His work hours are nine to six, with an hour for lunch. He has been consistently leaving without asking permission and without even putting the phones on voice mail."

"Have you spoken to him about this?"

"Several times. And that's not the only problem. This week he opened a letter that was addressed to me and marked 'Personal and Confidential.'"

"Assistants open their superiors' mail all the time. He probably just made a mistake."

"These are not isolated incidents. I've been keeping a file on his systematic dereliction of duty."

"Send it over. I'll take a look at it. Is that all?"

"I wish it were. Here, take a look at this."

As he said this, he opened Tom Soaring Hawk's desk drawer and gestured for her to look inside it.

"It's an invasion of an employee's right of privacy to go into his or her personal belongings."

"Not if there is a clear and present danger of criminal activity being perpetrated."

"What are you talking about?"

"Take a look." He gestured once more to the open desk drawer. Jasmine Liu moved slowly around the desk and bent down to see what was in the drawer.

"It's his toilet articles," she said.

"Take a look underneath. There's money."

"We have no policy against an employee keeping money in his or her desk drawer."

"What type of money is it?"

"I don't know. It looks foreign."

"It's euros, Jasmine. What would an employee of this division be doing with euros in his desk drawer?"

245

"Perhaps he's planning a trip to Europe."

"You may not be aware of this, but the *Warlord* project, which comes out of this division, is funded in euros. Doesn't it seem a little too coincidental that an assistant has one thousand euros in his desk drawer?"

"How do you know how much is there?"

"Because I counted."

"You went into his desk drawer without his permission?"

"I was looking for a paperclip. For chrissakes, Jasmine, you're making this seem like I'm the one out of line here."

"You are. You violated his right of privacy."

"I needed a goddamn paperclip!"

"You go next door and ask someone else. You don't open an assistant's drawer."

Norman took a deep breath and said, very slowly, "What if I had found an automatic weapon in there?"

"Then you would have reported it to Security, I should hope."

She stood there looking blankly at him. It was a similar look to the one he got from Tom Soaring Hawk—vapid and challenging at the same time. They would make a good couple, the two of them. Affirmative action in action.

After a moment of this weaponless Mexican standoff, she said, "Listen, Norman, I'll turn my back on this infraction, since it wasn't reported to me by Mr. Soaring Hawk himself. But keep in mind that all employees of this company have the same right to privacy."

Norman nodded slowly, not trusting himself to say anything.

"By the way, how're the sensitivity training seminars going?"

"Terrific."

"How many do you have left?"

"One."

"Good. I'm glad we took care of this."

* * *

When Barbara Walters decided to pass on flying to Uzbekistan to interview Ishrat Khana, even after the money had been cleared around the corner by Poindexter and North, the network had to make a tough call. Standing by ready to take her place was Carla Jann from *Entertainment Tonight*. Did they give the competition access to the set of their show and suffer the ratings hit that their own early prime-time lead-ins *Jeopardy* and *Wheel of Fortune* would take in exchange for seven million to ten million eyeballs' worth of free publicity for their ten o'clock Wednesday show?

Floyd ran a cost-benefit analysis and came up heads. In order to prepare the logistics of a set visit, he told Kara Kotch to contact their show runner in Uzbekistan directly, bypassing Norman Hudris, who, Floyd was beginning to think, was out to lunch. Both literally and figuratively.

"Every time I call him, his assistant says that he's out to lunch."

At the moment, Norman Hudris was, in fact, out to lunch. He and Howard Draper were at the Hercules Taverna in Glendale, eating *arni skaras* and sharing a half bottle of Liatiko, and discussing whether they wanted to get closer in or further out of the loop. *Warlord* was a loose cannon. A very hot loose cannon at the moment, but there was no telling which way the barrel was pointed.

"If it stays north, they're going to take all the credit," Howard said.

"I have documentation of our role in the development of the show."

"Which I've never seen."

"Which you didn't want to see."

"Be that as it may . . ."

"I can go to the press and tell the whole story, blow the skunkworks out of the water."

"Why the hell would you do that?"

"To protect my position."

"I wouldn't try it, Norman. You'd wind up in the Anaheim River chained to a slab of cement. Like Jimmy Hoffa. They'd never find your body . . ."

While this conversation was going on, Kara Kotch called the figuratively and literally out-to-lunch Norman Hudris's assistant and got the cell phone number of *Warlord*'s show runner.

"What's the time difference there?" she asked Tom Soaring Hawk.

"The time difference between there and where?" the assistant asked.

"Between here and Uzbekistan."

"He's not in Uzbekistan."

"I beg your pardon?"

"Charlie Berns is not in Uzbekistan."

"Where is he?"

"He's in Turkmenistan."

"I see. And what is the time difference there?"

"The same as in Uzbekistan?"

"Which is . . . ?"

"Thirteen hours."

"Thank you," she said, in a clipped tone. What were they putting in the water over in that division?

She added thirteen hours and determined that it was 2:00 a.m. in Turkmenistan. Nevertheless, she decided to call and leave her home number and a message on his voice mail to call her first thing in the morning his time, which would be evening her time in Tuloca Lake.

Knowing that disaster could strike at any moment, Charlie Berns always kept his cell phone switched on at his bedside. He had been asleep for only an hour—a deep, dreamless sleep after an exhausting day shooting Akbar riding his dirt bike in the hills around Dashoguz—when "The Volga Boatmen" dragged him back to the surface.

"What?" he growled into the phone.

"Oh, is that you, Charlie?"

"Who's this?"

"Kara Kotch at ABC in Burbank."

Who the hell gave *her* his number? And what was she doing calling him at 2:00 in the morning?

"Sorry to wake you. I was expecting to get your machine and leave a message."

"What can I do for you?" he uttered, trying to stuff a little civility into his voice. His head pounded—the onset of a vodka hangover, courtesy of Stalin, who earlier that evening at the hotel bar kept buying him drinks and insisting that he drink them.

"We'd like to arrange access to the set for some publicity."

"Publicity?"

"Yes. *ET* is interested in sending a crew over there to do the show.

It'd be fabulous publicity. They have a prime-time access audience of seven million."

"Uh . . . Karen . . ."

"Kara."

"Kara, I'm not sure that's such a good idea."

"Why not?"

"This is kind of a special set. It's a little . . . odd . . ."

"That's what makes it a good story. The odder the better. Chuck . . ."

"It's Charlie . . ."

"Charlie, people are very interested in the Kharkovs. They want to meet Izbul and Grushenka, see Ishrat Khana's room, visit Ali Mohammed in law school, talk to Ferghana and Akbar. It would be a slice of life—the Kharkovs at home."

"Listen, Izbul's a little jumpy now. You know, because of the truck bomb attack and the pressure from the Uzbeks . . . so this probably is not a good time . . ."

"But that's the whole point. They could film you filming all that, kind of a behind-the-scenes-type of thing."

"I have to tell you, they could be in serious jeopardy. They fire real bullets around here."

"That's great. They'll get a hell of a tune-in . . . *ET Goes to War,* something like that . . ."

"There're no first-class hotels or places to eat . . ."

"I'll have the field producer call you."

TWENTY-SEVEN

ET Goes to War

With the amazing success of *Warlord,* there was nothing but blue skies in Burbank. The company started cutting licensing deals hand over foot with international TV networks to produce their own versions of the smash reality show. The Russians got busy searching for an appropriate warlord in Chechnya; the French scoured Algeria for a radical Islamic terrorist chieftain; the Italians were in Yemen looking for a telegenic antigovernment sheik.

And as the ratings of the U.S version kept climbing, the marketing people were working night and day to capitalize on it. There was a *Warlord* Web site that got more hits than the biggest porno sites. The chat rooms were abuzz with opinions and theories about the Kharkovs. All over the talk-radio dial people were weighing in for and against the show. The religious right condemned it as godless and violent, while the nonreligious right thought it demonstrated the ineffectiveness of the gutless American foreign policy in the region. The gun lobby claimed the show supported the Second Amendment right of citizens to bear arms in the face of a weak central government. The feminists thought it was an egregious example of male-dominated culture, whereas the gay wing of the feminists was delighted by the relationship between Ferghana and Justyna. The shower scenes were taped off the air and passed around avidly in lesbian circles.

The other networks scrambled to counterprogram. Wednesday night at ten was becoming Death Valley for them. CBS merely surrendered the hour and used the time slot to burn off unmade pilots. *Law and Order: ECD* was getting beaten up so badly that NBC moved it and threw reruns of *Ed* in its place. Fox cut together the best moments of the most sensational tabloid news coverage it had in its archive—the O. J. Simpson white Bronco chase down the San Diego Freeway, Princess Di's car wreck, the Janet Jackson breast flash—and got a 0.2 rating, a tenth of a point below *Insulating Your Garage* on the Home Improvement Channel.

*   *   *

Langley pouched the TiVo-ed Episode 5 of *Warlord* to Curt Groner in Tashkent with an encrypted note that read: Recognize the Company "Handler"?

The CIA undercover agent put the videocassette into the VCR and watched the entire episode, pausing the machine at one point, then advancing frame by frame through a grainy scene behind a double-wide trailer outside the warlord's compound where Izbul Kharkov was having a conversation with a man who was identified in the subtitles as an intelligence asset named Herbert Karp. Curt Groner knew this man not as Herbert Karp, but as Kermit Fenster, aka Vernon Gough, aka Dwight Halloran.

The undercover CIA agent turned off the VCR, sat back on his poorly oiled Soviet-era swivel chair, and expelled a jet of stomach gas. Something was going on out there over the Turkmenistan border, something that Fenster-Halloran-Gough was involved in. And anything that *he* was involved in had to be hinky. The question was, What did Charlie Berns know? Or, even more interestingly, did the ABC television network and its parent company have any idea what they were sending into America's homes every Wednesday night at 10:00 p.m.?

Before he brought Langley in on this, however, he needed more information. He would go out there himself and find out what the hell was going on.

Curt Groner went to see the embassy's deputy chief of mission, Ira Prodny, a career diplomat who was so unwired at State that he wound up in Tashkent and had no idea that his cultural officer was CIA. He told Prodny that he was going to Nukus to give a talk on Ralph Waldo Emerson for the Western Uzbekistan World Civics Club. Then he packed his .38 Glock, gassed up the Land Rover and prepared to head west.

* * *

Meanwhile *ET*'s top correspondent, Carla Jann, her field producer Ted, her makeup person Esmeralda, her hair person Monte, her personal assistant Jewel, as well as a camera operator, a gaffer, and a soundman were also making preparations to visit the set of *Warlord*. They would be flying to Tashkent, then taking an Uzbekistan Airways 737 to Nukus, from where they would be met by a driver from the *Warlord* production office to take them to the set.

After Charlie Berns had balked at Kara Kotch's request to give the *ET* crew access to the set, he had gotten a phone call from a man who introduced himself as the "assistant to the CEO of the company that was paying his salary." The conversation had been brief and unequivocal.

The man had told him that a film crew from *Entertainment Tonight* would be on his set Monday and that he was expected to grant them access to interviews with anyone they wanted to talk to.

When Charlie had tried to explain the difficulties the crew would face, as he had done with Kara Kotch, the "assistant to the CEO of the company that was paying his salary" told him to overcome those difficulties.

So in the midst of all his other problems, Charlie would have to devote time and resources to dealing with eight Americans who would be soon arriving on his set. Izbul, of course, was delighted. He was a big fan of *ET*.

"Sending girl with big tit?"

"I don't know, Izbul."

"Mary Hartman. Nice rack."

Grushenka too was enthusiastic about being on American tabloid TV. Still under the impression that this was a fictional series, she had been walking around stricken by consumption, coughing fake blood into a handkerchief and delivering a series of deathbed soliloquies directly to camera, which Charlie and Buzz had transformed into lamentations about her AIDS symptoms.

Carla Jann had asked to interview Ali Mohammed at law school when they arrived in Tashkent. Charlie had told her that Izbul's son was on late spring break in Yalta on the Black Sea. The intrepid correspondent then suggested flying to Tashkent via Yalta. Charlie managed to dissuade her only by explaining that Izbul's son was engaged in highly sensitive undercover work for the Uzbek Anti-Terrorist Commando and that interviewing Ali Mohammed would not only blow the young man's cover but also compromise the series story line by giving the audience information they wouldn't be getting till Episode 10.

"I must impress upon you how delicate the information I just gave you is," he had told her in a grave voice. "If it gets out, not only is the series in trouble, but it would jeopardize the life of Izbul's son. And you don't want to be responsible for that, do you?"

"What about Ishrat Khana? Can we talk to her?"

Charlie had been less successful tap dancing around that one. He had told Carla Jann that although Ishrat Khana was back from Odessa, her plastic surgery scars hadn't healed yet and she didn't want to be on camera.

Ten minutes later Charlie had received another phone call from the "assistant to the CEO of the company that was paying his salary" and told to make sure that the ET crew had access to Ishrat Khana.

Now that they had been ordered to reveal Ishrat Khana to America, in an interview with Carla Jann that would play during prime-time access on three hundred syndicated TV stations, Charlie and Buzz had to figure out how to bring Nadira Beg out of the room as Ishrat Khana. And they had only six days' lead time before the ET crew showed up.

They game-planned scenarios, pacing back and forth in the production trailer.

"All right. Izbul kicks her out of the compound," Buzz hypothesized, "which means that Grushenka emerges victorious in the love triangle, right?"

"If he was going to throw her out, wouldn't he have already done it?"

"Okay, so we have her walk into the bedroom and confront Grushenka . . ."

"Who's dying of AIDS."

"So Ishrat Khana cuts her some slack . . ."

"She's not going to cut her any slack. Why should she? She's been fucking her husband while she was going under the knife in Odessa."

"How long has she back from Odessa?"

"I forgot."

"How long has Nadira Beg been in the room?"

"A week . . . but we haven't shipped any of the episodes we've cut her into yet . . ."

The logistics were getting more and more confusing as their fictional re-creation of the warlord's life diverged more and more from what was actually happening. Buzz stopped pacing, scratched his head, flashed a pained smile that indicated a possible solution.

"Why don't we just let her out? See what happens."

"When?"

"When *ET* shows up. We'll tell her to come out and talk to the nice people from America."

"She's a bipolar hash-addicted hooker."

"Who doesn't speak a word of English. I'll translate and make it up as I go along."

"So whatever happens, happens."

"Yeah. We'll just film it. I mean, this *is* a reality show, isn't it? We'll have a little reality for a change."

* * *

Earlier that day an official from the United States Trade Representative's Office had a meeting with Turkmenistan's minister of foreign affairs in the ministry's white marble neo-Roman monolith on Ulitsa Schevchenko in downtown Ashgabat. The purpose of the meeting was to enlist the Turkmen government's help with a problem that was becoming more and more prevalent throughout Asia, causing loss of revenue and aggravating the U.S. balance of payments deficit. The quid pro quo for this assistance was the renewal of Turkmenistan's most favored nations trading status with the United States.

Negotiations were painstaking. The Turkmen minister, Vepar Azadi, the nephew of Turkmenistan's president, Saparmurat Niyazov, had no authority beyond leaving the room every twenty minutes to confer with his uncle by cell phone.

For her part, the USTR official, Henrietta Bing, had a very focused agenda. She wanted the Turkmen government to issue a search warrant for the premises of a certain warlord who was currently eluding Uzbek authorities by hiding out in a small city in the north of Turkmenistan. In addition to the search warrant, she wanted Azadi to dispatch the one hundred troops it would take to enforce it.

Vepar Azadi said that they would have to have a magistrate from Turkmenistan's Supreme Court issue the warrant. Henrietta Bing pointed out, as diplomatically as possible, that the minister's uncle, President Niyazov, rarely bothered to consult his cabinet, let alone the courts, in governing the country. So why would he bother with such procedural niceties now?

The minister went out of the room again to confer with his uncle and returned with a proposal to provide the troops and the warrant if their cherished ally could provide them with fifty Bradley Fighting Vehicles to help them defend their border with Iran.

It took another hour for Henrietta Bing to bargain the minister down to a six BFVs, $3 million in agricultural credits and a state visit for President Niyazov sometime next year, which would include a Major League Baseball game and a visit to Disney World. After the deal was reached, they toasted each other with Stolichnaya and pledged mutual support in the fight against international terrorism, drug trafficking and the proliferation of nuclear weapons.

* * *

At approximately the same time that the USTR official was cutting a deal with the Turkmen minister of foreign affairs to conduct an armed search of Izbul's compound in Dashoguz, the warlord's estranged son, Ali Mohammed, was in Samarkand organizing a commando of Taliban fighters to shut down the television program that was being filmed about his father and that was a tool of American secular imperialism as well as a sacrilege. In spite of his visit to the producer of the television show, his cameras were continuing to record life at the compound and by so doing to spew forth lies and profanity.

Bootlegged copies of the series had found their way back to Central Asia and were shown in underground *chaikhanas* throughout the region, causing him great personal embarrassment and loss of face. His Taliban comrades called him "the lawyer," in reference to his having run away from this father's home to go to the nonexistent University of Tashkent Law School.

Ali Mohammed decided that there was no alternative but to terminate the show and anyone connected to it. This time he wouldn't screw up the job. He'd toss the grenade, not bounce it.

* * *

After watching *The Bachelor* one night, Gary Bowden, an accountant for a Snap-on Tools distributor in Boulder, Colorado, happened to stay tuned to the local ABC affiliate to catch a little of the new reality series that everyone at the office was talking about. After five minutes of strange dialogue between a man wearing a fleece vest over a flannel shirt, leather pants, and an embroidered skullcap and another man who looked like a Moslem version of a bar bouncer, the action cut away to a steam-clouded shower where two women were lathering each other up. This soft-core porn retained his attention for a while until they cut to a picture of what looked like a university somewhere in the Middle East and a voice-over in a strange language that was translated by subtitles as the voice of a son writing a letter home to his sister about his law school courses.

Gary Bowden was about to zap this with his remote and check out *Law and Order: ECD,* when they cut away again to a scene in which a group of men were playing blackjack in a large ornate room. This bizarre Central Asian private casino was populated by men in skullcaps with automatic weapons slung over their shoulders. His finger moved again to the remote button and was just about to press it when he saw something that stopped him cold. There in the back of the casino a pudgy teenage kid wearing an Eminem tee shirt was playing Ping-Pong with a young western-looking man in his early twenties with long hair and cowboy boots.

It couldn't be. His son was a Peace Corps volunteer in Samarkand teaching the Uzbeks how to build septic tanks, not a goon working for a warlord in Turkmenistan. Moving closer to the TV set, Gary Bowden waited for a close-up shot of the Ping-Pong player, and when it filled the screen he was able to make out the undeniable features of his younger son, Barrett.

First thing the following morning Gary Bowden got on the phone with Peace Corps headquarters in Washington and told someone in

Home Country Relations what he had seen. The woman he spoke to assured him that it was impossible. Peace Corps volunteers were not engaged in the kind of criminal activity that was portrayed in the TV show that was sweeping America. But, she promised, she would contact the local Peace Corps representative in Tashkent and make sure that Barrett Bowden was safe and sound and at his post in Samarkand.

As it turned out, the local Peace Corps rep, Robert "Bob" Ladl, hadn't seen the volunteer stationed in Samarkand for more than six months. He told the Home Country Relations person that he would check it out and get back to her. Robert "Bob" Ladl phoned the Uzbek Department of Public Works's liaison person in Samarkand and learned that six months ago Barrett Bowden had told him that he had been transferred to Dzhizak and left town.

Since there was no Peace Corps mission in Dzhizak, the local Peace Corps rep had to report back to Washington that Barrett Bowden was apparently AWOL. Washington told him to do everything in his power to find him and bring him safely back.

So Robert "Bob" Ladl got into *his* Land Rover and headed west, joining the CIA, the crew of *Entertainment Tonight*, a deputy from the USTR's office, one hundred crack Turkmen soldiers, and a Taliban commando of battle-scarred Afghan war veterans, all preparing to descend on Izbul Kharkov's compound in Dashoguz at about the same time.

Episode 9 of *Warlord* was shaping up nicely.

TWENTY-EIGHT

Ishrat Khana Dishes

"Can you fucking *believe* it? They booked *ET* to do a segment on *Warlord*. Kara went around me and *directly* to Charlie."

"Really?"

"It's *my* goddamn show. *I* developed it. *I* was the one who took the pitch, structured the deal, got the money, and now *I'm* out of the fucking loop . . ."

Jodie Jacobian listened to Norman Hudris whining with only half her attention. The other half was directed toward a brochure of paint samples for the redecoration of her new office. *When* she got into it. Although Brad Emprin had not yet approached her in response to her anonymous e-mail, she was convinced it was only a matter of time.

"You think I should hire a publicist to handle this? They cost a lot of money. Forty-five hundred, five grand a month for the cheap ones. I've got some cash-flow concerns at the moment. I've got a balloon payment coming up . . ."

Jodie Jacobian was no longer listening. Brad Emprin had just walked into her office. She covered the paint sample brochure with a script and looked up at the overdressed agent.

"Hey, what's up?"

Norman thought she was talking to him and said, "What do you mean, *what's up*? I've been telling you. They're keeping me out of the loop on *Warlord* . . ."

"Some of the best loops are the ones you're not in," Jodie Jacobian responded, oracularly, and hung up.

"Sit down. What's going on?" she said to Brad Emprin.

Brad Emprin did not sit down. He knew that all the agents' chairs at DBA were elevated to give them a height advantage over the people seated across their desks, affording the person behind the desk a subliminal power edge.

"We can do this either of two ways," said Brad Emprin, looking down at Jodie Jacobian.

"Do what?"

"Handle this negotiation. We can do it in code or we can do it out front."

Jodie Jacobian was five foot seven. Still, because he was standing, she was looking up at the five-foot-six-inch agent instead of down at him. She didn't like the power dynamic in the room. For all she knew, he could be wearing a wire.

"Let's do code."

"Okay. The English muffins are no longer in my possession. The accounting is buried so deep you couldn't find it with a Geiger counter. And I have downloaded copies of a certain extortionate e-mail on three different diskettes. One is in my wall safe, one is in the locked glove compartment of my car. And the third is in my safe-deposit box."

Over the years as an agent Jodie Jacobian had done her best to learn to detect the tells in people's voices when the bullshit was coming at her over the phone. Now she had it in front of her, and she wasn't getting a clear read.

"Extortion is a crime in this state," he said.

"So is embezzlement," she retorted.

"Only if you can prove it."

Believing he had established his leverage, Brad Emprin sat down, crossed one leg over the other, careful to preserve the crease in his chamomile-colored Prada trousers, revealing the bone china Nicole Farhi silk socks protruding from the double cream Roberto Cavalli suede loafers. Jodie Jacobian eyeballed the socks alone at fifty bucks, the shoes at four-fifty, on the inside, maybe six.

"Moving right along . . ." he said, pausing for a moment to let her twist in the wind before cutting to the chase. "Recently a certain agent in this agency took a trip to Cancún to visit the set of a client filming there. As it turns out, the client was filming in Vera Cruz, a distance of about seven hundred miles, as the crow flies, and the crow doesn't fly there. Mexicana flies there, and you have to make connections in Mexico City."

There was no point looking for the tell. He had her nailed to the wall. Three months ago she had extended a visit to a client working in Vera Cruz into a three-day holiday in Cancún with a hedge fund operator from Palos Verdes and written the whole thing off on her DBA expense account, including the two new bathing suits, the jade earrings and the hand-woven serape. She thought she had buried that one beneath Geiger counter range, but if this putz could dig it up, any half-competent auditor could.

She got up and walked melodramatically to her solitary window. The view was of a particularly unappetizing stretch of Santa Monica Boulevard—a Starbucks, a Kinko's, a dry cleaner's and a Middle Eastern export bank that nobody ever went into or came out of. She had been hoping to trade this in for the double exposure and the view onto Wilshire that looked across to Rodeo Drive and the Beverly Wilshire. She had already decided on caravan beige for the corner office's walls. What a fucking shame . . .

Slowly she turned back away and faced him. He was sitting on the chair blowing his nose into a monogrammed handkerchief.

"Your counter?"

"I think we have a push on the English muffins versus the Mexican hat dance."

"Embezzlement is a little heavier that padding an expense account."

"I don't know. You'd have to add up the hotel room, restaurant, bar charges and god know what else in Cancun. Could easily be more that a thousand or so . . . English muffins."

He had worked out the numbers. She was way over a grand on the bogus expense account. She waited a few more moments, to maintain a little dignity.

"All right, fine. We're even. That's it. Good-bye."

"We're not quite finished."

He was really pushing it now. She had half a mind to blow the deal and take him down with her. She would land on her feet. There had been some feelers out from CAA. They had offices there with two windows.

"*What?*"

"Reparations."

"What do you mean, reparations?"

"You started the war, you got to pay for it. Like the Treaty of Versailles."

"For chrissakes, Brad, what are you talking about?"

"I want your parking space."

"You're fucking kidding?"

"Nope."

Jodie Jacobian had the third-best parking space in the entire agency, three slots from the elevators. She had gotten it when one of the partners died and she simply painted her name over his before anyone else could claim it.

"You really are a shithead, you know that?"

"That's the highest form of compliment you can give an agent." He smiled and got up again. "Are we closed?"

"Fuck you!"

"I'll assume that means yes," he replied.

As he walked out of the office she could hear his balls clanging.

*　*　*

After his ploy to get Tom Soaring Hawk fired had blown up in his face, Norman Hudris reclaimed the 1,000 euros from his assistant's desk drawer and was debating whether he should return them anonymously to Brad Emprin or treat himself to a weekend in Vegas.

God knows he could use a little vacation. Even though Dr. Klezmer had reported that his prostate biopsy was negative, Norman wasn't entirely convinced he was out of the woods. The needle could have hit the good side of the gland. You never knew—a couple of centimeters away there could be an incipient malignant tumor that could be in his lymph nodes by Labor Day.

Nor were things going well with Jodie Jacobian. They hadn't had sex in three weeks. She told him that she had a yeast infection, but he suspected it was a pretext. So the car was back up on blocks, which, he conjectured, was responsible for the first nagging symptoms of the recurrence of his chronic prostatitis.

Nor was he dealing well with being marginalized on *Warlord*. Now that the show was a hit, it was as if the division didn't even exist. He hadn't even been consulted about the decision to send *ET* to the set. Kara Kotch had developed her own back-door channel to Charlie Berns.

So he was a little surprised, and not at all displeased, when Tom Soaring Hawk buzzed him to say that Charlie Berns was on line one.

"Charlie, how're you doing?"

"I'd be better if I didn't have eight Americans about to walk on my set."

"I did everything I could to stop it."

"Who's going to edit this footage they're shooting?"

"They are. It's their show."

"The network has no editorial control?"

"No. Why?"

"There's some stuff that shouldn't be seen by the public."

"Like what?"

"If I told you, Norman, I'd have to have you killed."

"Very funny, Charlie."

"I'm not being funny. Do me a favor, if anyone from the CIA contacts the network, let me know."

"The CIA?"

"Yeah."

"What do *they* want?"

"If I knew, I wouldn't be calling you to ask you to call me if they call you, would I? Don't fuck around, Norman, I have access to professional assassins over here. For two grand I can have you whacked. I could take the money out of the amort budget, and no one would ever know."

Before Norman could say anything, the line went dead.

* * *

Charlie heard the cars from Nukus coming through the gate of the compound. The two BMWs he had sent to the airport to transport Carla Jann arrived in a parade of dust. Izbul came out of his office wearing his best quilted robe and polished boots. He doffed his skullcap to the perky blonde getting out of one of the Beemers.

"Welcome, Mary Hartman, to my home."

Carla Jann offered her hand and explained that she was not Mary Hart, the co-anchor, but Carla Jann, the correspondent.

"Be it so."

Izbul's men formed an honor guard around the two of them, the barrels of their Kalashnikovs glinting in the midday sun.

"I feel like I already know you, Mr. Kharkov. From the TV show."

"Fuckink A."

"And this must be Merv," she said, smiling at Murv, who was standing at Izbul's side. Not understanding a word of English, Murv did not smile back. Instead his eyes scoured the crew for hidden weapons, while his men's eyes were all over Carla Jann and her personal assistant Jewel, a petite brunette in tight jeans and a revealing tee shirt.

Charlie welcomed the *ET* correspondent to the set of *Warlord.*

"It's a pleasure to be here," she replied, and then she introduced her crew, and everyone had to shake hands with everyone else. It took several minutes before they were able to go inside for Diet Pepsis and candied dates.

Sitting in Izbul's office in overstuffed armchairs, they made conversation in fits and starts as Carla Jann explained that she intended to be as unobtrusive as possible.

"Just pretend I'm a fly on the wall," she insisted.

"No flies on wall here," Izbul responded, defensively. "I see fly on wall, I cut it new one." He pretended to fire one of his pistols at an imaginary fly on the wall.

"What I mean is, ignore us. Just go about your business as if we weren't here. We'll try to be as unobtrusive as possible."

"Bada bink."

"So . . . maybe we ought to start setting up some interviews . . ."

Charlie quickly turned to Carla Jann and said, "I've got the whole interview schedule worked out in my office. Why don't we go over there and have a look, okay?"

And he was on his feet, ushering Carla Jann and Jewel out of the office before the delicate subject of Ishrat Khana came up.

On his way to the production trailer with the two women and the field producer, Charlie explained the tenuous domestic relations between Izbul and Ishrat Khana.

"She's back from Odessa, isn't she?"

"Yes. But they haven't seen each other yet. You see, she knows about Grushenka and she's pissed at Izbul. We don't know what's going to happen."

"What about Grushenka? Can we interview her?"

"If you want to expose yourself to infection."

"I thought she had AIDS. You can't get AIDS talking to someone."

"Unfortunately, her AIDS has lowered her resistance to other illnesses, and she's come down with a bad case of tick-borne encephalitis. She's coughing up blood and sending airborne bacteria into the air. Maybe if you were thirty feet away and wore a surgical mask . . ."

"Really?"

"Did you get inoculated against tick-borne encephalitis?"

"They said we didn't need it unless we were going to go trekking."

"Then I wouldn't risk it. Anyway, here's the deal with Ishrat Khana. We're going to do it in her room so that Izbul doesn't have to see her. There's no telling what he'll do if he sees you with her. The man's a psychopath."

Jewel's features whitened. "Maybe, we should just get some B-roll and do a stand-up with you describing the compound," the personal assistant offered.

"We've already promo-ed the interview with Ishrat Khana."

"Don't worry. He probably won't shoot all of us. At least not until we do his interview," Charlie said with a straight face. He was actually starting to enjoy himself.

* * *

Fifteen minutes later they were in the re-dressed Ali Mohammed's room, where the *ET* crew set up lights and Carla Jann's hair and wardrobe people prepped her for the interview.

Buzz had taken Nadira Beg into Akbar's room down the hall to give her a pipe of hash to mellow her out. She had bottomed out on the lithium and had been bouncing off the floor and on her way back up the elevator toward a manic high. This was an interview, he explained to her, conducted by UNESCO to study Uzbek women's views on domestic and family issues. He told her to speak quickly and with conviction and to rely on him for the translation.

Buzz and Charlie had been up half the night projecting the new story line, which would be leaked during the *ET* interview. They had decided to shift Ishrat Khana a bit more in the direction of empowerment and self-esteem, backing her away a shade from Tammy Wynette but not far enough to have her come off as Gloria Steinem.

When Esmeralda and Monte, Carla Jann's makeup and hair people, were satisfied that the correspondent was camera-ready, Charlie and Buzz went to get Nadira Beg. They walked into Akbar's room and saw that she had put some eye makeup on, highlighting pupils wide enough to drive a truck through.

"Buzz, she's stoned."

"Believe me, this is better than manic. Without it she could start to speed rap."

"You explained everything to her?"

"More or less."

The two of them took Nadira Beg down the hall and into the room with the *ET* crew and introduced her.

"What a pleasure to meet you," Carla Jann said with her big prime-time access smile.

A little slow on the uptake even when she wasn't stoned, Nadira Beg didn't reply until Buzz repeated the greeting in Uzbek. Then she said, "Welcome, UNESCO, to my home," which Buzz translated as, "It is my pleasure."

"May I call you Ishrat?"

Nadira Beg shrugged at that one, and Buzz decided it was an appropriate answer.

The two women took their seats. Carla Jann chattered away as the crew attached the lavaliere mikes and dabbed a little more powder on the correspondent's face. There was nothing they could do with Nadira Beg's face, hidden, as it was, behind the burka in order to hide the signs of her recent plastic surgery.

The first question that Carla Jann asked when they were rolling was, "So, how are you feeling?"

"Why shouldn't I be feeling fine?" Nadira Beg responded after Buzz translated the question.

"Very well, considering that I had recent surgery," Buzz translated the answer.

"You know, Ishrat, our viewers are interested in your plastic surgery. Tell us why you decided to get the work done."

"What work would I do?" she replied. "I'm a carpet merchant in Tashkent. My health isn't good. Sometimes I feel very blue. Medication is expensive in Uzbekistan, so I have to buy it on the black market, so to make ends meet I do business on the side having sex with men near the Juma Mosque."

Buzz translated this response as, "A woman has to choose between making herself attractive to her man and having enough self-esteem to expect him to love her even as she gets older and her body begins to deteriorate."

"So you want to fight for your man?"

"I wouldn't lift a finger for that pig." Nadira Beg nearly spit on the floor.

"I believe that, for better or for worse, a woman should stand by her man," Buzz translated.

As Charlie stood behind the *ET* camera and watched this high-wire act, Dostyk came into the room and whispered to Charlie that there was an American at the main gate of the compound trying to get in to see him. Murv's guards were threatening to shoot him on the spot.

Charlie hurried out of the room and downstairs to the gate, where he found Curt Groner in a Land Rover surrounded by a dozen men aiming assault rifles at him. The easiest thing to do would be to walk away and let Izbul make camel food out of him. But Charlie wasn't entirely sure what Groner might say to the warlord before he was taken out behind the barracks and shot. So he told Dostyk to tell Murv that Groner was a television executive who had come all the way from Hollywood, California, to visit the set.

Murv grunted something to his men and let Groner through the barrier.

"What the hell are you doing here?" Charlie asked the American diplomat as they walked from the Land Rover to the production trailer.

"I came here to tell you that you're really in deep shit."

"Tell me about it. I have a crew from *ET* on the set. I'm three days behind on cutting Episode Ten and I have airdates to meet."

"That's the least of your problems."

Groner reached into his shoulder bag and took a file folder out of it. "Here," he said, "take a look at this."

The file contained a half dozen photos of Kermit Fenster. Under each one was a different name. Besides Kermit Fenster, Dwight Halloran and Vernon Gough, there were seven other names. Skimming over the text, Charlie saw places and dates in Central Asia and the former Soviet Union. Stamped at the bottom of the file in large red ink was the word TERMINATED.

"If you're in business with Kermit Fenster, aka Dwight Halloran, aka Vernon Gough, you're in business with a seriously ill and dangerous man."

Groner referred Charlie to the medical records in the back of Fenster's file. There were a number of psychiatric reports describing Fenster as "delusional," "sociopathic," "violent," "dangerous."

"Okay," Charlie said, "so Fenster is a little cuckoo. Who isn't?"

"You know what he's doing here with Izbul Kharkov?"

"Helping me produce a reality television show for ABC."

"That's just his front . . ."

At this exact moment Charlie happened to glance up at the monitor showing the hallway outside Ishrat Khana's room and saw a woman dressed in a burka, a burka very much like the one that Nadira Beg was wearing, about to turn the corner that led to the room where the interview with the stoned, part-time-hooker Ishrat Khana impersonator was taking place.

"Excuse me," said Charlie and ran out of the trailer.

By the time Charlie reached the head of the stairs, he could already hear loud words in Uzbek. Inside the room two women in black burkas were shouting what he took to be insults at each other. In the middle of this, Carla Jann sat on her chair looking very perplexed, her eyes going from one woman to the other, while her crew shot the confrontation and Charlie's crew shot them shooting the two burka-ed women going at it.

"Catfight," Buzz explained to Carla Jann.

"Who's the other one?" the *ET* interviewer asked, having to repeat the question to be heard over the shrieking of the two women.

"She's Ishrat Khana's sister."

"What are they arguing about?"

"The sister, Bishkek Khana, is accusing Ishrat of having had an affair in Odessa when she was getting her face done."

"Can we interview Fishcake?"

"If she's still alive. Ishrat might kill her . . ."

As he stood there listening to the shrieking, Charlie began to feel it all start to crumble. It wouldn't be long before Murv or Izbul himself showed up to find out what was going on. And then it would hit the fan. In one big brown splotch. This whole intricate house of cards that he had been building painstakingly since he met Kermit Fenster at Debtors Anonymous in Brentwood last January was teetering precariously in the wind. He stood there trawling for an exit strategy, but, with the two burka-ed banshees going at each other, he could barely hear himself think. For the first time in a very long time, Charlie lost it.

"Shut the fuck up!" he shouted. Such was the force of his outburst that, though neither woman spoke English, they both stopped screaming.

Suddenly there was complete silence. The only sound that could be heard was the whir of the cameras. It seemed to extend in time, this silent, glaring standoff of burkas. It lasted fifteen, twenty seconds, maybe more, finally interrupted by the sound of a rumbling, consumptive cough coming from the hallway.

Charlie closed his eyes and grimaced, as Grushenka made her entrance, her red-stained handkerchief pressed to her lips. The Ukrainian diva waited a moment for dramatic effect, then, turning three-quarter profile to camera left, she looked from one burka-ed woman to the other and uttered a passionate, cough-splattered speech.

"Who's *she*?" Carla Jann whispered to Buzz.

"Grushenka."

"The home wrecker?"

"Uh-huh."

"I thought she had encephalitis."

"It's in remission . . ."

The presumably real Ishrat Khana then turned to the Ukrainian home wrecker and unleashed a torrent of abuse in Uzbek. Not to be outdone, Nadira Beg, coming down off her hash high, gave both women a piece of *her* mind. Now the shrieking was in both Uzbek and Ukrainian.

The *ET* DigiBetas didn't come up for air. Justyna fired from the hip. Charlie saw a gauze curtain descend in front of his eyes. It would all be over soon, one way or the other.

And as he was thinking about the prospect of being thrown to the camels, a grenade exploded in the middle of the courtyard. The compound shook. Everyone hit the ground. Except Justyna. She ran to the window and started to shoot back.

TWENTY-NINE

Gunfight at the O.K. Corral

Izbul was in his office watching *Oprah* with Akbar when the rocket-propelled grenade launcher fired into his compound. The force of the explosion knocked out his satellite dish, turning Oprah into shimmering lines. The warlord grabbed his Kalashnikov and ran out into the hallway, where he met Murv coming from the barracks.

They hurriedly set up a defensive perimeter, deployed soldiers on the roof and brought their own RPGL into position from behind the barracks. Izbul yelled at Akbar over the noise of the gunfire to get the television people into the cellar.

Akbar ran to the family wing and ordered them all out of the bedroom. The *ET* people went catatonic. Buzz told them to follow Akbar to safety, but they didn't move. He and Charlie practically had to lift them off the ground and push them toward the door.

The storage basement was beneath the kitchen. There was a dirt floor, cement walls and the dank odor of wet earth and vegetables. Cases of hijacked caviar, canned herring, Diet Pepsi and vodka were lined up against the wall, beside crates of cabbages. One naked lightbulb illuminated the entire area.

The three women rivals sat as far away as they could from one another. Carla Jann, Jewel, Esmeralda, Ted and Monte were huddled together in a corner, each trying to get a cell phone signal. Charlie told them they were being attacked either by a rival warlord from Ashgabat or by the Taliban.

Carla Jann looked panicked. "The Taliban? Oh, God. They do terrible things to women, don't they?"

"They just make you wear a veil," Buzz said, in an effort to comfort her.

"Ohmigod . . . ohmigod . . ." Jewel incanted, convinced that she was going to have to kneel down on a rug five times a day and not eat for an entire month during Rosh Hashanah.

Monte was the first to get a cell phone signal. He managed to reach his partner, Gavin, at the Peek A Boo Tanning Salon on Santa Monica Boulevard, in West Hollywood.

"Gavin," he whispered, "we're being attacked by the Taliban."

Gavin had Monte repeat this astonishing sentence several times before promising to call the marines, NATO and the UN and tell them that the crew of *Entertainment Tonight* was in Turkmenistan, in a dark cellar full of vodka bottles, under siege by heavily armed, America-hating religious fanatics.

Gavin Nussbaum had no idea how to get the marines, NATO or the UN on the phone, nor did anybody else at the tanning salon. They considered calling 911, the West Hollywood Sheriff's Station and the California Highway Patrol before settling on Fox News, which had a number you could call to report a breaking news story. If they used your story on the air, they sent you a pass to the set of *Malcolm in the Middle*.

A Fox News editor took the information down and promised to look into it, but thirty seconds later he got a call from someone who had seen Winona Ryder walking into a jewelry store on Montana with a large pocketbook and sent a team out to cover it.

The first person on U.S. soil to hear about the Taliban attack in Turkmenistan had been Curt Groner's control in Langley, Virginia. Groner, seeking shelter beneath a desk in the production trailer where Charlie had left him, had called him as soon as the gunfire started. He told the man on the other end of the line, whom he had never met and whose real name he didn't know, that he was outside Dashoguz under attack by what sounded to him like a rocket-propelled grenade launcher and that the lives of at least a dozen other Americans were at stake, including Carla Jann and her crew from *Entertainment Tonight*.

His control told him to sit tight until he could contact the Pentagon and see how long it would take to get aid to them. Groner gave him his location and shut the phone down to conserve the battery.

Under another desk, a few feet away, was a man in a skullcap.

"Assalom aleikum," Groner said.

"Zholov Dostyk. Producer, line. Please to meet you."

"Curt Smith. TV executive."

"CIA?" asked the line producer, having overheard the CIA agent's cell phone conversation with Langley.

"Nyet," Groner replied emphatically. He was in a rough enough position not to make matters worse by blowing his cover.

The CIA agent was considering whether to make a run for the compound when a volley of fire rattled the trailer and a split second later a man came flying in the door and hit the ground in an evasive action roll.

As bullets shattered the trailer windows, the man crawled on his belly further inside the door. A moment later the man looked up. He and Curt Groner exchanged looks.

"What the fuck are *you* doing here?"

"Hello, Fenster," Groner replied.

Fenster trained his Kalashnikov on Curt Groner, who pointed his Glock back at him. It would depend on whose reflexes were sharper. If they squeezed the triggers at the exact same moment, the Kalashnikov would do a lot more damage. But the Glock was no water pistol. It would blow a nice-sized hole in Kermit Fenster's chest.

* * *

Curt Groner's control at Langley was not about to call in Special Forces solely on the basis of a report from one field agent in Turkmenistan. As far as he knew, his undercover man in Tashkent was reliable, but there was no telling who might have gotten to him, or what the actual situation on the ground might be. Groner could have been on the phone with an Al Qaeda operative holding a gun to his head.

They could get a couple of hundred Special Forces personnel moving in twenty-four hours. If the Joint Chiefs didn't get involved. Then there'd be meetings. The president would have to be briefed.

He would call a National Security Council session. They would no-
tify the congressional leadership. Your basic group fuck.

So while the top people at Langley remained ignorant of the
events at Izbul Kharkov's compound in Dashoguz, the news reached
the West Coast of the United States when Monte got through to
Gavin again at the tanning salon and explained the situation in
greater detail. Gavin called back Fox News, who this time listened with greater attention after the Winona Ryder story didn't pan
out.

The Fox News editor got a few of the details wrong, principally
the location of the siege, which led to the streaming banner across
the bottom of the TV screen, ET CREW UNDER ATTACK IN TURKEY.

Among the people watching the Fox News Channel that morning
was Norman Hudris. In order to keep track of his dwindling stock
portfolio, Norman was in the habit of keeping FNC on constantly
with the sound off to track the twitching of the Dow. And so when
the news streamed across the bottom of his TV screen, he picked up
the phone and called Charlie Berns's cell.

Charlie was in the cellar with Buzz brainstorming how they were
going to work these events into the ongoing story line of *Warlord*
when he was Volga Boatmened by Norman Hudris.

"What are you doing in Turkey?"

"We're not in Turkey."

"Where the hell *are* you?"

"In the cellar under the kitchen of Izbul's compound in Dashoguz."

"They're saying on Fox News that you're in Turkey. And that
you're being attacked."

"There's some sort of shooting going on outside."

"Who's shooting?"

"Could be the Uzbeks, could be the Russian mob, could be the
Taliban . . ."

"The *Taliban*. Jesus . . ."

"Don't worry, Norman. My crew's getting it all on film."

"What about *ET*?"

Charlie glanced over at Carla Jann and her crew staring white-faced at their depleted cell phones. "They're looking a little unsteady at the moment."

"What's going to *happen*?"

"I don't know, Norman. This is reality television, remember? Whatever happens happens."

* * *

The story broke big and fast and in a number of permutations. In the hours following FNC's news banner about the situation in Turkey, the siege story, reported by Monte, through Gavin, had evolved into a hostage story, with Carla Jann and her *ET* crew having been taken hostage by Taliban guerrillas aided and abetted by a cell of Al Qaeda operatives. It would take a while before the truth was sorted out, and by that time the situation at Izbul Kharkov's compound outside Dashoguz would become even more complex.

Meanwhile a number of hastily called meetings were in progress. At CNN headquarters in Atlanta, executives were debating whether to send a news crew. They had people on the ground in Baghdad. For all they knew, however, the whole thing could be a publicity stunt by ABC to promote their new smash reality show, and since CNN was part of a different vertically integrated conglomerate, it was not anxious to give its opponents free airtime.

On the other hand, if the story panned out, CNN couldn't afford to be sitting with its thumb up its ass while Fox News was on the scene. So the decision was made to send a camera crew and reporter from Baghdad. They would rent a helicopter from Halliburton and have people on the ground in Turkmenistan within eight hours.

In Burbank, ABC Current Programming executives were vacillating between anxiety and exhilaration. The concern about the danger to their *Warlord* cast and production facility was counterbalanced by the excitement of the publicity surrounding the incident and the exposure of Izbul Kharkov and his family to an even wider TV audience. They waited for instructions from around the corner to be forthcoming. Nothing, however, but the usual opaque silence emerged from the Vatican.

No one in Burbank thought of contacting any of the people at ABCD in Manhattan Beach, namely Norman Hudris, who was the only person, besides Gavin, who had actually spoken to someone on the scene in Turkmenistan. Norman had tried to reach Howard, but the man he reported to was not taking his calls, or anyone else's.

Howard Draper was already in full damage control mode. Prophylactically. As soon as he saw the Fox News Channel banner, he left his office, by the stairway, got into his car and drove to Encino and told his wife that if anyone called he was visiting relatives in Schenectady, New York. Then he sat in his den and watched FNC on his forty-eight-inch flat plasma screen and waited to see which way the wind was blowing.

In Langley, Virginia, meanwhile, the agency was still checking out the story that FNC was carrying. Curt Groner's control went to the head of the Central Asian desk and reported what he had been told. The head of the Central Asian desk, covering *his* ass, notified his liaison at the Pentagon and told him what his subordinate had reported to him, qualifying it with enough caveats to cover him if the whole thing was bogus or, even worse, disinformation deliberately planted by Groner, in the employ of Al Qaeda.

While all this was going on, Charlie Berns and Buzz Bowden were at work. They were combat veterans by now, and a few grenades fired into the courtyard weren't going to stop them from brainstorming. Their main concern at the moment was how to get to Tashkent to cut Episode 9 in order to make their newly accelerated airdates. The show was so hot that the network had taken all their preemptions away.

"Should we go with the Taliban?" Buzz asked.

"What about the Turkmen mob, loyal to Murv?"

"I'm not sure we're ready to expose Murv as a traitor."

"Whatever we decide, we should tie it in to the catfight."

"So now we have two Ishrat Khanas on our hands."

"One's Bishkek, the sister."

"Right. What's she doing here again?"

"She's been here. It was Ishrat who was in Odessa . . ."

They were interrupted by more shouting from the two Ishrat Khanas. This time the real Ishrat Khana was laying it into Nadira

Beg, who was coming down badly from her cocktail of mood eleva-tors and was looking angrily in Buzz and Charlie's direction.

"What's she saying?" Charlie asked.

"She's calling Nadira Beg a piece of camel turd."

Not to be outdone, Nadira Beg turned toward Ishrat Khana and returned the volley. When Charlie asked for a translation, Buzz said, " '*You* ought to know—you have your tongue up the camel's ass.' Or words to that effect."

* * *

The firefight outside Izbul's compound between the Taliban com-mando and Izbul's soldiers became a three-way battle with the ar-rival of the hundred crack Turkmen troops who accompanied Deputy United States Trade Representative Henrietta Bing to arrest the Uzbek warlord hiding in Turkmenistan. As soon as their com-mander drove up the road to Dashoguz and heard the RPGLs firing, he ordered his men into defensive positions and phoned his uncle in Ashgabat for further instructions.

About an hour after the arrival of the Turkmen troops, U.S. Peace Corps Representative Robert "Bob" Ladl arrived in Dashoguz in his Land Rover to check on the whereabouts of the AWOL volunteer from Samarkand. Hearing the weapons fire coming from the com-pound, the Peace Corps rep went into the Hotel Diyabekir to see if he could find out what was going on. The hotel proprietor, used to hearing gunfire from the compound, merely shrugged and said they were probably just shooting camels.

The American was sitting at what passed for a bar at the Hotel Diyabekir—two stools and a piece of plywood—drinking an Oblo-mov and trying to decide whether he should brave the road to the compound, when Henrietta Bing walked in. Robert "Bob" Ladl of-fered to buy her a beer.

Henrietta Bing—hot and dry from the long trip across the Kara-Kum Plain from Ashgabat riding shotgun in the cab of a military transport truck, inhaling foul cigarette smoke and listening to Turk-men rap music—accepted.

"Bob Ladl. Pleased to meet you," he said as she sat down on the other stool in the makeshift bar.

"Henrietta Bing."

"What brings you to this part of the world, Ms. Bing?"

"Government business. What about you?"

"I'm with the Peace Corps. We have an AWOL volunteer holed up somewhere around here."

"Izbul Kharkov's compound?"

"How'd you know?"

"It's the only thing around here."

"You know what's going on?"

"Somebody's hurling grenades into the compound."

"No kidding. Who do you think it is?"

"Just about anybody. The man's got a lot of enemies. What's your Peace Corps volunteer doing in there?"

"We don't know. Someone spotted him on that reality TV show they're making there."

"He have a good lawyer?" Henrietta Bing asked as she took a pull off her Oblomov.

"Why?"

"He's going to need one."

* * *

The CNN people from Baghdad arrived just before sunset. They didn't stop at the Hotel Diyabekir. These people were battle-tested veterans of the war in Iraq, and it would take more than a few RPGLs to keep them away from the action. Within twenty minutes they had established communication with the Turkmen troops and were doing an interview with the nominally English-speaking commander, who explained their presence as "the enforcement of Turkmen territorial serenity in face of infraction by warlord Izbul Kharkov."

The mention of Izbul Kharkov's name stirred the few newsrooms across the United States that had not already picked up the story and run with it. And as the news rampaged across the country like a wildfire, the CIA, the State Department and, inevitably, the president himself, sprung into action.

The president called a National Security Council meeting and twenty minutes later donned his Iraq aircraft carrier landing flak jacket and went before the nation to announce that he had just ordered five hundred Special Forces troops out of Kabul to deploy immediately to Turkmenistan to defend American lives in jeopardy from worldwide terrorism.

"America means business," he said, from the White House press room. "Any terrorist who threatens America is going to be severely contradicted."

The national terrorist alert system clicked up a notch from yellow to orange. Flights in and out of Central Asia were grounded.

Just what was going on inside Izbul Kharkov's compound in Turkmenistan, however, was still unclear. CNN was outside the compound with a satellite telephone sending grainy blue pictures back to Atlanta of the three-way firefight between the Turkman soldiers, the Taliban attackers and the warlord's paramilitary forces.

But thanks to Monte's still-functioning cell phone, FNC was the only news organization with firsthand knowledge of what was going on within the walls of Izbul's fortress. The all-news station had dispatched a rapid response team with audio equipment to the Peek A Boo Tanning Salon in West Hollywood, where Monte was in communication with his partner Gavin.

Monte's voice was broadcast live over graphics of maps of the region and file photos of Carla Jann. The hairdresser did his best to describe the conditions inside the cellar and the sounds of battle around them.

"Carla was doing her sitdown with Ishrat Khana when the first explosion rocked the compound. They ushered us down here into a cellar under the kitchen. It smells from onions and there are all these cases of vodka . . . and it's like cold and damp . . ."

"Who's down there with you?" The Fox News Channel anchor asked him.

"Carla and her assistant Jewel, and Roberto the sound guy and our field producer Ted, and Esmeralda the makeup person and the people from the TV show . . . Charlie Berns and his writer . . ."

Monte was momentarily drowned out by a renewed volley of shrieking between the two Ishrat Khanas.

"Who's that?" the anchor asked.

"Ishrat Khana and her sister Fishcake. They don't like each other . . ."

"Doesn't sound like it. Can you put Carla on the line?"

A few moments later the people watching FNC heard, "This is Carla Jann reporting live for *Entertainment Tonight* from Dashoguz in northern Turkmenistan, where I have just interviewed the wife of noted warlord Izbul Kharkov about what it's like to be married to the most feared man in Central Asia. You know what she told me, Bill?"

"What's that, Carla?"

"That a woman has to balance devotion to her husband with self-esteem."

"Sounds like a remarkable woman . . ."

"You bet, Bill. She's just returned from Odessa, where she underwent cosmetic surgery—"

At that point, Grushenka got into the act, screaming at both women in Ukrainian.

"What was that, Carla?"

"That's Grushenka, the woman that Izbul's been having an affair with while his wife was out of town. Unfortunately, she's come down with a bad case of tick-borne encephalitis . . ."

And as she said those words the last bit of power drained from Monte's cell phone, and it expired, leaving America staring blankly into their TV sets and the news anchors vamping. Minutes later they were into sidebars, featuring retired army generals with pointers in front of maps of Turkmenistan and reporters doing stand-ups with Gavin and with Jewel's boyfriend in Studio City. They couldn't find anybody who knew Charlie Berns except his agent at DBA.

Brad Emprin told FNC that he was deeply concerned for the safety of his longtime friend and client Charlie Berns. ABC issued a brief statement to the effect that they were doing everything possible to protect the cast and crew of their show. A publicist for the parent company said that it had a policy of not commenting on ongoing political situations.

* * *

Although Charlie Berns still had a line of communication to the outside world, the executive producer of *Warlord* did not use his phone to call his agent in Beverly Hills, or Norman Hudris in Manhattan Beach, or FNC or CNN; he dialed Szczedrzyk's number to find out how his crew was doing.

"*Halo, slucham?*"

"Szczedrzyk, it's Charlie. You okay?"

"Why not?"

"Where are you?"

"Inside the gate. Shooting shit out of battle."

"It's not too dangerous?"

"*Nie.*"

"Where's Justyna?"

"On roof with wide angle."

"Tell her to be careful."

"*Tak.* Got the gunfire on the audio track. Great shit . . ."

Explosions could be heard over the line as the Polish director clicked off and went back to work. Charlie tried another number.

"What?" the acrid voice of Kermit Fenster answered.

"Fenster, what's going on out there?"

"You don't need to know, Charlie."

"Where are you?"

"In the production trailer. I got an Al Qaeda mole at gunpoint."

"What?"

"They planted this guy in the embassy in Tashkent. I'm going to terminate him with extreme prejudice as soon as I debrief him."

"Curt Groner's working for Al Qaeda?"

"You bet your bippy."

"I thought you said he was working for the Russians."

"That was just the cover for his cover. This guy's in Bin Laden's pocket. I got my Kalashnikov trained right between his eyes. He makes a wrong move, he's herring."

Charlie wished he had a cigarette. Two days ago he had decided to quit again. The timing couldn't have been worse.

* * *

Just before he and his men faded into the hills in the wake of news of the approaching U.S. Special Forces troops, the leader of the Taliban commando that had attacked Izbul Kharkov's compound gave a short interview to CNN's intrepid Baghdad-based war correspondent Lucien Alexander.

With sporadic gunfire all around them, the young warrior told the reporter that he and his men had declared a jihad against Izbul

Kharkov and the profane television show being disseminated from the compound. Kharkov was worse than an infidel, and sooner or later they would eliminate him and anyone else involved in the production of such filth.

The young man was dressed like a Taliban warrior—turban, dark brown robe, an AK-47 strapped across his chest. But protruding from his robe was a pair of Air Jordan XI Retros. This detail didn't escape the perceptive eye of Lucien Alexander, who, trying to lighten the interview, asked him where he had gotten the basketball shoes.

"In my old life. When I was living profanely."

Then in a sudden surge of self-destructive inspiration the young man announced to the satellite TV camera, "I am Ali Mohammed, formerly Utkur Kharkov. I will spill my father's blood to cleanse the earth."

And with that dramatic announcement, Ali Mohammed ordered his men to move out under the cover of darkness toward the hills in the south and eventually the Afghan border.

The image of Izbul Kharkov's eldest son, dressed like a Taliban guerrilla and pronouncing himself as his father's enemy, was not unlike the famous 1972 picture of Patricia Hearst in her black Symbionese Liberation Army beret with a machine gun in her hands. The shot made it on to CNN's Headline News and was used with permission and accreditation by the other networks, with the exception of ABC.

Across the United States the twenty-five million faithful viewers of *Warlord* were deeply perplexed. Phone calls flooded the ABC switchboard. The callers wanted to know what Utkur Kharkov was doing leading a Taliban commando attacking his father's compound in Dashoguz instead of studying maritime law in Tashkent.

THIRTY

Mopping Up

With the departure of the Taliban, the three-way firefight outside Izbul Kharkov's compound became a two-way siege. While the Hercules C-130 transport planes that would ferry the U.S. Special Forces soldiers were onloading equipment in Kabul, the Turkmen troops outside the walls of the compound in Dashoguz awaited further orders from President Niyazov in Ashgabat, and Henrietta Bing, at the Hotel Diyabekir, was on her cell phone to the United States trade representative himself, who was in direct contact with a highly placed White House official, who was keeping the president fully briefed on the developing crisis in Central Asia.

Just why the deputy USTR wanted admission to the Kharkov compound was at this point still classified information. The Turkmen commander's sound bite about "territorial serenity" was eventually translated into English and interpreted as an attempt by the Turkmen government to protect its territorial sovereignty by ridding the country of warlords.

Of course, anybody who was watching *Warlord* regularly at 10:00 p.m. Wednesday nights knew that the colorful Uzbek gangster was doing a number of things that were undoubtedly against the law, even in the Stans. Extortion, pistol-whipping, money laundering, camelcide were carried on routinely every week, if not every day. But no one had actually seen him kill anybody, push narcotics or peddle child pornography.

As news reports flowed in about the Turkmen troops and U.S. Special Forces, the American public wanted to know why they were persecuting the Kharkovs. Especially now, when things were going so badly for the warlord. His wife and his mistress were engaged in a bitter confrontation, complicated by the unexpected appearance of his sister-in-law. He'd had to go to the mattresses to ward off the co-ordinated attacks of his enemies. And, perhaps most devastating to Izbul, his son apparently was not only not in law school but had gone off to join the Taliban. This was a family in deep crisis.

The revelation of Utkur Kharkov's allegiance to the Taliban fragmented public opinion. Though there was very little sympathy for the beturbaned puritan ex-rulers of Afghanistan, the young man himself was popular with viewers. His letters from law school had won the audience's heart. Now they were being asked to believe that Izbul's son had been underground all this time in the Tora Bora caves with the Taliban instead of studying maritime law in Tashkent.

Internet chat rooms were full of heated debates over the veracity and meaning of this revelation. There was a strong feeling among hardcore devotees of the show that the interview that Utkur Kharkov had given to CNN was a sham, given by some Taliban double agent to discredit the young man. Or, worse, that it was disinformation fomented by Stalin or by the Uzbek mob in order to make inroads into Izbul's empire. In Utkur's last letter home to his sister, at the end of Episode 7, he had alluded to his having met a young woman at school that he wanted to bring home to meet his father. The audience was eagerly awaiting this moment when Izbul would be asked to give his blessing to his future daughter-in-law.

These events were going out raw to the world without Charlie and Buzz's ability to mold them into the story line. Trapped in the kitchen cellar, without a TV or radio, the two of them were unaware of the media circus going on in the outside world, as well as unable to spin what was going on at the compound by inventing suitable explanations for it in the subtitles.

When the shooting died down after the departure of the Taliban, Charlie and Buzz left the kitchen cellar in search of Izbul. They found the warlord sitting at the desk in his office wearing his combat uniform of Turkish fez, high leather boots, and fleece-lined ski vest. His TV was still on, but there was nothing but a jumble of lines flashing haphazardly across the screen.

"Look what they doink to my TV," he complained when he saw

the two Americans, as if they were responsible for his loss of reception.

"Who's attacking you?"

"Assholes."

"What assholes?"

"Taliban assholes, Turkmen assholes, Russian assholes. Cuttink them all new ones . . ."

At that moment, Murv entered the office, and the two men exchanged a few words in rapid, guttural Uzbek.

"Murv says it's the Turkmen out there," Buzz translated.

Izbul looked at Charlie and Buzz and, then, as if struck with a sudden inspiration, said to them, "You go talkink to them."

"Us?" Buzz asked.

"No. Just you. You goink out with white flag. You tellink them go away or I am killink Charlie Berns from Hollywood and Mary Hartman and everyone else."

Buzz said to Charlie, under his breath, "No way he does you."

"How do *you* know?"

"He can't do the series without you."

"What about the rest of the crew?"

"He could do them."

"You think he'd do Carla Jann?"

"He thinks she's Mary Hart."

They were interrupted by the arrival of Stalin. The lugubrious Georgian mob enforcer entered the room in his black overcoat and fedora, a long slim cigarette dangling from his lips. The conversation switched to Russian. It was heated and went on for ten minutes, with most of the talking being done by Stalin and Izbul. Buzz's Russian was rudimentary, but he understood enough to whisper to Charlie, "He says that they need to break out now. Before the Americans show up."

"The *Americans*?"

"Apparently the president has called in Special Forces from Kabul. It's on CNN in Tbilisi."

Buzz agreed to go out and cut a deal with the Turkmen. Izbul was offering to leave everyone alive in exchange for immediate safe passage through the Turkmen lines. The AWOL Peace Corps volunteer walked out of the main gate of the compound with a white flag improvised from a towel and a long kebab skewer.

His emergence from the compound was broadcast live over the CNN satellite equipment. The picture was transmitted around the world, notably to Boulder, Colorado, where Buzz's father Gary and his mother Marge watched dumbfounded as their son took a principal role in the drama that was unfolding in Central Asia.

"Holy mother of God," Gary Bowden exclaimed to his wife, "that's Barrett."

"He looks a little thin . . ."

Buzz made a brief statement to Lucien Alexander. "Everybody is well inside the compound. Nobody has been harmed."

"But what's going on?" the CNN reporter asked him.

"It'll all be explained in Episode Ten. Now if you'll excuse me, I have to go cut a deal so we can get to Tashkent and edit the episode. Otherwise there won't be an Episode Ten."

Buzz and the Turkmen commando leader disappeared inside the cab of one of the trucks. It didn't take long for Buzz to lay out Izbul's terms and hear the Turkmen officer tell him that he would have to get approval of any deal from Ashgabat, where President Niyazov was out to lunch. Buzz told him that the president better eat fast because the deal was on the table for exactly thirty minutes. He pointed to his Swatch and fixed a time, after which, he said, freely translating Izbul's language, the first dead body would be tossed over the compound wall.

On the way back he told Lucien Alexander and the worldwide audience that the discussions had been "frank."

"But what's the deal?"

"Stay tuned," said Buzz as he turned his back to the camera and walked back to the compound, his white flag draped rakishly over his shoulder.

* * *

The Hercules C-130 transport planes were already in the air while these negotiations were taking place. They were about ninety minutes from touchdown in Nukus, the ex-generals explained in front of maps showing the flight route from Kabul to Nukus.

These chalk talks enabled the viewing public to follow the developments as the noose tightened around the compound outside Dashoguz. They were becoming more familiar with the players as well. Newsrooms madly Googled everybody involved in the hostage situation. Gary and Marge Bowden's phone rang about fifteen minutes after their son first made his appearance on CNN.

The Bowdens repeated their story that Barrett was a Peace Corps volunteer building septic tanks in Samarkand, Uzbekistan, and that they had no idea what he was doing inside Izbul Kharkov's compound in Turkmenistan, let alone why he was negotiating with the Turkmen troops. In addition to the reporters' calls, Buzz's parents began getting calls from producers interested in tying up the rights to their son's story for television movies. CBS was already at $250,000 and consulting credit. Fox was offering to send them to Fiji with a group of attractive older people for a new show called *Celebrity Parents: South Pacific.*

Charlie Berns's Google was a little richer. It wasn't long before he was identified as the same Charlie Berns who a little more than four years ago had won an Academy Award for producing the best movie of the year, *Dizzy and Will.* File clips of Charlie standing at the dais of the Los Angeles Shrine Auditorium holding the statuette in his hand were shown and reshown. Reporters were assigned to ferret out the stars of that movie. Jeremy Ikon, the British actor who had played Benjamin Disraeli in the film, was reached by telephone in London and said that "Charlie Berns, if I recall, was altogether a decent chap." The screenwriter of the film, Lionel Traven-Travitz, contacted at his Mandeville Canyon home, said that his uncle had given him his first job in the movie business but that, since then, things had been a little slow. He then mentioned the name and phone number of his current agents and his Web site, where his credits could be accessed.

Xuang Duc, Charlie's debt consolidator, kept pencil and paper near his TV for the purpose of copying down information that could lead to locating the various deadbeats that his profession attracted. After seeing Charlie Berns's nephew on Fox News, he copied down Lionel's agency's name and found the address in the Beverly Hills phone book. Then he addressed the following letter to his debtor in care of his nephew, in care of his nephew's agency:

Dear Mr. Berns,

I am regretting to inform you that failing complete and imminent remission of sum of $695.50, plus delinquency interest in the amount of $43.19, representing our fees for servicing your account, I will be constrained in no uncertain terms to transfer such account to a collection agency that has affiliation in Turkmenistan and beyond, to mention only some branch offices. Only immediate FedExation of sum above in cashiers check can forestall this inevitability, which will promote irreparable harm to your credit rating.

Yours ever faithfully,

Xuang Duc, Personal Debt Counselor, Esq.

* * *

The conference in Izbul's office following Buzz's return from the truck cab confab with the Turkmen commando leader was both in Uzbek and Russian. Charlie didn't understood a word they were saying, but he could tell that there were disagreements by the amount of spitting on the floor. As usual, Izbul did most of both the talking and the spitting. He shouted and gesticulated and cupped his genitals, all gestures that Charlie recognized as a prelude to aggressive activity.

In the middle of Izbul's long tirade, the door to the office opened and Fenster walked in. As soon as Izbul saw the American, he yelled, "Fuckink Turkmen! We shoot our way out!"

"Forget the Turkmen. You got Special Forces on their way from Kabul."

"I am cuttink Special Forces new one."

"I wouldn't count on it. They have computer-guided missiles. All they got to do is dial in your coordinates and you're shish kebab."

"I am killink Mary Hartman."

"Don't waste your time. We got a ninety-minute window to get the fuck out of here."

"Where?" Charlie asked him.

Fenster looked at him as if noticing Charlie for the first time. "The show's over, Charlie."

"Why?"

"You'll find out in about an hour. See if you can work this one into your facacta story. *Salaam Aleikum.*"

"What about Groner?" Buzz asked.

"He's sleeping with the camels."

* * *

Curt Groner was not sleeping with the camels. He was sleeping with the line producer. Charlie found the two of them handcuffed to the video console desk in the production trailer.

"You got the keys?" he asked as soon as Charlie walked in.

Charlie shook his head.

"You better stop that maniac. He's going to come back and kill us."

Charlie ran back into the house and found Fenster in his room in the guest wing packing various currencies into a tote bag along with some boxer shorts.

"Give me the handcuff keys, Fenster."

"Why? So you can let that mole free? He sings, you're going to wind up doing time in Leavenworth. If you're lucky. They throw you in jail in this hellhole of a country, no one'll ever hear from you again."

"What the hell are you talking about?"

"Charlie, don't be a complete schmuck. Get the hell out of here. Right now. You can hire a cab in Dashoguz for a hundred bucks U.S. to take you across the Ustyurt Plateau into Kazakhstan. From there you can get to Bishkek and get the hell out of the Stans. There's no extradition between Turkmenistan and Finland, Portugal, Myanmar, Uruguay or Azerbaijan. Take your pick. You ought to have enough euros stashed away to buy yourself some papers and get back to the States in five . . . six years . . ."

"Why are they going to come after me? I'm just producing a television show."

"That's what you think."

Kermit Fenster flung his tote bag over one shoulder, his Kalashnikov over the over, blew Charlie a kiss and left.

THIRTY-ONE

Finding Nemo

Norman Hudris sat in his office in Manhattan Beach and, like just about everyone else on the planet, watched wall-to-wall cable news coverage of the drama playing out in Turkmenistan. After several attempts to reestablish contact with Charlie Berns by cell phone, Norman had stopped leaving messages on the producer's voice mail.

Howard had already jumped ship. He wouldn't hear from his boss until they went into active damage control mode, and maybe not even then. There wouldn't be any more lunches at the Hercules Taverna in Glendale. It was every man for himself at this point.

Things were eerily quiet throughout the entire division. It was as if they had been quarantined. Computer-generated interoffice memos and e-mail continued to arrive, like the twitching of an animal after it had died. But that was pretty much it.

Outside Norman's door, Tom Soaring Hawk sat at his desk working crossword puzzles with impunity and answering the stray phone call that managed to find its way in from the outside world. Since the confrontation over the euros, Norman's assistant had been even more literal with him. Norman had to be very precise about what he said. If he told Tom Soaring Hawk that he wanted lunch to be brought in, he had to indicate not only what he wanted but how he wanted it prepared—what type of salad dressing and whether the drink was large, medium or grande. Did he want a straw? How many napkins?

It was clear to Norman that this was payback time. As retribution, the Native American was going to drown his boss in literalness. It was even possible that Jasmine Liu had told him about the euro accusation, because Tom Soaring Hawk now locked his desk drawer when he went to the men's room.

Norman's relationship with Jodie Jacobian was continuing to degenerate as well. There hadn't been much contact with the DBA agent since the hostage crisis had begun. She claimed she couldn't afford to leave her TV set to have lunch, let alone to have sex. She TiVo-ed CNN at night in case she missed any developments.

The pace was so glacial that Norman began to nod off in his desk chair staring blankly at the grainy satellite images of the compound being sent back by the CNN people. He was, in fact, asleep when the point man on the scene, Lucien Alexander, announced dramatically that a convoy of armored BMWs was heading out of the compound gates.

Norman jerked himself awake and watched in astonishment as a phalanx of dusty BMWs with men in skullcaps firing assault weapons from all four windows went roaring out of the front gate followed by several vans.

"The Battle of Dashoguz has begun," Lucien Alexander said in a breathless tone.

*   *   *

As it turned out, the Battle of Dashoguz was pretty much of a dud. The Turkmen troops, not having received any orders from their president, who was still out to lunch, did not fire back. They merely kept their heads down and allowed the warlord and his army to penetrate their perimeter and escape. Not one round was fired.

Back in the TV studios, the ex-generals marveled at the audacity of the Kharkov troops and the complete lack of resistance on the part of the Turkmens. They speculated that perhaps it was some sort of trap, like a screen pass in football, where the offensive line let the defensive linemen through, only to attack them further down the field.

New maps were hastily produced, showing a wider area around Dashoguz, including Nukus, where the U.S. Special Forces team was about to hit the ground. The military experts vamped and speculated, calculating where the paths of the Americans and the warlord's army would cross. They kept cutting back to Lucien Alexander outside the compound, who was trying to ascertain just who was left inside, if there were still armed men holding them, and whether any hostages had been taken by Kharkov.

After the televised departure of the BMWs, there was great confusion among *Warlord*'s viewers. Where was Ishrat Khana? Where was Fishcake? What about Grushenka? Was Utkur Kharkov gone from the area? What about Akbar and Ferghana? And Ferghana's friendly Polish girlfriend? And what about Murv? Did the strong silent lieutenant break out with the warlord, or was he still in the compound holding the hostages? Or perhaps making his move on Ishrat Khana? Or on Grushenka?

Henrietta Bing and Robert "Bob" Ladl were on their bar stools at the Hotel Diyabekir still trying to get definitive instructions from their respective chiefs in Washington when the BMWs with Kalashnikovs protruding from their windows went roaring through town, scattering wild dogs and camels in their path.

"Who were they?" Robert "Bob" Ladl asked.

"I don't know," the deputy USTR replied.

They both looked up at the TV set over the bar, where the Uzbek folk dancing that had been playing was abruptly replaced by a talking head wearing a skullcap and a robe.

"What's he saying?" Robert "Bob" Ladl asked the desk clerk–bartender, who shrugged and said, "He speaks Uzbek."

The talking head dissolved, in turn replaced by satellite images from the compound outside of town. The two Americans sat there watching the same vehicles that they had just seen roaring down the street in front of the hotel blasting their way out of the compound in a blaze of automatic gunfire.

"Shit," Henrietta Bing muttered. "He's flown the coop."

"Who?"

"That was Izbul Kharkov in the Beemer. He's out of here."

Henrietta Bing was already off her bar stool and heading for the door, where her Turkmen driver was waiting for her.

Robert "Bob" Ladl followed her outside to his Land Rover, got behind the wheel and drove out of town after her.

* * *

As soon as Izbul and his men pulled off their daring breakout through the Turkmen lines, Charlie and Buzz went through the compound to see if anybody had been left behind. They found the office and barracks deserted. It appeared as if the only member of the warlord's immediate family left behind—with the exception of his wife, whom he had apparently not invited to leave with him— was his daughter Ferghana. They discovered her in the bedroom hauling cable for Justyna.

The Polish camerawoman was sitting on the sill of Ferghana's bedroom window, the DigiBeta perched on her shoulder like a grenade launcher, waiting for more action. Justyna's long blond hair streamed across her oval face and gave her the look of a Modigliani guerrilla warrior. Ferghana had shed her modest chador and was wearing a pair of khaki shorts and an Abba tee shirt.

"Are you all right?" Charlie asked Izbul Kharkov's daughter, stupidly. She looked better than he had ever seen her look.

"Of course."

"What about your father?"

"He wanted me to go with him. I refused."

"How about Akbar?"

"Akbar is with him."

The heir apparent. Of course.

"Where's Szczedrzyk?" Charlie asked Justyna.

Justyna shrugged her classic shrug of supreme weltschmerz. Who knew? What did she know about anything? Life was a veil of tears. You slogged through it as best you could. In Warsaw or on the shores of the Aral Sea or in a warlord's compound in Turkmenistan.

They tracked down Szczedrzyk in the production trailer using a screwdriver to try to open the handcuffs that attached Curt Groner and Dostyk to each other and to the console.

"We follow Izbul?" the phlegmatic Pole asked Charlie.

"Forget it," Groner said. "He's heading for Karakalpakstan. You'll have to shoot your way into the sand marshes to find him. Who's got the goddamn keys to these cuffs?"

"Fenster."

"Who's long gone, right?"

"I'm afraid so."

"Find a goddamn hacksaw and get me out of these cuffs."

"Be right back," Charlie lied, and he motioned for Buzz to join him outside the trailer.

"We better tell them outside there's no one left here," Buzz said, as soon as they were alone. "Before they start lobbing some more grenades in here."

"First there's something we have to check out," Charlie said.

"What?"

"We're going to need a hacksaw. Or maybe a gun."

*   *   *

President Niyazov finally returned from lunch at an Indian restaurant in Ashgabat to learn that a number of calls had come in for him from his commander in Dashoguz. He decided he'd take a nap before returning his brother-in-law's phone call. The curry lay heavy on his stomach.

So things were still status quo with the Turkmen troops outside Izbul's compound when Henrietta Bing and Robert "Bob" Ladl arrived from town. The commander told them that they were still waiting for official instructions from Ashgabat.

"Is there anybody still inside?" the deputy USTR asked.

The Turkmen soldier shrugged.

"Maybe we should go in there and find out."

"We can't put American lives in jeopardy," Robert "Bob" Ladl argued. "The *ET* crew is still in there, as well as my Peace Corps volunteer."

"But what if all Izbul's men are gone? We can just go in and free the hostages."

This exchange was picked up by one of the CNN ambient mikes and broadcast back to the States. People watching television had the same debate that Henrietta Bing was having with the local Peace Corps representative and with President Niyazov's brother-in-law. According to the ex-generals with pointers, the warlord's troops could have all escaped through the Turkmen lines. The question was would the Turkmen wait for the Americans before storming the compound. The U.S. Special Forces troops were on the road from Nukus, still almost an hour away.

In the Situation Room in the White House the president conferred with the Joint Chiefs. It was suggested that they liaise with the Turkmen authorities. The president put in a call to Turkmenistan's president, who was still sleeping off his curry in his palace in Ashgabat. He was told that the President Niyazov would call back at his earliest convenience.

* * *

Charlie and Buzz rushed back across the courtyard and inside the building. Having no idea where to find a hacksaw, they went into Izbul's office and found one of the warlord's personal firearms in the desk drawer. Though neither of them had ever used a firearm before, Buzz had experience with explosives while clearing land for septic tanks in Samarkand.

He shattered the padlock on the game room door with Izbul's nine-millimeter Beretta semiautomatic, and they entered the place that had been off limits to them for months. The room smelled of stale cigarette smoke and kebabs. The fluorescent light flickered. The Ping-Pong table and slot machines were still there, along with the green felt blackjack table. But there was something there that they had never seen before.

Along one entire wall cartons with Chinese lettering were stacked floor to ceiling.

"Heroin," Buzz said, eyeing the cartons.

They took a metal net support from the Ping-Pong table and, using the gun stock as a hammer, managed to pry open one of the stapled cartons.

Charlie reached inside the carton and found stacks of thin plastic containers. Cautiously, he lifted one out and held it in his hands for both of them to observe.

There in the dim light of Izbul Kharkov's game room, Charlie Berns and Barrett "Buzz" Bowden found themselves staring at the real reason they were in Turkmenistan. The television program had merely been a loss leader. The cash cow was bootlegged DVDs of *Finding Nemo,* one of the most successful films produced by the Walt Disney Company in recent years.

"Holy shit," exclaimed Buzz. "We're in the film piracy business."

"Big time."

"Holy shit . . ."

"You already said that."

THIRTY-TWO

The Infield Fly Rule

The U.S. Special Forces team from Kabul arrived outside the compound in the hills above Dashoguz in a convoy consisting of troop transport trucks, half-tracks and two Bradley Fighting Vehicles that had been transported from Nukus on a flatbed borrowed from the Uzbek government. Captain Phil Esposito, a battle-scarred veteran of the Afghan campaign, conferred with the Turkmen commander, President Niyazov's brother-in-law, who, still waiting for direction from Ashgabat, had very little tactical intelligence to offer.

The Americans had learned, largely from CNN, that the warlord and an undisclosed number of troops had left the compound hours ago. They had not crossed the Uzbek gangsters on the road from Nukus, and there was no indication of their whereabouts.

No one seemed to know how to establish contact with whoever was inside. There was no listed phone number for Izbul Kharkov in the Turkmen Telecom phone system. The *ET* crew's cell phones had all gone dead, which left the ABC production team.

Captain Esposito, in direct contact with the secretary of defense, who had now taken personal command of the operation after having undergone some serious dental work earlier in the day, explained the problem. The secretary telephoned ABC in Burbank. Never having had to speak to anybody at a television network before, he simply dialed the switchboard and asked for the guy running the show. He was eventually connected to Floyd, who, never having received a phone call from a cabinet official before, wasn't quite sure what the protocol was but nonetheless had his assistant ensure that the secretary was on the line before he himself picked up.

To complicate matters, the secretary's Novocain hadn't entirely worn off, making him sound as if he'd had a few drinks, and Floyd wondered if this call wasn't some sort of scam perpetrated by one of the rival networks to embarrass him.

"Do you know what the dickens is going on inside that compound, sir?" the secretary asked the head of the network.

"Only what I'm seeing on CNN, Mr. Secretary."

"Who's in charge?"

"Our executive producer." Floyd looked down at the cast and crew list provided by Kara Kotch and gave Charlie's name.

"Charlie who?"

"Berns."

"Do you have a cell phone number for this individual?"'

Floyd saw a blank space next to Charlie's name and said, "I'm afraid I don't."

"Let me ask you a question, sir. Are you telling me that this individual is running the operation for you and you don't have a way to get in touch with him?"

"Well, I suppose you could call his agent."

"His agent?"

"Uh . . . yes."

"Someone acting on his behalf?"

"No. The person who finds him work."

"How do I communicate with this individual?"

"You could call the Writers Guild and see if they have a contact number for him."

"The *Writers* Guild?"

"Perhaps not. He may not be a member. You see, we don't actually use writers on this show . . . Could I get back to you, Mr. Secretary?"

* * *

When Tamara Berkowitz took the secretary of defense's phone call, she asked him, as she had been instructed to ask all callers who were not on the agent's I-Want-to-Talk-to-Immediately list, if Mr. Emprin would know what this was regarding.

"This is the secretary of defense," he slurred.

The assistant put the secretary of defense on hold and buzzed her boss.

"There's a guy saying he's the secretary of defense on the line."

"*Whose* secretary?" The agent inquired, his congested sinuses making his hearing worse than usual.

"No. The secretary of *defense*. In Washington."

"He wants to talk to *me*?"

"That's what he said . . ."

Brad Emprin gave himself two quick squirts of Nasonex in each nostril, picked up the blinking line and said, "Colin, how are you doing?"

"This is the secretary of defense, not the secretary of state."

"Sorry. What can I do for you?"

"I need the cell phone number of one of your clients, a Mr. Charlie Berns."

"I can get a message to him if you like."

"Let's not be disingenuous, sir. Do we need to get to the bottom of this? You bet your bippy we do."

"The bottom of what?"

"Haven't you been watching television?"

Brad Emprin had been watching the Shopping Channel. He was in the market for a new pair of binoculars with which to watch his neighbors downcanyon have sex on their patio. He switched to CNN and saw the U.S. troops outside the compound in full battle dress.

"Yes, sir . . . it's a little tense over there in Iraq."

"It's in Turkmenistan."

"Of course. You want Charlie's cell number?"

"Asap."

"You know, I put him over there. Got him location scouting expenses and one hell of a per diem . . ."

* * *

While the secretary of defense was obtaining his cell phone number, Charlie was in the cellar with Buzz trying to explain to the hostages that they were no longer, strictly speaking, hostages. With Buzz translating into Uzbek for the benefit of Ishrat Khana and Nadira Beg, Charlie told them that Izbul and his men were gone and that there was nothing preventing them from just walking out of the compound.

"What about the Taliban?" Carla Jann asked.

Buzz explained that only the Turkmen were left.

"What are the Turkmen going to do with us?"

"Nothing. They came to get Izbul. And he's no longer here."

"So why don't *they* leave?"

"They're waiting for the Americans."

"The *Americans*?"

"They're on their way."

A sudden wave of relief went through the American ex-hostages upon hearing that their countrymen were coming to rescue them. But since Buzz could not confirm that the Americans had actually arrived yet, the *ET* crew decided to sit tight and wait for confirmation.

Nadira Beg was ready to go anywhere as long as she could get out of that cellar. She ranted at Buzz and ranted at Ishrat Khana and ranted at Charlie and even ranted at Carla Jann.

To escape the ranting, Charlie and Buzz withdrew to Izbul's office to discuss the situation.

"So what do we do?" Buzz asked, perching himself on top of the warlord's desk, still covered with kebab crumbs and Diet Pepsi cans.

Charlie sighed, shook his head. He had no idea what they ought to do at this point. A lot had gone down in the last few hours, and he still hadn't digested it all. The show was dead. Of course. He would have to find Izbul again, if he actually could, set up cameras, rehire a crew . . . but even if he did all that, the subtitle hoax had been blown. The audience now knew that Ali Mohammed had never been to law school, and they would soon find out that Nadira Beg was a bipolar Uzbek prostitute, that Ishrat Khana had never been to Odessa, that Ferghana had been taking showers with the show's camerawoman, and, worst of all, that there were several thousand DVDs of a very popular animated film in the game room that were undoubtedly being prepared to be shipped to street bazaars all over Central Asia.

"They could come after us," Buzz said.

"For what? Film piracy? We didn't know about it."

"Right. And we didn't see any money . . ."

"All we did is help launder the profits."

"Maybe we should talk to a lawyer anyway. Get somebody on the phone from the States to negotiate an immunity deal."

"We don't have any leverage."

"We got the *ET* crew in the cellar." The AWOL septic tank builder reached down and touched the Beretta in his belt to emphasize his point.

Charlie realized that after all these months his young partner was starting to unravel. The long hours, the crazy rhythms of their lives producing *Warlord,* the keeping the ball in the air as the story became more and more complex and improbable, had taken a toll. Buzz Barrett was no longer the happy-go-lucky hashish dealer living high off the hog in Tashkent, but a film pirate and money launderer with a cellar full of hostages in Dashoguz.

"You're not serious." Charlie said.

Buzz put the Beretta back in the desk drawer and shook his head. "Wow. Did I actually say that?"

At this point, "The Volga Boatmen" rang out from Charlie's pocket. "Hello?"

"Charles Berns?" An indistinct voice came over the satellite.

"Who's this?"

"This is the secretary of defense in Washington."

"You're putting me on."

"Do I impress you as a man who has the time to put people on?"

Charlie put his hand over the phone and said to Buzz, "There's a guy on the phone claims he's the secretary of defense in Washington."

"You think it's really him?"

"I don't know. He sounds like he's had a couple of drinks."

"Ask him to explain the infield fly rule. That's the way they used to tell who were spies in World War Two."

Charlie got back on the phone and asked the secretary of defense to explain the arcane baseball rule. There was a long moment of muffled silence as the secretary of defense had someone Google the infield fly rule. Then his Novocain-addled voice paraphrased from the laptop's screen: "You have runners on first or second, or first *and* second, and there's a pop fly to the infield, the batter's automatically out, runners advance at their own risk."

Charlie repeated the explanation to Buzz, who shrugged. "Beats the shit out of me."

Charlie got back on the phone and said, "What can I do for you, Mr. Secretary?"

"You can tell me who the Sam Hill is in there with you. For openers."

Charlie told him. The secretary then informed him that they were surrounded by five hundred U.S. Special Forces troops from Kabul who were equipped with logistic support consisting of two BFVs and a dozen RGPLs.

"That's very impressive," Charlie replied, "but we're on your side."

"That's for the Justice Department to decide."

* * *

Carla Jann and her crew were the first ones to leave the compound. They walked out, as instructed, their hands held high above their heads, while the Special Forces troops trained their weapons on them. The *ET* correspondent went running into the arms of the first U.S. soldier she saw as if she had just been freed from a bank hostage situation. Within minutes she was broadcasting live over the CNN satellite hookup.

Next came the Polish film crew, who had been instructed to leave their equipment behind. Justyna refused. She walked out, accompanied by Ferghana, aiming her DigiBeta directly into the trained rifles of the U.S. soldiers and shooting the whole confrontation.

The last people to leave, with the exception of Curt Groner and Zholov Dostyk, who were still handcuffed to the console in the production trailer, were Charlie, Buzz, Grushenka and Nadira Beg. Ishrat Khana refused to leave. She announced that she was going back to her room, even after Buzz explained to her that the compound was empty and would soon be searched by American soldiers. At the mention of American soldiers, she spit on the ground and headed off, presumably to her room. Grushenka, for her part, insisted on making a separate exit. A handkerchief to her lips, she walked out alone and squinted in the direction of where she thought the cameras might be.

When the CNN cameras picked up Nadira Beg in her burka, it

was assumed that she was Ishrat Khana, and Lucien Alexander broke off with Carla Jann to try to get a few words from the warlord's wife. When he stuck the microphone in her face, she ranted at him too.

"What's she saying?" the reporter asked Buzz.

"You don't want to know."

"Can we see her face-lift?"

"I would back off if I were you. She's extremely agitated."

"You're the Peace Corps volunteer, right?"

At this point Robert "Bob" Ladl broke through the line of soldiers and warned Buzz not to make a statement. He put his arm protectively around his charge and led him away from the cameras.

Which left Charlie standing alone and defenseless before Lucien Alexander and his camera.

"And you're Charlie Berns, the executive producer, right?"

Before Charlie could respond, a short woman in a dusty linen suit and flats approached and said, "Henrietta Bing, deputy United States trade representative. I have a warrant, issued by the minister of the interior of the Republic of Turkmenistan, for your arrest."

"My arrest?" Charlie repeated dumbly, seeing his entire sordid life flash before his bloodshot eyes.

"On charges of international film piracy in violation of the General Agreement on Tariffs and Trade, to which the governments of the United States and the Republic of Turkmenistan are signatories."

"I'm just a TV producer—"

"You have the right to remain silent. I would suggest you exercise it."

THIRTY-THREE

Habeas Corpus

As Charlie Berns was being handcuffed and led to one of the trucks that would transport him to Ashgabat to face indictment as a film pirate, he reflected upon the irony of his situation. Barely a year ago, in Hollywood, he couldn't get arrested. And here he was being led away in handcuffs in front of a worldwide TV audience.

Just before Charlie stepped up into the cab, Lucien Alexander shoved a microphone in his face and asked him if he had anything to say. Charlie looked back at the camera with a sleep-deprived glare and said, "You heard the woman—I have the right to remain silent." Then he turned his back to the camera, got into the truck and drove off.

"You work for CBS, right?" he said to Henrietta Bing as the truck bounced down the road to Dashoguz, from where it would turn south and head across the desert.

"What are you talking about?"

"They would do anything to shut the show down. We're kicking ass Wednesday nights at ten."

Henrietta Bing looked at Charlie, convinced that he was not only a film pirate but a lunatic.

"This is about film piracy. Plain and simple," she assured him.

"Do I look like a film pirate?"

"That's for Turkmenistan to decide. We have no jurisdiction here."

"You ought to be going after Izbul Kharkov and not me."

"We'll get him too."

"Lots of luck."

That was the extent of their conversation as they lurched over the rutted road south toward the capital city of a country that Kermit Fenster had characterized as the most fucked-up place in the Stans —a country, if he was not mistaken, where the president named days of the week after members of his family. And judging by the U.S.-issue military truck they were riding in and the arrest warrant they had provided the vigilante next to him, a country eager to curry favor with America. Turkmenistan would have little sympathy for a man who aided and abetted the most infamous warlord in Central Asia to commit crimes against the General Agreement on Tariffs and Trade. He was in the wrong country at the wrong time.

Nor would his own countrymen have much sympathy for him. He was an international film pirate, a man who was responsible for, among other things, the increasing U.S. balance of payments deficits, as well as the erosion of the collective bottom lines of the Hollywood movie studios. And perhaps worst of all, he was the perpetrator of an outrageous scam against the trusting American television audience—the large, demographically diverse group of viewers who had invested a great deal of emotional energy in characters whose lives he had shamelessly manipulated.

For that alone, he would be shot. Without a blindfold. On worldwide TV. During prime time.

* * *

In Burbank, meanwhile, the people who had financed the entire operation in Turkmenistan went into EDC mode. Extreme Damage Control was the purview of Poindexter and North, who had gamed situations like this one and were ready to implement a clearly delineated response procedure to minimize the company's exposure.

As soon as the CNN story about the film piracy ring in Turkmenistan broke, Mikey's point men sprung into action. They sealed off the facility in Manhattan Beach. Within an hour of the broadcast, the occupants of the building were ordered off the premises so that an imminent asbestos poisoning threat could be dealt with. Ten minutes after the last person was out of the building, the scrub team led by Poindexter and North moved in. Going from office to office, they deleted e-mails, shredded documents, stripped computer hard drives, disconnected phones and fax machines and had all incoming mail diverted from the post office. Another team worked in the parking structure removing parking permits from vehicles with a compound that left no traces.

By sundown, the building had been locked down. Norman Hudris sat parked around the corner—in his lap a carton of personal effects that had been carefully searched by the asbestos removal prep team for traces of the cancer-causing substance—and watched the place that he had worked for the last fifteen months be hermetically sealed.

He would never be permitted near that building again. It was clear to him that he would be either résumé scrubbed or scapegoated. Frankly, he wasn't sure which fate he preferred. Being scapegoated left you the option of going public, doing the talk shows, keeping your name in print. O.J. was still finding people to play golf with. But getting résumé scrubbed effectively left you with a gaping hole in your professional career. You had disappeared off the planet, and now you were reentering with the suspicious odor of anonymity. Better you came from jail or rehab with a recognizable name than right off the bus from East St. Louis.

Tomorrow he would make an appointment for a total body scan. Before they cut off his medical insurance.

* * *

Floyd didn't wait to have his hard drive deleted. As the network president on whose watch a scam reality show had been developed and aired, he was sitting with his thumb so far up his ass it was coming out of his nose. There were filmed records of his press conference of just a few months ago when he had trumpeted the arrival of *Warlord*. There were memos with his signature on them authorizing the expenditure of millions of dollars to produce the bogus series. There were interviews he had given in which he had basked in the glory of having a number-one show on his network. There was the letter from the Uzbek-speaking viewer who had written months ago to say that the subtitles were a complete fabrication.

Floyd issued a statement that he was stepping down in order to pursue opportunities that had presented themselves in the Internet business. His director of development, Kara Kotch, offered her sword as well. She announced that she had decided it was a propitious time for her to start a family and said that she was taking a leave of absence to devote herself to the task—a statement that was mercilessly lampooned on *Letterman* that night, with the host himself volunteering to help her with the job.

Within forty-eight hours of the CNN story exposing the series and the film piracy behind it, almost everyone connected with *Warlord*, at least those they could find, had either stepped down or been scrubbed. The company and the network announced, not without a certain amount of pride, that they had dealt thoroughly and swiftly with the scandal and had taken measures to prevent something like it from ever happening again. They were, in fact, stronger than ever, having confronted the problem and overcome it.

Which left Charlie Berns holding the bag. He was the man responsible for the entire unfortunate incident. He had taken cynical advantage of the American public. To set an example for anyone who might try to take advantage of the American public again, he was going to be prosecuted to the full extent of the law. The television industry would be purged of its asbestos-laden shell of poison and move on, stronger and more unified.

* * *

After an eight-hour truck ride in handcuffs across the Kara-Kum plateau, wedged between the Turkmen driver and the zealot from the United States trade representative's office, the international film pirate and reality show counterfeiter was remanded to a prison in Bekrewe, a village about ten kilometers west of Ashgabat.

It was the middle of the night when they pulled up in front of the low-slung stucco building in the foothills of the Kopet-Dag mountains. There was nothing else around except an abandoned pesticide factory. The chilly night air was redolent of rotting chemicals and camel manure.

"Could you get someone from the American embassy out here first thing in the morning?" Charlie asked Henrietta Bing, as he was helped out of the cab by one of the Turkmen soldiers.

"Tomorrow's Sunday. They're closed."

"This is an emergency."

"You'll survive till Monday morning."

"I'm an American citizen."

"You're an international felon."

And with that she climbed back into the truck as Charlie was led away into a dark courtyard by two prison guards.

"English?" Charlie asked them.

They shook their heads simultaneously and continued to frog-march him inside the building and along a dank, poorly lit corridor.

Charlie trotted out his cleaning-lady Spanish. *"Español?"*

They shook their heads again.

He took a stab at Latin. *"Habeas corpus?"*

Unlocking the heavy rusted door, they ushered him inside with a semibow, as if they were doormen showing him into the foyer of a luxurious apartment and not jailers locking him into a prison cell. The door closed behind him with the tinny sound of a 1985 Mazda.

In the faint illumination of the forty-watt lightbulb, Charlie took in his new accommodations: a twelve-foot-by-eight-foot room with a mattress on the floor, a threadbare blanket and a chamber pot. On the mattress was a copy of the Koran.

Charlie lay down on the mattress fully dressed, not even bother-ing to take off his shoes. He opened the Koran to the first page and let his eyes swim over the Arabic. He couldn't decide whether he wanted to laugh or cry. He did a little of both before drifting off into what passed for sleep at four o'clock in the morning on a ratty mat-tress in a twelve-by-eight cell in southern Turkmenistan.

* * *

Avery Cantrell, the political officer of the American embassy in Ash-gabat, found a message on his answering machine when he arrived at work Monday morning. He sat in his small office on the Mag-tumguly Prospekt with a view of the Arch of Neutrality, the garish rotating statue of Turkmenistan's president Saparmurat Niyazov, and listened to Charlie Berns ask him to please bail him out of jail as soon as possible.

Like just about everyone else who watched CNN, Avery Cantrell knew who Charlie Berns was and why he was being held in a Turk-men prison. He had discussed the situation with his DCM on Satur-day after the dramatic hostage rescue in Dashoguz. They had concluded that this arrest was a diplomatic hot potato, and they would wait for guidance from Washington before proceeding with anything beyond pro forma assistance to the prisoner.

Film piracy was a thorny issue these days. Like narcotics, it was becoming an important part of the black market economy of the region. This cash infusion was helping alleviate some of the dire poverty in Turkmenistan, and, accordingly, there was no real effort on the part of the Niyazov government to curtail it. Avery Cantrell sent a message back to the prisoner that he would be there at his earliest possible availability, which was two weeks from Friday.

Charlie appealed to the warden to allow him to call the United States and was told that prisoners could not make international phone calls. His money had been confiscated along with his cell phone when he had been arrested in Dashoguz. He didn't have a manat to his name with which to bribe the guards to get him a phone or, at least, a better mattress.

He was kept isolated in his cell, with only a few minutes every day of supervised bathing, which consisted of standing underneath a tepid drool of water with a thin bar of some form of soap substitute. He was not allowed contact with any of the other prisoners, though he could hear them in the yard playing soccer every afternoon.

So desperate was Charlie for some interruption of this dreary discomfort that he actually tried to read the Koran. Perhaps by sheer obstinacy, he theorized, he could teach himself to understand Arabic, or at least keep himself from losing what was left of his mind. After a day he thought that he could decipher the words for *the Prophet* and *Mecca*.

Then on a Wednesday afternoon, five days before Avery Cantrell was supposed to visit him, as he was fighting his way uphill though his Koran, he received the visit of another American. Bearing gifts.

* * *

Buzz Barrett had spent less than a week back with the septic tanks in Samarkand before jumping ship again. Though he had promised Robert "Bob" Ladl that he would serve out the remainder of his two-year Peace Corps assignment, a few days back in the field moving shit through chemicals convinced him that he was just not cut out for this type of work.

So once again he took off without leave, hitching a ride in a melon truck to Tashkent, where he had a chunk of cash from his hashish business stashed in a sleeping bag in the closet of a *pied à terre* in the old part of town near the Chorsu Bazaar. After making inquiries among friends and clients of his who were knowledgeable about Central Asian politics, he took a cab to the airport and caught an Air Turkmenistan flight to Ashgabat and then hired a taxi to drive him up into the hills west of the city.

There Buzz spread enough cash around among the warden and guards of the prison in Bekrewe not only to gain him admittance to see his friend but also to be able to smuggle in vitamin pills, halvah, candy bars, a small ball of hash and a fully charged cell phone.

He found his former writing partner lying unshaven on a mattress reading the Koran.

"Jesus, Charlie, did they get you to convert?"

"Just a little light reading," Charlie said, tossing the book aside and rising to greet his writing partner.

They embraced—the kind of sloppy shy hug shared by people who weren't really given to overt expressions of affection but were fond of each other.

"How the hell did you find me?"

"I've got friends in low places."

"Can you get me a lawyer?"

"I'm working on it. But it's going to take some time. Uzbek lawyers can't practice in Turkmenistan."

They sat side by side on the mattress and reminisced about the salad days in Dashoguz as Charlie ate the candy bars and Buzz lit up his hash pipe.

"Where's Izbul?"

"Probably over the border into Kazakhstan. In six months he'll be back in Nukus kicking ass."

"What'd you do about Nadira Beg?"

"She's back in front of the mosque selling rugs."

"You think Ishrat Khana's still in her room in the compound?"

"Where else would she go?"

"To Odessa, get her tits done."

The two of them slipped imperceptibly over the frontier into the fictional reality they had created together without missing a beat.

"What about Ali Mohammed?"

"Flunked out of law school."

"Is he marrying the American?"

"Only if she converts . . ."

As the sun lowered in the west, leaving the room to the meager light from the forty-watt bulb, they talked about the Kharkovs as if they were family they hadn't seen in a while.

"Too bad," said Buzz in a sudden surge of nostalgia. "It was a lot of fun."

"Yeah," Charlie nodded. "We were just beginning to cook."

"We'll wait a couple of years, do a reunion show . . ."

* * *

They kicked Buzz out after dinner. Before he left, the AWOL Peace Corps volunteer promised to try to find a lawyer in Ashgabat who would take Charlie's case.

"I'll give him a kilo of hash as a retainer."

Charlie waited till late at night for it to be morning on the West Coast of the United States, then took out his Nokia cell phone and called his agent in Los Angeles.

At 9:30 a.m. Brad Emprin was still in the 500 SL heading east in traffic along Wilshire when Tamara Berkowitz reached him from his office to ask if he wanted a call from a client patched through to the car.

"Who is it?"

"Charlie Berns."

"Charlie Berns? He's in jail. In Turkey."

"You want to talk to him?"

The agent had a quick discussion with himself about whether he wanted to take the call. The guy had fucked up big time. He had been arrested for film piracy, which in this town was right up there with child molestation. There was no way that anybody would go near him again. If he tried to set his foot on a studio lot, they would turn the attack dogs on him.

And yet . . . you never knew. Maybe he could work up a cable special on E! or on Bravo. Or a TV movie on the Recovery Channel. People watched specials on Charlie Manson. Why not Charlie Berns?

Brad Emprin told his assistant to patch the call through. As soon as he heard his client's voice, he said, "Charlie, good to hear from you."

"You know where I am, Brad?" Charlie whispered into the phone from the point in his cell that was farthest away from the door.

"Turkey?"

"Turkmenistan."

"Right. How're they treating you?"

"Like a piece of shit. I need a lawyer, Brad."

"I'll get on the blower with Legal . . ."

"This is not something that DBA's lawyers can handle. I need someone with experience in international law."

"You want me to call over to ICM? I know a couple of guys over there."

Charlie took a deep breath and tried not to lose it. This man was his lifeline at the moment. In his safe there should be $200,000 less commission in executive producing fees that he was supposed to be putting aside for his client. With this money, Charlie could try to buy his way out of Turkmenistan.

"Brad, I want you to listen very carefully, okay?"

"Can you speak a little louder? I can barely hear you."

"No. You got my checks, right?"

"You bet. Here in my safe just like you told me."

"I want you to use this money to hire the best international lawyer you can find."

"Uh, here's the problem, Charlie. The checks are made out to you."

"Brad, you know what a client trust account is?"

"Of course I do."

"I signed an authorization enabling you to cash checks made out to me and deduct commission. Remember? So cash a check, find a lawyer, pay him whatever he wants and get him on the phone to me over here. All right?"

"I'm on it, Charlie. Talk to you soon . . ."

"Brad!"

"What?"

"You're going to need a phone number."

"Shoot."

Charlie gave him the Nokia's number, told him to call only after midnight Central Asia time, and disconnected. As he heard the line go dead he had the sinking feeling that his fate depended on a man who could barely dial his own phone.

He took a deep breath and went back to his Koran for solace.

* * *

All the way into the office, Brad Emprin babied the big Benz through traffic and thought about what to do. The checks were in his office safe, in an envelope underneath the envelope containing a hard copy of the e-mail that Jodie Jacobian had sent him when she tried to shake him down for his office.

The matter of the under-the-table location expenses commission had not been entirely deep-sixed. It could still come up to bite him in the ass. He needed to be very careful. In these shark-infested waters, it was every man for himself.

Why go anywhere near the *Warlord* train wreck? Better to just walk away. They could execute Charlie Berns in Turkey, and then the whole matter would be buried with him. The guy was in jail on a cell phone. There wouldn't be any call log. No one except Tamara Berkowitz knew about the conversation that he just had with his client. His *former* client.

At Tuesday's staff meeting he would put Charlie Berns on the Terminated list. They would delete his name from the agency roster. Anybody called for him, they would be told that DBA no longer represented him.

When he arrived at his corner office in the DBA Building, he told Tamara Berkowitz that he was putting Charlie Berns on the Non-Accept List. This meant that the agent was either away from his desk, in a meeting, or out of the office any time that the client called.

Then Brad Emprin went into his inner office, closed the door, opened his safe and took out the envelope containing his client's checks net of commission. Rifling through his Rolodex, he found Charlie Berns's last known address in Mandeville Canyon. Using his left hand, he wrote the address on an envelope, sealed it and stuck it in his suit pocket. On his way home that night, he'd hop on the 405 and drive out to Pacoima, where he would drop it in the same mailbox he had dropped the euros he had sent Norman Hudris, the one next to the In-N-Out Burger.

THIRTY-FOUR

Digging Into the Koran

Within two weeks of Charlie Berns's arrest in Turkmenistan for film piracy, there was no longer any trace of the existence of ABC's secret division in Manhattan Beach. Not only did ABCD no longer exist, it never had. There was no record of it or of its employees on any company document or database. The building was leased to a truck rental firm, all signage removed, names scraped from parking spaces.

The employees who had worked there either were absorbed quietly back into the parent company or set adrift without a life raft. Those who were cut loose were given no severance pay or benefits; their health coverage was terminated, their comped passes to Disneyland invalidated. The rule of thumb was the closer you were to the action, the more likely you were to be vaporized. People like Howard Draper, Norman Hudris and Maxine Dyptich—the ones who knew where the euros were buried—were hung out to dry. There wasn't a trace of any of them left anywhere.

Norman had made a few unreturned phone calls to people he knew in Burbank and then simply gave up. Howard, of course, was not taking his calls at home. His wife Winnie said that he was in Schenectady, New York, visiting relatives and she didn't know when he'd be back.

Norman drove to Encino, rang the bell and told Winnie that he knew that Howard was not in Schenectady.

"He's in the garage," Winnie Draper admitted, seemingly relieved to see Norman. "He spends the whole day out there sitting in his car reading old copies of the trades. I'm afraid he's going to start the engine with the door closed. Would you please talk to him?"

She gave Norman a garage door clicker, and Norman went out to the front of the house and opened the door. Sitting in the middle of the neatest garage Norman had ever seen was a shiny 2004 Cadillac El Dorado. Inside the Caddie was the man he reported to, or at least used to report to, when they both existed.

Norman opened the passenger door and got into the car beside Howard. His boss was wearing a suit and tie and was cleanly shaven. His shoes were shined. He reeked of Mennen skin bracer. Beside him was a pile of *Variety*s and *Hollywood Reporter*s.

"Are you all right, Howard?"

Howard Draper, who was clearly not all right, looked at Norman and shook his head.

"Why are you sitting in your car in the garage?"

"I feel safe here."

"Howard, your wife is worried about you."

"She ought to be."

"Maybe you should talk to someone."

"I'm taping this conversation."

Howard reached into the backseat, where he had a small battery-operated tape recorder and put it on the seat between them. "I'm recording all my phone calls also. It could come in handy."

"For what?"

"For when they get to the indictment stage."

"There're not going to be any indictments . . ."

"Testing, one two three," Howard said into the machine. "I'm sitting here with Norman Hudris on Tuesday morning, July twelfth . . ."

"Howard, you don't understand. They don't need us. They got their guy. He's in jail in Turkmenistan."

"I don't know what you're talking about."

"Yes, you do. Charlie Berns, the man who sold us the show."

"Never met him."

"Remember *Warlord*? The show we produced? The show you went to Poindexter and North to get funded?"

"I can neither confirm or deny that statement."

313

"For chrissakes, Howard, you don't get it, do you? What they're doing to us is worse than an indictment. We're being obliterated. We don't exist anymore. The whole division, the whole goddamn skunkworks is gone. There's no record of it anywhere. ABCD never happened."

"Well, I was certainly never there."

"No, you weren't . . ." Norman sighed.

"And even if I had been, I would have had nothing to do with that criminal activity."

It was pointless to go on. The man was delusional. Norman leaned over close to the tape recorder and said, "Beam me up, Scotty . . ."

Norman left Howard in his Cadillac parked in his garage and drove aimlessly north on the 101. He would keep going till he ran out of gas. Better, he would check out right there on the Ventura Freeway. Find some tailgating asshole in a Hummer and jam his brakes on sharply in front of him. What difference did it make? He was already a dead man. They'd run the obit in the below-the-line section, reserved for grips and production auditors.

Dead television executive Norman Hudris, reportedly 43, died again on Tuesday as the result of a traffic accident on the Ventura Freeway. There is a completely unaccounted for 15-month gap in his résumé, during which time it is not known what he was engaged in. His credits were unavailable at press time, but he has been associated with various unsuccessful television pilots and overbudget films. He is survived by a geranium plant, a housekeeper to whom he owes three weeks' back pay . . . and a 2002 Lexus LS 430 with a bad engine valve . . .

* * *

Charlie Berns was not already dead, but he might as well have been. His only link to the outside world was the cell phone that Buzz had smuggled in for him. Its battery had one life to live. When it was gone, he would be completely incommunicado. Fearful that the phone would be confiscated, he waited till the middle of the night before whispering into the machine from the place in his cell farthest from the door.

He had managed to get the main number for the *New York Times* by dialing the foreign access code for the U.S. and then directory assistance for the 212 area code, but when he whispered into the phone asking to talk to a reporter, he was put on hold long enough that the number of bars indicating battery life was reduced by one and he disconnected. He tried the *Los Angeles Times* and was directed through their voice mail to an automated system for putting a vacation stop on his home delivery.

He finally got through to a live reporter at *Variety*. The reporter, Marja Rennholm, who handled television, said she was a little busy at the moment covering the new development season. Could he call back in August?

"I could be dead by August," Charlie whispered frantically into the phone.

"We all could be."

"Do you know who I am?"

"Actually, I don't . . ." the reporter admitted.

"The executive producer of *Warlord*."

"Oh . . . *you*. Aren't you in prison?"

"That's why I'm calling. I'm being held without a lawyer in Turkmenistan."

"I can barely hear you."

"That's because I'm on a smuggled cell phone. If they catch me, they'll cut off my fingers."

"Let me talk to my editor."

"Why? You're talking to me. Now."

"You know, the whole *Warlord* thing was a couple of weeks ago. I don't know whether it's still newsworthy . . ."

"It was the highest-rated show on television."

"Yeah, but it's off the air . . ."

After that phone call, he decided to conserve what was left of his battery life for incoming phone calls from Brad Emprin or from Buzz with news of a lawyer.

He went back to the Koran during the day, making little progress with his system of trying to infer words from context, studying the number of times they were used and then putting the letters together as if they were a cryptogram. It was about as inefficient a way to learn a language as there was, but there was nothing else for Charlie to do to survive the long hot July afternoons.

He began to lose track of time. Days and nights coalesced into one listless slog, punctuated by Koran studies, fitful sleeping, the unappetizing meals of hard rice with thin slices of overspiced lamb and watery tea.

His system alternated erratically between diarrhea and constipation, his head ached constantly. He had an exotic rash on his genitals that he couldn't bear even to look at. As his resolve to stay on top of things gradually dissolved, he began to recognize signs of serious depression. He had started to explore different ways of committing suicide.

Killing himself, however, presented practical problems. They had taken away his belt, and there was nothing in the cell with which to hang himself. There was no heavy object to bash his skull in beside the Nokia, which happened to be very light, just as its advertising claimed. He considered eating the phone. It was small enough to swallow. If he harvested enough grease from the mutton at dinner maybe he could lubricate the phone to slide down his throat . . .

At night he would fall asleep amid these increasingly creative suicide schemes in the tepid glow of the forty-watt lightbulb that was never turned off. He would sleep restlessly in a light patina of sweat and anxiety, to be awakened by the muezzin's call to prayer at some godawful hour in the morning to face another long, hot day of fruitless Koran studies and suicide fantasies.

In the middle of one of these amber nights, as he tossed and turned on the pancake-thin mattress, Charlie awoke abruptly to find the guard who brought him his food standing over him and speaking.

Charlie sat up and repeated the few words he had inferred from the Koran. This was their usual manner of communication, with neither man understanding the other one. Eventually, they slipped into minimalistic sign language, which was usually sufficient to communicate within the narrow limits of what had to be communicated.

But on this night, the guard, whose name was either Dag or Dug, went through a more elaborate choreography of sign language to indicate that Charlie should get up and follow him. When Charlie rose, the guard picked up the copy of the Koran beside the mattress and put it into Charlie's hands.

The perspiration already gathered in the various recesses of Charlie's body turned cold. *Come with me and bring your Koran.* What could that mean other than they were going to take him out and shoot him? Even though he had been entertaining suicide plans, the thought of being lined up against a wall and summarily shot in the middle of the night terrified him.

Charlie began to tremble. Dag or Dug tried to reassure him in pantomime that everything would be all right, but Charlie wasn't buying. This was it. The United States trade representative, tired of waiting for the wheels of justice to grind in Turkmenistan, had ordered his execution. An unfortunate prison accident. The international felon was shot trying to escape.

A form of shivering catatonia overcame him, to the extent that Dag or Dug had to grab his arm to steady him and lead him out of the cell. Charlie trudged alongside his jailer, past the cells of sleeping men and out into the courtyard, his bowels quivering. Dead man walking . . .

As he reached the entrance to the courtyard, Charlie looked around for the squad of soldiers with rifles, but instead, in the middle of the improvised soccer field, there was an automobile with a driver behind the wheel. Dag or Dug led Charlie over to the passenger door of the small black car, opened it, then leaned over and air-kissed him on both cheeks.

The kisses of death. Soon they would offer him the blindfold and the cigarette. Charlie mumbled a word from the Koran that he thought meant farewell and got into the car. Without a word, the man started the engine and drove out of the courtyard and into the dark countryside.

* * *

While Charlie Berns was being driven to his execution in Turkmenistan, the garage door to Howard Draper's three-car garage in Encino opened and a tall bearded man in navy blue sweats approached the El Dorado, opened the door and got in.

"Who are you?" Howard Draper asked the man who had just gotten into his car beside him.

"My name is Eli Horowitz, and your wife asked me to come out here to talk to you."

"About what?"

"About why you are spending your days sitting in your car."

"It's none of your goddamn business."

"Perhaps. But by acting this way you're making it the business of other people."

"Who are you, some sort of shrink?"

"No. I'm just a facilitator," Eli Horowitz said, reaching over and removing the keys from the Caddie's ignition. "I'm going to help you."

"Give me those keys," Howard squawked.

"Not until you leave the car."

"I'm not leaving this car."

"Then you're not getting the keys."

"What the hell is this, some kind of psycho bullshit?"

"It's called an intervention. It's basically a concerted effort by people who love you to get your life back on track."

Howard reached into the backseat and got the tape recorder.

"There's going to be a record of this."

"Good."

Howard spoke into his machine. "This is Howard Draper and I'm being intervened against my will by a man I've never seen before. I take no responsibility at all for this incident."

"So, Howard, let's talk. What's going on?"

* * *

The man driving Charlie to his execution smoked cigarettes that smelled as if they were made of yak dung. As the minutes passed, and as they joined the main road to Ashgabat, Charlie began to consider the possibility that he wasn't going to be shot immediately. Instead he was going to be taken to a prison in Ashgabat to be tortured before being shot.

It was still dark when they reached the outskirts of the surreal city, a theme park of elaborate buildings and monuments to President Niyazov against a backdrop of dreary Soviet-era apartment houses and parched green spaces that had turned brown. The chain-smoking driver drove perilously fast through the deserted streets and parked the car abruptly in an alley behind a gas station.

Another man emerged from the alley, took the place of the chain-smoker, started the engine and drove off without a word. He wore a black turtleneck sweater and had a ripe-looking scar on his cheek.

"You speak English?" Charlie tried.

"Of course," the man responded in a Russian accent.

"Where are you taking me?"

"To Turkmenbashi."

"Why am I going to Turkmenbashi?"

"Because there is boat there."

"Why am I going on a boat?"

"Because you leave Turkmenistan on boat, you don't show no papers."

"I don't understand."

"You are herring fisherman. Going out to catch herring."

"Where?"

"In Caspian Sea."

Charlie closed his eyes and tried to sleep as the car bounced along the semipaved highway that presumably went west to Turkmenbashi. Soon he would be in the penal colony of whatever country was on the other side of the Caspian Sea. Or he would be sleeping with the herrings. At this point it didn't make a whole lot of difference.

* * *

Twenty-seven hours later—ten hours to drive the six hundred kilometers of the two-and-a-half-lane highway that connected Ashgabat with the Caspian Sea port of Turkmenbashi, formerly known as Krasnovodsk, two hours sitting around breathing in the smell of salt refineries and rotting fish before boarding the forty-seven-foot herring boat for the fourteen-hour trip across a rough sea, and one hour sitting in a dank seaside tavern in Baku, the capital of Azerbaijan—Charlie Berns learned why he had been brought there.

A man walked in the door, a man whom he had expected never to see again in his entire life—a man whom, Charlie had resolved, he would never speak to again, and in the event that he should appear in his path, he would reach for the nearest weapon and, failing that, turn around and walk, not run, as fast and as far away as he could.

"How are you doing, Charlie?" Kermit Fenster asked. "Buy you a slivovitz?"

T H I R T Y - F I V E

Auf Wiedersehen

"You fuckhead!" Charlie Berns shouted at Kermit Fenster in the dingy longshoreman's bar in the Caspian Sea port of Baku.

"Keep your voice down."

"No, I will *not* keep my voice down! I shouldn't even be talking to you!"

"Charlie . . ."

"I want to know how you pulled this off."

"You don't need to know."

"Yes I do. That's what got me in trouble in the first place. Not needing to know. You fucked me over, Fenster! You manipulated me, you lied to me, you traded on my reputation to set up your fucking scam and left me holding the bag, so I'm not talking to you . . . And, by the way, fuck you!"

"You through, Charlie?"

"No. And unless you tell me what the fuck's going on, I'm leaving."

"You're a fugitive from justice."

"I don't care. I'll blow the whistle. I'll spill my guts. I'll go to the papers. I'll go to Fox News . . ."

The slivovitz arrived in dirty brandy snifters. Fenster took a pull off his, then said, "All right, Charlie, I'm going to answer this one question. One time. Only because you're distraught. You want to know how I got you here? I had an asset in Ashgabat spread two hundred thousand manats around the prison."

"How much is two hundred thousand manats?"

"A hundred and fifty dollars."

"That's *all*?"

"For three hundred thousand manats I could've had you killed. You see, Charlie, you're just an encumbrance to the Turkmens right now. You're an embarrassment. You managed to make Izbul Kharkov world famous right under their noses. You made them look like assholes. They don't like you. They prosecute you, you become a news story. They just want you to go away. I did them a favor."

"What about the Americans? What if I tell them everything, the whole scam, the euros, the subtitles . . . ?"

"The Americans aren't going to do dick for you. You're a bigger embarrassment to them than you are to the Turkmens. You made a film pirate out of one of the top three entertainment conglomerates in the world. You jerked off the American public. You profaned the god of television. You might as well having taken a dump on the flag."

"I'll plea bargain . . ."

"You don't get it—nobody gives a shit about you anymore. You're yesterday's sound bite. You're a living reminder of the whole mortifying affair. You're a national shame. Nobody wants to talk to you, not even a goddamn grand jury. I got to tell you, Charlie, you couldn't even get arrested in Azerbaijan."

At this point, as the truth began to sink in, Charlie drank the slivovitz. It took only a half snifter full of the potent Croatian plum brandy to send him to the toilet to recycle the kebabs he had eaten on the herring boat, the last vestige inside him of Turkmenistan.

He returned to the table, white and weak, sat down and asked Kermit Fenster point-blank, "Why'd you go to all this trouble, Fenster?"

"I like you, Charlie."

"Now give me the real reason."

"How'd you like to get back in the movie business?"

Charlie screwed up his eyes and looked carefully at the features of his former partner, half-expecting him to break out laughing. But he remembered that Kermit Fenster never laughed.

"It's just like falling off a bicycle," Fenster continued. "You got to get right back on."

"Do you think I'm fucking stupid?"

"Just listen to the idea, will you? After you hear it, you don't want in, it's okay with me. No hard feelings. Want a little borscht?"

Charlie shook his head and Fenster called the waiter over and ordered borscht for both of them. Then he put his elbows on the table, folded his hands in front of him and leaned over the table toward Charlie, in much the same manner that he had done six months ago in Starbucks.

"You know what the biggest growth industry in this facacta country is? You're going to say oil or caviar, right? Forget it. Oil is controlled by the cartels, with the government siphoning off a nice chunk at the source. And the Caspian Sea is so polluted the sturgeon are dying of emphysema. So what do people do in this godforsaken place besides drugs? They sit in front of their DVD players and watch movies. And what type of movies do they watch? *Lord of the Rings? Finding Nemo?* Uh-uh. The bootleg market's drying up. You didn't help things by getting nailed in Dashoguz . . ."

"*Me?*"

"There's not a whole lot of markup on Hollywood films anymore. The studios are cracking down on piracy. Now there's too many people to grease. What I'm talking about is making our own product. We own it one hundred percent. We make it, ship it, sell it. And we print money."

"You want to make movies in Azerbaijan?"

"Not just any movies."

Though there was nobody in the bar who looked like they understood English, Fenster lowered his voice and said, "Porno movies."

Charlie actually smiled at Fenster. He didn't think he was capable of smiling at the man again, but he couldn't help himself. "You want me to make porno movies?"

"What'd I just say?"

"What the hell do I know about making porno movies?"

"What's to know? You get some lights and a camera, a bed, a little KY Jelly . . . I'll supply the girls. They love Asians here. I got people in Bangkok'll send me over a stream of them—cute little things with long black hair and tight butts . . . sell like kebabs. So what do you say?"

"Is this an offer I can't refuse?"

"Charlie, you hurt my feelings."

"I'm sitting here in a bar in a country I entered illegally. Thanks to you. I'm a fugitive from justice. I don't have a dime. I don't have a passport. Where am I going to go?"

"You want a passport, I'll get you a passport. I'll give you money. Enough for an airline ticket back to the States. Then you can make your decision. What do you say?"

The borscht that Charlie didn't want arrived, along with two more snifters of slivovitz. Fenster said something else to the waiter, who nodded, went to get a camera and pointed it at Charlie.

"What the hell is he taking my picture for?"

"For your new passport. Smile, Charlie."

* * *

Fenster had Charlie driven to the Radisson on Kasparov Prospekt, named after the world-renowned Azerbaijani chess player, where he checked him into a luxurious suite, told him to order whatever he wanted from room service and get a good night's sleep.

"Watch a movie on the sex channel. You'll see how bad the porn is in this country. I'll be by in the morning. We'll talk."

Exhausted, filthy and finally hungry, Charlie ordered an onion omelet and an Oblomov from room service and ran the water for a bath. Then he sat in the tub, ate his omelet and drank his beer. As he leaned his head back against the edge of the bathtub and closed his eyes, his mind filled with images of his recent odyssey—the endless Kara-Kum desert that he had been driven across from Dashoguz, the twelve-by-eight cell in Bekrewe, the small springless Volga that drove him to Turkmenbashi, the herring boat and the pier in Baku. Standing alone at the end of the pier was Kermit Fenster. He was holding a football.

Go ahead, kick it, Charlie. Right through the uprights.

He emerged from the tub, dried off, took one look at the TV with the HBO and pay movie channel hookup, and got into bed with his Koran instead. Half a page later, he was fast asleep.

* * *

True to his word, Fenster showed up at noon the next day with a United States passport and ten thousand U.S. dollars in nonconsecutive one-hundred-dollar bills. In a shopping bag marked Banana Republic Baku were a silk polo shirt, a pair of casual fit cotton slacks, Ralph Lauren boxers, beige socks and size 9½ docksiders.

Fenster laid it all out on the settee in the corner of the room, helped himself to some coffee from the room service cart containing the remainder of Charlie's breakfast, then sat down on the ottoman.

"Sleep okay?"

Charlie stared down at the passport in his hand. It had his name, his date of birth, his address in Mandeville Canyon. The photo made him look as if he had aged ten years from his last passport photo. He felt as if he had aged twenty-five years.

Fenster took the remote and clicked on the TV, hit a few more buttons until the TV screen on the other side of the room was filled by a badly lit close-up of an overweight woman with dripping eye makeup performing what was presumably oral sex but was difficult to determine in the soft focus of the camera work. The fellatrix breathed loudly through her nose over a tinny soundtrack of vaguely Central Asian music. The same angle stayed on the screen endlessly, as if they had simply shot the whole sequence without any editing.

"Take a look at this shit," Fenster said. "You see this, you don't want to jerk off, you want to throw up."

Charlie had seen better stag films at fraternity smokers in the '60s, when they used to set up a projector in the basement of the frat house and watch fat Mexican hookers from Tijuana blow guys with masks and black socks on.

"I'm going to pass, Fenster."

"Charlie, this is a ground-floor opportunity. A hundred grand gets us up and running. Six weeks from now we're making a profit."

"You don't need me. You can get anybody to do this shit."

"I want a pro handling this."

"Thanks, but I'm going to take a little hiatus from the movie business."

"Why?"

"I'm homesick."

"For what? L.A.? You got nothing there but debts."

"I've got some money there that I had put away for me. I can clear my debts and get into something else."

"Charlie, nobody's going to give you the time of day there. You're public enemy number one."

"Maybe, Fenster, but that was over three weeks ago. By now nobody even knows who I am anymore, right?"

Fenster held Charlie's eyes for a moment, then shrugged. He got up from the chair and looked over at the open book on the night table.

"One piece of advice before you get on a flight to L.A.?"

"What's that?"

"Lose the Koran."

Fenster opened his wallet, took out a card and handed it to Charlie. "Give me a ring if you change your mind. Any time, day or night."

On the card was the name Julian Hanauer. There was a P.O. box in Montevideo, Uruguay, and a phone number.

* * *

That night Charlie was on an Aeroflot 747 to Moscow, where he transferred to Frankfurt to catch a Lufthansa flight to Los Angeles. In the transit lounge at the airport in Moscow he bought a copy of *Time*.

The magazine had a cover date of July 31, only three weeks after he had been arrested in Dashoguz. He scanned it carefully for any references to him or to *Warlord* but came up with nothing except a review of the show that was going to replace the hit reality show Charlie had produced on Wednesday nights at 10:00 p.m. on ABC. The new show was called *Trista and Ryan's Divorce.* It was, according to the review, the riveting real-life story of the harrowing divorce between the two young people who only eight months ago had gotten married in prime time after Trista, the blond bachelorette, had chosen Ryan after ten weeks of competition among a dozen men for her favors. In this, the opening episode, they raced around town interviewing lawyers to see which one offered the best deal and learned how to hide their assets.

The network had high hopes for the show, which, they believed, was the type of entertainment that America would embrace. There was no mention of the show it was replacing. Or of the producer who had provided it. Or of Izbul Kharkov. Or of Turkmenistan, film piracy, Murv's power play, or Ishrat Khana's face-lift. *Sic gloria transit television* . . .

Charlie slept most of the way from Frankfurt to Los Angeles, waking as the landing gear locked down. He rubbed his eyes and opened the window shade to look at his home city as the big Airbus lowered altitude over downtown and moved west along the Harbor Freeway toward the airport. He could see the already heavy early-morning traffic edging along in all ten lanes and the forlorn palm trees shivering in the damp fog. The whole city was spread out and enormous beneath him, slumbering over the fissures of past earthquakes.

As they taxied to the gate, the air hostess welcomed them in German and in impeccable English to Los Angeles International Airport. The local time was 8:07 a.m. The temperature was 63 degrees Fahrenheit, 17 degrees Celsius. Thank you for flying Lufthansa. *Auf Wiedersehen* and have a nice day.

THIRTY-SIX

The Exhaust Pipe, Take Two

After the last of his script deals collapsed and three of his four vehicles were repossessed, Lionel Traven-Travitz's live-in girlfriend and closet organizer Shari—the woman who had color-coordinated his seven bathrooms and transformed his pool house into an office for her organizing business—left him. She drove away with her Latvian personal trainer and sent her sister Rita, the woman whose Honda Civic Lionel's uncle Charlie had driven while she was recovering from periodontal surgery, to collect her things. She didn't leave a note. Instead she left a bill. On the $4,200 burled wood desk that Lionel had bought for her she left an invoice for the time she had spent organizing Lionel's life. Two hundred five hours at $125 an hour. It came to $25,625.

Following Shari's departure, Lionel's depressive Estonian cleaning lady Glinka departed, owed five weeks' salary. She, too, left a bill. As did Mr. Kim, Lionel's anal-compulsive pool man, who, when Lionel failed to remit for three months in the little envelope that was stuffed under the pool house door, backwashed the pool motor with mayonnaise.

Then the above-the-line staff checked out. His agent stopped taking his phone calls; his lawyer sent letters threatening serious legal action while simultaneously billing his ex-client for the time writing the letters, as well as for the messenger service that delivered them; his accountant sent overdue bills accruing 18 percent annual interest along with notices from the IRS on penalties due to the unjustified write-off he had taken for the medical building in Costa Mesa, which, perversely, had started to generate positive cash flow.

Then came the foreclosure letters from the bank that had written the mortgage on the highly-leveraged 6,200-square-foot house on the top of Mandeville Canyon. In ninety days the property would be seized by the bank and sold at auction unless Lionel repaid the $32,000 plus late pay charges overdue.

So, in the little more than four years since he had ridden into town and achieved fame and fortune with his first screenplay, Charlie Berns's nephew Lionel was back where he started. Or worse. Then he'd had $200 to his name.

He could raise what money he could from his Writers Guild award nomination plaque by auctioning it off on eBay and buy a one-way bus ticket back to Parsippany, New Jersey, to face his friends and relatives to whom he had shamelessly boasted of his success. Or he could kill himself.

He could take a flyer off one of the pedestrian bridges that crossed over the Hollywood Freeway or seal off the pool house windows and run a hose full of Porsche exhaust into it. Either one would spare him seventy-two hours in a Greyhound and the faces of his parents as he rang their doorbell with a duffel bag full of dirty color-coordinated towels.

On a foggy morning in late July, Lionel went outside to see if he could get the soon-to-be-repossessed Porsche Turbo Carrera GT close enough to the pool house to run a hose from the exhaust pipe through a window. He backed the vehicle through the narrow pool gate opening and was able to get it within twenty feet of the pool house. As he was trying to estimate the length of the garden hose that his departed gardener Reynaldo Ramirez-Bernstein had left uncoiled when he, too, had quit, Lionel heard a car engine climbing the long driveway to the house.

It was undoubtedly a process server or a realtor that the bank had sent over to appraise the house. But as the car negotiated the turn in the driveway and came into view, Lionel could see it was yellow with a sign on top of it advertising a revival of *Cabaret*.

Imagine Lionel Traven-Travitz's reaction when the taxi stopped in front of the house and his uncle Charlie, who was supposed to be in jail in Turkey, stepped out carrying a Lufthansa flight bag.

Charlie walked through the pool gate, took one look at his

nephew, the Porsche incongruously parked near the pool house, the uncoiled garden hose and did the math. Been there, done that.

"You don't look so hot, Lionel," he said, shaking his nephew's hand.

"I'm not doing so hot?"

"You have anything to drink inside the house?"

"Got milk?"

"Let's hoist a few and talk things over."

* * *

"What do you *mean,* I don't qualify?" Norman Hudris said to the desiccated clerk in the crinkly JCPenney $5.99 shirt at the Unemployment Office on Santa Monica Boulevard in Hollywood. "I've been working for the past fifteen years."

"Maybe, but there's no record of employment for the past fifteen months. And without that, you're not eligible."

"Social Security taxes were deducted from my salary."

"There's no record in Sacramento of any FICA being filed in your name."

"But . . ." The words dissolved in his mouth. What was the point of arguing with a man in a $5.99 shirt? Not only had his résumé been scrubbed but so had his tax payments.

Norman turned around and walked away, past the line of out-of-work actors filing claims. Outside he squinted into the percolating heat and considered what to do. He had a dollar fifty in his pocket, a quarter short of getting him on a bus home. Even though his MasterCard was overdrawn, he could take a shot at an ATM at the bank on Highland. Maybe he'd get lucky.

As he trudged west along Santa Monica he saw a billboard with a smiling man sitting across the desk from a competent looking Asian guy with a pocket protector and a calculator. The tag line read: IN DEBT? Underneath the large letters, the copy said that Silver Lake Debt Consolidation Service could make your debt problems manageable with one easy phone call. There was an 800 number in bright red.

If the ATM didn't pay off, Norman would panhandle the quarter, take the bus to Coldwater, walk up the hill to his house and dial the number. He'd do it today. Before they disconnected his phone.

* * *

Charlie and Lionel sat in the lime green kitchen, which, deprived of Shari's organizing attentions, had gradually drifted entropically back into its natural state of disorder. As they drank glasses of milk from a container that had passed its sell-by date a week ago, Lionel recounted the accumulation of woes that had driven him to backing the Porsche up to the pool house.

"I don't think I'd actually have done it?" he claimed. "But I was interested in exploring my options?"

"I know how you feel," Charlie nodded, with sympathy.

Was there any point in admitting that a little more than four years ago he, too, had explored that option—to the extent of actually taping up the windows of his house—and that had it not been for Lionel's fortuitous arrival, he may have actually gone through with it?

Instead he told his nephew about his incarceration and liberation, his trip across the Caspian Sea in a herring boat, his being offered a ground-floor piece of a porno production business in Azerbaijan.

"Porno? No kidding?"

"I passed."

"So what are you going to do now?"

The truth was that Charlie hadn't thought that far ahead. He had escaped from Central Asia while the going was good. He was out of range of the Turkmens, of Izbul Kharkov, of Murv, of Stalin, of Kermit Fenster. He had prevailed. He hadn't eaten his Nokia. The souring milk rose in his stomach, but Charlie fought it back down. He had handled Korean noodles in Nukus, lamb fat and rice in Bekrewe, slivovitz in Baku. He could handle milk seven days past its time.

There was an envelope with his name written on it sloppily in pencil and no return address lying on a throwaway newspaper on the kitchen counter.

"This for me?"

"Oh yeah, that came last week? I thought it was junk mail? I've been meaning to throw it out?"

The letter had a Pacoima postmark. Could anything with a Pacoima postmark be good news? Grabbing a butter knife from the knife drawer, still arranged according to size and degree of serration, Charlie slit open the envelope. Inside he found eight DBA client exchange checks made out to him for $22,500 each, representing his *Warlord* fees net of commission.

"Lionel, how much money do you need to dig yourself out of this mess?"

"I owe thirty-two grand on the house? The IRS wants eighteen-five? I'm into my lawyer and accountant for maybe ten grand between them . . . ?"

"You got any gas in that Porsche?"

"Not a whole lot?"

"You can coast down the hill in neutral. There's a gas station at Barrington."

"Where we going?"

"To the bank."

THIRTY-SEVEN

Step Thirteen

At 10:30 the following Saturday morning, Charlie Berns drove his rented Ford Thunderbird convertible, its tank full of 91 octane, down Mandeville Canyon. Hooking a left on Sunset, he drove east to Kenter, turned right to San Vicente and parked in a supermarket lot right under a sign that said that unauthorized vehicles would be towed at the owner's expense.

Charlie got out of the car and didn't look back. It would take more than a tow truck to intimidate a man who'd had grenades tossed at him by the Taliban. Crossing the street against the light, he entered the courtyard of the church. He walked up an interior stairway and down an outside walkway past the small rooms of intense-looking people getting their lives together.

At eleven sharp he opened the door to room 2D and took a chair in the rear of the room, facing the blackboard, his back to the door. The room smelled of burnt coffee and ammonia. There were a dozen or so people scattered around on the folding chairs, avoiding eye contact.

The recovering debtor du jour got up from his chair and led the group in the recitation of the twelve steps. The group humbly asked Him to grant them the serenity to know the things they couldn't change, the courage to change what they could change and the wisdom to know the difference. The meeting lurched forward. The designated speaker spoke of his getting up the courage finally to confront his cousin about his having left pizza droppings on the front seat of his car when his cousin had borrowed the car, when he still had a car. He felt good about getting that off his chest. The group applauded, acknowledging his courage in dealing with the problem.

Phyllis, the group leader, asked if anyone else wanted to share. As she said this, her eyes landed on Charlie and stuck. They stayed there, ferret-like, searching for recognition. Somewhere in her large data bank of debtor faces she thought she recalled this one.

At this moment, just as Charlie and Phyllis were getting reacquainted, the door opened and a latecomer arrived. Phyllis took her eyes off Charlie to welcome the latecomer. The others in the group welcomed him.

The man took a seat three folding chairs away from Charlie, who turned to offer a reassuring smile. And as he did, he almost broke out laughing. He couldn't believe it. Of all the twelve-step programs in the world, why'd he have to walk into this one?

As Charlie Berns nodded cordially to Norman Hudris, he raised his hand and was recognized by Phyllis.

Slowly he got up and faced his fellow deadbeats. He took a moment to compose himself and then said, "Hi, my name is Charlie, and I'm a film pirate."

"Hi, Charlie . . ."

Later he would put one of Kermit Fenster's nonconsecutive Franklins in the collection basket and reminisce about old times with Norman Hudris over coffee and bagels. Then he'd find out where they towed the T-bird, get it out of hock, drive home and figure out what to do with the rest of his life.

Epilogue

After the siege of Dashoguz was lifted, Szczedrzyk and his crew returned to the Aral Sea to resume their documentary film on the ongoing ecological disaster there. In the approximately five months they had been gone, it had shrank another 16,549 acres and lost an additional 255,655,900 gallons of water. They decided that they would simply put a graphic on the screen saying "Five Months Later" . . . and continue filming.

* * *

One member of the crew did not return to the Aral Sea with them. Justyna Klarwiszki went to Dubrovnik with Ferghana Kharkov, where they opened a juice bar together. They adopted a Dalmatian from a Dalmatian rescue service and named her Wanda Landowska after the renowned Polish lesbian harpsichordist. They are living together in a small apartment over the Polska-Uzbek Juica Kafé featuring a king-size futon and a commodious shower.

* * *

Ferghana's father Izbul Kharkov and his men went into hiding in the rugged hills just over the Uzbek border in Kazakhstan. They took over an abandoned convent near Kulundy and installed a satellite dish on the roof of the chapel. The warlord has scattered enough euros around from his film piracy business to guarantee protection against being extradited to Uzbekistan.

* * *

His first lieutenant Murv left to start his own warlordship after Izbul refused to give him a bigger cut of the revenues amassed from hijacking drug caravans crossing the desert en route to Riga and points west. Murv failed to kill his ex-boss in an abortive coup attempt, during which he himself was shot in the calf by none other than Izbul's son Akbar, the heir apparent, who, no longer having to pull his own pud, shows signs of being a chip off the old block.

* * *

The former heir apparent, Utkur Kharkov, aka Ali Mohammed, returned to the Tora Bora caves, where he began to see that his career path in the Taliban was obstructed. He tried to network with his fellow fundamentalist terrorists but found that his blood connection to the man against whom a *fatwa* had been declared was holding him back. After some soul searching, he decided to emulate his fictional counterpart from *Warlord* and enroll in law school. He is now studying international maritime law at the University of Cairo.

* * *

His mother, Ishrat Khana, remained in her room at the compound in Dashoguz while Turkmen government agents, accompanied by the deputy U.S. trade representative, combed the place for pirated DVDs. She refused to leave, even when directed to at gunpoint. As far as anyone knows, she is still there. Locals report occasionally spotting her in her burka shopping for rice and pistachio nuts in Dashoguz.

* * *

Ishrat Khana's stand-in, Nadira Beg, returned to Tashkent and resumed her career selling carpets in front of the Juma Mosque and turning the occasional trick to keep herself in lithium and hashish. Her interview with Carla Jann on *ET* was purchased from Paramount Domestic Syndication for an inordinate amount of money by a company called Acme Receivership, Inc. and has never aired.

* * *

Nadira Beg's lithium and hashish dealer, Barrett "Buzz" Bowden, sold his business to a local drug dealer, sent a resignation letter to Robert "Bob" Ladl claiming that building septic tanks had exacerbated his chronic asthma, and went home to Boulder, Colorado, where he took an online TV writing course before moving to L.A., signing with DBA for representation and landing a job as staff writer on *The Gilmore Girls*. He does not list *Warlord* on his résumé.

* * *

Robert "Bob" Ladl spent an inconclusive night with Henrietta Bing in the Hotel Diyabekir before returning to Tashkent to complete his service as Peace Corps country rep. He returned to his home in Los Angeles and, following a distinguished career as head counsel for Universal, works as a legal consultant to Local 36 of the Pipe Fitters union.

*   *   *

Upon her return to Washington, Henrietta Bing filed a full report on the film piracy operation in Turkmenistan with the Office of the United States Trade Representative. Her report was accidentally shredded during the PEDRP (Periodic Excess Document Removal Program) mandated under the federal paperwork reduction statute. She has left the public sector and now owns a knitting supply store in Bethesda, Maryland.

*   *   *

Grushenka Malkadovna spent a week living like a Bedouin in a tent on the Kazakhstan border before leaving Izbul Kharkov after a scene of operatic intensity and returning to Kiev to resume her career as an actress in Georgian soap operas. The cough she had developed thanks to her sympathetic case of consumption stayed with her until she went to see a doctor who found actual lesions on her lungs. The doctor wrote an article for the *Ukrainian Journal of Pulmonary Medicine* on his discovery of this rare case of hysterical tuberculosis.

*   *   *

Josef Djugashvili, aka Stalin, parlayed his cut of the *Warlord* TV series profits and its ancillary revenue stream into a majority position in an escort service in Tbilisi. He remains available as a production consultant to any film company that is contemplating shooting a movie anywhere between Bulgaria and Tajikistan.

*   *   *

Khabib Ghofur had to close down his Uzbekfilmlabaya after thugs broke into the facility and took a chainsaw to his Avid, not only destroying the machine but all the files on it. Though the vandals were never found, a Uzbek forensic crime scene investigator, with an uncanny resemblance to the American actor William Petersen, discovered fibers that he was able to link by computer imaging to an Old

Navy clothing store on Olive Street in Burbank, California. His report to the Uzbek minister of justice was placed in a file for illegal grain subsidies and never read by anyone.

* * *

After having his handcuffs blown off with an acetylene torch, Curt Groner left Dashoguz and returned to Tashkent to resume his cover job as cultural officer at the American Embassy. In between trips to Uzbek high schools where he distributes Uzbek-language translations of Washington Irving's *The Legend of Sleepy Hollow,* Groner has followed the crumbs left by Kermit Fenster, aka Dwight Halloran, aka Vernon Gough to Baku, where the rogue ex-CIA agent was reported to be in the herring business. "If he's in the herring business, I'm Barbra Streisand," he said on a secure line to his control in Langley.

* * *

Langley's Central Asian desk liaised with their FBI counterparts to investigate Kermit Fenster, aka Dwight Halloran, aka Vernon Gough. They sent an agent out to Los Angeles to look into the connections between the ex-CIA operative and the Hollywood company that had financed the film piracy operation. Working methodically, Special Agent Maurie Shreveport went to the ABCD facility in Manhattan Beach only to discover that it had been shut down and the building leased to a truck rental firm. Using new FBI top-secret e-mail retrieval software, which permits the restoring and opening of previously deleted e-mails, he was able to identify people who had once been employed there.

* * *

The first person he tracked down was Norman Hudris's former assistant, Tom Soaring Hawk, who was working as a director of Comedy Development at the network itself. Following a poor grade on its most recent diversity evaluation, ABC was eager to find qualified members of underrepresented groups. He is the only Native American employed by the network, which elevates it to the 97th percentile among entertainment companies when ranked by diversity. Tom Soaring Hawk told Maurie Shreveport that he had never met anyone named Kermit Fenster, etcetera, and referred him to his ex-boss Norman Hudris.

* * *

Norman Hudris is working at the regional offices of Toys "R" Us, where the former television executive has landed a job in Quality Control. The job consists of visiting the toy giant's Southern California outlets and randomly taking toys home to test then for safety and durability. His Van Nuys apartment, where he moved after losing the Coldwater Canyon house to foreclosure, is full of toys. In spite of his steady employment and the downgrading of his spending habits, he continues to attend Debtors Anonymous meetings on a regular basis.

* * *

The man whom Norman Hudris tried to report to, Howard Draper, finally left his garage after Eli Horowitz's forty-eight-hour intervention succeeded in getting him out of his car. He is interviewing for jobs at various talent agencies in town, including DBA, the agency that had provided the talent for the reality television program that his division created and that, he maintains, was developed beyond his back and completely without his knowledge.

* * *

DBA's hot young agent Brad Emprin has left the agency to become a personal manager to Ice Cube. Before leaving, he recommended that his assistant, Tamara Berkowitz, be promoted to the rank of junior agent after the previously out-of-work-actress signed an affidavit attesting to the fact that she had no knowledge of any location scout expense commission money.

* * *

Upon his departure, Brad Emprin's corner office, with a view of both Wilshire and Santa Monica Boulevards, was occupied by fellow agent Jodie Jacobian, who moved all her things in the night Brad Emprin moved his things out. The following morning she had painters do the walls eggshell with mauve trim, and as soon as the paint was dry she put up her favorite print of Renoir's *Mona Lisa*.

* * *

Over the hill in the San Fernando Valley, John Poindexter and Oliver North continue to handle damage control for the Burbank-based entertainment conglomerate, whose stock didn't even flicker after the

Warlord fiasco, largely because, as far as anybody on Wall Street, or anyplace else for that matter, knew, they had nothing to do with the reality series.

* * *

Their boss, the CEO of the company, has stated in a press release that he has never heard of the program and expressed surprise to learn that it had been broadcast on his network. Preoccupied as he has been with fighting off a series of hostile takeover attempts, he admits to not being as aware as he should be about the day-to-day activities of the company's television division.

* * *

Xuang Duc, Charlie Berns's debt consolidator, finally tracked down his client on the top of Mandeville Canyon and presented him a bill for $854 ($693 plus accrued interest). Charlie paid him with the last of Kermit Fenster's hundred-dollar bills, and, as he was instructed by Step 9 ("make amends to all the people we have harmed"), apologized to the Vietnamese debt counselor.

* * *

Charlie and his nephew Lionel are living a freewheeling bachelor's existence in the house they retrieved from the bank. They have taken up golf, spending at least three afternoons a week playing eighteen holes on local courses. Occasionally, they bat around ideas for television programs or for movies, realizing that one of these days, after the *Warlord* money starts to run out, they may actually have to get serious about selling something. But for the moment they are both happy to be alive, a feeling that is reinforced every time one of them passes the neatly coiled hose outside the pool house and realizes that it's long enough to fit through the window.

* * *

At the moment there are five different Jimmy Smits projects in development at various production companies and networks

.

About the Author

Peter Lefcourt is the author of six previous novels: *Eleven Karens, The Woody, Abbreviating Ernie, Di and I, The Dreyfus Affair,* and *The Deal.* He is also an award-winning writer for film and television. He lives in Santa Monica, California, and at his timeshare in Tashkent.